PRAISE FOR THESE AWARD-WINNING AUTHORS

New York Times bestselling author
ELIZABETH LOWELL

"For smoldering sensuality and exceptional storytelling
Elizabeth Lowell is incomparable."
—*Romantic Times Magazine*

"I'll buy any book with Elizabeth Lowell's name on it!"
—*New York Times* bestselling author Jayne Ann Krentz

New York Times Extended bestselling author
DIANA PALMER

"Diana Palmer is a mesmerizing storyteller who
captures the essence of what a romance should be."
—*Affaire de Coeur*

"Diana Palmer is a unique talent in the romance
industry. Her writing combines wit, humor,
and sensuality; and, as the song says,
nobody does it better."
—*New York Times* bestselling author Linda Howard

Award-winning author
JOAN ELLIOTT PICKART

Joan Elliott Pickart "makes love magical, special, real,
natural and oh, so right!"
—*Rendezvous*

"Joan Elliott Pickart weaves a sensitive love story..."
—*Romantic Times Magazine*

Elizabeth Lowell

New York Times bestselling author Elizabeth Lowell has won countless awards, including the Romance Writers of America Lifetime Achievement Award. She also writes mainstream fiction as Ann Maxwell and mysteries with her husband as A. E. Maxwell. She presently resides with her husband in Washington State.

Diana Palmer

has a gift for telling the most sensual tales with charm and humor. With over 40 million copies of her books in print, Diana Palmer is one of North America's most beloved authors and is considered one of the top ten romance authors in America.

Diana's hobbies include gardening, archaeology, anthropology, iguanas, astronomy and music. She has been married to James Kyle for over twenty-five years, and they have one son.

Joan Elliott Pickart

is the author of over seventy novels. When she isn't writing, she enjoys watching football, knitting, reading, gardening and attending craft shows on the town square. Joan has three all-grown-up daughters and a fantastic little grandson. In September of 1995 Joan traveled to China to adopt her fourth daughter, Autumn. Joan and Autumn have settled into their cozy cottage in a charming, small town in the high pine country of Arizona.

ELIZABETH LOWELL

DIANA PALMER

JOAN ELLIOTT PICKART

&

HEAVEN ON EARTH

Silhouette® Books

Published by Silhouette Books

America's Publisher of Contemporary Romance

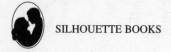 SILHOUETTE BOOKS

ISBN 0-373-48448-8

HEAVEN ON EARTH

Copyright © 2001 by Harlequin Books S.A.

The publisher acknowledges the copyright holders of the individual works as follows:

FEVER
Copyright © 1988 by Two Of A Kind, Inc.

EYE OF THE TIGER
Copyright © 1986 by Diana Palmer.

APACHE DREAM BRIDE
Copyright © 1996 by Joan Elliott Pickart.

CONTENTS

FEVER
by Elizabeth Lowell

To Francis Ray
salt of the earth
and sweetness, too

One

Ryan McCall climbed out of the battered ranch pickup and instantly began unbuttoning his city shirt. He had flown from Texas to a small local landing strip in Utah where he kept one of the few luxuries he had bought for himself—a plane that could get him in and out of his father's life in nothing flat. From the airstrip he had driven in the pickup over increasingly primitive roads until he reached his home in the early afternoon. He had loved every rough inch of the way, because each rock and rut meant that he was farther removed from the father he loved and could not get along with for more than a few minutes at a time.

"It was worth it, though," Rye told himself aloud as he stretched his long, powerful arms over his head. "That Angus bull of his is just what my herd needs."

Unfortunately it had taken Rye two weeks to convince Edward McCall II that his son would not, repeat *not*, marry some useless Houston belle just to get his hands on the Angus bull. Once that was understood, the negotiations for the bull had gone quickly.

Rye turned his face up to the afternoon sun and smiled with sensual pleasure at the warmth pouring over him. The Texas sun had been hot. Too hot. He preferred the golden heat of Utah's mountain country, where the lowland's fierce sun was gentled by altitude and winds smelling of piñon and distant pines. The air was dry, brilliant in its clarity, and the small river that wound through the Rocking M was a cool, glittering rush of blue.

Eyes closed, shirt undone, Rye stood and let the peace he always felt on his own land steal over him. It had been a long two weeks. His father had just turned sixty. His lack of grandsons to carry on the family name had been duly noted—about six times an hour. Even his sister, who was normally a staunch ally, had told him sweetly that she would be bringing up a very special girl for the end-of-the-summer dance Rye always held at his ranch. Rye had ignored his sister, but he hadn't been able to ignore the endless stream of moist-lipped debutantes or accomplished divorcées who were trembling with eagerness to get their perfectly manicured claws into the McCall pocketbook.

Rye's mouth shifted into a sardonic smile. He could afford to be amused by the women's transparent greed now; he was home, beyond their reach, and he thanked God for every instant of his freedom. Whistling softly, he pulled out his shirttails and leaped onto the porch without touching any of the three steps. The movement was catlike in its speed, grace and precision.

Since Rye had come into his mother's small inheritance at twenty-one, he had spent his time digging postholes, felling trees and riding thousands of miles over his own ranch. The hard labor showed in his powerful body. The lithe flex and play of muscles beneath tanned skin had attracted more than one feminine glance. Rye discounted his appearance as any part of the reason women lined up at his door, however. He had seen his father and his younger brother fall prey to too many greedy women to believe that any woman would want him for any reason other than his bank account, which meant that he had very little use for women at all.

The instant Rye walked into his house, he knew that someone else was there. The room smelled of perfume rather than the sunshine and fresh air that he preferred. He turned and saw a woman standing in the dining room. She had pulled open a sideboard drawer and was looking at its utilitarian contents with a combination of curiosity and disbelief.

"Taking inventory?" Rye asked coolly.

The woman made a startled sound and spun to face him. The movement sent black hair flying. There was no shifting of cloth, however; the clothes she was wearing were too tight to float with any movement she made. Big, dark eyes took in every detail of Rye's appearance. They widened at the breadth of his shoulders and the thick mat of hair that began at his collarbone and disappeared beneath the narrow waist of his pants. The speculation in the woman's eyes increased as she approvingly inspected the fit of his slacks.

A single fast look told Rye that his father had gone all out this time. The woman was built like a particularly lush hourglass and had paid a tailor to prove it. Not a single ripe curve went unannounced. The blouse was too well made to strain at the buttons with each breath she took, but it was a near thing. Automatically Rye put her in the "experienced divorcée" category.

"Hello," she said, holding out her hand to him and smiling. "My name's Cherry Larson."

"Goodbye, Cherry Larson. Tell Dad you tried, but I threw you out so hard you bounced. He might feel sorry enough for you to buy you a trinket." Rye's words were clipped, as cold as the gray eyes staring through Cherry, dismissing her as he turned away.

"Dad?"

"Edward McCall II," Rye said, heading for the staircase, pulling off his shirt. "The Texan who paid you to seduce me."

"Oh." She frowned. "He told you?"

"He didn't have to. Overblown brunettes are his style, not mine."

The bedroom door slammed, leaving Cherry Larson to examine the stainless steel flatware in peace.

A few moments later Rye emerged in boots, Levi's and work shirt. Cherry was still standing in the dining room. He passed her without a look, lifted his hat from a peg by the kitchen door and said, "I'm going for a ride. When I get back, you won't be here."

"But—but how will I get into town?"

"Wait around for a silver-haired cowboy called Lassiter. He loves taking women like you for a ride."

Rye walked to the barn with long, angry strides. The first thing he saw was Devil, his favorite mount. The big horse was tied to the corral fence, swishing flies with a long, black tail. Saddled, bridled, ready to go.

Instantly Rye knew that at least one of the cowhands had realized
how he would react when he saw the woman lying in wait for him in
his own home. He'd bet that the thoughtful cowhand had been Jim.
He was happily married, yet he fully sympathized with his boss's desire to stay single.

"Jim, you just earned yourself a bonus," Rye muttered as he untied
the reins and swung onto the big black horse.

Devil bunched his powerful haunches and tugged impatiently at the
bit, demanding a run. He hadn't been ridden by anyone during the
weeks that Rye had been gone, and Devil was a horse that had been
born to run.

There was no one in sight as Rye cantered out past the barn. For a
moment he wondered about the fact that none of his men had turned
out to say hello, then he realized that the hands were probably back
in the barn somewhere, laughing at his reaction to the lushly baited
trap set in his lair. The men could have warned him about Cherry's
presence, but that would have spoiled the joke, and there was nothing
a cowboy loved better than a joke—no matter who it was on. So they
had just made themselves scarce until the fun was over.

Reluctantly Rye smiled, then laughed out loud. He spun the big
horse on its hocks just in time to see several men filing out of the
barn. Rye waved his dark hat in a big arc before spinning Devil around
again and giving the horse the freedom to run that it had been begging
for.

As the trail to McCall's Meadow glided by under Devil's long stride,
Rye relaxed again, relishing his freedom. The high, small meadow was
his favorite part of the ranch, his ultimate retreat from the frustrations
of being Edward Ryan McCall III. Usually he was one of the first
people to reach the mountain meadow after the snow melted in the
pass, but the melt had come very late this year. He hadn't had time to
get to the meadow before he had gone to Houston to negotiate for the
purchase of one of his father's prize bulls.

Before Rye had bought the ranch, the various high meadows had
been used as summer pasture for cattle and sheep. Most of the meadows still pastured cattle. The small, high bowl that had come to be
called McCall's Meadow hadn't been touched for ten years. Dr.
Thompson had been very eloquent in his plea that Rye, as one of the

few ranchers who could afford it, should be the one to lead the way in allowing a small part of his land to return to what it had been before white men had come to the West. The resulting patterns of regrowth in the plants and the return of native animals would be studied in detail, and what was learned would be used to help reclaim other lands from overgrazing.

In truth, Rye hadn't needed much persuading to participate in Dr. Thompson's study. Rye might have been born in the city but he had never loved it. He loved the rugged land, though. He loved riding through sunlight and wind and silence, and seeing mountains rise above him, their flanks a magnificent patchwork of evergreen forest, blue-gray sage and quaking aspen that turned from green to shimmering silver under a caressing breeze. The land gave him peace.

And if a man took care of the land, unlike a woman, the land would take care of him in return.

That same afternoon Lisa Johansen sat by a mountain stream and slowly trailed her fingers through the cool, clean water. The sunlight that smoothed over her was as warm and sensual as her daydream, making a languid heat uncurl deep within her as she stretched to meet her dream. *He will be like the mountains, strong and rugged and enduring. He will look at me and see not a pale outsider but the woman of his dreams. He will smile and hold out his hand and then he'll gather me in his arms and...*

Whether she was awake or asleep, the dream always ended there. Wryly Lisa acknowledged to herself that it was just as well; she had a thorough intellectual understanding of what came next, but her practical experience in a man's arms was one zero followed by another and another, world without end, amen. Isolation from her peers had been the biggest drawback to the kind of life she had led with her parents, who were anthropologists. There had always been men about, but none of them were for her. They had been tribal men who were cultural light-years apart from herself and her parents.

With a sigh Lisa scooped up a palmful of water and drank, letting the shimmering coolness spread through her. After two weeks, she still didn't take for granted the mountain water flowing clean and sweet and pure, day and night, a liquid miracle always within her reach. As she bent to drink again, the muted sound of hoofbeats came to her.

Lisa straightened and shaded her eyes with her hand. At the entrance to the high, small valley were two riders. She stood up, wiped her dripping hand on her worn jeans and mentally reviewed her meager supplies. When she had taken the job of watching over McCall's Meadow through the brief, high-country summer, she hadn't realized that she would need to buy so many supplies from her tiny food budget. But then, she hadn't realized that Boss Mac's cowboys would be such frequent visitors to the meadow. Since she had first met the cowboys ten days ago, they had been back almost every day, swearing that nobody made pan bread and bacon like she did.

The shorter of the two cowboys took off his hat and waved it in a wide arc. Lisa waved back, recognizing Lassiter, Boss Mac's foreman. The man with him was Jim. If they had other names, the men hadn't mentioned them and she would never ask. In many of the primitive tribes among which she had been raised, to ask someone for his full name—or for any name at all—was unspeakably rude.

"Morning, Miss Lisa," Lassiter said, dismounting from his horse. "How're them seeds doing? They slipped through that old fence and flown away yet?"

Lisa smiled and shook her head. Ever since she had told Lassiter that she was here to watch the grass seeds growing within the big meadow fence, he had teased her about runaway seeds that needed to be "hog-tied and throwed 'fore they learned their rightful place."

"I haven't lost any seeds yet," Lisa said gravely, "but I'm being real careful, just like you told me. I'm particularly watchful when the moon is up. That's when all sorts of odd things take a notion to fly."

Lassiter heard Lisa's precise echoes of his earlier deadpan warnings and knew that she was gently pulling his leg. He laughed and slapped his hat against his jeans, releasing a small puff of trail dust that was almost as silver as his hair. "You'll do, Miss Lisa. You'll do just fine. Boss Mac won't find one seed missing when he gets back from Houston. Good thing, too. He's hell on wheels after a few weeks of having his pa parade eager fillies past him."

Lisa smiled rather sadly. She knew what it was like to disagree with parents on the subject of marriage. Her parents had wanted to her to marry a man like themselves, a scholar with a taste for adventure. So they had sent her to the United States and their old friend Professor Thompson with instructions to find her a suitable mate. Lisa had come, but not to find a husband. She had come to see if the United States would be her home, if she would finally find a place that would hold the answer to the hot restlessness that burned like a fever in her dreams, in her blood.

"Hello, Miss Lisa," the second man said, climbing down and standing almost shyly to the side. "This here mountain must agree with you. You're pretty as a daisy."

"Thank you," Lisa said, smiling quickly at the lanky cowhand. "How's the baby? Has he cut that tooth yet?"

Jim sighed. "Durn thing's stubborn as a stump. He keeps a-chewin' and a-chewin' and nothin' happens. But the missus says to thank you. She tried rubbing that oil you gave her on the gum and the baby was right soothed."

The smile on Lisa's face widened. Some things didn't change, no matter the culture nor the country. Oil of cloves was an ancient remedy for gum troubles, yet it had been all but forgotten in America. It pleased Lisa that something she had learned half a world and cultural centuries distant from Utah's mountains could help the fat-cheeked baby whose picture Jim proudly displayed at every opportunity.

"You and Lassiter are just in time for lunch," Lisa said. "Why don't you water your horses while I build up the fire?"

As one, Lassiter and Jim turned toward their mounts. Instead of leading the animals away, both men untied gunnysacks that had been secured behind the saddles.

"The missus said you must be getting right tired of bread and beans and bacon," Jim said, holding out a sack. "Thought you might like some cookies and things for a change."

Before Lisa could thank him, Lassiter held out two bulging sacks. "Cook said he had more food hanging around than he could set fire to 'fore it went bad. You'd be doing us a favor if you took it off our hands."

For a moment Lisa could say nothing. Then she blinked against the stinging in her eyes and thanked both men. It was very comforting to know that generosity, like a baby's first tooth, was a part of human experience everywhere in the world.

While the men watered their horses, Lisa added a few more sticks to the fire from her dwindling supply of wood, mixed up a batch of dough and checked the soot-blackened kettle that served as a coffeepot. To her joy, a generous supply of coffee had been included in the supplies that the men had packed up the trail for her. There was also dried and fresh fruit, more flour, dried beef, fresh beef, rice, salt, oil and other packages she didn't have time to investigate before the men came back from the stream. The sacks were a treasure trove to Lisa, who had been accustomed to seeing food measured out carefully except for the rare feast days.

Humming happily, Lisa planned meals that would have been impossible before Lassiter and Jim had come riding up the trail with their generous gifts. She had come to America with almost no cash. If there had been any money left over from the grants that supported her parents, it had always gone to help out the desperately poor among the natives. Nor did the job of being caretaker in McCall's Meadow pay anything beyond a roof over her head, a fixed amount of money for supplies and a stipend so small it could only be called an allowance.

The cabin itself was ancient. Previous students had joked that it had been built by God just after He finished the mountains surrounding it. There was a hearth, walls, floor, roof and not much else. The lack of electricity, running water and other such amenities didn't bother Lisa. She would have loved to have some of the beautiful carpets that the Bedouin tribes used to brighten and soften their austere lives, but she was more than content with the gentle sun, clean air, abundant water and near absence of flies. To her, those things were true luxuries.

And if she wanted to touch something soft and exquisitely made, she had only to open up her pack and admire her parents' parting gift to her. The yards of cloth were a linen so fine that it felt like silk. One piece was a luminous dove gray meant to be made into a swirling dress. The other piece was a glowing amethyst that was the exact color of her eyes. It, too, was destined to be made into a dress.

Despite their alluring beauty, Lisa hadn't cut into either length of cloth. She knew that they were meant to help her find a husband. She didn't want that. She wanted more from life than a man who saw her as a cross between a producer of sons and a beast of burden. Few of the native marriages Lisa had seen aroused in her anything but a mixed admiration for the women's stamina. Intellectually she knew why the nubile girls her age and younger had watched men with dark, speculative eyes and measuring smiles. Emotionally Lisa had never felt the strange fever that she had seen burning in other girls' blood, making them forget the lessons of their mothers and grandmothers, aunts and sisters.

Secretly that was what Lisa had always hoped to find somewhere in the world—the fever that burned through body and mind, the fever that burned all the way through to the soul. Yet she had never felt farther away from it than in America, where the boys her own age seemed very young, full of laughter and untested confidence, untouched by famine and death. During the few days that she had lived with Professor Thompson, waiting for the pass into McCall's Meadow to open, she had met many students; but not once had she looked at the males around her with ancient female curiosity in her eyes and fever rising in her blood.

She had begun to doubt that she ever would.

Two

"**S**ure smells good," Lassiter said, coming up behind Lisa as she cooked. "You know, you're the only one of Professor Thompson's kids we haven't had to teach how to make real camp coffee."

"In Morocco, coffee isn't coffee until it's so thick it barely pours," Lisa said.

"Yeah? You'll have to make that for me someday."

"Bring lots of tinned milk, then. And sugar."

"Think so?"

She nodded.

"Real horseshoe floater, huh?"

Lisa hadn't heard the phrase before. The image it conjured in her mind made her laugh. "Actually, it would probably float the horse, too."

Chuckling, Lassiter looked around the camp, approving of the order that Lisa had brought to the area. Twigs for kindling and thicker sticks for burning had been stacked within easy reach of the campfire, along with a few larger pieces of wood. The ground itself had been recently swept with a broom made of twigs. The various tools that had been broken or abandoned by other students had been gathered by Lisa and laid out neatly on a log. The tools ranged in size from a slender awl to a battered wedge and sledgehammer used for splitting logs. The big, double-edged logger's ax that came with the cabin showed recent signs of having been sharpened, although Lassiter couldn't imagine what Lisa had used to hone it. Nor could he imagine her using the ax itself. The handle was four feet long, and she was only a few inches over five feet.

The ax reminded Lassiter that he had meant to see how Lisa was fixed for firewood. Unlike the other students, she cooked her food over a campfire rather than on a camp stove. Lassiter suspected that she didn't even have such a stove. In fact, he suspected that she didn't have much at all beyond the clothes she stood in and the bedroll that was being aired right now over a small bush. Yet despite her obvious lack of money, she had never begrudged him or any of the McCall cowhands a meal, regardless of how many men there were or how often they showed up. She had always offered food no matter what the time of day, as though she knew what it meant to be hungry and didn't want anyone to leave her camp with an empty belly.

"Jim, why don't you and me snake a few logs on down here," Lassiter said, settling his hat on his head firmly. "We won't have time to cut them up today, but we can get them ready. Twigs and sticks are all well and good, but a proper fire needs proper wood."

"You don't have to," Lisa began. "I can—"

"Durn things are blocking the trail," Jim interrupted, mumbling. He snagged the heavy ax in one hand and turned to his horse. "Boss Mac would have our hides if a horse tripped on 'em and came up lame."

"Miss Lisa, you'd be doing us a favor just burning them up," Lassiter said firmly as he stepped into the stirrup.

Lisa looked from one man to the other, then said simply, "Thank you. I could use some more wood." As the men rode off, Lisa suddenly remembered. "Be sure that you don't take anything from inside the fence!" That was why she was here, after all. She was to protect everything behind the fence from the interference of men, so that the meadow could slowly revert to its natural state.

"Yo," Lassiter said, raising his hand in acknowledgment.

The men didn't have to go more than a hundred feet to find the kind of wood they wanted—pine logs no bigger than ten inches in diameter, the remains of trees that had fallen and had been cured through the following seasons. As Jim and Lassiter worked, preparing the logs to be dragged to the cabin, their voices carried clearly through the mountain silence.

Lisa listened to the men while she cooked, smiling from time to time at their colorful phrases when a log was especially stubborn. When the conversation shifted to the mysterious Boss Mac, she found herself holding her breath so as not to miss a word. She knew only two things about the absent owner of McCall's Meadow: his father urgently wanted Boss Mac to marry and have a son, and his men respected Boss Mac more than anything else except God.

"Then he told that redhead if'n she wanted a free ride, she should go down to the highway and wiggle her thumb," Lassiter concluded, laughing. "She was so mad she couldn't talk for a minute. Guess she thought a few nights in town with the boss meant wedding bells." The sound of the ax rang out as branches were trimmed from the log. "And then that redhead found her tongue," Lassiter continued. "Ju-das Priest! I ain't never heard such language. An' her with such a sweet smile, too."

"You get a look at the one layin' in wait for him now?" Jim asked.

He grunted with effort as the heavy ax bit into wood, making a notch for the rope to rest in while the log was dragged over to the cabin. Lassiter secured the rope around the log, then mounted his big horse and took a few turns on the rope around the saddle horn. At a touch of his heels, the horse slowly began pulling the log toward the cabin.

"Well, did you get a look?" Jim asked again as he mounted his own horse, wondering what the latest candidate for McCall's bed was like.

"Sure did." Lassiter's admiring whistle lifted musically on the mountain air. "Big dark eyes to put a deer to shame. Black hair down to her bosom—and a mighty fine bosom it was, too, all full and soft. And hips? Lordy, it was enough to make you weep. I tell you, Jim. I don't know a man alive that wouldn't want to climb into that saddle."

"Hell you don't," grunted Jim. "What about Boss Mac?"

"Oh, I wasn't talking about *marrying* it," Lassiter said. "Didn't your pa tell you? A smart man don't marry a horse just cuz he enjoys a ride now and again. Look at me.''

"I'm lookin','' Jim retorted, "and I'm thinkin' most women would rather have the horse.''

Lisa couldn't completely hide her laughter. When the men heard, they realized that their conversation had carried very clearly to the camp. As they rode in, both of them looked embarrassed.

"Sorry, Miss Lisa,'' Jim mumbled. "Didn't mean to be sayin' such things in front of a girl.''

"It's all right,'' she said hastily. "Really. We used to sit around the campfire and talk about Imbrihim's four wives and eight concubines and no one was embarrassed.''

"Four?'' Jim asked.

"Eight?'' Lassiter demanded.

"For a total of twelve,'' Lisa agreed, grinning.

"Lor-dy,'' said Lassiter in admiring tones. "They make 'em strong over there, don't they?''

"Dumb,'' Jim muttered. "They make 'em dumb.''

"Just rich,'' Lisa said cheerfully. "You herd cattle and Imbrihim herds camels, but things are pretty much the same underneath—in both places a strong, dumb rich man can have as many pretty, dumb women as he can afford.''

Lassiter threw back his head and laughed. "You're one of a kind, Miss Lisa. But don't you go to thinking the boss is dumb. He ain't.''

"That's God's truth,'' Jim said earnestly. "Boss Mac don't catch near as many girls as throw themselves at him. I'll bet he don't do nothing with the one waiting at the ranch now but kick her out on her high-rent keister. 'Scuse me, Miss Lisa,'' he added, flushing. "I forgot myself. But it's true just the same. Boss Mac is a good man and he'd be a happy one, too, if'n his pa would stop running secondhand fillies past him.''

"I don't know about the one at the ranch,'' Lassiter said, smiling a very male smile. "Wouldn't surprise me a'tall if he kept her around. If nothing else, he needs a date for the dance, otherwise every gal in two hundred miles will be all over him like flies on fresh…er, honey.''

"The dance is six weeks away,'' Jim protested. "He's never let a woman stay around that long.''

"He's never had a woman that looked like this one," Lassiter said flatly. "She's the kind to make a man's jeans fit too tight, make no mistake about it."

Lisa made a strangled sound and nearly dropped the frying pan as a blush climbed up her fair skin at the image that came to her mind with Lassiter's words. She couldn't help wondering what it would be like to make a man burn with that kind of elemental fever. Then she remembered Lassiter's description: *Big dark eyes…black hair down to her bosom…all full and soft. And hips. Lordy!*

Glumly Lisa prodded the pan bread, knowing that the only thing a pale, slender, inexperienced blonde was likely to set fire to was lunch.

Black nostrils flared as Devil drank the wind sweeping down out of the high country. He snorted and pulled hard at the bit. There were two trails to the meadow. One followed an old rough wagon road that had been built when the meadow was first homesteaded more than a century ago. That was the trail cattle had been driven over when the meadow was used for summer pasture. Rye could tell from the hoofprints that his men had been riding that road with unusual frequency in the past weeks. Two sets of very fresh prints told him that Lassiter's big bay and Jim's smaller cow pony had just come down out of the meadow and headed east to check on the range cattle.

The second trail hadn't been touched since the last storm. The route was precipitous, narrow, and the path all but invisible. Rye had stumbled onto it six years ago and had since used it when he was too impatient to get to the meadow's peace to take the long way around. Most horses would have balked at the path. Devil took it with the confidence of an animal born and raised in steep places.

After a long series of breathtakingly rugged switchbacks, the trail clawed up a talus slope and into a mixed grove of aspen and evergreens. The weathered cabin was just beyond the grove, at the edge of the remote meadow that was slowing reverting to its primal state. As Rye approached it, he heard the raucous cry of a whiskey jack flying through the trees and an odd series of noises that sounded rather like someone chopping wood. Rye listened for a while and then shook his head, unable to identify the sounds. The noises were too few and far between and too erratic to come from the rhythmic motions of a man chopping wood.

The horse's hooves made no sound on the bed of evergreen needles as Rye rode around the back of the cabin into the meadow. What he saw thirty feet away made him rein in the horse and shake his head in a combination of approval and disbelief. The odd sounds were indeed those of wood being chopped, but the axman who had his back turned to the woods was a flaxen-haired college kid not much taller than the ax itself. No matter how high the boy stood on his toes or how hard he swung, he lacked the size and muscle to handle the heavy ax the way it had been designed to be handled.

But the kid was getting the job done anyway. There was a ragged, gnawed-looking pile of firewood on one side of the chopping stump. On the opposite side was a much bigger, much more intimidating pile of untouched logs.

Rye reined the big black horse closer. He had cut enough wood to know that the boy was overmatched. Game, but in way over his head. He'd be all summer and well into winter before he gnawed his way through that pile of logs.

Then the kid turned around at the sound of Devil's restless snort… and Rye felt as though he had been kicked.

The "boy" was a young woman with the kind of willowy, long-legged, high-breasted body that made a man's blood run hot and thick. What he had thought was a boy's short hair was a mass of platinum braids piled high above a delicate face. Her eyes were a clear amethyst that took away what little breath remained to Rye. She watched him with a combination of curiosity, poise and innocence that reminded him of a Siamese kitten.

Suddenly Rye felt rage replace desire in his blood. *Innocence?* Like flaming hell! She was just one more freeloading female lying in wait for his money—and she had the raw nerve to do it in his favorite retreat.

Rye spurred Devil closer. The girl was not intimidated by the big horse. When Devil's shoulder was no more than a foot away from the girl, Rye reined in and looked her over, trying to reconcile his certainty that she was a cunning gold digger with the slender, delicately beautiful, almost solemn girl who stood watching him with fathomless amethyst eyes, her hand on Devil's shoulder as she absently soothed the restless horse.

Lisa noticed Rye's blunt appraisal for only an instant before she was shaken by a soft, slow explosion deep inside herself, an explosion that sent shock waves all the way to her soul. Emotions sleeted through her, a wild exhilaration mixed with fear, a confused feeling of having lost her footing in reality while at the same time never having felt more alive. And above all she knew a primal certainty that grew with every second she stood motionless watching the stranger who had ridden up and turned her life inside out without saying a word: she had been born to be this man's woman.

There was no hesitation, no withdrawal, no questioning within Lisa as she looked at him. She had lived on the edge of life and death in too many different cultures to flinch from the truth now simply because it was new or strange or utterly unexpected.

She could not look away from him. In electric silence she stared at his dusty boots, his powerful calves and thighs, his narrow hips, his shoulders wide enough to block out the sun, his hard jaw and shadowy beard stubble and curiously sensual mouth—and his eyes the color of rain. She was far too riveted to conceal her fascination with him, and too innocent to understand the currents of sensuality and desire that stirred her body, bringing a slow fever to her flesh.

Rye saw the subtle flush of response in her heightened color and felt a hot shaft of answering desire. Reluctantly he conceded that his father's taste in sexual bait had made a quantum improvement. This candidate was definitely not a thick-hipped, overblown rose. There was an essential elegance to the girl that made him think of the transparent, burning grace of a candle flame. There was also a shimmering, almost hidden sensuality in her that made his body harden in anticipation.

"You're something else, little girl," Rye said finally. "If you'll settle for a diamond bracelet instead of a diamond ring, we'll have a good time for a while."

The words came at Lisa as though from a distance. She blinked and took a deep breath, composing herself in the face of the overwhelming truth of the hard-looking, rough-voiced stranger.

"I beg your pardon?" she asked slowly. "I don't understand."

"The hell you don't," he retorted, ignoring the leap of his blood when he first heard the husky softness of her voice. She was young, almost a girl, but the eyes that watched him were as old—and as curious—as Eve. "I'm a man who doesn't mind paying for what he wants, and you're a girl who doesn't mind getting paid. Just so long as we understand that we'll do fine." His pupils darkened and widened as she took a sudden, sharp breath. "Hell," he added roughly, "we'll do better than fine. We'll burn down the whole damned mountain."

Lisa didn't even hear the last words. Her mind had come to a quivering halt over the description of herself as *a girl who doesn't mind getting paid*. Prostitutes were prostitutes the world over; being described as one by the man who had turned her world inside out just by riding into view made her furious. She realized that he had felt none of the soul-deep awareness that she had felt, had known none of the utter rightness of being with him that she had felt. He had seen only a piece of merchandise he wanted and had set out to purchase it.

The amethyst eyes that examined him were different this time. They noted that his shirt collar and cuffs were badly frayed, a button was missing where the material stretched across his chest, his jeans were faded and worn almost to transparency, and his boots were scarred and down at the heels. This was the wealthy sultan insulting her by offering to rent her body for a while?

Caution vanished in a searing instant, taking with it Lisa's usually excellent self-control. She did something that she hadn't done since she was eight years old. She lost her temper. Completely.

"Who are you trying to fool?" Lisa asked in a voice that had lost all softness. "You couldn't afford a glass stickpin, much less a diamond bracelet."

The look of shock on the man's face made Lisa feel suddenly ashamed of herself for attacking him on the basis of something that she cared nothing about—money. Her shame deepened as she realized that, given the way she had been staring at him, it wasn't surprising that he had assumed she would be pleased rather than angered by his blunt proposition.

Lisa closed her eyes, took a deep breath and remembered something that didn't vary from culture to culture across the world: men, especially poor men, had a great deal of pride, and they were inclined to be quite abrupt when their stomachs were growling.

"If you're hungry, there's bread and bacon," Lisa said in a quiet voice, automatically offering him what food she had. "And cookies," she added, remembering.

The corner of Rye's mouth kicked up in amusement. "Oh, I'm hungry all right," he drawled, "so let's decide on a price."

"But it's free!" Lisa said, shocked that he would expect to pay for a simple meal.

"That's what they all say, and every last one of the poor little dears ends up whining for a diamond ring."

Belatedly Lisa realized that the word *hungry* could have more than one meaning. Her anger flashed again, surprising her. Usually she was the kind of person to laugh rather than swear when things went wrong, but the heat racing through her blood owed nothing to her sense of humor. The man's off-center, lazy, terrifyingly sexy smile made her furious.

"Are you this rude to everyone?" she asked, clipping each word.

"Only to little darlings who ask for it by lying in wait for me in my favorite places."

"I'm here because it's my job. What are you doing in McCall's Meadow besides wasting Boss Mac's time?"

Again, Rye couldn't keep his shock from showing. "Boss Mac?"

"Yes. Boss Mac. The man who pays you to herd cattle. Surely you recognize the name?"

Rye barely swallowed a hoot of incredulous laughter as he realized that the girl had been sent out to trap a man she didn't even know on sight. As he opened his mouth to straighten her out about Boss Mac's true identity, Rye saw the humor of the situation—and the potential for teaching what was obviously an amateur gold digger the rules of the game she had chosen to play.

"I surrender," he murmured, smiling and holding his hands in the air as though she had drawn a gun on him. "I'll be good if you don't report me to, um, Boss Mac." Rye looked down at her and asked innocently, "How well do you know him?"

The change from blunt to charming unsettled Lisa. "I've never met him," she admitted. "I'm just here for the summer, making sure nothing goes wrong with Dr. Thompson's experiment," she added, waving her hand toward the rustic split-rail fence zigzagging across the end of the meadow.

Rye strenuously doubted that she was here only to watch the grass grow, but all he said was, "Well, you watch out for Boss Mac. He's hell on women."

Lisa shrugged gracefully. "He's never bothered me. Neither have his men. All of them have been very polite. With one exception," she added coolly, looking directly at him.

"Sorry about that," Rye said sardonically, lifting his hat in a polite salute. "I'll be real polite from now on. I know Boss Mac well enough to be dead scared of his temper. Is that offer of bacon and bread still open? And cookies."

For a moment Lisa could only stand and look up at Rye's powerful, rangy frame and feel odd sensations shivering throughout her body. The thought of him being hungry, of him needing something that she could give to him, made her feel weak.

"Of course," she said softly, appalled that he would think her so mean as to turn a hungry man away from food. "I'm sorry if I've been rude. My name is Lisa Johansen."

Rye hesitated, unwilling to end the game so quickly. When he spoke it was curtly, and he gave only the shortened form of his middle name, Ryan. "Rye."

"Rye..." Lisa murmured.

The name intrigued her, as did the man. She wondered if it was his first or his last name or a name he had chosen for himself. She wondered, but she did not ask. She was accustomed to primitive peoples; for them, names were potent magic, often sacred, and always private. She repeated the name again, softly, enjoying it simply because it was his and he had given it to her.

"Rye.... The bacon and bread will be ready in a few minutes. If you want to wash up, there's a pan of water warming in the sun around at the side of the cabin."

Rye's eyes narrowed into glittering silver lines framed by sable lashes that were as thick and as long as a woman's. It was the only hint of softness about him as he studied Lisa, searching for any sign that she was pretending not to know who he really was. He saw absolutely nothing that indicated she knew that he was Edward Ryan

McCall III, called Ryan by his dead mother, Rye by his friends, Little Eddy by his father—and Boss Mac by his hired hands.

Rye watched the gentle swinging of Lisa's hips as she walked to the campfire and didn't know whether to be furious or amused that she knew so little about her intended quarry that she didn't even recognize his nickname.

"Little girl, you've got a lot to learn," he muttered under his breath. "And you've come to just the man who can teach you."

Three

As Rye watched Lisa's easy, economical movements around the campfire, he decided that his father's latest candidate was different in more than her unusual, delicate beauty. Whatever else Rye might think about her, she wasn't afraid of work. Not only had she been willing to tackle a log with an ax that was old, dull and far too big for her, she had also taken the time to clear up the clutter that had slowly gathered around the cabin over the summers of student use. Used aluminum cans, plastic containers and glass bottles, as well as other flotsam and jetsam of modern life, were all stacked in neat piles at the side of the cabin.

"Next time I come, I'll bring a gunnysack and pack out that trash for you," he offered.

Lisa looked up from the frying bacon. The pan was perched on a warped, blackened grate, which was supported by the rocks that she had brought from the stream to make a fire ring. "Trash?"

"The bottles and cans," he said, gesturing toward the side of the cabin.

"Oh."

Lisa frowned slightly as she turned the bacon. Where she had come from, the pile would have been viewed as raw materials rather than junk. Broken glass would have been patiently ground into jewelry or pressure-flaked until it was a knife edge that could cut tough fibers or hides. It was a technique that she had used more than once herself, when they had lived with tribes that were too poor or too remotely located to replace steel knives when they broke or were lost. Modern steel kept its edge miraculously, but it was an expensive miracle. As for the tough, resilient plastic bottles, they would have been used to carry water, seeds, flour or salt—or even, on the shores of an African lake, as floats for fishing nets. The aluminum cans would have been worried over until they became something useful or were reluctantly discarded somewhere along the way.

"Thank you," Lisa said carefully. "If it's all right, I'd like to hang on to some of those things for now. The gunnysack would be very nice, though, if you're through with it. That way I can soak clothes in the stream and not lose them. The water runs awfully fast."

Rye stared, unable to believe that he had heard correctly about the collection of junk along the side of the cabin and washing clothes in the stream. Even if he put the question of trash aside, the other student caretakers had gone into town once a week for supplies and laundry and had carried enough equipment up the trail in the first place to make two of his best packhorses groan.

With the exception of the frying pan and bucket, it didn't look as though Lisa had carried anything new to the cabin. Her clothes were clean but showed signs of long wearing. There were patches on her jeans and shirt that had been sewn on with incredibly tiny, even stitches. He had assumed that the patches and fading were part of the new fashion trend that had clothes looking old the first time they were worn out of the shop. Now he was beginning to wonder. Maybe it was simply that she preferred to wear old, comfortable clothing as he did.

Or maybe she just didn't have a choice.

Lisa didn't notice Rye's suddenly speculative look at her clothes. She was busy cutting another piece of bacon from the slab that Lassiter had brought. She was using a broken jackknife she had discovered among the weeds in the front yard. Unfortunately she hadn't discovered a whetstone with the knife. She had ground off the rust on a convenient rock, but the blade would have had a tough time gnawing through butter.

With a muttered word in another language, Lisa set aside the hopelessly dull knife and went to the side of the cabin. She selected a piece of glass, examined its edge and returned to the fire. Casually she went back to work on the bacon, holding the glass between thumb and forefinger and cutting with light, quick strokes. When she was finished, she set the impromptu blade aside on top of a flat rock that she had found and carried to the fire for just that purpose.

"Hell of a knife," Rye said, not bothering to conceal his amazement.

"It won't hold its edge for long," Lisa said, laying the strip of bacon in the cast-iron pan, "but while it does, it's sharper than any steel."

"Lose your knife?" he asked, approaching the topic from another angle.

"No. It's just that the one I found was pretty rusty. Must have been here for a long time."

"Umm. I'll be going into town tomorrow. Want me to pick up a new knife for you?"

Lisa glanced up and smiled at Rye, silently thanking him for his thoughtfulness. "That's very nice of you, but I found enough glass around here to last for several summers."

She turned back to the bacon, missing the look that crossed Rye's face.

"Glass," he said neutrally.

She nodded. "And there are enough antlers around to keep an edge on."

"Enough antlers."

Something in Rye's tone caught Lisa's attention. She looked up, saw his face and laughed softly, realizing how she must have sounded.

"You use a point of the antler to pressure-flake the glass when the edge goes dull," she explained. "Glass has a conchoidal fracture. It breaks in tiny curves rather than a straight line. So you just put the point of the antler on the edge of the glass, press, and a tiny curved flake comes off. You do that all the way down the edge and then up the other side if you want to be fancy. The blade you get is pretty uneven, but it's hellishly sharp. For a while."

There was a silence while Rye assimilated what had been said and tried to match it with Lisa's deceptively fragile beauty.

"Are you one of those crazy physical anthropology students who run around trying to live like Stone Age men?" he demanded finally.

Lisa's soft laughter and amused amethyst eyes made tiny tongues of fire lick over Rye's nerve endings.

"Close," she admitted, still smiling. "My parents are anthropologists who study the daily life of the most primitive cultures on earth. Hunter-gatherers, nomads—you name it and we've lived it. Mom got interested in rare grasses, so she started collecting seeds and plants wherever we were and sending them on to university seed banks. The people who were working to develop high-yield, disease-resistant crops for Third World countries would use the plants in their experiments. That's why I'm here."

"You're disease resistant and high yield?" Rye offered dryly. He was rewarded by musical feminine laughter that shortened his breath.

"No, I'm an experienced seed collector who is used to camping out."

"In a word, just right for a summer stint in McCall's Meadow."

She nodded as she looked around at the clean, fertile meadow and the aspens shivering against a bottomless blue sky. "Of all the places I've been, this is the most beautiful," she said softly, closing her eyes for an instant to drink the sensual pleasures of the meadow. She inhaled softly, her lips slightly parted as she tasted the untamed wind. "Sweet, pure, perfect," she murmured. "Do you have any idea how very rare something like this is?"

Rye looked at Lisa's sensual appreciation of the sun and sky and wind for a long moment. The certainty grew in him that he had been wrong about her. She was what she had called the meadow—sweet, pure, perfect and very, very rare. She wasn't just another woman lined up for a lifetime of easy living as a rich man's wife. She couldn't be. Every one of the women who had come hunting him at the ranch had been appalled by the lack of amenities in the ranch house—the bare wood floors and stainless steel silverware, the ancient kitchen—and by his blunt promise that any work that got done around the house would be done by his wife rather than a pack of servants. And that went for the stables, as well. Any woman who wanted to ride could damn well shovel out stalls, polish saddles and bridles, and in general earn the right to put a horse through its paces.

Every single one of the women had told Rye to go to hell and had left without a backward look—which was exactly what he had had in mind. He didn't think Lisa would do that. She didn't have fancy nails to worry about. Hers were short enough not to get in the way, and they were as scrupulously clean as the wisps of platinum-blond hair that clung to her delicately flushed face. Nor did the thought of physical labor dismay her. He could still see her in his mind's eye, stretching up on tiptoe in a futile effort to bring the ax blade down with enough force to take a decent bite out of the log. She had spent a long time working on that log, long enough to leave red marks on the palms of her small hands.

He could see those marks clearly as she piled steaming, herb-scented bread and evenly cooked, crisp bacon on a plate for him.

"After dinner, I'll chop some wood for you," Rye said, his tone gruff. The thought of Lisa struggling to chop enough wood simply to cook his food disturbed Rye in ways that he didn't understand.

Lisa's hands paused as she put bacon on the battered tin plate. She didn't want Rye to feel that he had to repay her for the food he was eating. The longer she looked at his clothes, the more she doubted that he could afford even the most token amount of cash in payment. Nor did she want it. At the same time, she knew how proud a poor man could be.

"Thank you," she said softly. "I'm not very good with an ax. The places where we've lived didn't have pieces of wood big enough to need chopping before they were burned in cooking fires."

Rye bit into the camp bread and closed his eyes in pure pleasure. Tender, fragrant, steamy, exotic, the bread was like nothing he had ever eaten before. Food always tasted better in the meadow's crisp, high-mountain air, but this was extraordinary.

"Best bread I've ever eaten," he said simply. "What did you put in it?"

"There's a kind of wild onion growing near the stream," Lisa said as she settled cross-legged on the ground. "There was something that smelled remarkably like sage, too, and another plant that was very like parsley. I could see that deer had been browsing on the plants, so I knew they weren't poisonous. They tasted good when I nibbled on them. Kind of clean and crisp and lively. I put a little of each in for flavoring. Bread may be the staff of life, but variety is the spice.''

Rye's grin flashed suddenly, making a hard white curve against his tanned face. Then he frowned as he thought over what she had said about tasting the various meadow greenery. ''Maybe you better take it easy on the plants.''

Her head snapped up. ''I didn't go into the fenced part of the meadow.''

''That's not what I meant. Some of those plants might make you sick.''

''Then deer wouldn't eat them,'' Lisa said reasonably. ''Don't worry. Before I came up here, I spent some time in the university library. I know exactly what the local narcotic and psychoactive plants look like.''

''Psychoactive? *Narcotic?*''

''Ummm,'' she agreed, swallowing a bite of bacon. ''Hallucinations and delirium or narcosis and full respiratory arrest, that sort of thing.''

''From my meadow plants?'' he asked incredulously.

Lisa smiled over Rye's proprietary ''my'' in reference to the meadow. She knew just how he felt. After only two weeks in the meadow, she felt as though it were her home.

''There's a plant growing not thirty feet from here that can cure the symptoms of asthma, make you crazy or kill you, depending on the dose,'' she said matter-of-factly. ''It's called datura. Grows everywhere in the world. I recognized it right away.''

Rye looked suddenly at the bread he had been wolfing down.

''Don't worry,'' Lisa said quickly. ''I wouldn't touch datura. It's simply too powerful. The only herbs I use are for flavoring or for simple things like a headache or a stomachache or to soak my hands to help them to heal faster after hard work.''

''There are things for that around here?'' Rye asked, looking at the meadow and forest with new interest.

Lisa nodded because her mouth was too full to talk politely. Other cultures didn't object to a person chewing and talking at the same time, but Americans did. Her parents had been quite emphatic on that point. Burping was also prohibited. On the plus side, however, it was not considered a sign of demonic possession in this culture to eat with the left hand. That was quite a relief to Lisa, because she was naturally left-handed.

"Almost all modern drugs are the result of research into what is called 'folk medicine,'" Lisa continued. "Outside of the industrialized nations, people still depend on herbalists and home remedies to heal the sick. For ordinary discomfort such things work quite well and, compared to Western medicines, they cost almost nothing. Of course, when they get the chance, every tribe, no matter how primitive, inoculates their children against contagious diseases, and families will travel hundreds of miles at terrible hardship to take a sick or badly injured child to a hospital."

Rye savored the subtly flavored bread as he asked questions and listened to Lisa talking matter-of-factly about exotic cultures and various tribes' special expertise in medicine or animal husbandry or astronomy. Before he had finished eating, he had begun to wonder about his definition of "primitive." Lisa had been raised among tribes that could be described in no other terms than savage, primitive, Stone Age, yet there was a sophistication about her that had nothing to do with fine clothes, finishing schools or the other hallmarks of modern civilization. Lisa accepted human diversity with tolerance, humor, appreciation and intelligence. She was the most cosmopolitan and at the same time the most innocent person he had ever met.

The longer Rye sat with Lisa, the more convinced he became that the patches on her clothes weren't a fashion flourish but a necessity. Nor was the fact that she gathered trash for future use an attempt to be eccentric or ecologically trendy; she did indeed have a specific use for what she kept. She sat with lithe grace on the ground not because she had taken yoga or ballet, but because she had been raised among cultures that had no chairs.

"Amazing," he muttered to himself.

"I suppose so," Lisa said, grimacing. "I never went in for fermented mare's milk myself. The smell is indescribable. I guess that by the time we moved in with the Bedouins, I was just too old to be flexible in my tastes."

Rye realized that she had overheard him and thought that he was commenting on the Bedouin passion for fermented mare's milk rather than on his own awareness of how different Lisa was from other women he had met.

"I'll stick to bourbon," Rye said, trying and mercifully failing to imagine what fermented mare's milk would taste like.

"I'll stick to mountain air," Lisa said. "And mountain water."

The tone of her voice told Rye that she meant it. Having been raised in a dry, hot part of Texas, he could understand her passion for altitude and cold, sweet water.

"Time to earn my meal," he said, coming to his feet.

"You don't have to."

"How about if I admit that I like chopping wood?"

"How about if I admit that I don't believe you?" she retorted, looking at her own reddened palms.

He grinned. "I'm a lot tougher than you are. Besides, there's something satisfying about cutting wood. You can see exactly what you've done. Beats hell out of pushing papers and sitting on twelve corporate boards."

"I'll have to take your word for it," she said, glancing up at him curiously.

Abruptly Rye realized that a down-at-the-heels cowboy wouldn't know anything about corporate boards. He ducked his head and examined the ax blade carefully, cursing his heedless tongue. He was almost sure that Lisa didn't have the slightest idea who he was—either that, or she was a world-class actress. Somehow he doubted that she was. He did know one thing: innocent or actress, he didn't want her to realize that he was rich. He didn't want the flashes of elemental feminine appreciation that he had seen in her eyes when she looked at him turn into an equally elemental feminine calculation as she added up her own poverty and his real net worth.

"Both blades look like they've been used to quarry stone," Rye muttered.

He went to where he had tied Devil and fished around in the saddlebags he always carried. A few moments later he came back to the campfire with a whetstone in his hand and went to work sharpening the ax. Lisa watched, admiring his unusually long, strong fingers and the skill with which he worked to bring an edge up on the steel.

Once Rye glanced up and saw Lisa looking intently at his hands.

He thought of what it would be like to be touching her silky body instead of cold steel, and to have her watching him. Immediately the fever that had been prowling in his blood became hotter, heavier, like his heartbeat. He bent over and went back to work on the ax, not wanting the direction of his thoughts to be revealed by his hardening body.

"Better," he grunted finally, touching his fingertip to the edge, "but it needs a lot of work before I'd want to shave with it."

Rye stepped up to one of the logs that Lassiter had dragged into camp, swung the ax and felt the blade sink into the wood. He had learned a lot about chopping wood the summer he made the split-rail fence that kept cattle from grazing in McCall's Meadow. Barbwire would have been easier to install but he had preferred to look at weathered wood zigzagging over the remote, beautiful meadow.

When Lisa finished cleaning up, she found a spot that was covered with pine needles and warmed by the fading sun. She sat and watched Rye, fascinated by his combination of power and masculine grace. The sound of the ax biting into wood was clean, sharp, rhythmic. It went on without pause or change until he bent to reposition the log. Then the rhythm resumed as muscles bunched across his shoulders, straining the fabric of the old shirt. The pile of cut wood grew with astonishing speed as the late-afternoon silence was punctuated by the whistling strike of steel against wood and the small sounds of chips falling to the ground amid dry aspen leaves.

Suddenly Rye's shirt split as the worn fabric gave up the unequal contest against the shifting power of his shoulder muscles.

Lisa leaped to her feet and ran toward him. "Your shirt!" she said, dismayed.

The back of Rye's shirt had parted in a wide, straight tear. Between the pieces of faded blue cloth, his skin gleamed over the flex and play of his muscles as he continued chopping wood without pausing to assess the damage to his clothes. Lisa's breath wedged in her throat and stayed there. The satin heat of him was tangible, as was the raw strength that had torn apart the cloth. Watching him sent the most curious sensations through her body, a shimmering feeling that made her skin flush as though with fever.

"No problem," Rye said, glancing at Lisa as he lifted the ax again.

"But you wouldn't have ruined your shirt if you hadn't been chopping wood for me," she said, biting her lip.

"Sure I would have." Rye paused to balance a chunk of log on the chopping stump. He raised the ax and brought it down on the wood with a smooth, uninterrupted motion. The wood split apart and the halves tumbled to the ground. "The shirt's nearly as old as I am. I should have tossed it out long ago. I just kind of liked it."

"Toss it? Do you mean throw it away?"

He smiled. She made it sound as though throwing away the worn shirt was unthinkable.

"Oh, no, don't," Lisa said, shaking her head in a quick negative. "Leave it with me. I'll mend it."

"You'll mend it?" he asked in disbelief, looking at the frayed cuffs. The shirt wasn't worth the thread that it would take to fix it, much less the time.

"Of course," she said. "There's no need for you to buy a new shirt to replace this one. Really."

Rye sank the ax blade into the chopping stump and turned toward Lisa. She looked as unhappy as her voice had been when she had told him that it was her fault that his shirt was ruined.

"Please," she said softly, putting her hand on his arm.

"It's all right, honey," he said, touching her cheek with gentle, callused fingertips. "I don't blame you."

Lisa couldn't control the quiver of awareness that swept through her at Rye's touch. When he saw the telltale trembling of her flesh, heat flooded violently through him. He looked from her fingers tightening on his arm to her suddenly dilated pupils and knew that she wanted him. She believed that he was too poor to replace a worn-out shirt, yet she shivered helplessly when he touched her.

The realization swept through Rye, and with it came the knowledge that he had never wanted a woman half so much as he wanted the one who stood only inches away, watching him with wide amethyst eyes as she tried to still the trembling of her lower lip by catching it between her small teeth.

"Lisa..." he whispered, but there were no words to tell her about the fever raging just beneath the surface of his control.

He fitted his hard hand beneath her chin and bent down to her. It took an agonizing amount of willpower to do no more than barely brush his lips over hers, soothing their trembling. She stiffened at the touch and then shivered wildly once again.

Rye forced himself to release Lisa when all he wanted to do was to undress her, to pour over her like a hot, heavy rain, to feel her pouring over him in turn....

Then he looked at her eyes. They were wide with surprise and curiosity and perhaps desire. He didn't know. She hadn't responded to his kiss by offering more of her mouth to him or by putting her arms around him. Perhaps she sensed the desire running through him in a savage flood and was afraid of him. She was barely more than a girl, and she was alone in a remote place with a man who was easily twice her strength—a man who wanted her with a violence that he could barely control.

The realization of his own savage need and Lisa's helplessness shocked Rye.

"It's all right, little one," he said huskily. "I won't hurt you."

Four

The memory of Lisa's trusting, almost shy smile stayed with Rye all the way down the mountain. So did the heat in his blood. He had intended to teach her how to use the ax. He hadn't dared. He hadn't trusted himself to stand that close to her. He had ached to take more from Lisa than that single, brushing kiss, yet he hadn't allowed himself even to touch the tip of his tongue to her soft lips. Smelling the sunshine scent of her hair, seeing the tiny trembling of her lips, breathing in the sweetness of her breath… It had been all he could do to keep from unwrapping her shining braids and pulling her unbound hair around him, binding them together in a world that began and ended with their joined bodies.

With a throttled groan, Rye turned his thoughts away from the shimmering temptation of Lisa Johansen. It didn't seem possible that any girl in that day and age could be so innocent, yet she had acted as though she had never been kissed. Certainly she hadn't seemed to know how to return even that chaste caress with a gliding pressure of her own lips.

The thought of such complete innocence shocked, intrigued and aroused Rye. The women he had known before had been experienced, sophisticated, sure of what they wanted from him. Sometimes he had taken what they so willingly offered. Most of the time he simply had walked away, disgusted by seeing dollar signs reflected in the women's eyes rather than real desire.

More than Lisa's delicate beauty and her unusual upbringing, it was her honest sensuality that made her so compelling to Rye. She didn't know that he was rich. She didn't look at him and see more money than a reasonable person could spend in a lifetime. She looked at him and saw a man.

And she wanted the man she saw.

Rye had sensed Lisa's passionate fascination with him as surely as he had sensed her inexperience. The fact that he himself—rather than his bank account and future inheritance—aroused Lisa was so unexpected that Rye could barely allow himself to believe it. The fact that his touch made her shiver with sensual fever rather than with greedy fantasies of money everlasting was so compelling that Rye hadn't been able to trust himself to remain with Lisa in the meadow's sun-drenched intimacy.

By the time he reached the ranch house, he had decided that he must have an objective way to judge Lisa's apparent innocence and honesty. It was as obvious as the fit of his jeans that he wanted her too much to trust his own judgment of her character. He very much wanted to believe that she was exactly what she seemed, completely unawakened yet feeling the slow heat of desire spreading through her innocence whenever she looked up at him.

Rye pulled off his torn shirt and wadded it up for the wastebasket. Just before he let go of the cloth, he hesitated. He had finally promised Lisa that he would let her try to mend the shirt. She had been so relieved that he had almost told her that he could buy all the shirts he wanted, anytime he wanted them. Then the thought of her slender hands working over the shirt, touching each fold and seam, leaving something of herself in the cloth and then giving it back to him had changed his mind. He would far, far rather have her believe that he was too poor to buy himself a shirt than to have her know that he was rich and getting richer with every day.

Ignoring the ranch account books that lay waiting within the floppy disk, Rye bypassed the computer for the telephone. He dialed a number, waited and heard Dr. Thompson answer on the fourth ring.

"Ted? This is Rye McCall. I want to talk to you about that student you sent up to watch the meadow this summer."

"You mean Lisa Johansen? She's not a student, at least not officially. She challenged our anthropology department. As soon as the tests are graded, I'm willing to bet she'll be a graduate, not a student. Of course, with her parents, it's not surprising. The Drs. Johansen are world-famous experts on—"

"Challenged?" interrupted Rye quickly, knowing that if he didn't get Dr. Thompson off the subject of anthropology, it could be a long time before they got back to the subject of Lisa Johansen. The professor was a wonderful teacher and a good friend, but he could talk a mountain flat.

"Challenged. As in took final exams in certain courses without having taken the courses themselves," Dr. Thompson said. "When you have someone with Lisa's unconventional educational background, it's the only way to test academic achievement. The poor girl's never been in a real classroom, you know."

Rye hadn't known, but beyond making appropriate encouraging noises, he said nothing. He had Dr. Thompson steered in the right direction. Now all Rye had to do was settle into a comfortable chair and let nature take its inevitable course.

"Oh, yes, it's true," Dr. Thompson continued. "She speaks several exotic languages, she can transform unspeakable things into savory stews over a campfire, and she can do clever things with her hands that make some of my physical anthropology students' eyes pop. Wait until you see her make a deadly little knife out of a piece of broken beer bottle."

Rye's gentle murmur of encouragement was lost in the professor's rushing words.

"She's a darling child, too. Such eyes. My Lord, I haven't seen eyes like that since her mother was my first and best student years and years ago. Lisa's a lot like her mother. Fine mind, healthy body, and not enough money to make a call from a pay phone—not that she would know how to, either. Lisa, that is, not her mother. Poor child barely knew how to flush a toilet when she got here. As for a modern kitchen, forget it. My electric stove frustrated her, the dishwasher made her jump and the trash compactor completely boggled her. Rather unnerved me, if you want to know the truth. Now I know how the natives feel when my eager students follow them around taking notes on odd indigenous customs. She learns fast, though. A very bright girl. Very bright indeed. Still, her parents waited too long to send her here. Now all she's suited for is the life of a vagabond herder.''

"Why?"

"Time. Yesterday, today, tomorrow.''

"I don't understand.''

The professor sighed. "Neither does Lisa. Civilized man divided time into past, present and future. Many tribes don't. To them, there are only two kinds of time. There is a very vague 'time before' and then there is the vast, undifferentiated *now*. That's where Lisa lives. In the endless tribal present. She no more understands the Western concepts of hourly work and weekly wages than I understand Zulu. As for typewriters, filing cabinets, computers and that sort of thing...well, there's just no possibility. The only suitable job I could find for her on short notice was watching grass grow in your meadow until the school year begins in the fall. Then her scholarship money should take care of her until Geoffrey gets back from Alice after Christmas.''

"Geoffrey? Alice?'' asked Rye, wondering how the conversation had been sidetracked.

"Geoffrey is the brightest anthropology student I've had since Lisa's mother. Alice Springs is in Australia's outback. Geoffrey is doing research for his Ph.D. on the oral traditions of Australian aborigines, with particular emphasis on the use of—''

"Does Lisa know this Geoffrey?'' Rye interrupted impatiently, feeling an irrational shaft of jealousy.

"Not yet, but she will. She's going to marry him.''

"What?''

"Lisa's going to marry Geoffrey. Haven't you been listening? Lisa's parents sent her to me so that I could find a suitable husband for her. I have. Geoffrey Langdon. Her skills are admirably matched with his professional needs. She'll be able to run the camp while he works. Who knows? If she shows the same flair her mother did for fieldwork, Lisa might be able to help Geoffrey on his research.''

"What does Geoffrey think of all this?''

"I haven't got an answer from him yet, but I can't imagine that he would be anything except enthusiastic. She's a pretty little thing and her parents are very, very well respected within academic circles. That sort of thing matters to young academics, you know. He might even get to work with her parents, perhaps even to collaborate with them on a paper or two. That would be a colossal boost for his academic career."

"What would Lisa get out of this love feast?" Rye asked, trying to keep the irritation from his voice.

"'Love feast?' Oh, dear, you *are* a child of Western culture, aren't you? Love has nothing to do with it. Lisa will get out of the arrangement exactly what women have always gotten out of marriage—a lifetime of food, shelter and protection. In Lisa's case, that's much more necessary than love. She simply isn't prepared to cope with the modern Western world. That's why her parents sent her to me when it came time for her to marry."

"She came here to find a husband?" Rye asked harshly.

"Of course. She could hardly marry a Bedouin herder, could she?"

There was a silence, which was immediately filled by Dr. Thompson's blithe retelling of the life of a Bedouin wife. Rye barely listened. He was still caught in the moment when his worst fears had been confirmed: Lisa was one more woman looking for a lifetime meal ticket. Innocence had nothing to do with it. The game was as old as Adam and Eve—male lust and female calculation joined in unholy matrimony.

And Rye had nearly fallen right into the musk-scented tiger trap.

Afterward Rye couldn't remember the rest of the conversation. He showered and changed clothes in a bleak rage, not knowing whether he was more angry with Lisa for being so innocently, deliciously treacherous or with himself for almost falling into her hands as though he had no more brains than a ripe apple.

Yet no matter how he swore at himself or at her, the memory of Lisa's trembling mouth haunted him, and when he fell asleep it was to dream of velvet heat enfolding him, caressing him, arousing him until he awakened with a stifled cry on his lips. His body was sweating, hard, heavy with a desire so great it was almost unbearable.

It was no better the following morning. Rye stepped into the bathroom cursing. After fifteen minutes he decided that cold showers were vastly overrated as a means of subduing lust. He stamped into his boots and ate a cold breakfast, because he knew that the smell of bread toasting would have brought back memories of camp bread and Lisa watching him, her fingers trembling almost invisibly as she handed him the fragrant, steaming food she had prepared for him.

Rye slammed the kitchen door and strode out to the barn, wishing that he could slam the door on his thoughts half so easily. In the east, rugged peaks were condensing out of the dawn sky. The cowhands were straggling out to the barn. Horses nickered and milled in the corral, waiting for men to single them out with flying lariats and gentle words.

"Morning, Boss Mac. Old Devil looks like he got some of the starch taken out of him yesterday."

Rye recognized the pale silver of Lassiter's hair even before the cowhand's drawl registered. "Morning, Lassiter. I took Devil up the back way to the meadow. You look a little tuckered around the edges yourself. Tough ride?"

The cowhand grinned, lifted his hat to smooth his prematurely silver hair and seated his hat once more with a swift stroke. "I was meaning to thank you. Cherry said you particularly told her to look me up for a ride. That filly was prime, really prime."

"Bet she came with a meat inspector's stamp on her haunch to prove it, too," Rye said sardonically.

Lassiter shook his head. "Boss, you shouldn't take it so personal. When a gal that looks like that is ready, willing and by God *able*, why the least a man can do is meet her halfway."

"That's why I have you around. Fastest zipper in the West."

The retort and the cowhand's hoot of laughter drew smiles from the men who were hauling saddles out to the corral fence. Lassiter's ability to get women into bed was legend. No one knew whether it was his silver hair, his slow smile or his quick hands. Whatever it was, the women loved it.

"How did the meadow look?" Lassiter asked innocently.

"Better than my dining room."

"Yeah, Cherry mentioned something about that. Was she really checking the silver?"

"She sure as hell was. Did she take the fillings out of your teeth?"

"It was worth every last one. Did you eat supper there?"

"In the dining room?"

Lassiter's eyes twinkled. "In the meadow."

Rye grunted, then gave in. Lassiter would keep waltzing around the subject of Lisa until he found out how Rye had reacted to having his private domain invaded by yet another woman. If there was anything on earth the cowhands loved better than a joke, Rye hadn't found out what it might be.

"At least she can cook," Rye said obliquely.

"Easy on the eyes, too. Skinny, though, 'cept up top."

Rye started to deny that Lisa was skinny anywhere, then caught the gleam in Lassiter's eyes. Rye laughed and shook his head.

"I should brand your tail for not warning me about Cherry or Lisa," Rye said.

Lassiter's teeth flashed. "You find a filly that can rope and hog-tie me, and you can put that brand anywhere you please."

"I think I already found one."

"Yeah?"

"Yeah. You've been up to the meadow so often your bay's big hooves left a trench."

Slowly Lassiter shook his head. "Not that filly. Miss Lisa's too innocent for the likes of me."

"Besides," Jim called from the corral, "she ain't given him nothing but the same sweet smile she gives every other hand. And bread and bacon that would make a stone weep. Lordy, that gal can make camp-fire food sit up and do tricks."

Rye was relieved to hear that Lisa hadn't responded to any of the cowhands as she had to him. However, that did nothing to cool his anger at himself for almost being taken in by her.

"Innocent? Maybe, but she's after the same thing Cherry was—a diamond ring and a free ride for life. Only difference is that Lisa doesn't know who I am."

"Didn't you introduce yourself?" Lassiter asked, surprised.

"Sure. As just plain Rye."

Instantly Lassiter saw the humorous possibilities in the situation. He smiled slowly, then laughed and laughed. Reluctantly Rye smiled.

"She thinks you're just another hand?" Jim asked, looking from Lassiter to Rye.

"Yeah," Rye said.

Jim chuckled. "An' she's looking for a husband?"

"Yeah."

"An' she don't know who you really are?"

"Yeah."

"I don't believe it. She's no hip-swinging city hussy."

"Ask Dr. Thompson the next time he comes up to the meadow," Rye said in clipped tones.

"Well, shoot," Jim complained. "She sure didn't let any of us in on the game. Don't blame her for passing up old Lassiter as hitching material, but she didn't give Blaine a second look, neither. Ain't that so, Blaine?"

"That's right," called a tall, lean young man who was squatting on his heels in front of the corral, smoking a cigarette. "An' the good Lord knows I'm a durn sight prettier than Lassiter."

There were catcalls and howls from the cowhands as they compared Blaine's prowess and physical attributes to Lassiter's. Both men took the chaffing with good nature. They had played too many jokes on the other cowhands to object when their own turn came to be the butt of rough humor. Rye waited until there was a pause in the raillery before he got down to implementing the decision that he had made in the small hours of the night when he had awakened sweating with desire.

"Well, I'm tired of being chased and cornered on my own land," Rye said flatly.

There were murmurs of agreement on the part of the hands. A man's ranch was his castle—or ought to be. Boss Mac had their sympathy in his struggle against matrimony.

"Lisa doesn't know who I am and I want it to stay that way. As long as she thinks I'm just one of the hands she'll treat me like one of you. That's what I want. Otherwise I won't be able to spend any time in the meadow at all without being pestered to death."

There was another round of agreement from the men. Each of them knew how much Boss Mac loved to spend time in his meadow. They also knew that without the meadow to soothe him, Boss Mac had a temper that would back down a hungry bear.

"Now, I know one of you would call me Boss Mac if I went up to the meadow with you, so I won't. When I go, I'll go alone. Got that?"

There were grins all around as the men thought about the dimensions of the unfolding joke. There was Lisa up in the meadow hunting a marriageable man, and the most hunted, marriageable man in five states would be slipping in and out of the meadow without her even suspecting it.

"And I want you to stop going up there."

The grins vanished. A joke was one thing. Leaving a small bit of a girl out in the wilderness completely on her own was another. No matter how well she cooked over a fire, and no matter how game she was in taking on a man's tasks, she was neither as big nor as strong as a man. In the West, such distinctions still brought out latent stirrings of chivalry. The cowhands would tease Lisa unmercifully, play a thousand jokes on her without a second thought, but they would never do anything that they believed would actually harm her.

As one, the men looked to Lassiter, who was their unofficial spokesman as well as the Rocking M's foreman.

"You sure that's wise, boss?" Lassiter asked softly. "That there meadow is a long ways away from anywhere. What if she turned her ankle on a wet rock or the ax slipped when she was chopping wood or the summer flu got her and she was too weak to carry a bucket of water from the stream?"

Only the rosy flush of dawn kept Rye's face from showing a sudden pallor. The idea of Lisa being hurt, alone and stranded up in the high meadow camp was unthinkable. She had been so at home around the camp, so supremely suited to her surroundings, that he had forgotten the true primitiveness of the meadow.

"You're right," Rye said instantly. "I should have thought of that. Go up, but not as often as you've been going, or else no work will get done and I'll never have the meadow to myself." He looked slowly from man to man, including everyone in the cool glance. "But if any man touches her, he'll be looking for a new arm and a new job, in that order. Understood?"

Male smiles flashed briefly in the dawn. They understood very well, and they approved.

"Sure thing, boss," Lassiter said. "And thanks for the visiting privileges. She makes the best bread I ever ate. Think maybe she'd like to be a ranch cook after she's through watching grass grow this summer?''

"Doubt it. By then she'll have given up on Edward McCall III and moved on to greener pastures.''

Rye stood in the flooding rush of dawn and wondered why the thought of Lisa leaving brought restlessness rather than relief.

Five

Polaroid camera in hand, Lisa slipped through the split-rail fence into the meadow preserve. She went to the nearest numbered stake—number five—knelt and looked through the viewfinder. The silvery-green grass in front of the stake was slender and delicate, almost fragile appearing, but it had grown inches in the past week.

"Good for you, number five," she muttered. "Keep it up and you'll go to the head of Dr. Thompson's list of hardy, useful grasses. Your children will be fruitful and multiply in pastures all over the world."

She let out her breath, squeezed the button and heard the surprisingly loud clack and grind of the Polaroid's mechanism as the camera went to work. Instantly a featureless square popped out of the bottom of the camera box. She shielded the print from the sun by putting it in her shirt pocket where the exotic chemicals could develop in peace. After weeks in the meadow, the process of development was no longer so fascinating that she watched each print as it condensed out of nothing until it filled the odd paper square. These days she contented herself with sneaking quick peeks as the photo developed. She couldn't quite take the process for granted. There were too many parts of the world where the camera and its instant images would have been considered magic, and she had lived in most of them.

The tribal view of photographs as magic was one that Lisa came close to sharing. Even after Dr. Thompson had given her a book on the photochemical process, she still felt like a magician with a very special kind of magic wand every time she wielded the Polaroid and came up with precise, hand-sized images of the world around her. It was certainly easier than the painstaking process of exactly reproducing the appearance of all the plants with paper and pencil, as her mother did.

Lisa went through the meadow, photographing the plants in front of each numbered stake, changing packs of film several times. If Boss Mac's cowhands hadn't delivered fresh film, she would have been forced to go "down the hill" and into town every week. She preferred staying in the meadow, where time had nothing to do with clocks.

Seasons she understood. There was a time of fertility and a time of growth, a time of harvest and a time of barren fields. That was predictable and natural, like the rising and setting of the sun or the waxing and waning of the moon. It was just the artificial nature of weeks that took some getting used to. She suspected that for the rest of her life she would think of a week as the time it took to use up five packs of Polaroid film in McCall's Meadow.

As Lisa worked she kept pausing to stand on tiptoe and peer toward the grove of mixed aspen and evergreens at the back of the cabin. Rye would come up that way, when he came. If he came. Since the first time he had visited the meadow, he had returned twice a week and had hardly spoken to her at all. Once she had followed the tracks of his horse to the sheer trail zigzagging down the shoulder of the mountain. None of Boss Mac's other cowhands had come into the meadow by that route. Nor were there other tracks on the trail besides those of Rye's big black horse. Apparently it was a trail only Rye knew about— or dared to take.

Would he come today?

The thought brought a surge of the same restlessness that had claimed Lisa's dreams since the first time she had met Rye. She had enjoyed the visits of Boss Mac's men, but Rye's visits the past few weeks had been different. His effect on her was too vivid, too overwhelming, to be described by a word as bland as "enjoyment." He was a summer storm sweeping down from the peaks, leaving everything in his path wind-tossed and shivery and glistening with new possibilities.

She could relive in her memory the single time he had kissed her weeks before, the slow brush of his lips over her mouth, the warmth of his breath, the heat radiating from his big body into hers. When he had kissed her, she had been too shocked by the sensations bursting through her to do more than stand motionless, consumed by the instant when she had first known a man's kiss. By the time she had truly realized what was happening, he was already stepping away from her. He had gone back to chopping wood as though nothing had happened, leaving her to wonder whether he had been half so shaken by the caress as she had been.

"Of course he wasn't," Lisa muttered as she switched a used film pack for a fresh one and aimed the viewfinder at another numbered stake. "If he had been, he would have kissed me again. Besides, kissing isn't unusual here. Look at the kids who were in Dr. Thompson's eight o'clock class. Half of them were late to class because they were kissing their lovers goodbye in the corridor. The rest of them brought their lovers right into class and—oh, darn it, I ruined another one!"

Glumly Lisa stuck the botched photo in her rear pocket without waiting to see how badly out of focus the print was. She had to stop thinking about Rye and kissing and lovers. It made her whole body tremble. That was the third photo she had mangled so far today. At that rate she would need an extra shipment of film before the week was out.

Maybe Rye would bring it.

With a groan of exasperation at her own unruly mind, Lisa went to the next stake—and saw Rye walking across the meadow toward her. She knew him instantly, even though he was too far away to make out his features. No other man moved with just that blend of male grace and power, his long-legged stride eating up the distance between them. No other man had shoulders like that, a breadth and strength balanced above lean hips. And, Lisa thought as Rye drew closer, no man had ever watched her the way he did, with a combination of curiosity and hunger in his eyes. And wariness.

The wariness had been there the second time Rye had visited Lisa in the meadow, and it hadn't changed since then. She had noticed his attitude immediately and had wondered what had caused it. The wariness certainly hadn't been there the first time he had met her. She would have seen it. She had been watched by too many strangers in too many strange places not to recognize wariness when she saw it.

Seeing it now so clearly in Rye's glance made Lisa feel suddenly awkward. She wondered wildly whether she should hold out her hand to him for the brief, firm clasp of greeting that was so essentially American. And then she wondered what Rye was doing inside the meadow preserve. None of the other cowhands had so much as set foot beyond the split-rail fence.

"Good morning, Rye," she said, and her voice caught at the hunger that flared visibly when his glance traveled over her body.

"Good morning."

Without realizing it, Lisa simply stood and memorized the features of Rye's face. She loved the forelock that had escaped from his hat to lie in sable profusion across his forehead. The very dark, shining brown color was matched in the steep arch of his eyebrows and in the long, dense eyelashes that were almost startling against the hard planes of his face. His eyes were very light, a glittering, crystal gray that was shot through with tiny shards of blue and surrounded by a thin rim of black. He hadn't shaved recently. Stubble darkened his face, gave it texture and made the contrasting paleness of his eyes even more pronounced. His mouth was wide, his upper lip cleanly shaped and his lower lip just full enough to remind her of the instant of brushing contact when he had kissed her. His caress had been unexpected, firm and soft at once, and his lips had been a teasing resilience that she wanted to experience again.

"Is my nose on straight?" Rye drawled.

Lisa felt a flush climbing up her fair cheeks. Staring was staring, no matter what the culture, and she had been caught with her eyes wide open as she drank in his appearance. No wonder he was wary of her. Around him, she wasn't quite sane.

"Actually, no," she said, rallying. "Your nose looks a bit crooked."

"The first bronc I rode bucked me into next week. Broke my nose, two ribs and my pride."

"What did you do?"

"Breathed through my mouth while I learned to ride. For a city boy, I didn't do too bad after that."

Lisa's shock was clear on her face. "You were raised in a city?"

Rye started to curse his loose tongue before he remembered that many modern cowhands started out on paved streets. A man couldn't help it if his parents had bad taste in living places. "For my first fifteen years. Then my mother died. My dad remarried and we moved to a ranch."

Lisa started to ask where Rye's father was now, then hesitated. Before she could remember if it was polite to ask about a man's relatives, Rye was saying something about the meadow. The change of subject was so swift that Lisa wondered if talking about family was a social taboo among cowhands. But if that was true, why was Jim so forthcoming on the subject of his own family?

Sunlight glancing off Rye's gray eyes distracted Lisa, making her forget what her question had been. She was accustomed to people with eyes that varied from dark brown to absolutely black. The lightness of his eyes was fascinating. Not only were there shards of blue, but in direct light there were luminous hints of green, as well.

"...think so?" he asked.

Abruptly Lisa realized that she was staring again. "I'm sorry. I didn't hear you."

"Must have been the whiskey jack making all that racket," he said dryly, knowing very well that he had been the distraction, not the raucous bird.

"What's a whiskey jack?"

"The mountain jaybird that sits on that bare pine branch near the cabin and waits for you to turn your back on a piece of bread."

"Is that what you call it—a whiskey jack?"

"Not when it steals my lunch."

There was an instant of silence before Lisa's laughter pealed. Rye felt the sweet sounds sink into him as surely as the warmth of the sunlight and the slow caress of the wind. The temptation to take her lips beneath his had never been greater. They were parted now, glistening with the recent touch of her tongue, flushed with the vitality that shimmered just beneath her skin. It would be so easy. He could almost feel how it would be, the softness of her flesh beneath his palms, the rush of her breath over his mouth, the sliding heat of her tongue rubbing against his....

Lisa realized that Rye was staring at her mouth with an intensity that made her feel both weak and curiously alive. Prickles of awareness shivered over her skin. She wondered what he was thinking of, what he wanted, and if he remembered that single, fleeting moment when his lips had touched hers.

"Rye?"

"I'm here," he said, his voice husky, deep.

"Is it rude to ask what you're thinking?"

"Not particularly, but the answer might shock you down to the soles of your little feet."

She swallowed. "Oh."

"How about if I ask you what you were thinking instead?"

"Oh!" she said, her amethyst eyes wide with dismay. "Er, that is, I wasn't really, I was just..." She tried to look away from the off-center curve of Rye's smile. She couldn't. "I wasn't thinking, not really. I was just wondering."

"What were you just wondering?"

She took a deep breath and let it out. "How your mouth could look so hard and have felt so velvety."

The pulse just beneath Rye's temple leaped visibly, reflecting the sudden hammering of his blood. It was why he had stayed away from her after that one, brief kiss.

And it was why he couldn't stay away from her.

"Did my lips feel like velvet?" he asked softly.

"Yes," she whispered.

Before the last breath left her lips, she felt the brush of his mouth against hers.

"You sure?" he murmured.

"Mmm."

"Is that a yes?" He caressed her lightly again. "Or a no?"

Lisa stood utterly still, afraid to move and thus end the moment. "Yes...." She sighed.

Rye had to clench his hands into fists to keep from pulling Lisa into his arms. All that prevented him from grabbing her was his own wariness of the heat sweeping through him, changing his body to meet the elemental femininity of hers. There was no doubt that she had wanted his kiss. There was also no doubt that she had done nothing to return it. He was hard, hot, ready, and she was standing there, watching him with curious amethyst eyes, catlike in her poise and stillness.

"Now that we've got that settled, how's the meadow doing?" Rye asked, keeping his voice normal with an effort as he stepped back from her.

The change in him dismayed Lisa. She wondered why he had stopped kissing her, if she had done something that she shouldn't have, but when she tried to ask him, the words dried up on her tongue. He was looking around the meadow as though nothing had happened between them. In fact, it was as though she weren't there at all.

"The meadow?" she asked, her confusion clear in her voice.

"Yeah. You know. Grass without trees. Meadow."

Suddenly Lisa realized that she was swaying toward Rye, her breath held, her mind quivering like an aspen leaf. And he was watching her with something very close to amusement gleaming in his uncanny eyes. For the first time she wondered if he wasn't simply teasing her to watch her blush. It would be the kind of joke that cowhands loved to play on the uninitiated, and when it came to being kissed by a man, she was definitely a novice. If it was a joke, it would explain why her heart was going crazy and her body felt like sun-warmed honey, while Rye was glancing around the meadow as though he had come to see it rather than her.

The joke was on her, Lisa admitted to herself ruefully. What was the idiom that the cowhands had used? Something to do with fishing…hook, line and sinker. That was it. She had fallen for Rye's skillfully presented bait and taken it in a single gulp.

Yes, the joke was definitely on her. Unfortunately her normal sense of humor seemed to be asleep, leaving her to flounder on unaided. Then she remembered Rye's question about the meadow. Gratefully she grabbed the neutral topic.

"Some of the meadow grasses," Lisa said quickly, "are growing at a rate of several inches a week. Number five has been especially productive. Yesterday I checked it against last year's records. There are more stems per plant and the stems themselves are significantly taller. I understand that the thaw was late this year. Perhaps number five does better in a cold, wet climate than the grasses it's competing with. If so, Dr. Thompson will be delighted. He's convinced that too much effort is being spent on desert grasses and not enough on the sub-Siberian or steppe varieties. Number five might be just what he's looking for.''

Normally Rye would have been interested in the idea that his meadow preserve was being useful to hungry people halfway across the world, but at the moment the only hunger he could think of was the heavy beat of his own blood.

"Boss Mac must be a very generous man,'' Lisa continued. As she spoke, her natural enthusiasm for the meadow project replaced the cold disappointment she had felt when she realized that Rye had only been teasing her in his own way, like Lassiter with his solemn warnings about flying seeds and full moons. "This meadow would be a rich summer pasture for his herds, but he set it aside for research that will have no benefit for his ranch.''

"Maybe he just likes the peace and quiet up here.''

Lisa's serene smile transformed her face. "Isn't it beautiful?'' she said, looking around. "I was told that Boss Mac loved to spend time here, too, but he hasn't been to the meadow the whole time I've been here.''

"Disappointed that he hasn't come calling?''

The sardonic curl to Rye's mouth surprised Lisa. "No, I'm just sorry that the poor man is too busy to enjoy his favorite place.''

"Oh, he's busy, all right. So busy that he told me to take over his meadow watching this summer. He just won't have time to get up here and check on things.''

As Rye spoke, he watched Lisa closely, searching for signs of disappointment in her expressive face when she discovered that her carefully laid matrimonial trap wasn't going to work on Edward McCall III.

"Oh,'' Lisa said. "Well, what sort of thing did Boss Mac usually do up here? Will you need any help? Dr. Thompson didn't mention anything but taking notes on the growth of his grasses, taking pictures, and labeling them, and keeping the daily weather log.''

The clear amethyst eyes looking at Rye revealed nothing. Lisa was watching him, but not with the breathless anticipation she had shown a few minutes before. She was as relaxed and yet as subtly wary as a doe grazing at the margin of the meadow, alert for the first hint of a predator gliding close.

"He just sort of kept a general eye on things," Rye said casually. "He spent a lot of time by the creek. Guess he liked to watch the reflections in the water."

"I can understand that. There's nothing more beautiful than cool, clean water, not even the first light of dawn."

Rye heard the note of certainty in Lisa's voice and looked at her speculatively at her. "You sound like a West Texan."

"I do?"

"Yeah. I was raised there. They love water, too. They have so damn little of it."

Lisa smiled and began to walk slowly toward the next numbered stake. "Sounds like dryland herders all over the world. There's never enough water to go around."

After an instant of hesitation, Rye followed Lisa deeper into the meadow. Her faded jeans looked soft, supple, and they fit the curve of her bottom with loving perfection.

"They must wear jeans everywhere in the world," he said.

"What?"

Rye realized that he had been thinking out loud. "Your jeans have seen a lot of use."

"They belonged to one of Dr. Thompson's students. She was going to throw them out until I showed her how to put on patches. She liked the result so much that she went out and bought new jeans, faded them in bleach and then spent hours sewing patches on perfectly good cloth." Lisa laughed and shook her head. "I still don't understand why she didn't just keep the old ones."

Rye smiled slightly. "Fashion isn't supposed to make sense. It's supposed to attract men."

Lisa thought of the dark blue tattoos, chiming anklets, nose gems and kohl eyeliner that were fashionable in various parts of the world. "It must work. There are a lot of children."

Before Rye could say anything, his breath wedged in his throat as Lisa knelt gracefully, straining the fabric across her bottom for an instant. She took the picture quickly and then rose to her feet once more with an ease that made him think how good her body would feel locked with his in a slow act of love. She had a supple, feminine strength that would mate perfectly with his male power. She would be like the meadow itself—generous, elegant, fragrant, a sun-warmed richness that would surround him, drenching his senses.

Abruptly Rye realized that he was going to have to think about something else or start wearing his hat on his belt buckle.

"What are you going to do after summer is over?" he asked.

For a moment Lisa said nothing, then she laughed.

"Let me in on the joke?" he said.

"Oh, this one is on me, too," she assured him wryly. "It's just that your question didn't make sense to me for an instant. You see, I keep slipping back into tribal time. No tomorrow, no real yesterday, just every day lived as it comes along. According to tribal time, I've always lived in the meadow and I always will. Summer will never end. It's hard to fight that way of looking at the world. Especially here," she added, watching the grass rippling in the breeze. "Here the seasons are the only hours that matter."

He smiled slightly, knowing what she meant. "And the days are just minutes marked off by the sun."

Lisa turned and looked up at Rye with an intensity that was almost tangible. "You understand."

"I feel the same way about the meadow. That's why I come here as often as I can."

Rye's quiet words confirmed Lisa's earlier guess. The meadow rather than her own presence was the lure that had drawn him up the mountain. She sighed.

"Have you worked for Boss Mac a long time?" she asked.

"Tribal time or real time?"

Lisa smiled slightly. "'Real' time. I have to adjust to this culture just as I did to the others. So...have you worked for Boss Mac a long time?"

"I've been here as long as he has. More than ten years."

"It's a long way from West Texas. Do you see your family much?"

"Too much," he muttered. Then he sighed. "No, that's not fair. I love my dad, but I have hell's own time getting along with him."

"You and your boss have a lot in common."

"Oh?" Rye said, his expression suddenly wary.

"You both love the meadow and you both have trouble with your father. At least, Lassiter says that Boss Mac has trouble. Apparently his father wants heirs to the McCall empire and Boss Mac is in no hurry to provide them."

"That's what I hear, too," Rye assured her, his voice dry.

"I wonder why? Most men are eager to have sons."

"Maybe he hasn't found a woman who wants him as much as she wants his money."

"Really? Is he that cruel?"

Rye looked startled. "What?"

"A woman might refuse to marry a man who is too poor or too lazy to provide for the children she would have," Lisa explained patiently, "but the only time I've ever seen a woman refuse to marry a rich man was when he was simply too cruel to be trusted with her life, much less that of any child she might have by him."

"That is not Boss Mac's problem," Rye said flatly. "He just wants a woman who would want him even if he didn't have two dimes to rub together in his pocket."

Lisa heard the tightness in Rye's voice and knew that he spoke for himself, as well. He was poor and very proud. She had seen enough of American life to know that dating cost quite a bit of money; it was rather like an informal "bride price" that men were required to pay before being granted the right to marry. Rye obviously didn't have any money to spend. It must have stung his pride not to be able to court a woman.

"Maybe," Lisa said carefully, "Boss Mac has been looking at the wrong kind of woman. My father never had money and never will. My mother never cared. They share so many things in common that money just isn't important to them."

"And I suppose you would be happy living the rest of your life in a skin tent and eating from a communal pot."

The sarcasm in Rye's voice made Lisa wince. He must be very raw on the subject of women and money.

"I could be happy, yes."

"Then why did you come here?" he demanded.

"I was...restless. I wanted to see my own country."

"And now that you've seen it, off you'll go again, following your husband from one outback outpost to the next."

Lisa blinked, wondering if she had missed something in the previous conversation. "My husband? The outback?"

Rye silently cursed the anger that had loosened his tongue. Boss Mac might know about the future love life of Dr. Thompson's charge, but a broke cowhand called Rye wouldn't.

"Since Boss Mac won't be showing up in the meadow this summer, you'll be going back to school in the fall, won't you?" demanded Rye.

Lisa wondered what Boss Mac's presence—or lack of it—had to do with her going back to school in the fall, but Rye looked so fierce that she simply said, "Yes, I guess so."

"Well, it doesn't take a genius to figure out that you'll meet some anthropology type at school and marry him and go skipping off around the world to count beads with the natives." Rye glared at the camera. "You finished yet?"

"Er, not quite."

Rye grunted. "When you're finished, come to the cabin. I'll teach you how to use an ax so that you and your overeducated husband won't freeze to death in the middle of some damned forest."

Speechless, Lisa watched as Rye strode angrily across the meadow without a glance back over his shoulder. A phrase she had heard Lassiter use came to her mind.

Who put a nickel in him?

Six

The sound of steel sinking into wood rang across the meadow in a steady rhythm that paused only when Rye bent to reposition the shrinking log. Usually the act of chopping wood soothed his temper, so long as he didn't think about what had made him angry in the first place. With each stroke of the ax Rye promised himself that he would watch his tongue more carefully when he was around Lisa. It was none of his business what she did or didn't do when she left his meadow. She could marry a Zulu warrior for all he cared. Hell, she could marry ten of them.

The ax sank so deeply into the wood that Rye had to stop and lever the steel loose. Cursing, he examined the cutting edge of both blades. It was a moment's work to touch up the edges to lethal sharpness with the whetstone. Then he peeled off his shirt, tossed it onto the woodpile and settled in for some serious exercise. He was careful to think of something besides Lisa while he chopped. Thinking about her had a ruinous effect on his self-control.

Gradually Rye gave himself over to the age-old rhythms of physical work. Swinging the heavy ax correctly required both power and finesse. There was an elemental grace in the repetitious movements that became almost an end in itself. Like the beating of drums in an unvarying rhythm, the act of chopping wood suspended time.

Lisa stood motionless beneath a trembling canopy of aspen leaves just beyond the stream, watching honey-colored chips of wood leap from beneath gleaming steel. Rye wielded the big ax with liquid ease, as though the long hickory shaft and four-pound ax head were an extension of himself. As he worked, sunlight and sweat ran in golden rivulets down his back, making his naked skin glow. The black, wedge-shaped mat of hair on his chest glittered with random drops of sweat. His arm muscles flexed and then his arms straightened and swept down. Steel whistled through air into wood.

Rye twisted, lifted the ax, then brought it down again with a sleek, powerful motion that fascinated Lisa no matter how many times she saw it repeated. She didn't know how long she had stood there watching Rye before he finally set aside the ax, went to the stream and scooped up water in his big hands. He drank deeply, then sluiced his head and shoulders with great handfuls of water, washing away sweat. When he was finished he knelt for a few moments by the stream, tracing ripples and currents with his fingertips. There was a sensual delicacy to the gesture that contrasted vividly with the blunt power of his body.

When Lisa looked from Rye's hand to his eyes, she saw that he was watching her. For an instant it was as though he had been tracing the outline of her body instead of the surface of the cool, rushing water. Warmth stirred within her. It expanded slowly, sending soft tongues of fever licking through her.

With a single lithe motion Rye stood and walked toward her. When he stopped, his body was only inches away from her. The scent of cool water and warm male flesh curled around her, making her breath catch. He was so close that she could have licked drops of water from his skin. The thought of doing just that sent more heat sliding softly through her.

"What are you thinking?" Rye asked, his voice low, husky.

Very slowly Lisa lifted her glance from the diamond drops of water nestled in his thick, dark chest hair to the clarity of his eyes watching her. She tried to speak but could not. Unconsciously she licked her lips. She sensed as much as heard the sudden intake of Rye's breath as he watched her tongue.

"Thinking?" Lisa made a choked sound that could have been a

laugh or a cry of despair. "What I do around you doesn't qualify as thinking." She swallowed and rushed on, saying the second thing that came to her mind, because the first thing would have been to ask if she could sip the water from his skin. "Do you think I'd chop wood better if I were stripped to the waist, too?"

She had meant it as a joke, but the way Rye's glance traveled slowly over the buttons of her blouse was no laughing matter.

"Hell of an idea," he said, his voice deep, his hands reaching for the top button. "Wonder why I didn't think of it."

"It was a joke," she said desperately, grabbing his hands. They were hard, warm and had a latent strength that shocked her.

"Take your blouse off and we'll see who laughs first."

Lisa tried to speak, couldn't and then saw the glint of amusement in his eyes. She groaned, caught between relief and something very close to disappointment.

"I've got to stop doing that!" she said.

"Offering to take off your blouse?"

"No! Falling for that deadpan humor of yours. You get me every time."

"Little one, I haven't even gotten you once."

Suddenly Lisa realized that she was holding both of Rye's hands within her own, hanging on to him as though she were drowning. And that was how she felt when she looked in his eyes. Falling and drowning and spinning slowly, held in the gentle storm of the fever stealing through her in shimmering waves.

"How about it?" he said.

"Getting me?" she asked in a high voice.

His slow, off-center smile made her heart turn over.

"Would you like that?"

"Help," she whispered.

"That's what I was offering to do."

"You were?"

"Don't you want to learn?"

"Learn...what?"

"How to chop wood. Why, did you have something else in mind?"

"I have no mind around you," she said. "How could I have anything in it?"

Rye threw back his head and laughed, a sound as rich and warm as sunlight itself. Lisa found herself laughing with him in turn, not minding that it was herself she was laughing at. There was no malice in Rye, simply a sensual teasing that she had never before encountered and could neither resist nor resent.

"I'll get better at this," she warned him.

"At what?"

"Teasing."

He gave her a startled look followed by a smile that made her toes curl. "You like teasing me, do you?"

She grinned. "Sure do."

"It's called flirting," he said. "Most people like it."

It was Lisa's turn to look startled. "Is this how cowboys flirt?"

"It's how men and women flirt, honey. How did they do it where you came from?"

Lisa thought of sidelong looks from sloe eyes, lush hips moving that extra inch, breasts swaying proudly. "With their bodies."

Rye made a strangled sound and burst out laughing again. "Tell you what. You teach me how to do it with my body and I'll teach you how to chop wood."

Lisa had the distinct feeling that the "it" he was referring to and the "it" she was referring to weren't the same thing. She opened her mouth to point that out, only to stop as she saw the laughter lurking just beneath Rye's carefully neutral surface. He was waiting for her to walk into the gently baited trap.

"No you don't," Lisa said quickly. "Uh-uh. Not this greenfoot or tenderhorn or whatever you cowboys call idiots like me. If I ask you what this 'it' is that I'm supposed to teach you to do with your body, you'll ask me what I think 'it' is and then I'll start telling you and you'll laugh and there I'll be with my tongue tied in knots and my face the color of dawn."

"Can you really tie your tongue in knots?"

"No, but I can fold it up at the edges just like Mother could. See?"

Lisa stuck her tongue out flat, then folded it neatly up so that the opposite sides almost touched each other. An instant later the delicate pink flesh vanished behind her teeth once more.

"Again," he demanded.

He watched in fascination as she repeated the process. "I'll be damned. Now I know how butterflies do it."

"Do what?"

"It, what else?"

"Hook, line and sinker," Lisa groaned.

"Sounds like a painful way to do it." Rye ducked and laughed at the same time. "If you push me into the stream, you're going to get wet."

Lisa measured Rye's size against her own and sighed. He was right.

"You're taking unfair advantage of someone who's smaller than you are," she pointed out.

"Clever of you to notice."

"Where's your sense of fair play?"

"I took it off with my shirt." Rye waited for a moment, watching Lisa struggle to control a rush of incautious words. "Let me do that for you."

"What?"

"Bite your tongue. I'd do it very gently. I wouldn't even leave a mark."

Suddenly Lisa couldn't breathe. She looked at Rye with a combination of curiosity and yearning in her amethyst eyes. Then she remembered that this was simply Rye's way of teasing a girl who wasn't accustomed to the deadpan, leg-pulling Western style of humor.

"I'll settle for having you teach me how to leave marks on a log," Lisa said. "Big marks."

For an instant she would have sworn that Rye looked disappointed, but the moment passed so swiftly that she wasn't sure.

"Big marks, huh?" he asked.

"Chunks. Like the ones you get."

Rye's mouth turned up at one corner. "Don't hold your breath, honey. To chop like me you'd have to be built like me." He looked at the pronounced rise of Lisa's breasts and the flare of her hips and wondered how he ever could have mistaken her for a boy, no matter what the distance. "You definitely aren't built like me."

"It's just as well," Lisa said solemnly. "I'd look terrible with a dark beard."

Amusement flared in his pale eyes. The curve of a smile showed briefly beneath the dense shadow of beard stubble. "Let's see what we can do about your chopping style."

Rye held out his hand. Lisa took it without hesitation. The hard warmth of his palm sent a shiver of sensation through her that made her breath catch.

"Ready?" he asked.

She started to ask what she was supposed to be ready for, then decided that so long as Rye was holding her hand she was ready for anything.

"I'm ready."

"Okay." He turned toward the small stream. "On three. One, two, *three.*"

Still holding Lisa's hand, Rye took two long running steps and then leaped the sparkling ribbon of water. Lisa was right beside him, launching herself into the air without hesitation. Laughing, holding on to each other, they landed on the far side just beyond the silver margin of the stream. They were still smiling as they walked to the chopping stump. Rye levered the ax free using only one hand, for the other was still held within Lisa's gentle grasp.

As Rye looked down at Lisa's unusual, vivid eyes and unselfconscious smile, it occurred to him that it had been a long time since he had felt so at peace with himself and the world. Being with Lisa put him in touch with a kind of laughter that he had rarely known since his mother had died so many years before. Lisa had the same ability that his mother had shown, a way of finding joy no matter what the circumstances in which she found herself, and sharing the joy with a smile or a glance or a word, making everything around her somehow brighter than it had been before.

For the first time Rye wondered if it hadn't been his father's search for just that rare quality of joy that had sent him on an endless round of dating and mating which had brought pleasure only to the women who had cashed his checks. It had been the same for Rye's younger brother, who had married and divorced twice before he turned twenty-five. At least their sister, Cindy, had learned very quickly to tell the difference between men who wanted her and those who wanted only an entrée into the McCall checking account.

That was one thing Rye didn't have to worry about with Lisa. She couldn't be smiling at him because of his money for the simple reason that she thought he was too poor to buy a new work shirt much less to pour diamonds into her hands. But she watched him with admiring eyes anyway. That made her smile all the more beautiful to Rye. Not having to question why Lisa enjoyed being with him was a luxury that money literally could not buy. It was a unique, addictive experience for Rye; for the first time in his life he was positive that he was being enjoyed simply as a man.

Belatedly Rye realized that he was standing with an ax in his right hand, Lisa's warm fingers in his left and an unaccustomed grin on his lips.

"You have a contagious smile," he said, squeezing Lisa's fingers once before he released them and handed her the ax. "You'll need both hands for this. When I chop, I hold the ax down at the bottom of the handle. You shouldn't do that. The length of your arm is a bad match for the length of the handle. Hold it farther up. When you swing the ax back, let your right hand slide up the handle. When you swing the ax forward, let your right hand slide down again. But whatever you do, always hold on hard with your left hand. Like this."

Rye demonstrated the proper technique. Lisa tried to keep her eyes on the ax and his hands. It was impossible. The supple flex and play of his back muscles moving beneath his sun-darkened skin fascinated her.

"Want to try it?" he asked.

Lisa barely prevented herself from asking just which *it* he was offering to let her try. When she took the ax, her fingers brushed over his hands several times. The vitality of him radiated through her at each touch, a warmth that was more than simple body heat. Her hands were unsteady when they closed around the smooth, hard shaft of the ax. She mentally reviewed what he had just told her, took a deep breath, lifted the ax and brought it down on the chopping stump.

The ax head bounced once, barely scratching the scarred wood. She repeated the motion. The ax head bounced. She tried again. The same thing happened. Nothing.

"Did I forget to mention that you're supposed to put your back into it?" Rye asked after the third swing.

"'It' is quite busy enough already without having to deal with my back, as well," muttered Lisa.

For a moment Rye was nonplussed. Then he remembered just how many subjects had been covered—or uncovered—by the word *it* so far today.

"It has been very busy," Rye agreed.

"It certainly has. As a matter of fact, it just went on strike. No its allowed. Be specific or be quiet."

His lips twitched with his efforts not to smile. "Right. Here, let's try it—er, chopping—this way. This should give you an idea of the right rhythm and swing."

Rye stepped behind Lisa and reached around her until his hands were positioned above and below hers on the long handle. Every time she breathed in, a blend of evergreen resin and warmth and man filled her senses. His skin was smooth against hers, hot, and the hair on his arms burned beneath the sun in shades of sable and bronze. She could feel his breath stir the wisps of fine hair that had escaped her braids.

With each motion Rye made, his chest brushed against Lisa's back, telling her that barely a breath separated their bodies. The realization was dizzying, like feeling the earth turn beneath her feet. She hung on to the ax handle until her knuckles whitened, because the smooth wood was the only solid thing in a world that was slowly revolving around her.

"Lisa?"

Helplessly she looked over her shoulder at Rye. He was so close that she could have counted his dense black eyelashes and each splinter of color in his gray eyes. His mouth was only inches away. If she stood on her tiptoes and he bent down, she could know again the sweetness and resilience of his lips.

Rye took the ax from Lisa's unresisting hands and sank the blade into the stump with a casual flick of his wrist.

"Come closer," he whispered, bending down to her. "Closer. Yes, like that."

Rye's last words were breathed against Lisa's lips as his arms tightened around her, arching her into his body. She felt the warmth of his chest, the hard muscles of his arms and then the pressure of his mouth moving over hers. Blindly she put her hands on his biceps, bracing herself in a spinning world, holding on to his muscular strength as she savored the sweet resilience of his lips and the contrasting roughness of his beard stubble, and she wished for the moment never to end.

Suddenly Rye's arms loosened and Lisa found herself set away from him once more.

"What's with you?" Rye asked curtly. "You come on to me like there's no tomorrow, but when I kiss you, nothing happens. I might as well be kissing my horse. Is this your idea of a joke?"

Conflicting waves of heat washed over Lisa, desire and embarrassment by turns staining her face red. "I thought it was yours."

"It?" he said sardonically.

"Kissing me," she said. "It's a joke for you, isn't it? But the joke's on me." She took a deep, uncertain breath and rushed on. "I know that you're showing me just how much of a tenderfoot I am and I'm trying to be a good sport about that, because you're right, I'm a total tenderfoot when it comes to kissing. I've never kissed anyone but my parents and whenever you kiss me I get hot and cold and shivery and I can't breathe and I can't think and—and I don't know anything about kissing and—and the joke's on me, that's all. When you finish laughing you can go back to teaching me how to handle an ax, but please don't stand so close because then the only thing I can think about is you and my knees get weak and so do my hands and I'll drop the ax. Okay?"

The tumbling words stopped. Lisa looked anxiously at Rye, waiting for his laughter.

But he wasn't laughing. He was staring at her, hardly able to believe what he had just heard.

"How old are you?" he asked finally.

"What day is it?"

"July twenty-fifth."

"Already? I turned twenty yesterday."

For a long, electric moment Rye said nothing. Lisa stood without moving, afraid to breathe. He was looking at her from the shining platinum crown of her braids to her toes peeking out from her frayed sneakers. The look he was giving her was as intense as it was—possessive.

"Happy birthday," he murmured, as much to himself as to Lisa.

After a last, lingering glance at her pink lips, he met her eyes. "There's a fine old American custom on birthdays," he continued, smiling gently at her. "A kiss for every year. And, little one, when I kiss you it will be a lot of things, but it sure as hell won't be a joke."

Lisa's lips parted, but no words came out. She was looking at his mouth with a curious, sensual hunger that was as innocent as it was inviting. Rye saw the innocence now, whereas before he had seen only the invitation.

"No one but your parents?" he asked huskily.

She shook her head without looking up from his lips.

He took her hand, gently smoothed it open with his fingertips and kissed the center of her palm.

"That's one." He kissed the ball of her thumb. "That's two." The tip of her index finger. "Three."

Lisa couldn't stifle a small, throaty sound when Rye's teeth closed slowly on the pad of flesh at the base of her thumb. She felt no pain, simply a sensuous pressure that sent pleasure flaring out from the pit of her stomach.

"F-four?" she asked.

He shook his head, rubbing his cheek against her palm. "There's no limit on bites. Or on this."

His head turned slowly. The tip of his tongue flicked out to touch the sensitive skin between her first and second finger. Before he moved on to the second and third finger he tested the resilience of her flesh with his teeth. He did the same all across her hand, the tender vise of his teeth followed by hot, humid touches of his tongue. When he caught her smallest finger between his lips and pulled it into his mouth, stroking her skin with tongue and teeth, she shivered wildly. Very slowly he released her, caressing her every bit of the way.

"Do you like that?" he asked.

"Yes," she sighed. "Oh, yes, I like that."

Rye heard the catch in Lisa's voice and wondered what it would be like to hear that again and then again, yes and yes and yes as he tasted every bit of her until she moaned the final *yes* and he eased into her untouched body. The thought of being inside her made him clench with urgent need. Feeling the slow, hidden tremors sweeping through her flesh from her toes to her fingertips did nothing to cool the heat and heaviness of his own desire.

"Did you like having my lips on yours?" he asked.

But before Rye finished asking the question he was bending down to Lisa, for he had seen the answer in the sudden darkening at the center of her eyes. Her amber eyelashes swept down, shielding the telltale expansion of her pupils as she turned her face up to him with the innocence and trust of a flower drinking in the morning sun. Her innocence pierced his desire with a sweetness that was also pain. He knew he should tell her not to trust him so much; he was a man and he wanted the untouched secrets of her body, he wanted to caress and possess every aspect of her, he wanted to feel her softness yielding to his hard flesh, clinging to him, sheathing him in ecstasy.

"Closer," he whispered. "Closer. I want to feel you going up on tiptoe against me again. Closer...*yes*."

Rye made a thick sound of pleasure when Lisa put her hands on his naked shoulders and arched into his arms. He caught her lips almost fiercely, kissing her hard, feeling her stiffening in surprise when his tongue prowled the edges of her closed lips. With an effort he forced himself to loosen his grip on her supple, responsive body. He leaned his forehead against the pale coils of her braids, fighting for control of his breath and his unruly passion.

"Rye?" Lisa asked, troubled, unsure.

"It's all right." His head lifted and then bent to her again as he nuzzled at her lips. "Just let me...just once...your mouth...oh, honey, let me in. I'll be gentle this time...so gentle."

Before Lisa could say a word, Rye's lips were brushing over hers once more. Again and again he savored the softness of her lips, skimming gently, barely touching, increasing the contact so slowly that her arms locked around his neck, pulling him closer in unconscious demand. When she felt the hard edge of his teeth close tenderly on her lower lip, her breath rushed out in a soundless moan.

"Yes," he murmured, licking the tiny marks he had left. "Open for me, little one, want me."

Lisa's lips parted and she shivered as Rye's tongue licked over her sensitive flesh as though it were his own. The shifting, elusive pressure of his caress teased her lips farther and farther apart until no barrier to his possession remained.

"Yes," he said thickly. "Like that. Like *this*."

The gliding, sensual presence of Rye's tongue within Lisa's mouth wrung a small cry of discovery from her. A wave of heat swept out from the pit of her stomach, a fever that turned her bones to honey. She clung to Rye's strength without knowing it, for all she could feel was the rhythmic penetration and retreat of his tongue caressing her. She abandoned herself to the rising heat of her own body and to him, returning the gliding pressure of his tongue with her own, enjoying the intimacy of his taste and textures, lured deeper and deeper into his hot mouth until she was giving back the kiss as deeply as she was receiving it.

After a long, long time Rye slowly straightened. He held Lisa gently against his chest, trying and failing to control the shudders of desire that swept through him. When he realized that the same wild trembling was sweeping through her body, he couldn't stifle a thick masculine sound of triumph and need. She was utterly innocent, yet a single kiss had made her shiver with desire for him.

"Five," Lisa murmured finally, dreamily, rubbing her cheek across Rye's bare chest. "I can hardly wait for six."

"Neither can I. But I'm going to if it kills me. And I think it just might."

Rye saw the puzzlement in Lisa's eyes and smiled despite the clenched need of his body. "You're like a curious little kitten. Didn't your daddy ever tell you that curiosity killed the cat?"

And satisfaction brought it back.

The childhood retort echoed in Rye's head, but it brought him no comfort. He wasn't about to take advantage of Lisa's innocence by seducing her before she ever had a chance to object. His conscience wouldn't let him take a woman who didn't even know his name. Nor would he tell her who he was. He didn't want to see dollar signs replace sensuality when she looked at him.

Yet he still wanted her. He wanted her until he shook with it. But he wasn't going to take her. Sex he could have from a thousand women. Lisa's innocent smile could come only from her.

Seven

Lisa hummed softly as she worked on making Rye's new shirt. Gray, luminous, with subtle hints of blue and green, the color of the fine linen cloth she was cutting reminded her of nothing so much as his eyes when he watched her. And Rye always watched her. From the moment he rode his big black horse into the meadow until the last look over his shoulder before Devil plunged down the steep trail to the ranch, Rye watched her.

But that was all he did. He didn't kiss her. He didn't hold her. He didn't take her hand or offer to teach her how to use the ax. It was as though those incandescent moments near the chopping stump never had occurred. He still laughed with her, teased her until she blushed and looked at her with hunger in his eyes, but he never touched her. The one time Lisa had brought up the custom of birthday kissing—and missing kisses—he had smiled rather grimly and told her that it wasn't his birthday.

That was when Lisa had realized that not only wasn't Rye going to kiss her again, he was careful not to touch her even in the most casual ways. Yet he came up to the meadow nearly every day, if only for a few minutes. Despite his baffling sensual distance, Lisa instinctively knew that it was more than the meadow itself that was bringing Rye up the long trail from the ranch.

He's just poor and proud, that's all, Lisa told herself as she finished cutting out the final piece of the shirt. *He can't afford to date and he has too much pride to court a woman unless he has money in his pocket. But Boss Mac's party is free.*

Then why hasn't Rye asked me to go? said a mocking voice at the back of her mind.

Because nice shirts cost money, and everyone wears nice clothes to a party, that's why. But this shirt will be free, and he can't refuse to take it because it's just a replacement for the one he ruined chopping wood for me.

Pleased with her logic, Lisa hummed to herself as she set out the simple tools she would use to sew the shirt. Needle, thread, scissors and the skill of her own fingers were all that she would use, because that was all she had. It was also all she needed. She had been sewing clothes of one kind or another since she had been old enough to hold a needle without dropping it. The pattern for the shirt had been taken from Rye's old one, which she had carefully picked apart into its individual pieces. Using the old pieces, she had cut new ones. The only alteration she had made was to add nearly two more inches in the shoulders of the linen shirt, for the old shirt had been cut too small to stretch across the bunching of Rye's powerful back and shoulder muscles when he worked.

What to use for buttons had bothered Lisa. She had thought of asking Lassiter to buy buttons for her, but he came to the meadow only once a week. Besides, she didn't think it would be fair to ask him to spend his free time shopping for just the right buttons for another man's shirt. She had tried to carve buttons from wood, but the result had simply been too rough-looking against the fine linen. Then she had discovered the solution to the problem literally at her feet. Each year the deer shed their old antlers and grew new ones. The technique of shaping antlers into useful tools was very old, far older than civilization. Carving antler and bone was one of the arcane arts that Lisa had learned along with how to pressure-flake glass into a makeshift knife.

As with most primitive techniques, about all that was required for a finished product was time, patience and more time. That wasn't a problem for Lisa. In the meadow she had fallen back under the spell of the slow rhythms of tribal time, when patience wasn't difficult because there was nothing to hurry toward. She had enjoyed watching the buttons gradually take shape. She had enjoyed painstakingly polishing each one and thinking of the pleasure Rye's sensitive fingertips would get from the satin smoothness of the buttons. It was the same while she worked on the incredibly fine texture of the linen itself; much of her satisfaction came from the knowledge that the soft cloth would bring pleasure to Rye while he wore it.

Humming a work song whose rhythms were as old as the techniques she used, Lisa basted pieces of the shirt together for later sewing. When she finally stopped for lunch, she remembered that she had been warming water to wash herself. She tested the temperature of the water in the barrel that Rye had moved to a sunny spot for her. The liquid was silky and warm. She dipped out a pan of water, carried it into the cabin and bathed with the efficiency of someone to whom bucket baths were an accepted part of life. When she was clean, she put on a pale blue blouse that had come from an open-air market half a world away. One of her two pairs of patched and faded jeans had finally worn completely through at the knees, so she had followed local custom and cut the legs off to make a pair of shorts. In August, the high meadow was more than warm enough for her to enjoy having her legs bare.

When Lisa went back outside, she carefully refrained from looking in the direction of the steep trail. If Rye came to the meadow at all today, it would be late in the afternoon. Often he only stayed for a few minutes, asking her if she needed anything from "down the hill," or if she had been feeling well, or if she had any cuts or sprains that might need attention. She would answer no and yes and no, and then they would talk for a bit about the meadow and the grasses and the turning of the seasons.

And they would look at each other, their eyes full of all that hadn't been said or done.

Lisa's mouth made a bittersweet curve as she caught her reflection in the water remaining in the barrel. The time she had spent in the meadow had brought a golden sheen to her skin, a hint of sensual ripeness that had been absent before. It was the same for her mouth. Her lips were somehow fuller, more moist, a rosy invitation for Rye's caressing kiss—yet his touch never came. She would awaken from forgotten dreams with her breasts full, aching, her body in the grip of the shimmering, elemental fever that Rye had called from her very core.

Lisa dipped another bucket of water from the barrel, unbraided her hair and submerged the pale blond mass in the bucket. She stayed outside to wash her hair, knowing from experience that the process was too sloppy for a cabin or even for a tent. She didn't mind the mess. She luxuriated in the fragrant mounds of lather and the clean, warm water that left her hair silvery with life and light. Unbound, her hair was hip-length, thick and very softly curling. She toweled the long strands thoroughly and combed out her hair with steady sweeps of her arm. Then, feeling lazy, she carried her bedroll through the fence and into the meadow itself. There she stretched out on her stomach, letting her hair fan across her back and hips to dry. The languid breeze, warm sunlight and drowsy humming of insects soon made her eyelids heavy. After a while she gave up fighting the peace of the meadow and slept.

When Rye slipped through the fence and into the meadow, for one heart-stopping moment he thought that Lisa was naked except for the hair curled caressingly around her hips. Shimmering with every shift of breeze, her hair was a silken cloak whose beauty had only been hinted at while coiled in braids atop her head. He stood transfixed, barely breathing, feeling as though he had trespassed on the privacy of a nymph who had been shielded until that moment from human eyes.

Then the breeze shifted again, smoothing platinum hair aside to reveal the earthbound color of worn cutoffs. Rye let out his breath in a soundless rush. He knew that he should turn around, run back to the cabin, untie Devil and ride like hell down to the ranch. He knew if he went and knelt next to Lisa, he wouldn't be able to stop himself from touching her.

And he knew that once he had touched her, he might not be able to stop at all. He wanted her too much to trust himself.

So tell her who you are.

No! I don't want it to end so soon. I've never enjoyed being with anyone so much in my life. If we become lovers I'll have to tell her who I am and then everything will be ruined.

So don't touch her.

But Rye was already kneeling next to Lisa, and the silken feel of her hair sliding through his fingers drove everything else from his mind. Gently he lifted the hairbrush from her relaxed fingers and began brushing the silvery cascade of hair. The long, soft strands seemed alive. They arched up to his touch, curled lovingly around his hands and clung to his fingers as though in a silent plea for more caresses. Smiling, he brushed with slow, gentle strokes, and when he could resist it no more he eased his fingers deep into the sun-warmed, shimmering depths of her hair. The exquisite softness made an involuntary shiver run through him. He lifted her hair to his lips and buried his face in the shining strands, inhaling deeply.

Lisa stirred and awakened languidly, caught in the dream of Rye that had haunted her every time she slept. When her eyes opened she saw the flexed power of his thighs pressing against his taut jeans and the pale delicacy of her unbound hair clinging to his body. She sensed as much as felt the weight of her long hair caught in his hands, a sensuous leash made of countless silky strands, and each strand bound her to him—and him to her. Slowly she turned her head until she could see his face buried in her hair. The contrast of dark and fair, of hard masculine planes and soft femininity, made her breath fill her throat.

Then Rye opened his eyes and Lisa couldn't breathe at all. Passion burned behind his black eyelashes, a turmoil of need and emotion that exploded softly inside her, bringing fever in its wake. She looked into his eyes and saw the truth that she had sensed the first time Rye had ridden into the high meadow and found her trying to chop wood. She had no defenses against that elemental truth of his passion, no defenses against him.

"I tried not to wake you up," he said huskily.

"I don't mind."

"You should. You're too innocent. You shouldn't let me near you. You trust me too much."

"I can't help it," Lisa said, her voice soft, unhesitating. "I was born to be your woman. I knew it the instant I turned around and saw you sitting like a warrior on a horse as black as night."

Rye couldn't bear the honesty and certainty in Lisa's beautiful amethyst eyes. His black lashes closed and a visible shudder ran through his body.

"No," he said harshly. "You don't know me."

"I know that you're hard and more than strong enough to hurt me, but you won't. You've always been very careful of me, more gentle and protective than most men are with their own wives and daughters. In every way that matters, I'm safe with you. I know that, just as I know that you're intelligent and hot tempered and funny and very proud."

"If a man isn't proud and hard and willing to fight, the world will roll right over him and leave him flatter than his shadow in the dust."

"Yes, I know that, too," Lisa said simply. "I've seen it happen in every culture, no matter how primitive or how civilized." She looked at Rye's head bent over her hair as he smoothed it against his cheek. "Did I mention that you're very handsome, too, and have all your own teeth?"

Helplessly Rye laughed. He had never known anyone like Lisa—wry, sensual, honest, with a capacity for joy that glittered through everything she said and did.

"You're one of a kind, Lisa."

She smiled sadly. She had been one of a kind wherever she had gone with her parents. Always watching, never being a part of the colorful, passionate pageant that was humanity. She had thought it would be different in America, but it hadn't been. Yet for a time, when Rye had been near, she hadn't felt separate. And when he had kissed her, she had felt the slow, sweet fever of life steal through her, joining her to him.

Tentatively Lisa traced the full curve of Rye's lower lip with the tip of her index finger. He flinched away from the innocent, incendiary touch, not trusting his self-control. She dropped her hand and looked away. She was too unsophisticated to conceal her bafflement and hurt at his withdrawal.

"I'm sorry," she said. "When I woke up and saw you, and you had your face buried in my hair..." Her voice died. She looked back over her shoulder, giving him an apologetic smile. "I guess I'm too much of a tenderfoot with men to read the signs right. I thought you wanted..."

Lisa's voice faded again. She swallowed, trying to read Rye's expression, but there was nothing to read. Only his eyes were alive, glittering with the fever that he was fighting to control. She didn't know that; she only knew that he had flinched when she had touched him. When he closed his eyes, she saw the rigid line of his clenched jaw, and she believed that he was forcing himself to be kind and say nothing.

She turned away from Rye, only to find herself still bound to him by the shining lengths of her hair caught between his fingers. She tugged very lightly once, then again, trying to free herself without drawing his attention. Gradually she realized that there was a gentle, inescapable force pulling her back toward him, reminding her that there were two ends to the silken leash of her hair. When she faced Rye again he was watching her with eyes that blazed.

"We have to talk, little one, but not now. Once, just once in my life, I'm going to know what it's like to be wanted as a man. Just a man called Rye."

"I don't understand," Lisa whispered as Rye bent down over her, filling her world.

"I know. But you understand this, don't you?"

A small sound escaped Lisa as she felt the sweet firmness of Rye's lips once more. The caressing pressure slowly increased, parting her lips, preparing her for the tender penetration of his tongue. Yet he withheld even that small consummation from her while he rocked his mouth languidly against hers, sensitizing lips that turned hungrily to follow his seductive motions. She said his name, and the sound was as much a sigh as a word. Hearing it sent fire licking over him.

"Yes?" Rye murmured, nuzzling Lisa's soft lips.

"Would you...?"

Her words broke softly when his teeth captured her lower lip. She made a tiny, throaty sound of pleasure, but the caress lasted only an instant.

"More," she murmured. "Please."

Lisa felt as much as heard Rye's laughter. She opened her eyes to find him watching her with an intensity that was almost tangible.

"Shouldn't I have said that?" she asked.

"Say anything you like," he said, his voice almost rough with the hammering of his blood. "I love hearing it, feeling you turn to follow my lips, knowing that you want me. I love that most of all. Having you want me and knowing that it's me, just me, that makes you tremble.''

"Is that part of it?''

"It?'' he asked, smiling crookedly.

"This.''

Lisa eased her fingers into his thick, warm hair and pulled his mouth down to hers. With the same sensual deliberation that he had shown to her weeks ago, she traced the outline of his lips with the tip of her tongue before she closed her teeth with exquisite care on his lower lip. When she felt the shudder that rippled through his powerful body, she smiled and slowly released him.

"Trembling is part of the velvet fever, isn't it?'' she asked softly.

Rye closed his eyes and counted his own heartbeat in the violent race of his blood. The thought of making love with a woman as honestly sensual and sensually honest as Lisa nearly made him lose control.

But she was so innocent that he was afraid of shocking her long before he would be able to fully arouse her.

"Will you…?'' She touched his lips with her fingertip.

"Do you want me to kiss you?'' he asked, opening his eyes, looking into the amethyst depths of hers.

"Yes,'' she sighed.

"How do you want me to kiss you? Like this?'' Rye's lips skimmed over Lisa's. "Or like this?'' He skimmed again, then returned to linger. "Or like this?'' His tongue drew a warm, moist line around Lisa's lips, between them, inside them, until she whimpered softly and opened herself for a deeper kiss. "Is this what you want?'' he whispered.

When Lisa finally felt the moist invasion of Rye's tongue, her whole body tightened. He began stroking her mouth in slow, sensual rhythms that made her melt against him, moving as he moved, slowly, deeply. What had begun as a simple kiss became the sensuous consummation she had longed for. She clung to him, forgetting his warning against trusting him, knowing only that she was in his arms and it was even better than her dreams. When he would have finally ended the embrace she made an inarticulate sound of protest and tightened her arms around his neck, wanting more of his heat and sweetness.

"Shh," Rye said, biting Lisa's tongue delicately. "I'm not going anywhere without you. You're going to be with me every inch of the way if it kills me...every last inch."

He shifted slowly, lowering himself onto the blanket, kissing the silky radiance of her hair as he fanned it out above her head in a silver-gold cloud. Watching her eyes, he stretched out beside her and traced the line of her cheekbone first with his fingertip, then with the back of his fingers. She caught his hand and pressed a kiss into it before biting him not quite gently on his callused palm. His response was a low, very male laugh. His eyes turned the color of smoked crystal as he looked at her mouth and the curve of her breasts beneath her blouse.

"Do you want me to kiss you again?" he asked in a low voice.

"Yes," she said, meeting his eyes. "Oh, yes, Rye. I want that."

"Where? Here?"

Lisa smiled when his fingertips touched her lips.

"Or here?"

She shivered when he traced the delicate rim of her ear.

"Or here?"

His fingertip smoothed over the line of her throat, pausing at the pulse that beat quickly just beneath her skin.

"How about here?" he murmured.

The back of Rye's fingers caressed the hollow of Lisa's throat and then slowly slid beneath the collar of her blouse. There was no bra between his skin and hers, nothing to dull the sensation when he stroked the firm rise of her breast and caught her nipple between his fingers. She cried out in surprise and passion and put her hand over his as though to stop him from caressing her so intimately again.

"Are you saying that you don't want this?" Rye asked softly, tugging at her velvet nipple with gentle, skillful fingers.

Sensations speared through Lisa, making speech impossible. She moaned softly and arched against Rye's touch, holding his hand in place on her breast.

"That's it," he murmured, thumbing her nipple and listening to her sweet cries, feeling the echoes of her pleasure tighten his body, filling him with a heavy rush of blood. "Tell me what you want, little one. I'll give it to you. All of it, everything you can imagine."

"I want—" Lisa's voice broke as Rye rolled the nipple between his hard fingers, sending pleasure bursting through her. "I—" Her voice fractured again.

Lisa gave up trying to speak. She held Rye's hand against her breast and pressed herself into his palm, silently asking for more. Smiling, he slid his hand from beneath hers, ending the caresses that had flushed her skin with passion.

"Rye?"

"Yes?" he asked. His fingers flicked open first one button on her blouse, then a second, then a third. As he started to pull the cloth aside, Lisa made a startled sound. Her hands came up to hold the edges of the half-unfastened blouse together.

"Don't you want me to touch you?" Rye asked softly.

"I—I've never—I don't know."

"Your body does. Look."

Lisa looked down at her breasts. The nipples that ached so sweetly were erect, pushing against the soft cloth, begging to be touched again. While she watched, Rye's fingers circled the tip of one breast, then the other, making the nipples stand even higher and sending sensations spearing through Lisa all the way to the soles of her feet.

"It will feel even better without the cloth," Rye whispered, smiling as he listened to the soft whimpers he was drawing from Lisa. "Let me see you, baby. I won't touch you unless you want me to. All right?"

Slowly Lisa nodded her head, not trusting her voice to speak. She didn't care what Rye did, so long as it meant that the ache in her breasts would be answered by his caresses.

Looking only at Lisa's eyes, Rye slowly pulled aside one half of the partially undone blouse. With teasing, sensuous care, he tugged the cloth across the hard, high peak of her breast before tucking the loose folds beneath the firm flesh. He saw her eyes half close, felt her shivering sigh as her breast tightened at the first warm wash of sunlight across it. The nipple pouted in deepening shades of pink, revealing the heightened rush of blood through her body.

"Yes," Lisa whispered, moving languidly, arching slightly. "Yes. The sunlight feels so good it makes me ache, but it doesn't feel nearly as good as your hand."

He barely stifled a groan at the sudden hammer blows of need that made him painfully rigid. She was more beautiful than he had expected, more beautiful than seemed possible. Her breast was smooth and full, the skin flawless as a pearl, and her nipple was a raspberry waiting to be tasted by his tongue.

Lisa saw the fierce clenching of Rye's body and the sudden stillness of his face as he looked at her breast nestled among folds of blouse.

"Rye?"

Heat pulsed through Rye as he heard Lisa call his name in a voice made husky by the same passion that was driving him to the very edge of his control. His whole body tightened until he could barely speak.

"You're burning me alive," he said hoarsely, "and I've barely touched you. You're so innocent. But I'm not. I want you so badly that I feel like my guts are being torn out. I want to undress you, to hear you cry my name when I touch you where no one ever has. I want to kiss every bit of you, to lay my cheek against your waist, to trace the curve of your bare belly with my tongue, to taste the smooth skin inside your thighs, to touch you every way a man can touch a woman. But you're so damned innocent, I'd shock you even if I did no more than kiss the tip of your breast."

Lisa tried to speak, but could not. Rye's words had been like caresses, stealing her breath.

"Do you understand what I'm saying?" he asked roughly. "I'm not talking about a few more hot kisses and then I ride back down the hill. I'm talking about lying naked with you and touching you in ways you can't even imagine, and when you're hot and crying for me, I'll begin all over again until you're so wild you won't even know your own name."

Lisa's eyes widened and her lips parted over a silent rush of air.

"That's when I'll take you and you'll take me and for a time there will be no you, no me, only us locked together in the kind of pleasure that people kill or die for," Rye finished roughly. "Do you understand that? If I touch you the way you're begging to be touched, you won't leave this meadow a virgin."

Eight

Eyes wide, Lisa watched Rye. She opened her mouth to speak, licked her lips and tried to think. It was impossible. His words kept echoing inside her, making her tremble. She hadn't thought beyond the pleasure of his kisses. She should have, and she knew it. She was innocent but she wasn't stupid.

"I'm s-sorry," she said helplessly, hating to know that she had caused him pain. "I wasn't thinking how it would be for you. I never meant any hurt."

When Rye saw Lisa's taut expression he swore harshly and sat up in a single, savage movement. Then he closed his eyes, because if he kept on looking at her, he would reach for her, kiss her slowly, deeply, seducing her before she had a chance to say yes or no.

Suddenly he sensed the warmth of her breath against his hand in the instant before her lips touched his skin. When she held his hand against her cheek and whispered apologies, he felt the trembling of her body and knew that right now there was as much fear and unhappiness as passion in Lisa. The realization chastened him, cooling the fever that had been on the edge of burning out of control.

"It's not your fault," Rye whispered, pulling Lisa gently onto his lap, soothing her with a gentle hug. "It's mine. I knew where I was going. You didn't." He smiled wryly. "But I didn't know I could want a woman the way I want you. It took me by surprise.'' He brushed his lips over her cheek and tasted tears. ''Don't cry, baby. It's all right. I know myself better now. I won't take either one of us by surprise again, and I won't do anything you don't want. You can have as few or as many of my kisses as you like, however you like them, wherever you like them. Just don't be afraid of me. I'd never force anything from you, Lisa. You know that, don't you?''

The words reassured Lisa, but not as much as the soothing, undemanding kisses that Rye gave to her forehead and cheeks, the tip of her nose and the corners of her mouth. After a few moments she let out her breath in a long sigh and relaxed against his chest. He swept up her hair and draped it over his shoulder so that silky strands cascaded down his back. He wished that he was naked so that he might feel the texture as well as the weight of her beautiful hair. He turned his face into the pale, fragrant strands and inhaled deeply, stroking her hair with his dark cheek.

Seeing the sensual pleasure that her hair gave to Rye sent curious tremors through the pit of Lisa's stomach. She remembered the moment when she had awakened to find him turning his face from side to side in her hair as though he were bathing in the warm, flaxen cascade. She remembered a few weeks before, when he had nuzzled his teasing, sensual mouth into her palm, his tongue licking intimately between her fingers, his teeth closing on her skin until she couldn't stifle a moan. The thought of having her whole body caressed like that made her skin flush with sudden heat and sensitivity. The breeze blew and she stifled a tiny gasp at the feather touch across her still-bare breast.

''Lisa,'' whispered Rye.

She turned and saw that he was looking at her breast rising between folds of pale blue cloth.

''Do you trust me enough to let me touch you again?''

''Yes. No. Oh, Rye, I trust you but I don't want to make it worse for you. It isn't fair that you should hurt when you make me feel so good.''

''It's all right,'' he said, smoothing his hand from Lisa's knee to her hip to her waist. ''It's all right, baby. This will feel good to both of us. Unless you don't want it?'' His breath wedged as he controlled himself, keeping his hand just below her breast, waiting.

"It?'' she said in a high voice, caught between a virgin's nervousness and the fever that was burning down through her bones to her very soul.

He smiled crookedly. "My hand, and then my mouth. Here. Sipping on you, tasting you, loving you.''

He bent down and almost touched his lips to the ruby peak that was reaching toward him even as he moved. Instead of cupping or kissing the sensitive flesh, he blew on her as though she were a birthday candle. Lisa's broken laugh at the teasing caress become a choked cry as his warm palm took the weight of her breast. Yet still he ignored the tight, pink crown, as though he didn't know that it ached for his caress.

Without thinking, Lisa arched her back, trying to close the distance between Rye's mouth and her breast. The world spun as he lifted her, turned her, stretched her out on the blanket once more. He swept up the weight of her hair, letting it tumble wildly above her head, and then buried his left hand in the silky warmth, twisting it slowly around his fingers until her head tilted backward, arching her back.

"More,'' Rye said huskily.

Lisa didn't understand, but the feel of his fingers kneading her scalp was so unexpectedly sensual that she tilted her head back even farther and rubbed against his hand like a cat. Her back arched more with the motion, tightening her bare breast, making the nipple stand even higher.

"That's it, baby,'' Rye murmured, flexing his fingers against her scalp, urging her to draw herself even closer to his mouth. He moved in slow motion as he bent down to her, teasing both of them by not quite touching her despite the mute pleading of her arched back. "Yes, higher. You'll like it even better that way…and so will I.''

With supple grace Lisa arched her back fully, brushing the tight crown of her breast against Rye's lips. Only it wasn't his lips that touched her, but the hot, moist tip of his tongue. The unexpected caress made her back curve like a drawn bow. His right arm slid beneath her, holding her while his mouth slowly closed over her breast, gently devouring first her hard pink crest and then the velvet areola and not stopping until he was filled with her and his tongue was shaping her and his teeth were a sensual vise that made her writhe with pleasure. Her nails dug into his powerful shoulders as she called his name with each breath she took, ragged breaths that echoed the rhythms of his mouth tugging at her breast, setting fire to her body.

With a swift motion of his head, Rye turned and claimed Lisa's other breast, raking lightly through the cloth with his teeth until the nipple stood forth proudly. His teeth closed through the cloth with exquisite care despite the hunger that was making shudders run through his body.

Lisa's voice splintered as waves of pleasure visibly swept through her. She didn't feel the rest of her blouse being unbuttoned or cloth being peeled away from her skin. She felt only his hot, wild caresses on her naked breasts as fever raced through her. When he laced his fingers through hers and stretched her arms above her head, she arched gracefully toward his mouth, her back a taut curve, her breasts full and flushed with the heat of his kisses.

"Don't stop," Lisa moaned, twisting beneath Rye, trying to ease the throbbing of her nipples against his hard chest. "Please, Rye, don't stop."

The hard thrust of his tongue between her teeth cut off her pleas. She returned the kiss fiercely, wanting to crush her body into his, shaking with her wanting. His lips pressed down into hers, controlling her wild motions, slowly transforming them into the rhythmic movements of the act of love. She didn't protest. She wanted it as much as he did. She had never wanted anything half so much. She felt his hips settle between her legs, opening them. Then he arched suddenly against the hidden center of her passion, and she cried out in fear at the sensations that speared through her.

"Rye!"

"Easy, baby, easy," he said, fighting the urgent hammering of his own blood. "It's all right." He turned onto his side, bringing Lisa with him. For long moments he gentled her with voice and touch and body, phrases and caresses that soothed rather than set fire to her. "That's it, honey. Hold on to me. There's no hurry. There's just the two of us enjoying each other. Just us and all the time in the world."

Lisa clung to Rye while he stroked her slowly, calmly, his voice soft despite the tremors of passion that ripped through him at every shift of her breasts against him. After a few minutes he slowly unbuttoned his shirt, and his breath came out in a ragged sigh when he felt her nipples nuzzle through the black thatch of his hair until they pressed against his sun-darkened skin. The contrast of satin breasts and work-hardened muscle made his erect flesh strain even more tightly against the confinement of his jeans. He ignored the harsh urgency of his sex, knowing that whether Lisa became his lover that day or took no more from him than his kisses, she deserved better in her innocence and honesty than a hurried, nearly out-of-control man.

"You're more beautiful every time I look at you," Rye said, his voice deep and his breath warm against Lisa's ear. He bit her ear delicately, then with more power, enjoying the way she moved toward rather than away from his caresses. His strong hand stroked against her back, rubbing her gently against his chest. "Do I feel nearly as good to you as you do to me?"

Lisa laughed shakily, no longer frightened by the intense, unexpected sensations that had taken her body without warning. She was curious now, restless, hungry to feel that transforming pleasure again. "You feel twice as good. Five times. Nothing could feel better than you do."

As she spoke, she responded to the gentle pressure of Rye's hand by twisting in slow motion against him, savoring the shivery feelings that went from her nipples to the pit of her stomach and then radiated out softly, hotly, turning her bones to honey.

"Do you like—" Lisa's voice broke suddenly as Rye's knee moved between her legs, opening them. The warm, hard weight of his thigh slid upward until it pressed against her softness, rocking, sending a slow, sweet lightning radiating throughout her body. She made a low, involuntary sound of surprise and looked at him with dazed amethyst eyes. The sensation wasn't as sharp as it had been the first time, when he had lain between her legs, yet still the pleasure could hardly be borne.

"Do I like...?" Rye asked, moving deliberately between Lisa's thighs, accustoming her to being caressed. His body tightened hungrily when he felt the sudden, humid heat of her as she was taken by waves of pleasure.

"D-do you like being touched?" she asked, her voice trembling.

"Yes." He bent and kissed her slowly. "Do you want to touch me?"

"Yes, but..."

"But?"

"I don't know how," Lisa admitted, biting her lip. "I want it to be good for you, as good as you make it for me."

Rye closed his eyes for an instant, fighting the urge to pull Lisa's hands down his body until they rubbed against the hard, urgent flesh between his legs.

"If it gets any better for me," he said almost roughly, "it could be all over." He smiled crookedly at her. "Put your hands on me. Anywhere. Everywhere. Whatever you like. I want to be touched by you. I need it, baby. You don't know how I need it."

Lisa's hand trembled as she lifted it to Rye's face. She traced the dark arch of each eyebrow, the line of his nose, the rim of his ear. When that caress made his breath catch audibly, she returned to the sensitive rim, but this time it was her mouth that caressed him. With catlike delicacy she sketched the curves of his ear using the tip of her tongue, spiraling down and in until she felt the sensual shudder that rippled through Rye's body.

"You like that," she murmured.

"Oh, I don't know," he said huskily. "Could have been a coincidence. Maybe you better try it again."

She looked startled, then smiled. "You're teasing me."

"No, baby. You're teasing me."

He gave a low growl when her teeth closed on his ear in a caress that she had learned from him.

"Should I stop teasing you?" she asked, laughing at his soft growl.

"Ask me again in an hour."

"An hour?" Lisa said. The words were a soft rush of air against Rye's sensitive ear. "Can people stand that much pleasure?"

"I don't know," he admitted, "but it would be worth dying to find out."

Lisa's answer was muffled because her lips had become intrigued by the difference in texture between Rye's jaw and his ear. He didn't complain about the lack of conversation; he simply turned his head slightly, offering easier access to the soft explorations of her mouth. Too soon she encountered his shirt. He drew away for a moment, shrugged out of his shirt and threw it aside without a glance. But when he turned back to Lisa, he was afraid that taking off his shirt had been a mistake. She was staring at him as though she had never seen a man bare to the waist.

"Should I put it back on?" he asked quietly.

She dragged her glance slowly up to his intent eyes. "What?"

"My shirt. Should I put it on again?"

"Are you cold?"

The low sound that came from Rye could hardly have been called laughter. "Not very damn likely. You just seemed…surprised…when I took off my shirt."

"I was remembering when you came to the stream after chopping wood. You rinsed off your chest and shoulders and when you stood up the drops were like liquid diamonds in the sunlight. I wanted to sip each one of them from your skin. Would you have liked that?"

"Oh, baby," he whispered.

Rye caught Lisa's mouth beneath his and kissed her, loving her with slow movements of his tongue, both shaken and fiercely aroused by what she had said. Finally, reluctantly, he released her, because he knew that he was right on the edge of his self-control. He lay back on the blanket, his fingers interlaced beneath his head so that he wouldn't reach out to the pink-tipped breasts that peeked out so temptingly from her unbuttoned blouse.

"How good a memory do you have?" he asked huskily.

"I'm told it's very good."

"Close your eyes and remember every drop of water you saw on me. Can you do that?"

Eyes closed, smiling dreamily, Lisa said, "Oh, yes."

"They're yours, every one of them. All you have to do is take them."

Her eyes snapped open. She looked at Rye stretched out before her, watching her with a mixture of humor and sensual intensity that made her breath stop. Slowly she bent down to him, shivering as he did when her lips first touched his skin.

"There was one here," she said, kissing the base of his neck. "And here…and here," she continued, nuzzling the length of his collarbone toward the center of his chest. "And there was a tiny silver trickle here."

Rye closed his eyes as Lisa's pink tongue licked down the centre line of his chest, burrowing through his thick hair to the hot skin beneath.

"The drops went all the way down to your buckle," she said, hesitating, a question in her voice.

"God, I hope so."

Smiling, Lisa continued down past Rye's ribs, smoothing her mouth along the center of his body, testing the resilience of his flesh with her teeth and her tongue. When she reached the buckle she stopped, and Rye was tempted to tell her that the water had run beneath his clothes all the way to the soles of his feet. His breath came out in a rush when she kissed the skin just above his belt, nibbling all along his flat stomach. He locked his fingers together above his head to keep from reaching for her as her soft lips caressed in a random pattern across his ribs, stopping just short of a nipple hidden beneath curling black hair. When she continued on up to his collarbone without a pause, he made an inarticulate sound of disappointment.

"You missed some drops," he said thickly.

"I did? Where? Here?" Lisa asked, touching Rye's collarbone with the tip of her tongue.

"Lower."

"Here?" Her lips caught and tugged playfully on the hair curling in the center of his chest.

"That's closer. Now go to the right."

"Your right or mine?"

"Either way, honey. You'll find it."

Suddenly Lisa understood. She laughed softly. "Of course. How could I have forgotten that water gathered there?"

Rye couldn't answer, for she had found a flat nipple and was teasing it delicately, hotly, using teeth and tongue as he had on her. He made a hoarse sound of pleasure. When her fingers began to knead through the thick mat of his chest hair, he twisted his torso slowly, increasing the pressure of her touch. Her nails sank into his skin as she flexed her hands, loving the feel of the crisp hair and hard muscles rubbing against her palms. Her hands roamed up and down his chest, stroking him, enjoying the sensual heat of his skin.

In time she discovered that the hair beneath Rye's arms was as soft as a sigh. The ultrafine texture fascinated her. Her fingers returned to it again and again, just as her mouth kept returning to the tiny, rigid points of his nipples until he could bear it no longer. His hands unclenched and pulled her across his body until she was straddling him. Before she could say a word her blouse was pushed off her shoulders and discarded, leaving her breasts completely bare. The tips hardened as he looked at them, telling him that she wanted his touch as much as he wanted to touch her.

"Rye...?"

"Come here, little love," he said huskily.

Slowly Lisa leaned forward, bringing her breasts into Rye's hands. When his warm fingers found her nipples, she shivered with the exquisite, piercing pleasure his touch gave to her. She couldn't control the cries that rippled from her any more than she could stop the fever that flushed her body, heightening her sensitivity. She twisted slowly in his hands while he drew her ever farther up his body. She saw his lips open, saw the hint of his teeth as his tongue circled her nipple and then she was inside his mouth, captive to his hot, moist caresses. With a moan she stretched out full-length on his body, giving herself to his loving.

Rye's hands closed around Lisa's narrow waist, kneading it even as his mouth tugged on her breast. He shaped the rich curve of her buttocks, sinking his fingers into her flesh in a caress that made her bones loosen. His long fingers rubbed down her thighs, then swept back up again and down and up in a rocking motion that made her tremble. He slid his thumbs beneath the bottom edge of her cutoff jeans, tracing the full curve of her bare flesh.

"Rye," Lisa said, then shuddered as his thumbs burrowed farther up beneath the faded cloth.

"What?" he murmured, turning his head so that he could caress her other breast.

"I feel...dizzy."

"So do I, baby."

"You do?"

"Bet on it. If I weren't lying down, I'd be lucky to crawl."

Lisa's laugh was shaky but reassured. "I thought it was just me."

"Oh, it's you, all right. There's enough heat in that lovely body of yours to melt this mountain all the way to its core."

"Is that…all right?"

"No," he said nuzzling her breast. "It's much better than all right. It's incredible and sexy as hell. I've been missing you all my life and didn't even know it."

Lisa's laughter turned into a gasp as sensations streaked through her from the sensuous tugging of Rye's mouth on her breast. His hand moved between her legs, cupping her intimately in his palm, and she stiffened at the unexpected caress.

"This is part of it," Rye said, watching Lisa's eyes as his palm rubbed against her.

"It?" she said breathlessly.

And then her thoughts shattered into a thousand brilliant shards of pleasure with each motion of his hand. She moved helplessly against his palm, sending a cascade of shining hair sliding over him. He shivered at its whispering caress.

"This is the home of the velvet fever," he whispered against her lips. "Can't you feel it, honey? Hot and sweet, hungry and beautiful…so beautiful."

Rye made a low sound as Lisa shuddered against his hand, for the spreading heat of her body answered him better than any words could have. His hands moved and the snap closing the waist of her cutoff jeans gave way, followed by the soft hiss of the zipper sliding down. Gently, inevitably, his fingers eased inside the waistband. She lay full-length on top of him, trembling, saying nothing as she felt the last of her clothes sliding down her legs, baring her to the sunlight and to the man whose eyes blazed brighter than any sun.

Rye held Lisa naked on top of him, soothing her with long, gentle strokes of his hands, trying to still the wild need in his own body.

"R-Rye?"

"Hush, baby. It's all right. I'm not going to do anything that you don't want me to do."

She let out a shaky breath and slowly relaxed against him.

"That's it," he murmured. "Just relax and enjoy the sun while I enjoy you."

After a few moments the sun and Rye's soothing, loving hands made Lisa's uneasiness at being nude vanish. She sighed and stretched sensuously. Soon her hands itched to stroke Rye as she was being stroked, but when she ran her hands from his shoulders to his waist, his jeans were there, a barrier that reminded her that she was naked and he was not.

"This isn't fair," she whispered.

"I'll survive," Rye said tightly, misunderstanding.

"No, I meant your jeans."

"What about them?"

"They're in my way."

There was an electric silence, then, "How shockproof are you?"

"Quite."

"You're sure?"

"Yes," Lisa said simply, meeting his glance. "Very sure."

Rye went utterly still when he realized what Lisa was saying.

"You don't have to," he said, his voice rough with the restraint he was imposing on himself.

"I know. I want to…"

"But?" he asked tautly, reading the question in the unfinished sentence.

"I don't know how. And I want to please you. I want that so much."

Rye held Lisa close as he turned onto his side and kissed her tenderly. "You please me," he said huskily.

He gave her tiny, biting kisses before thrusting his tongue into the sweet darkness of her mouth. She opened to him, drawing him in even more, wanting the mating of tongues as much as he did. Reluctantly he ended the kiss and stood up. He took off his boots and socks, unfastened his belt buckle and looked down at Lisa.

She was lying on her side, her hair flying around her in silken disarray, her pink nipples peeking out from the white-gold strands. The curtain of her hair parted on either side of her hip, revealing a pearly curve of flesh and a pale tangle of much shorter, curlier hair.

"It's not too late to change your mind," Rye said, wondering if he lied.

Lisa smiled.

Watching her, he unfastened the fly of his jeans and peeled them down his body, taking his underwear in the same motion. He kicked the clothes aside and stood with his breath held, praying that she was as shockproof as she had said, for he was more aroused than he had ever been in his life. He wanted her to take the same pleasure in that as he did, but she was innocent and he expected her to be afraid.

Lisa's eyes widened until they were amethyst pools within her shocked face. She saw the violent pulse leaping at his temple and throat and farther down, where he thrust rigidly forward.

And then he was turning away, reaching for the clothes he had just discarded.

"No!" Lisa said, coming to her knees in a cloud of flying hair. She flung her arms around Rye's legs and pressed her face against the top of his hard thigh. "I'm not afraid. Not really. I've seen men wearing almost nothing, but not…not… It just startled me."

Rye stood and trembled when Lisa's hair settled over his hard flesh like a loincloth of silk. "It?" he asked, his voice like a rasp. "You do love that word, don't you?"

She looked up and saw the humor glittering through the passion that made his eyes blaze and his skin burn hotly beneath her cheek. She knew at that instant that her instincts had been right; Rye wouldn't hurt her, no matter how great his strength or his need.

"This," Lisa said, brushing her cheek over the full length of his erect flesh, "startled me."

"Baby," Rye whispered, sinking to his knees because he could stand no longer, "you're going to be the death of me. And I can hardly wait."

His fingers skimmed beneath the shimmering curtain of Lisa's hair, then curved around the back of her thighs, rocking her up against his body. Her breath caught and held as his fingers stroked down her thighs and then returned to the bottom of her buttocks again and again, each time sliding deeper between her legs, parting them just a bit more with every caress.

"Do you know what it did to me when you rubbed your cheek over me?" he asked, biting her ear and then thrusting in his tongue.

"N-no."

"This," he whispered.

Lisa bit back a moan as his palm smoothed down her belly and his fingertips parted her tight curls, seeking and finding skin that was moist, unbelievably soft. With each gliding motion of his fingers she trembled more. Her eyes closed and she swayed in front of him like a flower in the wind.

"Put your arms around my neck," Rye whispered, sliding farther into her body, preparing her for the much deeper joining to come.

Blindly Lisa did as Rye asked, clinging to him because he was the only real thing in a world that was spinning faster and faster with each touch of his fingers inside her. She felt neither self-consciousness nor shyness at the increasing intimacy of his caresses, for the elemental fever he had discovered in her had burned through everything, leaving only heat and need.

"That's it, baby. Hold on tight and follow me. I know where we're going."

Rye found and teased the sensitive bud that was no longer hidden within Lisa's softness. With each circular caress she moaned, feeling waves of shimmering heat sweep through her until she could hold no more and her pleasure overflowed.

"Yes," he said, biting her neck with enough force to leave tiny marks, teasing her now with the flesh that was as hard as she was soft. "Again, baby. Again. Share it all with me. It will make it easier for you, for me, for both of us. That's it. *Yes.*"

Lisa barely heard the words that wrapped around her, joining her to Rye as surely as her arms holding on to him and his body probing gently against hers. She felt herself lifted and carefully lowered to the blanket once more. Though he lay between her legs, he did not touch the moist flesh that he had teased into life. Her eyes opened and her head moved restlessly, feverishly.

"Rye?"

"I'm right here. All of me. Is that what you want?"

"Yes," she whispered, reaching down to touch him as intimately as he had touched her.

Rye closed his eyes as a shudder ran through his whole body. The feel of Lisa's small hand closing around him was more exciting than he would have believed possible.

"Baby," he whispered, "let me…"

He took her soft mouth with every bit of the fever that was burning him alive. When her tongue rubbed hungrily over his, he eased himself into her body until he felt the fragile barrier of her innocence.

"Rye?" she said. *"Rye."*

Deliberately he slid his hand between their partially joined bodies, rocking his hips slowly, caressing the hard bud of her passion.

Lisa moaned suddenly as fever flared wildly through her, a fever spreading up from Rye's hand and his hard flesh. He filled her slowly, moving gently, caressing her with his hand and body until pleasure swept through her in rhythmic waves, pleasure so great that it utterly consumed her, melting her over him again and again, and each time she called his name. She wanted to tell him she could feel no greater pleasure without dying, and yet he caressed her still, rocking within her. Deep within her. And then he was motionless, savoring the agonizing pleasure of being fully sheathed within her.

"Lisa," Rye whispered. "Baby?"

Her eyes opened slowly, dazed by the shimmering heat of being joined with him. "I thought…I thought it would hurt," she admitted.

"It did," he said huskily. "But the pain was buried by so much pleasure that you didn't know. Does this hurt now?"

He moved slowly. She made a soft, broken sound that was his name.

"Again," she said brokenly. "Oh, Rye, *again*." She looked into the gray blaze of his eyes. "Or doesn't it feel as good to you?"

"Good?" Rye shuddered as he buried himself fully within Lisa again and withdrew and penetrated her once more. "There are…no words. Come with me, baby. Take me where you've already been."

He moved in an agony of restraint, holding back with all his strength. He had never felt anything to equal the velvet fever of Lisa's body, had never known a physical sharing half so deep, had never believed himself capable of anything that approached the intense sensual involvement he was feeling. He moved slowly within her, deeply, his expression both tormented and sublime, wanting it never to end and knowing if he didn't let go soon he would die of the sweet agony.

Lisa's cries glittered through the fevered darkness that had claimed Rye, telling him that she was on the other side of ecstasy, calling to him. He wanted to go to her and he wanted to stay where he was, stroking the fever in both of them higher and higher while a darkness shot through with colors swirled around him, a thousand tiny pulses of ecstasy pricking his nerves into full life, shimmering, pressing, demanding.... With a hoarse, broken cry he arched into her until he could go no deeper, and then he surrendered to the sweet violence ripping through his control, demanding to be released.

Rye's last coherent thought was that he had lied; he hadn't known where they were going. Lisa had taken him to a place he had never been before, wrapping him in the velvet fever of her body, burning away his flesh, killing him softly, fiercely, burning with him soul to soul in a shared ecstasy that was death and rebirth combined.

Nine

Lisa sighed and carefully pulled out the tiny stitches she had spent the last hour sewing into the fine linen. She had been thinking about Rye rather than about keeping the proper tension on the thread. As a result, the seam was too tight, bunching the supple fabric. Patiently she smoothed out the cloth with her fingers before running long basting stitches down the length of the seam once more, holding the two pieces together until she could sew the finished seam with much smaller stitches. It had taken her many practice attempts on scraps before she had begun to master the trick of the flat fell seams that she had seen for the first time when she had picked apart Rye's old shirt. The neatness of the seams had fascinated Lisa; not a single raw edge could be seen anywhere on the shirt. She wanted it to be the same for his new shirt, nothing unfinished inside or out.

And that was the way it would be, despite the added work such seams made for Lisa. The additional time to be spent on the shirt didn't register as a problem with her. There was no time in McCall's Meadow, simply the brilliant clarity of summer flying like a banner from every mountain peak. Were it not for the growth of the grasses she photographed faithfully every seven days, she wouldn't have had any idea at all of the passage of time. Summer was a long, sweet interlude punctuated by the sight of Rye riding his powerful black horse into the meadow's radiance.

The thought of grass growing reminded Lisa to check her makeshift calendar. She looked up at the windowsill of the cabin's only window. Six pebbles were lined up. Today would be the seventh. Time to take pictures again. Not only that, but sunlight had begun to creep across the windowpane, which meant that it was after the noon hour. If she didn't get busy, Rye might come riding into the meadow and find her working on his shirt. She didn't want that to happen. She wanted the new shirt to be a complete surprise.

The thought of how much Rye would be pleased by the shirt made Lisa smile. He would be relieved and happy to be able to ask her to Boss McCall's dance at last. There had been many times during the past weeks when he had started to say something to her and then had stopped, as though he weren't certain how to say it. She suspected that he was trying to ask her to the dance, or to explain why he wouldn't be comfortable going there in his worn work clothes. The last time he had started to speak to her only to stop for lack of words, she had tried to tell him that it didn't matter to her whether his clothes were expensive or threadbare, it was enough for her just to be with him, but he hadn't let her finish. He had stopped her words with hungry movements of his tongue, and soon she had forgotten everything but the fever stealing through her body.

Remembering the intensity of Rye's lovemaking caused Lisa's hands to tremble. The slender needle slipped from her fingers. She retrieved it, took a deep breath and decided that it would be better if she didn't work any longer on Rye's shirt. She would probably prick herself and bleed all over the fine, pale fabric.

A horse's snort carried through the clear air, startling Lisa. She came to her feet in a lithe rush, only to see that it was two horses walking up the old wagon road from the valley below rather than one horse alone. Even though one of the horses was dark, she knew that its rider wasn't Rye. When he came to the meadow, he always came alone. While he was in the meadow, no matter how long he stayed, no one else came.

The thought made Lisa freeze for a moment, asking herself why Rye was always solitary. Lassiter usually came with Jim. Sometimes

Blaine and Shorty or one of the other cowhands would show up with film or supplies or a hopeful look in the direction of the campfire. Always the cowhands stayed only long enough to eat and check on her before they tipped their hats to her and moved on as though they sensed that somewhere out beyond the rim of the meadow, Rye was waiting impatiently for them to leave.

And Lisa was waiting impatiently for him to arrive.

"Yo, Lisa! You in the cabin?"

"I'll be right out, Lassiter," she called, hurriedly putting the shirt pieces on top of the closet shelf.

"Want me to stoke up the fire?"

"I'd appreciate that. I haven't eaten lunch yet. How about you and Jim?"

"We're always hungry for your bread," Jim called.

Lisa walked quickly out onto the porch, only to stop uncertainly as both men stared at her.

"Is—is something wrong?" she asked.

Lassiter swept off his hat in a gesture curiously like a bow. "Sorry. We didn't mean to stare. You always wear braids on top of your head, and now your hair is all loose and shiny. Lordy, it's something. Eve must have looked like you at the dawn of creation."

Lisa flushed, surprised by Lassiter's open admiration. "Why, thank you." Automatically her hands went to her hair, twisting it into a thick rope that could be coiled on top of her head and held with pieces of polished wood that were rather like chopsticks.

"Don't hide all that glory on our account," Lassiter said.

"I don't have much choice if I'm going to get close to a cooking fire."

"You have a point," he said, replacing his hat, watching sadly as the shimmering, gold-white strands vanished into smooth coils.

"Amen," Jim said. "Long hair and a campfire could put you in a world of hurt. Boss Mac would never forgive us if anything happened to you."

Lisa paused in the act of securing her hair on top of her head. "Boss Mac?"

Lassiter threw Jim a hard look, then turned back to Lisa. "Boss Mac is real particular about the health of the people that work for him. He told us to take special care of you, what with you being up here alone and all, and being such a little bit of a thing.''

"Oh." Lisa blinked. ''That isn't necessary, but it's very thoughtful of him.''

"Beg pardon," Jim said, ''but it's real durn necessary. All us cow-hands take Boss Mac's words to heart, 'specially that Rye. Why, he must be up here to check on you pretty near every day lately.''

Lisa flushed and looked down, missing the glare that Lassiter gave to Jim.

''The boys and me, we figure he might be getting sweet on you,'' Jim continued, ignoring Lassiter's narrow-eyed look. ''That would be a real wonder, him being such a loner and all. Why, I'll bet—''

''Thought you said you were hungry,'' Lassiter interrupted.

''—we can look forward to seeing you at the dance, can't we,'' finished Jim, smiling widely.

Lisa sensed that she was being teased again but couldn't guess where the joke lay, unless it was in Jim's delight at seeing a ''loner'' like Rye asking a woman to the dance.

''Don't count on Rye asking me,'' she said, forcing herself to smile as she stepped off the porch and walked between the two men. ''As you said, he's a loner. Besides, not everyone has extra money for party clothes.''

''What do you mean? Boss Mac has enough money to—ow, Lassiter! That's my foot you're tromping on!''

''Doubt it,'' Lassiter muttered. ''You already got both of them in your big mouth.''

''What the hell you jawing…'' A look of comprehension settled onto Jim's earnest face. ''Oh. Well, shoot. What's the point of a joke if'n there's no punch line?''

''The only punch you got to worry about is on the end of Big Mac's fist. Savvy?'' Lassiter shot a quick look in Lisa's direction. She was bending over the fire, stirring up the ashes. He bent closer to Jim and said in a low voice, ''Listen, hoss. You better stay down the hill until Boss Mac's through with his joke. You spoil his fun and you're going to be looking for some far-off piece of range to ride. What would Betsy think of that, with you two having another little one on the way an' all?''

"Well, *shoot*," Jim said, frustrated. "You hold on to a joke too long and it's no fun a'tall."

"That's Boss Mac's problem. Yours is to keep your trap shut unless it's to shovel in food."

Grumbling beneath his breath, Jim followed Lassiter to the campfire.

Papers were scattered all across Rye's desk. Each one had a small yellow square of sticky paper attached to the much larger white square. The yellow was covered with detailed instructions as to what needed to be done. He squinted down at one of the little sticky squares, discovered that he couldn't decipher his own hurried note and swore. He grabbed a tablet of tiny yellow squares and began to write.

The ballpoint pen had gone dry. Disgusted, he threw it into the metal wastebasket with enough force to leave a dent.

"First thing this fall, I'm going to hire an accountant," he muttered. "I should have done it years ago."

But he hadn't. He had been determined to handle every aspect of ranch business by himself. That way no one could say that Edward Ryan McCall III hadn't earned his own fortune. Unfortunately, bringing the ranch back from the state of near ruin in which he had found it took an enormous amount of time. Never before had it bothered him that running the ranch left him with no time for a private life. The women who had found their way to his door hadn't tempted him away from his work for any longer than it took to satisfy a simple physical urge. Being with his family had held no real allure for him, either; in fact, listening to his father's long-winded lectures on the necessity of continuing the McCall dynasty had been a real deterrent to frequent family visits on Rye's part.

He glared at the papers and wondered if he shouldn't just pick up the telephone and order a bookkeeper the way he would a half ton of oats. Why bother with interviews and checking references and all the other time-consuming things that had prevented him from getting an accountant in the first place? Just pick a name, grab the phone and walk out of the office a few minutes later with the job done. Devil would be looking over the fence right now, waiting impatiently for his rider to appear.

But Rye wouldn't be appearing. If he didn't input into the computer at least some of the paperwork laid out before him, the ranch accounts would be in such a snarl that he would never untangle them—not even this fall, when there would be day after day after day of nothing but ranch work to look forward to.

Frowning, Rye turned his mind away from the end of summer. He never thought of endings when he was in the meadow with Lisa. There, time didn't exist. She had always been there, she always would be there, no past, no future, just the elemental summer that knows no time. Like Lisa. There was a timeless, primal quality to her that was both fascinating and compelling. Perhaps it was her capacity for joy. Perhaps it was simply that she was able to live entirely in the instant, to give her undivided attention to each moment with him. Time as he understood it had no meaning to her. No yesterday, no tomorrow, nothing but the endless, shimmering present.

Yet summer would end. Rye knew it, although when he was with Lisa he didn't believe it. When he wasn't in the meadow, everything looked different. Outside of the meadow, his conscience goaded him for not telling her that he was the owner of McCall's Meadow, not simply a threadbare cowhand with no past and no future. But when Rye reached the meadow, whatever he was or wasn't when he was down the hill simply faded beneath the incandescent light that was Lisa. Whether he lay with his head in her lap while he talked about cattle and men and changing seasons, or whether he lay deep within her and felt her passionate cries piercing his deepest silences, with Lisa he had found a peace that transcended ordinary boundaries of time and place.

That was why his words stuck in his throat and refused to budge when he started to tell her his full name. Each time he was with her, what they shared became more and more valuable, until now it had become so precious that it didn't bear thinking about. If he told her who he was, he would lose something that was beyond price. She would look at him and see Edward Ryan McCall III instead of a cowhand called Rye. The instant she knew who he was, time would flow in its regular channels once more. That would happen soon enough, at the end of summer, when she would leave and the meadow would be empty once more.

And so would he.

That's why I won't tell her. Either way, I lose. Each day that I don't tell her is a day stolen out of time. Summer will end, but it won't end one second before it must.

The phone rang, disturbing Rye's thoughts. As he reached for the receiver he looked at the clock and realized that he had spent the past half hour staring through the papers on his desk and thinking of a meadow and a woman who knew no time. The yearning to be with Lisa twisted suddenly in him like a knife, a pain surprising in its intensity.

To hell with the ranch accounts. I need to be with her. There's so little time left.

The phone rang for the fourth time.

"Hello," Rye said.

"Goodness, what a bark. It's unnerving to know that your bite is even worse."

"Hello, Sis," he said, smiling. Cindy was the only member of his family whose call was always welcome. "How's the latest boyfriend?"

"Funny, Bro. Really funny."

"That fast, huh?"

"Faster. We hadn't even ordered dinner before he led the conversation around to my family. I was using Mother's maiden name at the time, too. There I was, Cinderella Ryan, being wined and—"

"Cinderella?" interrupted Rye, laughing.

"Sure. A name that outrageous has to be real, right?"

"You've got a point."

"I should have used it to stick him to a board with the other insects in my collection," she said glumly. "They're getting smarter, but no more honest."

Rye grunted. He knew that "they" were the fortune hunters of the world. He despised all such people, but he reserved special contempt for the male of the species.

"Come live with me, Cinderella. I'll vet them for you. I can smell a money hunter ten miles away."

"I wish Dad could."

"Is he at it again?"

"In spades."

"Don't tell me. Let me guess," Ryan said. "She's tall, brunette, 42-25-40, and her major talent consists of getting clothes that fit."

"When did you meet her?" Cindy demanded.

"I haven't."

There was silence, then rueful laughter. "Yeah, I guess he's pretty predictable, isn't he?"

"Not surprising. Mother was tall, dark and beautiful. He's still looking for her."

"Then he should add IQ to his list of numbers," Cindy retorted. "Just because you're built doesn't mean that you have the brains of a double cheeseburger with no mustard."

Rye smiled to himself. Cindy was the image of their dead mother— tall, brunette, curvy and very bright.

"Speaking of which," Cindy continued.

"Which what?"

"Good question. When you have an answer, you know my number."

Laughing, Rye kicked back in his office chair and put his cowboy boots on the papers. It occurred to him that Cindy and Lisa would enjoy each other. The thought took the smile off his face, because Cindy would never have the chance to know Lisa.

"...my college roommate. You remember her, don't you? Susan Parker?"

"Huh?" Rye said.

"Ryan, brother dear, monster of my childhood years, this is your wake-up call. *Wake up.* You're having a roundup or hoedown or whatever in a week. A dance. Correct?"

"Correct," he said, smiling.

"I am coming to your ranch in a week," Cindy continued, speaking slowly, clearly, as though her brother were incapable of comprehending English spoken normally. "I am bringing with me a woman called Susan Parker. She went through college with me. We shared a room. After college, she made an obscene amount of money smiling for photographers while wearing the most hideous clothes woman-hating male designers ever fashioned. Are you still with me?"

Rye's inner warning system went into full-alert status. "Beautiful and rich, right?"

"Right."

"Wrong. You're welcome anytime, Cinderella, but leave your matchmaking kit at home."

"Are you saying that my friends aren't welcome at your ranch?"

Rye opened his mouth for a fast retort and then stopped, defeated. "Cindy, you're my favorite sister and—"

"Your only one, too," she interjected.

"Will you zip up?"

"Well, since you asked so nicely, I'll be glad to—"

"Cynthia Edwinna Ryan McCall, if you don't—"

"Shut up," Cindy continued, interrupting, her timing perfect.

Rye sighed. "Cindy. Please. No matchmaking. Okay?"

There was a brief pause, followed by, "You really mean it, don't you?"

"Yes."

"Have you finally found someone?"

Pain turned in Rye again, drawing his mouth into a thin line.

"Ryan?"

"You're welcome to come to the dance. Bring what's her name with you if it makes you happy. I'll even be polite to her. I promise."

"What's she like?"

"Hell, Cindy, she's your friend, not mine. How would I know?"

"No. Not Susan. The one you've found."

Rye closed his eyes and remembered what Lisa had looked like asleep in the meadow, sunlight running through her hair in shimmering bands of pale gold.

"Her name is Woman...and she doesn't exist," Rye said softly. "Not really. She lives outside of time."

There was a long pause before Cindy said, "I don't understand. I don't know whether to be happy for you. You sound...sad."

"Be happy. For a time I've known what it is to be loved for myself alone. She thinks I'm just a cowhand with patched jeans and frayed cuffs and she doesn't give a damn. She treats me as though I've poured diamonds into her hands, and I haven't given her one single thing."

"Except yourself."

Rye closed his eyes. "That's never been enough for other women."

"Or men," Cindy said, her voice low as she remembered her own painful discovery that it was her money, rather than herself, that had attracted the man she had loved. "I'm happy for you, Ryan. However long it lasts, I'm happy for you. I can't wait to meet her."

"Sorry, Sis. It just isn't in the cards."

"Won't she be at the dance? Oh. Of course not. She doesn't know who you are. Damn."

He smiled despite the pain twisting through him. "She wouldn't be able to come even if I were able to ask her. She hasn't the money to buy a decent pocketknife, much less something as useless as a party dress. Patched jeans or silk, it wouldn't matter to me, but I'd cut off my hands rather than make her feel out of place."

"So buy her a dress. Tell her you won the money in a poker game."

"She'd tell me to get a new shirt for myself—and mean it."

"My God. Is she bucking for sainthood?"

Rye thought of the sensual pleasure Lisa took in his body, of the feel of her soft mouth and hot tongue exploring him.

"Sainthood? No way. She's just too practical to spend money on a onetime dress when her man is too poor to buy a new work shirt for himself."

"I want to meet her."

"Sorry. Summer will end soon enough as it is. I love you, Sis, but not enough to shorten my time with her by so much as an hour just to satisfy your curiosity."

Cindy muttered something Rye chose not to hear. Then she sighed. "What does she look like?"

"Lassiter told me a few hours ago that Eve must have looked like that at the dawn of creation."

What Rye didn't add was that he had nearly decked Lassiter for even looking at Lisa.

"Lassiter said that? Holy cow. She must be a real world-burner."

"He was more respectful than lustful."

"Uh-huh. Sure. If you believe that, you better have your IQ recounted, Brother. With Lassiter, lust is a state of being."

"I didn't say he was *only* respectful. It's just that there's a quality of innocence about her that defeats Lassiter's standard approaches."

Cindy laughed. "That I believe. Only a true innocent wouldn't know who you are. Where has she lived all her life—Timbuktu?"

"Among other places."

"Such as?"

"She's a world traveler."

"Jet-setter? Then how come she didn't recognize you?"

"Cindy, I'm not—"

"No fair," she said, interrupting. "You won't tell me what she looks like and you won't tell me her name and you won't tell me where she lives."

"But I did tell you. She lives in a place out of time."

"So where do you meet her?"

"There."

"'In a place out of time.'" Cindy hesitated, then asked wistfully, "What's it like in that place out of time?"

"There are no words...."

For several moments Cindy closed her eyes and simply hung on to the phone, fighting the turmoil of emotions called up by the bittersweet acceptance in her brother's voice.

"My God, Ryan. You should be happy, yet you sound so...bleak."

"Winter is coming, little sister. We're supposed to have a killing frost in the high country before the week is out. Summer will be much too short this year."

"And you'll miss being in your meadow, is that it?" Cindy asked, knowing how much peace Ryan found in the high meadow he had let go back to a wild state.

"Yes. I'll miss being in my meadow." Rye's gray eyes focused suddenly on the peak that rose above McCall's Meadow. "That reminds me. I've got to get a batch of film up there before dark."

"I can take a hint, especially when it's delivered with a sledgehammer. See you next weekend."

"I'll look forward to it," Rye said.

But it was the mountain he was looking toward when he spoke.

He hung up the phone, grabbed the bag of film from the top of a filing cabinet and headed toward the barn with long strides. He had a sense of time unraveling faster and faster, pulling apart the fabric of his unexpected summer happiness. The feeling was so strong that he had a sudden rush of fear.

Something has happened. She's hurt or she found out who I really am. Something is wrong. Something.

The sense of imminent danger goaded Rye all the way up the steep trail. He urged Devil on in a fever of impatience, testing the big horse's agility and endurance. When he burst through the aspen grove at the rear of the cabin, there was no one waiting for him by the campfire. He spurred Devil into the opening of the meadow where the split-rail fence zigzagged gracefully over the land.

From the corner of his eye Rye caught a flash of movement. Lisa was running toward him, an expression of joy on her face. He slid off Devil, took three running steps and caught Lisa up in his arms. His hand moved over her hair, releasing it from its bonds. He buried his face in the flying, silver-gold cloud and held her hard, drinking in her warmth, telling himself that summer would never end.

Ten

Lisa looked at the pebbles on the windowsill. Five. She glanced at the long-legged bay gelding patiently waiting in the aspen grove. The horse had been on loan to her ever since she had bruised her bare foot wading in the stream and had wistfully asked Jim if she could borrow his horse in order to check the meadow fence. After letting her ride for a few moments under their watchful eyes, Lassiter and Jim had been surprised at her skill on horseback. They had also been full of advice on how to treat a bruised foot.

It had been the same when Rye had made an unexpected return trip to the meadow just before sunset that same day, leading the gelding called Nosy. He had watched critically while she rode Nosy, approved her style and told her gruffly that Boss Mac should have thought of giving her a horse to ride sooner. If she needed something, she could ride to the ranch, and if she was hurt and couldn't ride, all she had to do was turn Nosy loose. He would go back to the ranch better than any homing pigeon.

Lisa's glance went from the pebbles to the angle of the sunlight slanting through the windowsill. It was at least two o'clock.

He's not coming back again today and you know it, she told herself silently. *He said that Boss McCall was keeping everyone hopping getting ready for the dance.*

Rye had ridden up to the meadow that morning, coming to her with the dawn, teasing her from sleep into sensual wakefulness with a tender persistence that had made her shiver with the fever stirring in her blood. He had made love to her as though she were a virgin once more, caressing her until she was flushed with passion, then beginning all over, stroking her body until she was wild—and then he had begun yet again, loving her with his mouth instead of his hands, teaching her of a honeyed intimacy that stripped the world away, leaving only the velvet fever of her body and his intertwined.

The memory of Rye's hot, unbearably knowing mouth loving her made Lisa's hands shake. He had made her feel like a goddess worshiped by a sensual god, and when she thought she could bear no more, he had come to her, teaching her that there was no end to ecstasy, simply beginnings.

With trembling hands, Lisa reached for the brown paper shopping bag that she had set out by the door. She had almost given Rye the shirt that morning, when dawn had turned his skin a rich gold and made his eyes incandescent with pleasure. But she had wanted the shirt to be perfect, and she hadn't had time yet to master completely the old flatiron she had found in the cabin's only closet—along with a rusted Spanish spade bit, a broken hammer and a handful of square nails that had to be older than the flatiron itself. Cleaning and using the ancient, heavy iron had tested her patience and ingenuity to their limits, but it had been worth it. The shirt was beautifully smooth now, and the cloth shimmered as though it were alive.

For the tenth time Lisa assured herself that Boss Mac wouldn't be angry if she used his horse for a nonemergency trip to the ranch. The meadow wouldn't be hurt by her absence. All her photos and logbooks were caught up. Surely Boss Mac would understand....

Quit stalling, she told herself firmly. *Rye said that he wouldn't be able to come to the meadow for a few days, and the dance is the day after tomorrow. If I don't give him the shirt today, he won't be able to ask me to the dance at all.*

Lisa took a deep breath, picked up the paper bag and went out to saddle Boss Mac's horse.

Rye cursed the walleyed cow in terms that would have made a rock blush. The cow, however, was not a rock. She was a cow, which was something entirely different. Compared to a cow, a rock was intelligent.

"Boss Mac? You in there?" Lassiter yelled.

"Where the hell else have I been for the last hour?" Rye snarled, unhappy at being interrupted yet again. He had put off so many things since he had become Lisa's lover that the men were after him every ten minutes to make a decision on something that should have been settled weeks ago.

"You still doctoring that fool cow?" Lassiter asked.

"Hell, no. I'm making a damn paper doily."

Lassiter looked over the stall just as the cow's long, ropy, far-from-clean tail swished across Rye's face with deadly accuracy. The cowhand listened with real respect while Rye described the cow's ancestry, personal habits, probable IQ and certain resting place after death in searing, scatological detail. Meanwhile Rye continued swabbing antibiotic on the many cuts that the old cow had received when she had stubbornly tried to walk through a barbwire fence. And tried, and tried and then tried again.

"She sure did take a notion to leave that pasture, didn't she?" Lassiter observed.

Rye grunted and made another pass with the dripping swab. "You want something from me or are you just exercising your jaw?"

"Your sister just called," Lassiter said quickly. "Your pa's coming with her to the party, unless there's a meeting and he misses the early plane. If that happens, you'll have to pick him up in the city. He's bringing a pack of his friends. 'Bout eight, near as I can tell. Miss Cindy tried to talk him out of it. Didn't work, I reckon. Like death an' taxes, he's coming."

Eyes closed, jaw clenched, Rye controlled the impulse to take a swing at the bearer of bad news.

"Wonderful," Rye said through his teeth. "Just wonderful." Then he had a thought that made his lips twitch into a reluctant smile. "I can just see his latest glitter baby's face when she realizes that the dance floor is the bottom of a barn and the band isn't plugged into anything but two hundred years of tradition."

Quietly Lassiter let out the breath that he had been holding and smiled. "Yeah, that should be worth seeing. How long has it been since your pa came up here?"

"Ten years."

"Been a few changes since then."

"Dirt is still dirt, and fresh cow pies still stick to your boots."

"Boss, those things ain't never gonna change."

Rye took a last pass at the cow's right side, then moved to her left.

"The way she's cut up, it'd be easier just to finish the job and barbecue the old she-devil," Lassiter offered.

"We'd wear out our teeth on her."

Lassiter grinned. He knew that Rye had a sentimental attachment to the walleyed cow. She had been the first cow to calve after he had bought the ranch. She had had twins nearly every year after that, healthy calves every one. Ugly as she was, Rye called her his good-luck charm.

"I've got a call into Doc Long," Rye continued. "When he's through stitching up the Nelsons' crazy quarter horse, he'll come here."

"Did that old stud go through the fence again?"

"Nope. Barn wall."

"Lordy. That's one determined stud."

"Some damn fool tied a mare in heat just outside."

Lassiter laughed softly.

Beyond the big, open doors of the barn, someone began hollering for Boss Mac.

"Go see what he wants," Rye said, ducking another swipe of the cow's tail.

Lassiter left and came back within minutes. "Shorty wants to know how deep to dig the barbecue pit."

"What? He's from Texas, for God's sake!"

"Oklahoma. Stockbroker's son. Shaping up into a real good hand, though. Better with horses than anyone except Jim."

Rye sighed. "Tell Shorty to make the hole big enough to bury a steer."

Shaking his head, Rye went back to working over the tattered old cow. He was interrupted six more times before he finished going over the cuts. Between getting normal ranch work done and getting everything lined up for the dance, it seemed that no one could do without Boss Mac's guidance for more than ten minutes at a stretch.

Finally Rye straightened, stretched the kinks out of his back and went to the huge porcelain sink he had installed when he had built the barn. He sluiced off the worst of the dirt and spilled medicine, stretched his aching back again and thought longingly of Lisa up in the high meadow. But no matter how many times he rearranged what had to be done in his mind, he couldn't find the hours to ride to the meadow and hold Lisa once more.

Suddenly, savagely, he cursed the work that prevented him from being with her. He was still scowling blackly when he stalked back down the line of stalls to take a last look at the old cow. He discovered that in his absence she had left a present for him. Muttering beneath his breath, he grabbed a manure fork, not wanting to risk any more infection in the old cow's cuts.

"Rye? Are you in here?"

At first Rye thought he was dreaming. He spun around and saw her standing on tiptoe in the broad center aisle, peering into various stalls.

"*Lisa.* What the hell are you doing here?"

She turned quickly at the sound of Rye's voice. The smile she had on her face faded into uncertainty when she saw his expression. As he shut the stall door behind him and walked toward her, Lisa's fingers tightened even harder on the paper bag she was carrying.

"I know how busy you are and I don't want to get you in trouble with Boss Mac," Lisa said hurriedly. "It's just that I had something for you and I wanted to give it to you and so I rode down the hill and—" she thrust the bag into Rye's hands "—here it is."

For an instant Rye was too stunned to do more than stare at Lisa. Into the spreading silence came Jim's clear voice shouting across the barnyard.

"Boss Mac? Yo, Boss Mac? You around?"

"In here!" Rye shouted, answering reflexively.

Lisa's eyes widened. No wonder Rye seemed so shocked to see her. Boss Mac was close by and she was interrupting Rye's work. She had heard enough about Boss Mac's temper not to want to make Rye the target of it. She looked around frantically, wondering where Boss Mac was.

"Shorty wants to know how deep the bed of coals should be laid an' Devil just threw a shoe an' Lassiter told me to tell you that Doc Long has to check on a mare with colic before he can sew up your durn fool walleyed cow," Jim said as he entered the barn. The change from bright sunlight to the muted interior illumination made him blink. "Where the blazes... Oh, there you are. Shorty swears he saw that bay gelding you gave to Lisa tied behind the barn. You want me to check?"

"No," Rye said curtly.

"You sure? If'n Nosy threw her or..." Jim's voice trailed off into silence as his vision cleared and he saw Lisa standing just beyond Rye. "Oh, Lordy, Lordy. Me and my big mouth. I sure am sorry, Boss Mac."

Lisa didn't hear Rye's response. She was still paralyzed in the first shock of discovery.

"You're..." Her voice dried up. She swallowed convulsively as she looked at Rye's tight, bleak expression. "Boss Mac."

"Yes," he said, and his voice was as hard as his face.

Lisa stared at Rye, trying to order her chaotic thoughts. "I..." She made a small, helpless gesture with her hand when her voice failed her again.

"I'm sorry, Boss Mac," Jim mumbled. "I sure didn't mean to spoil your joke."

Jim might as well not have spoken. Rye stood motionless, his attention focused solely on Lisa as he waited for calculation to replace passion in her eyes when she looked at him.

All trace of blood left Lisa's face as Jim's apology to Rye sank through her paralysis.

I sure didn't mean to spoil your joke.

She didn't notice the cowhand's rapid, silent retreat from the barn, for she had suddenly remembered the first words Rye had ever spoken to her: *You're something else, little girl. If you'll settle for a diamond bracelet instead of a diamond ring, we'll get along fine for a while.*

Now, too late, she knew what that "something else" was.

A fool.

Rye had warned her in the clearest possible words that he wanted only one thing from her, but she hadn't listened. She had taken her loneliness and nameless yearning and she had created a beautiful dream: a poor cowhand called Rye.

I sure didn't mean to spoil your joke.

Jim's words echoed and reechoed in Lisa's mind, haunting her.

A joke, joke, just a joke…all of it, from the first instant, a joke. Rye was Boss Mac, the wealthy womanizer, the man who wouldn't settle down and provide his father with an heir. Boss Mac, who came from so much money that no one in his family bothered to count it anymore. Like his women. No one bothered to count them, either.

Lisa's amethyst eyes went to the brown paper bag that held the shirt she had made for Rye. She could imagine what he would think of clothing made under the most primitive circumstances, clothing that had all the myriad flaws of handwork. The shirt's stitches weren't perfectly even; there were no two buttonholes precisely the same size; the finished shirt had been pressed by an antique flatiron heated on a stone hearth. And the buttons themselves were appallingly unsophisticated.

Color returned in a flaming wave to Lisa's face when she thought of the buttons, no two alike, carved from antler and crudely polished by hand. She looked at Rye with stricken eyes, trying to find words to explain that she had meant well, she just hadn't known who he was or she never would have presumed…

Another realization came to Lisa in a wave of color that surged and faded as quickly as her heartbeat.

No wonder Rye didn't ask me to the dance. He isn't just one of the cowhands. He's the owner of the Rocking M. Whoever comes to the dance with him won't be a girl who has no money, no formal education, and social graces learned around primitive campfires.

What a joke. On me. Definitely on me.

Wild laughter clawed at Lisa's throat, but she had just enough self-control not to give in. She knew with certain humiliation that if she did, the laughter would soon turn into a raw sound of pain. That wouldn't do. She was in civilization now, where people masked their emotions. That was a social grace she simply had to learn. Immediately. Now. This instant.

And then Lisa realized that she couldn't smile and congratulate Rye on his droll Western foolery. She simply wasn't that sophisticated. She never would be. She was like the meadow—open to both sunlight and rain, lacking protection, a haven with no barriers.

That was what she needed right now. The meadow's generous, un-calculated warmth.

Lisa turned and ran until she found herself in the blinding sunlight outside the barn. She raced toward Nosy and mounted with the wild grace of someone who had been raised riding bareback. The horse spun on its hocks in answer to the urgency of its rider, but a powerful hand clamped onto the reins just below the bit, forcing the animal to stay in place.

"Whoa, boy! Easy, there. Easy," Rye said, bracing himself against the horse's attempts to free itself. When Nosy snorted and settled down, Rye looked up at Lisa but did not release the reins.

The first thing Rye saw was her unnaturally pale skin, her face drawn into taut lines. Her expression was that of someone who had been struck without warning and was searching for a way to avoid further blows. She was looking away from him, toward the peak that rose above McCall's Meadow, and her body fairly vibrated with her urgency to flee. He knew without asking that she was longing for the meadow's timeless summer, its silence and peace. He longed for the meadow, too. But it was gone now, yanked from his grasp by a cow-hand who couldn't keep his mouth shut.

Rye hissed a single, vicious word. Lisa flinched and tried to rein the gelding away from him. It didn't work. Rye's fingers were immovable.

"I tried to tell you a hundred times," he said harshly.

Lisa tugged futilely on the reins. There was no give. She realized that she wasn't going to get to the meadow's gentle embrace without first confronting Rye. Grimly she clung to what remained of her self-control.

"But you didn't tell me," she said, watching the meadow rather than Rye. She tried to smile. It didn't work. "Telling me would have spoiled the joke. I understand that. Now."

"Not telling you didn't have a damn thing to do with a joke. Not after we became lovers."

Rye saw Lisa flinch at the word *lovers*, saw the hot flush of em-barrassment rising up her skin. She looked vulnerable, defenseless.

Innocent. But she wasn't. He had taken that innocence from her. No. She had given it to him, hadn't she?

She gave it to a cowhand called Rye. But I'm Boss Mac. Why didn't I tell her?

Swearing at himself and the world, his temper slipping away word by hot word, Rye ducked under the horse's neck without releasing the reins and forced Lisa to face him.

"I don't know why I'm feeling so damned guilty," he snarled. "I had a good reason for not telling you who I was!"

"Yes, of course," she said politely, her tone uninflected, her eyes fixed over Rye's head on the peak that rose above the meadow. She pulled discreetly on the reins. Nothing moved. "May I go now or do you want your horse back?"

Lisa's careful, polite words had the effect of adding a torch to the spilled gasoline of Rye's temper.

"You know why I didn't tell you, so don't play innocent!" he said angrily, clenching Nosy's reins in one hand and the forgotten paper bag in the other.

"Yes. Your joke."

"It wasn't a joke and you damn well know it! I didn't tell you who I was because I didn't want you to look at me with dollar signs rather than desire in your eyes! Why the hell should I feel guilty about that? And before you answer, you better know one more thing. I know that you came to America because you wanted to find a husband who could either live like your parents or had enough money so that you wouldn't have to adjust to clocks and a forty-hour work week."

Lisa's expression became more confused with each of Rye's words. Seeing that didn't improve his temper.

"You weren't raised to live in the real world and you know it," he said roughly. "Tribal time just doesn't fit in twentieth-century America. So you went head-hunting a rich man or an anthropologist and you ended up giving yourself to me despite the fact that I was poor and sure as hell wasn't bent on studying Stone Age natives. I took what you offered and never promised you one damn thing in the way of marriage or anything else. So you can just drop the wounded-innocent routine. You knew that summer would end and so did I, and then you would ride down the hill into the arms of that jackass an-thropologist Ted Thompson has all picked out for you.''

Rye didn't ask himself why even thinking about the unknown man waiting for Lisa made his own body tighten in a killing rage. He didn't ask himself about the meaning of anything that he was feeling—he was too angry at sensing summer slip through his clenched fists as irretrievably as sunlight sliding into night. He needed Lisa's sweet fire and shimmering warmth. He needed it as much as he needed air; and he was fighting for it in just the same way as he would fight for air, no holds barred, no quarter given, no questions asked or answered, nothing of softness in him.

And he was losing anyway. Losing her. He had known he would, but he hadn't known it would come this soon and hurt this much. The pain enraged him, and the loss.

He felt the reins being tugged slowly from his clenched hand.

"No!" he snarled, tightening his grip. "Talk to me, damn it! Don't just ride out of here like I don't exist!"

The demand penetrated Lisa's single-minded determination to es-cape. For the first time she looked directly at Rye.

He had expected to see calculation and money dreams in her eyes. He saw nothing but the same darkness that he felt expanding through his own soul. Pain and loss and grief, but not anger.

The lack of anger baffled Rye until Lisa began to speak. The very care with which she chose her words, the ruthless neutrality of her voice, the slow trembling of her body—each told him that she was stretched almost beyond endurance. She wasn't angry because she couldn't afford to be without losing all control over herself.

"I don't know anything about an anthropologist, jackass or other-wise," Lisa said. "My parents sent me here to find a husband, but that's not why I came. I wanted to find out who and what I am. I didn't fit into any of the cultures I grew up in. I was always the white, skinny outsider, too aware of other traditions, other gods, other ways to live. I thought I must belong here, in America, where people come in all colors and traditions are something families invent as they go along. I was wrong. I don't belong here. I'm too…poor.''

"That doesn't say anything about us, about you and me," Rye coun-tered coolly.

Lisa closed her eyes as pain twisted through her, leaving her shaken. "What do you mean?"

"You're hurt and upset because I fooled you, and right now I'm mad as hell at everyone involved, including myself. But underneath it all nothing has changed between us. I look at you and I want you so bad I can hardly stand up. You look at me and it's the same. We're a fever in each other's blood. That hasn't changed."

Lisa looked at Rye, at the hard line of his mouth and the blazing gray of his eyes, and knew that he was right. Even now, with anger and pain churning inside her, she could look at him and want him until she was dizzy with it.

Fever.

Rye saw the answering desire in Lisa's eyes and felt as though the claws that had been twisting in his guts were being slowly withdrawn. The end of summer would come…but not today. Not this instant. He could breathe again. He let out a long, harsh breath and released the reins, transferring his hand to the worn softness of the fabric stretched across Lisa's thigh.

"There's one good thing to come out of this mess," he said roughly. "Now that you know who I am, there's no reason you can't come to the dance."

As soon as Rye mentioned the dance, Lisa remembered the wretched shirt concealed within the bag he still held. Suddenly she knew that she could survive anything but him looking at that shirt and seeing all of her shortcomings so painfully revealed.

"Thank you, that's very kind of you," Lisa said quickly, "but I don't know how to dance."

She smiled at him, silently pleading that he understand that it wasn't anger or pride which made her refuse. She was out of place down here, and she knew it.

But Rye wasn't in an understanding mood.

From the front of the barn came Lassiter's voice calling for Boss Mac. Rye swore viciously under his breath.

"I'll teach you how to dance," he said flatly.

She shook her head slowly, unable to speak.

"Yes," he countered.

"Yo! Boss Mac! You in the barn?" yelled Lassiter, his voice fading as he went into the barn. "You got a call from Houston waiting on…"

"You'd better go," Lisa said, gently pulling on the reins again.

Rye lifted his hand from her thigh and held on to the reins. "Not until you agree to come to the dance."

"Boss Mac? Yo! Boss Mac! Where in hell are you!"

"I don't think that would be a good idea," Lisa said hurriedly. "I really don't know anything about American customs or—"

"Shove customs," Rye snarled. "I'm asking you to a dance, not to take notes about quaint native practices!"

"Boss Mac! Yo!"

"I'm coming, damn it!"

The horse shied nervously at Rye's bellow. He simply clamped down harder on the reins and glared up at Lisa.

"You're coming to the dance," he said flatly. "If you don't have a party dress, I'll get you one."

"No," she said quickly, remembering all too well his comment about giving her a diamond bracelet if she pleased him. "No dress. No diamond bracelet. Nothing. I have everything I need."

Rye started to argue, but a single look at Lisa's pale, set expression told him that it would be useless.

"Fine," he said in a taut voice. "Wear your damn jeans. It doesn't matter to me. If you don't want to dance we'll just listen to the music. That doesn't require anything but ears, and you damn well have two of them. I won't have time to come up to the cabin and get you. I've spent too many hours away from here in the past weeks. If I don't get to work, there won't *be* a dance—or a ranch, either, for that matter."

Lisa smiled sadly as she saw Lassiter approaching from one direction and Jim coming at a trot from another, men descending on Rye like flies on honey. The thought of how much time he had stolen from his work to be with her was both soothing and disturbing. Rye might have had that kind of time to spare; Boss Mac obviously did not.

"I'll send Lassiter for you tomorrow afternoon," Rye said. "Early."

Hesitantly, knowing that it was a mistake, Lisa nodded her head. She could no more resist seeing Rye again than water could resist running downhill.

Relief swept through Rye, an emotion so powerful that he nearly sagged beneath its weight. He looked up searchingly at Lisa, trying to see beyond the shadows in her eyes to the warmth and laughter that had always been beneath.

"Baby?" he said softly, tracing Lisa's thigh with his knuckles while he held on to the paper bag. "I'm sorry that I didn't tell you sooner. I just didn't want things to…change."

Lisa nodded again and touched Rye's hand lightly. When one of his fingers reached to curl around her own, she removed the paper bag from his grip, squeezed his hand and simultaneously tugged on the reins, freeing them from his grasp. By the time he realized that the bag was in her hands, Nosy had backed up beyond his reach.

"Lisa?"

She looked at him, her face pale, her eyes so dark that no color showed.

"Didn't you ride all the way down the hill to give me that bag?"

She shook her head and tried to make her voice light. "This was for a cowboy called Rye. He lives in the meadow. Boss Mac lives down here."

Rye felt the cold claws sliding into his guts once more. "Rye and Boss Mac are the same man."

Lisa reined the horse toward the mountains without answering.

"Lisa?" Rye called. "Lisa! What did you want to give me?"

The answer came back to him, carried on the wind sweeping down from the high peaks.

"Nothing you need…."

Rye stood for a long time, hearing the words echo in his mind. He sensed something sliding through his grasp, something retreating from him. He told himself that he was being foolish; Lisa had been shocked and hurt and she had taken back whatever present she had intended to give him, but she was coming to the dance with him. He would see her again. Summer hadn't ended yet.

Nothing you need.…

Suddenly he sensed an abyss opening beneath the casual words, a feeling that he had lost something he could not name.

"Nothing has changed," he told himself fiercely. "She still wants me and there's no money attached to it. Nothing has changed!"

But he didn't believe that, either.

Eleven

The morning of the dance, Lisa awoke to an unearthly landscape of glittering diamond dust and a sky of radiant sapphire. Aspen leaves shivered in brilliant shades of citrine that made nearby evergreens appear almost black by contrast. Lisa's breath was a silver cloud and the air itself was so cold and pure that it shone as though polished. She stood in the cabin's open door and drank the meadow's beauty until her own shivering could no longer be ignored.

Only once did she think of Rye, who was Boss Mac, who was not Rye.

No. Don't think about it. There's nothing I can do to change what happened any more than I can run back through the night into yesterday's warmth. I have to be like the aspens. They would love to have the sweet fever of summer forever, yet they aren't angry at its end. They save their greatest beauty for the final, bittersweet moments of their summer affair.

And so will I. Somehow.

The jeans that Lisa pulled on were stiff with cold and patched in as many colors as the morning itself. She finished dressing quickly in a T-shirt, blouse, sweatshirt, wind-shell, socks and shoes, all but emptying out the closet.

Outside, the sunlight was so bright that the campfire's flames were invisible but for the subtle distortion of the heat waves rising into the intense blue of the sky. The coffee smelled like heaven and tasted even better as it spread through Lisa's chilled body. The contrast between cold and heat, frost and fire, heightened all her senses. Suspended like the aspens between the season of fire and the coming of ice, she watched in rapt silence while frost crystals sparkled and vanished as shade retreated across the meadow before the still-powerful sun.

When the final gleaming hints of frost had gone and all the plants were dry, Lisa slipped through the meadow fence with the camera in her hand. It would be the last time she recorded the height of plants against their numbered stakes, for the frost had been as hard as it had been beautiful; it had brought the end of growth in its glittering wake.

The meadow had not been taken by surprise. It had been preparing for that diamond-bright morning since the first tender shoots of new growth had unfurled beneath melting spring snow months before. The feverish rush of summer had already come to fruition. Grasses nodded and bowed to each passing breeze, their plumed, graceful heads heavy with the seeds of the next summer's growth. Beyond the grasses, aspens trembled and burned, their leaves such a pure, vivid yellow that Lisa could not bear to look at it without narrowing her eyes.

She moved through the meadow with the silence and ease of a wild thing. Her hands were light, quick and sure as she cut seed heads from grasses, taking only what Dr. Thompson needed from each plant and leaving the rest for the meadow and its creatures. Back at the cabin she sorted the numbered collection bags and set them aside. She pasted the pictures she had just taken into the log, entered the necessary comments and put the notebook aside, as well.

The angle of the sunlight and Lisa's growling stomach told her that it was past noon. The realization yanked her from the tribal time into which she had retreated, letting its slow, elemental rhythms soothe the turmoil inside her. She ate a cold lunch while she heated water for washing her hair. Long before the smoke-blackened bucket began to steam, she heard hoofbeats. Her heart beat wildly, but when she turned around it was only Lassiter.

What did I expect? Rye—Boss Mac—said he would send Lassiter, and that's just what he did.

"Hello," Lisa said, smiling through stiff lips. "Have you eaten lunch?"

"Afraid so," Lassiter said regretfully. "Boss Mac didn't want me to fool around up here before I brought you down the hill. Then just as I was leaving his pa called. The boss had to drive all the way into the city to pick him up. I'll tell you true, Miss Lisa, by the time Boss Mac gets back this evening, he'll be in a temper that would shame a broken-toothed grizzly."

"I see. Well, pour yourself a cup of coffee anyway while I get some things from the cabin. I won't tell Boss Mac we took a few extra minutes of his time if you won't."

Lassiter swung down from his horse and walked toward Lisa. His eyes searched her face. "You feeling okay?"

"I'm fine, thank you. And no, I didn't cut myself or sprain anything, and I don't need supplies or film from down the hill," she added, forcing herself to smile as she went through the familiar list.

Lassiter smiled in return, even though his question hadn't been meant as part of the quiz Boss Mac administered to any cowhand who had seen Lisa. Lassiter watched Lisa closely while she put out the small campfire with a thoroughness that spoke of long practice. He sensed something different about her, but he couldn't decide just what it was.

"I see you got a good frost last night," he said finally, looking from the blazing yellow aspens to the deceptively green meadow.

"Yes," Lisa said.

"It will stay hot for a few days more, though."

"Will it? How can you tell?"

"The wind shifted late this morning. It's from the south now. Guess we're going to have an Indian summer."

"What's that?" Lisa asked.

"Sort of a grace period between the first killing frost and the beginning of real cold. All the blessings of summer and no bugs."

Lisa looked toward the aspens. "False summer," she murmured, "and all the sweeter for it. The aspens know. They're wearing their brightest smiles."

She ran quickly to the cabin and emerged a few moments later carrying her backpack, her braided hair hidden beneath a bright scarf tied at the nape of her neck. Lassiter had saddled and bridled Nosy for her while she was in the cabin. As he handed over the reins, he looked at Lisa and realized what had been missing. There was no laughter in her today, but yesterday laughter had been as much a part of Lisa as her matchless violet eyes.

"He didn't mean no harm," Lassiter said quietly.

She turned toward him, confused, for her mind had been with the transformed aspen leaves burning like thousands of candle flames against the intense blue of the autumn sky.

"Boss Mac," Lassiter explained. "Oh, he's got a temper on him sure enough, and he won't back up for man nor beast, but he's not small-minded or vicious. He didn't mean for his joke to hurt you."

Lisa smiled very carefully, very brightly, her eyes reflecting the blazing meadow aspens. "I'm sure he didn't. If I haven't laughed in all the right places, don't worry. I just don't understand all the fine points of Western humor yet."

"You're sweet on him, aren't you?" Lassiter said quietly.

Her face became expressionless. "Boss Mac?"

Lassiter nodded.

"No," she said, reining the gelding toward the wagon trail. "I was 'sweet on' a cowhand called Rye."

For a moment Lassiter simply stood with his mouth open, staring at Lisa as she rode away. Then he mounted quickly and followed her out of the meadow. All the way down to the ranch he was careful to keep the conversation on Jim's teething baby, Shorty's barbecue pit and the walleyed cow that had more stitches in her hide than a pair of hand-tooled boots. Though Lisa still smiled far too little to suit Lassiter, she was more like herself by the end of the ride, and if sometimes her smile didn't match the shadows in her eyes, he saw no need to make an issue out of it.

When Lisa and Lassiter rode into the yard, there were expensive cars parked every which way, their paint gleaming like colored water beneath a coating of dust from the rough ranch road. There were battered pickups from nearby ranches, plus several strange horses in the corral. A big, candy-striped awning stretched down one side of the barn, protecting long tables from the afternoon thundershowers that often rumbled down from the mountain peaks. People shouted greetings and called to one another as they carried huge, covered dishes from their cars to the ranch kitchen. Everyone seemed to know everyone else.

A familiar feeling came back to Lisa, a combination of wistfulness and uneasiness that came from being the one who didn't belong at the gathering of clans. Welcome—yes. But a member of the tribe? No.

"Well, I see the Leighton kids came in over High Pass the way they used to 'fore the state highway come through," Lassiter said.

Lisa followed his glance to the corral, where three strange horses lipped hay from a small mound that had been dropped over the rails. "High Pass?"

"The trail you asked about just before we crossed the first stream and after Boss Mac's shortcut comes into the wagon road. The trail goes out over the mountain to the Leighton place. From there it's only a mile or two into town." Lassiter scanned the parked vehicles again and swore beneath his breath. "I don't see Boss Mac's pickup. That means his pa missed the early plane. Hellfire and damnation," Lassiter said, sighing and pulling his hat into place with a sharp motion of his hand. "The boss will be chewing nails and spitting tacks, no two ways about it. C'mon, let's get you settled so he won't have that to jaw at me about."

"Settled?"

"Boss Mac said for you to put your gear in his room." Lassiter spoke casually, looking anywhere but at the sudden rush of color on Lisa's face. "It's the big one just off the living room. His sister and her friend and his pa and his friends will take over the rest of the place," Lassiter continued hurriedly, "so there wasn't much choice."

"No problem," Lisa said tightly. "I won't be staying the night, so I'll need the room only long enough to wash up and change clothes."

"But Boss Mac said—"

"Shall I put Nosy in the corral or the pasture?" Lisa interrupted, her words crisp.

The thought that Rye—no, not Rye, *Boss Mac*—had assumed that she would calmly move into his bedroom infuriated Lisa. For the first time since she had discovered who Rye really was, she felt not only sad and foolish but insulted, as well. She could accept the end of summer without real anger, for living among various tribes had taught her that the passage of seasons was as inevitable as the progression from light to dark and back to light again.

But she could not accept becoming the latest of Boss Mac's women.

"I'll put Nosy in the barn," Lassiter said, watching Lisa warily, seeing the anger that had replaced the first flush of humiliation. "He could use some oats after being on grass for the last few weeks."

"Thank you," she said, dismounting. "Will you leave the tack on the stall door?"

"He told me to put it away. He told me you wouldn't be needing it anymore, or the horse, neither." Lassiter cleared his throat and added uncomfortably, "It's pretty plain that Boss Mac expects you to stay here."

"In his bedroom?" Lisa inquired, raising one platinum eyebrow in an elegant arc. "With him? That's not very likely, is it? I just met the man yesterday. He must have me confused with one of his other women."

Lassiter opened his mouth, closed it and smiled reluctantly. "He didn't say nothing about where *he* was planning to sleep. Just where he was planning for *you* to sleep. He's never had a woman here overnight. Not once."

"Good heavens. I certainly wouldn't want to spoil his spotless record. Especially on such short acquaintance."

Slowly Lassiter's smile dissolved into laughter. He leaned over the saddle horn and looked at Lisa admiringly. "Guess you're gonna get some of your own back, huh?"

"I'm going to what?"

"Get even," he said succinctly.

The idea hadn't occurred to Lisa in just those terms. Once it had, the temptation was very real. Then she thought of the aspens burning silently, each yellow leaf a proclamation both of the summer's bounty and the end of heat. She had no more chance to beat Rye at his own game than the aspens had of staying green through winter.

Lisa dismounted, resettled her backpack and went into the house as Lassiter led Nosy away. Even to her uncritical eye, the ranch house's furnishings were Spartan, with the exception of the office. There was nothing spare, worn or second-rate about the computer, just as there was nothing cheap about the cattle, the horses or the wages of the men who worked for Boss Mac.

I wonder what he pays his women?

The answer to that unhappy thought came as quickly as the question had.

Diamond bracelets, of course.

There was no doubt as to which bedroom was Rye's. It was the only one with a bed big enough for him. Attached to the bedroom was a bathroom with an oversized shower. Lisa shot the bolt of the bedroom door behind her. She removed the length of amethyst cloth from her backpack, shook out the long piece of linen and hung it over a hanger in the bathroom. She took a long, luxuriant shower, relishing every hot drop of water, feeling like a queen in a palace bath. When she finally emerged from the shower, the steam had removed most of the wrinkles in the linen. The rest succumbed to the small iron she found in Rye's closet.

After a few tries she got the knack of the bright pink blow-dryer that had been left out on the bathroom counter. She couldn't imagine Rye using the device any more than she could imagine him using the scented soap and shampoo that had been in the shower. She almost hadn't used them herself, because the bottles had been unopened.

Maybe Rye brought women here more often than Lassiter thought.

Unhappily Lisa brushed her hair until it was a fragrant, silver-gold cloud clinging to everything it touched. She outlined her eyes in the manner of Middle Eastern women since the dawn of time. Mascara made her long amber lashes as dark as the center of her eyes. She colored her lips from the glossy contents of a fragrant wooden pot no bigger than her thumb. The scent she used was a mixture of rose petals and musk that was as ancient in cosmetic lineage as the kohl lining her eyes.

She gathered the silky wildness of her hair and wove it into a gleaming, intricate mass, which she secured on top of her head with two long ebony picks. The picks were inlaid with iridescent bits of seashell, as were the six ebony bracelets she put on her left wrist. Slipper-shoes of glittery black went from the backpack to her feet. She picked up the rich amethyst strip of linen and began winding it around herself in the manner of an Indian sari. The last four feet of the radiant cloth formed a loose covering over her hair and made her eyes look like huge amethyst gems set in skin as fine grained and luminous as pearl.

"Lisa? Are you in there? Open up. I have to take a shower and Cindy's camped in the other bathroom."

Lisa jumped at the unexpected sound of Rye's voice. Her heart went wild.

That can't be Rye. It's too soon.

A quick glance out the bedroom window told Lisa that the afternoon had indeed slipped away. She started toward the bedroom door, only to stop as her hand touched the bolt. She wasn't ready to face Rye and smile as brightly as the meadow aspens. She wasn't sure that she would ever be that brave.

"Lisa? I know you're in there. Open the damned door!"

Before she could speak, Lassiter's familiar cry rang through the house.

"Boss Mac? Yo, Boss Mac! You in the house? Blaine says that walleyed cow is chewing out her stitches. You want to call the doc again or you want to sew up the old she-devil yourself?"

What Rye said in response convinced Lisa that Lassiter had been correct; right now Rye was in a mood to give a sore-toothed bear lessons in how to be obnoxious. She heard his boot heels punctuate every one of his strides between the bedroom and the front door. When the sound of his swearing faded, she peeked out, saw no one and hurriedly left the bedroom. As she rounded the corner into the living room, she nearly ran into a tall, slender woman who had hair the color of freshly ground cinnamon, the carriage of a queen or a model—and a very expensive diamond bracelet on her elegant wrist.

"My God," the woman said, staring at Lisa. "Since when did Ryan start keeping a harem?"

"Ryan?"

"McCall. As in Edward Ryan McCall III, owner of this ranch and a few million other odds and ends."

"Oh. Another name. Wonderful. Good question about the harem," Lisa said, giving the word its Middle Eastern pronunciation—har*eem*. "I'll bet he has the answer. Why don't you ask him the next time he buys you a diamond bracelet?"

"Excuse me?"

"There you are, Susan," said another woman. "I thought I'd lost you to that silver-haired, silver-tongued devil."

Lisa turned and saw a tall, young, beautifully curved woman walking in from the front porch. Her skin was flawless, her eyes were like clear black crystal, and she was wearing a red silk jumpsuit that had Paris sewn into every expensive seam.

"My God," Lisa said, unconsciously echoing Susan. "He does have a harem?"

"Lassiter?" asked the black-eyed beauty. "Why, yes, I'm afraid so. But we forgive him. After all, there's only one of him and so many, many needy women."

"Not Lassiter—Rye. Ryan. Boss Mac. Edward Ryan McCall III," Lisa said.

"You left out Cindy's brother," said the brunette dryly.

"Who?"

"Cindy," Susan said, smiling, "introduce yourself to this little houri before she stabs you with one of those elegant ebony hair picks. Where did you get them, by the way?"

"In the Sudan, but they were trade items, not a local craft," Lisa said absently, not taking her eyes from the tall brunette. Next to her and Susan, Lisa felt like a short fence post wrapped in a secondhand rag.

I should have stayed in the meadow. I don't exist down here. Not really. Not the way these women do. My God, but they're beautiful. They belong. They're real. And I'm not. Not here, with all these people who know each other and Rye/Boss Mac/Ryan/Edward Ryan McCall III.

"And the eye makeup came straight from Egypt, too, about three thousand years ago. The dress is a variation of the sari," Susan said, ticking off each item on her fingers, "and the shoes are Turkish. The eyes are right out of this world. The coloring is Scandinavian with that perfect Welsh complexion thrown in, and the body is beautifully proportioned, if a bit short. Heels would solve that problem. Why don't you wear them?"

"Susan is a former model who is now running a fashion house. She doesn't mean to be rude," the other woman explained.

"*Moi?* Rude?" Susan said, lifting her perfectly shaped brows. "The ensemble is unusual but absolutely smashing. Is it rude to point out that the effect would be enhanced by heels? I'd offer mine, but you'd have to cut them in half. God, I'd kill for such delicate feet. And those eyes. Is your hair really platinum blonde, or did you cheat just the tiniest little bit?''

"Cheat?'' Lisa asked, puzzled.

Susan groaned. "It's real. Quick, put her in a closet or none of the men will look at me.''

Lisa blinked, too surprised at being envied by the tall, cinnamon-haired beauty to say anything.

"Let's start all over again,'' the brunette said, smiling. "I'm Cindy McCall, Ryan's sister.'' She laughed as Lisa's expressive face revealed her thoughts. "That look of relief is more flattering than a wolf whis-tle,'' Cindy said. "Not that I blame you. Competing for Ryan with Susan around would be more than enough trouble for anyone, without throwing an overbuilt brunette into the bargain. Unfortunately I'm afraid you're both out of the running for my brother. Ryan already has found someone and it's all very hush-hush. But there are other single men here, lots of good food, and I even saw some wine lurking at the bottom of the beer cooler. In short, there are more reasons to smile than to wail.''

Lisa closed her eyes and stifled her cry of disbelief as Cindy's words echoed silently. *Ryan already has found someone.*

"She doesn't believe you,'' Susan said. "Do you think she has a name, or did Tinkerbelle drop her off on the way to chase an alliga-tor?''

"I think it was a crocodile,'' Cindy said.

Susan shrugged. "Either one makes great shoes. Ah, she's back. If we're very quiet, maybe she'll tell us her name.''

Lisa smiled wanly. "I'm Lisa Johansen.''

"Ah, I was right about the Scandinavian genes,'' Susan said tri-umphantly.

Lassiter suddenly appeared behind Susan. He bent slightly, said something only she could hear and was rewarded by a heightened sparkle in her eyes and an outstretched hand slipped into his.

"Bring her back before dawn,'' Cindy said, watching Lassiter and Susan leave.

"You have any particular day in mind?" asked Lassiter.

Cindy laughed and shook her head. Lisa looked closely but saw no jealousy or pain in Cindy's face.

"You don't care?" Lisa asked.

"Lassiter and Susan?" Cindy shrugged. "They're of legal age. I'd hoped that she might catch Ryan's eye, but there's no chance of that now that he's otherwise involved."

"Where is she n-now?" Lisa asked, stumbling over the last word.

"Who?"

"Rye's—Ryan's woman."

Cindy smiled oddly. "Do you know any place around here where they don't keep time?"

"What?"

"He told me that 'her name is Woman' and she 'lives in a place out of time.' He goes to her there. That's why I can't meet her. Too many clocks at the ranch."

Bittersweet tears burned behind Lisa's eyes when she realized that she was the one whom Rye had described to his sister—and he knew, too, that Lisa didn't exist down here. She existed only in the meadow, which knew no time, where a poor cowhand called Rye came to see her whenever he could.

"But I want to see them together," Cindy continued wistfully. "Even if it's only at second hand, I want to see what it's like to be wanted for yourself, not for your bank account."

Lisa heard both the yearning in Cindy's voice and the echoes of Rye's determination. *Once, just once in my life, I'm going to know what it is to be wanted as a man. Just a man called Rye.*

Lisa hadn't understood what he meant at that time. She did now. She understood, and it hurt more than she would have believed possible. Not for herself, but for Rye. She loved him as he had always wanted to be loved, and he would never believe it, for he wasn't a cowhand called Rye. He was Edward Ryan McCall III, heir to too much money and too little love.

"Oh, look at that gorgeous baby," Cindy cried softly.

Lisa glanced over her shoulder and saw Jim holding a baby in his arms. The cowhand appeared both proud and a bit apprehensive at being left in sole charge of his son. Jim's expression changed to pure pride when he spotted Lisa and hurried over.

"There you are. Betsy told me to be sure to show off Buddy's new tooth."

The baby waved his fat fists and stared with huge blue eyes at Lisa. She smiled in delight. After an instant, Buddy smiled back. The new tooth gleamed in solitary splendor against the baby's healthy pink gums. One fist wobbled erratically, then found its target. Buddy gummed his fingers with juicy intensity.

"He's cuttin' another one, too," Jim said, his tone divided between pride and resignation. "Teething babies are 'bout as touchy as a rattler in the blind."

Cindy blinked. "Beg pardon?"

"A rattlesnake that just shed its skin can't see," Jim explained. "It'll strike at anything that moves. Rest of the time rattlers are pretty good-natured."

"If you say so," Cindy answered dubiously.

Buddy whimpered. Jim shifted him uneasily, much more at home with a rope or a saddle than his baby son. Buddy sensed that very clearly. His whimper became a full-fledged announcement of impending unhappiness. Jim looked stricken.

"May I?" Lisa asked, smiling and holding out her arms.

With a look of pure relief, Jim passed over the baby. "He's so durn little I'm always afraid I'll break him or something."

Lisa's laugh was as soft as her smile. Automatically she rocked Buddy slowly in her arms while she spoke to him in a low, gentle voice. His eyes fastened on the bright amethyst cloth draped over her head. Little fingers reached, connected and pulled. Cloth tumbled down and gathered around her shoulders like a shawl. The baby's attention immediately went from the cloth to the pale crown of her hair where the shell-inlaid ebony sticks glittered. With tiny hands he reached for the tantalizing ornaments, only to discover that his arms were much too short. His face reddened and clouded with frustration.

Before he could cry, Lisa plucked out both sticks, knowing that if she left one in place, that would be the one Buddy wanted. The baby gurgled and reached for the black sticks, only to be sidetracked by the rapidly unraveling cloud of Lisa's hair. Long strands slid downward slowly, then with greater speed, until everything was undone and her hair hung like a heavy silk curtain all the way to her hips.

"Oh, Miss Lisa, now he's gone and messed up your party hairdo. I'm sure sorry," Jim said, a stricken expression on his face.

"That's all right," she said softly. "Buddy's just like children everywhere. He loves things that are soft and shiny."

She tucked the ebony sticks into her bodice, picked up a handful of her own hair and began stroking the baby's cheeks with it until he laughed in delight, displaying both his new tooth and the reddened spot nearby where another tooth was attempting to break through.

"Sore gums, little man?" she murmured.

Gently Lisa rubbed her fingertip on the spot. Instantly Buddy grabbed her finger and began gumming and drooling in earnest, a blissful expression on his face. Laughing softly, rocking slowly, she hummed an intricate African lullaby to him, as lost to the outer world as the baby in her arms was.

Cindy stared, caught by the image of the baby sheltered within shimmering veils of Lisa's unbound hair. The slow movement of her body as she rocked sent light rippling the length of each silken strand, but as extraordinary as her hair was, it was not as astonishing as the wordless, elemental communication shared between herself and the child.

Her name is Woman and she lives in a place without time.

Cindy didn't know that she had whispered her thoughts aloud until she heard Rye's bleak voice beside her.

"Yes."

Lisa's head came up slowly. Rye looked into her eyes, afraid to see the very money hunger for which he was searching—and finding only darkness and violet mystery, the essential Lisa retreating from him, gliding away among the shadows of all that had not been said.

"Where'd Little Eddy run off to?" boomed a male voice from across the room.

"He's with me, Dad," Cindy said, turning to look over her shoulder.

"Well, drag him on over here! Betty Sue and Lynette didn't fly all the way out from Florida just to talk to an old man."

Rye set his jaw and turned to give his father the kind of bleak stare that would have stopped any other man in his tracks. The stare was met by Big Eddy's determined smile. Eddy put a hand on each woman's bell-shaped fanny and shooed them toward his son.

"There he is, girls, my oldest child and heir, the only person on the face of the earth who's more stubborn than yours truly. First gal that gives me a grandson will have more diamonds than she can hold in both little hands."

A wave of laughter rippled through the room.

"I begged him not to do this," Cindy whispered.

Rye grunted.

"Introduce him to Lisa," Cindy said quickly. "Maybe he'll get the picture."

"The only way he'll get the picture is when it's tattooed on his nose with a sledgehammer. You know something? I'm looking forward to it."

"Ryan, you can't!"

"The hell I can't."

"He's your father. Even worse, it won't do any good. He's so desperate for an Edward McCall IV that he's been trotting eager studs through *my* house lately."

"So that's why you dragged what's her name up here."

"Er...ah..."

Rye hissed a savage word as his father appeared two steps away, a well-developed brunette clasped in each hand.

Cindy closed her eyes, thought a fast prayer and said quickly, "Hi, Dad. I'd like you to meet someone very special. Her name is Lisa Johansen and she...she..." Cindy's voice died as she turned around to draw Lisa forward.

No one was behind Cindy but Jim and the baby son sleeping peacefully in his arms.

Twelve

Though a full moon shone brilliantly, drenching the land in silver light, Rye didn't dare take the steep, rugged shortcut to the meadow. Instead he took the wagon road, following the single set of hoofprints that had been incised into earth still damp from a late-afternoon thundershower. He concentrated only on those hoofprints and let the rest of the world fade into nothingness. He didn't want to think about the shouting match he had had with his father in the barn, or about the shadows in Lisa's eyes, or about the anger and cold fear he had felt when he had turned and found her gone as though she had never existed, leaving not even a word for him, not a touch, nothing.

Summer isn't over, he thought fiercely. *She can't leave.*

Thin, windswept clouds rippled in sheer veils across the face of the moon, softening its brilliance briefly before dissolving until only night and stars remained. Evergreen boughs sighed and moaned as their crowns were combed by transparent fingers of wind. It was the same everywhere he looked, bush or grass, tree or silver stream. The night itself was subtly restless, caught between heat and chill, breezes turning and twisting, returning and unraveling, never still, as though the air were seeking answers to unasked questions in the darkness that lay beneath the blind silver eye of the moon.

But the meadow was hushed, motionless except for the spectral stirring of aspen leaves whispering softly of summers come and gone. A horse's low nicker rippled through the night. Devil answered and trotted quickly toward the rope corral that had been strung among a grove of aspens.

The sound of hoofbeats brought Lisa upright in a tangle of sheets and blankets. She hadn't slept for more than a few moments since she had returned to the meadow. She had hoped that Rye would come to her after the dance, but she had been afraid that he wouldn't. Even now she didn't trust her own ears. She had wanted to hear hoofbeats coming into the meadow so much that she had heard them every time she drifted off to sleep, and then she had awakened with her heart hammering frantically and hoofbeats echoing only in her mind.

But this time the sounds were real.

She came to her feet in a rush and opened the cabin door. Aspen leaves shivered in slow motion, each languid rustle a whispered reminder of long hours spent sated beneath the sun. Her hair stirred in a vagrant breeze, shining as the aspen leaves shone, silver echoes of summer past.

"Lisa?"

She ran to him through the moonlight, unable to conceal her joy. He caught her in his arms, held her high and close, let her hair fall in moon-bright profusion around his shoulders. The heat of her tears on his skin shocked him.

"I was afraid you wouldn't come," she said again and again, smiling and crying and kissing him between words. "I was so afraid."

"Why did you leave?" he demanded, but her only answer came as tears and kisses and the fierce strength of her arms around his neck. "Baby," he whispered, shaken by emotions he couldn't name, feeling his eyes burn as hotly as her tears. "Baby, it's all right. Whatever it is, it's all right. I'm here...I'm here."

He carried her into the cabin and lay with her on the tangled blankets, never releasing her, his own anger and questions forgotten in his need to comfort her. After a long time the hot rain of tears slackened, as did the sobs that turned like knives in his heart.

"I'm s-sorry," Lisa said finally. "I was going to b-be like the aspens. They smile so brightly, always, no matter what, and suddenly I c-couldn't and I...I'm sorry."

Rye hushed her with gentle kisses brushed across her lips and tear-drenched eyelashes, and then he held her closer still, wrapping her hair around his shoulders, letting her presence sink into him like sunlight into the meadow. Slowly Lisa relaxed, absorbing him even as he was absorbing her. She became supple once more, her softness fitting perfectly against each muscular ridge of his body. He closed his eyes and held her, breathing in her fragrance, savoring her gentle weight and warmth until her breathing was even and deep once more. He felt the gentle kisses she pressed into his neck and he smiled, feeling as though a weight had been lifted from his heart.

"Ready to tell me what that was all about?" Rye murmured, rubbing his cheek against the cool silk of Lisa's hair.

She shook her head and looked at him through shining veils of hair, her eyes glowing with something close to desire and not far from tears.

"It's all right now," she said, nuzzling against his cheek, breathing in the scent of him. "You're here."

"But what…?"

Rye felt the heat of Lisa's tongue gliding along the rim of his ear and forgot the question he had been trying to ask. His hands shifted subtly on her back, savoring rather than comforting her. The change was rewarded by a hot tongue thrusting into his ear.

"You're going to get into trouble doing that," he warned softly.

"I'd rather get into your shirt," she murmured, running her right hand delicately over his chest, lightly raking his nipple to attention.

His breath broke. "Let's compromise. How about my pants?"

She smiled and bit his ear with sensual precision. When she turned to capture his mouth he was waiting for her with a hungry smile. She teased him as he had once teased her, nuzzling lightly at his mouth, running her tongue along the sensitive inner surface of his lips until he could bear it no longer. He moved swiftly, trying to capture her mouth for the deep kiss he wanted so badly that he groaned when she eluded him.

"Come here," Rye said, his voice gritty, hungry.

Lisa's laughter was a soft rush of air against his lips as she obeyed. She sought him in the warmth and heat of his own mouth, shivering violently as his taste swept across her tongue. The kiss deepened and then deepened again until it was the slow, sensual mating of mouths that she had learned from him.

And that was just one of the things he had taught her.

A tremor of anticipation shook Lisa at the thought of the many ways in which Rye had teased and pleasured her. She wanted to arouse and to satisfy him in those same ways, if he would allow her the freedom of his body. Would he mind being loved by her hands, her mouth? Would he sense in her touch all the things that she couldn't say, the meadow being transformed silently by frost, the aspens blazing their most beautiful smiles in the face of the certain loss of summer?

"Rye...?"

"Kiss me like that again," he said huskily, seeking Lisa's mouth even as he spoke. "No ending, no beginning, nothing but the two of us."

Lisa fitted her mouth to Rye's, seeking him as hungrily as he sought her, sinking into him while time hung suspended between the season of fire and the coming of ice. The kiss changed with each breath, now teasing, now consuming, always touching, sharing, growing until both of them could hold no more. But no sooner had the kiss ended than he pulled her mouth down to his once more with an urgency that could not be denied.

"Again," Rye whispered against Lisa's lips. "Don't stop, baby. I need you too much. When I looked for you at the ranch, you weren't there. *You weren't there.*"

Lisa heard all that Rye didn't say, his anger and his bafflement, his wordless rage that everything had changed before he had been ready for any change at all, frost-scattered light blinding his eyes, summer's end.

"I don't belong down there," Lisa whispered, kissing Rye between words, loving him, preventing him from saying any more. "I belong up here in a summer meadow with a man called Rye. Just a man called Rye...."

The slow, deep kiss Lisa gave Rye made him groan with the passion that had grown greater every time she had satisfied it. Beneath his clothes, his powerful body became hot, taut, gleaming with the same hunger that had his mouth seeking hers, finding, holding, drinking with a thirst that knew no end. Beneath her searching fingers, the buttons of his shirt opened and the cloth peeled away. He groaned with the first sweet touch of skin on skin, no clothes between, nothing but her warm hands caressing him, smoothing the way for her teeth and the hot tip of her tongue.

"Baby, come closer," Rye whispered, pulling Lisa across his body until her legs parted and she half sat, half lay on top of him. "I need your mouth. I need…"

Lisa felt the shudder that ran through him when she slid from his grasp, evading him until her teeth closed delicately on his tiny, erect nipples. Teasing him, hearing him groan, feeling his skin grow hotter with each of her caresses, excited her almost beyond bearing. She forgot everything except the man who was giving himself to her sensual explorations, watching her with eyes blazing hotter than a summer sun.

She smoothed her face from side to side on his hard chest while her hands kneaded from his shoulders to his waist. Her fingers slid beneath his waistband, searching blindly, stroking, caressing, nails raking lightly over hard bands of muscle until she could bear the restraints of cloth no longer. She reached for his belt buckle, her hands shaking, wanting him.

And then Lisa realized what she was doing. She looked up at Rye, silently asking him if he minded. The glittering passion in his eyes made fever burst in the pit of her stomach, drenching her with heat.

"What do you want?" he asked in a voice so deep, so caressing, it was like a kiss.

"To undress you."

"And then?" he asked, smiling.

"To…pleasure you," she whispered, biting her lower lip unconsciously, then licking the small marks. "If you don't mind?"

Lisa felt the lightning stroke of response that went through Rye, tightening his whole body.

"I always hoped that someday I'd die of your sweet, hungry mouth," he whispered.

She said his name, husky and low, a promise and a breathless cry of pleasure at the same time. He reached for her but she slid through his fingers again, down the length of his body, leaving his hands softly tangled in the silken ends of her long hair. Her hands closed around first one of his boots, then the other, then his socks, until there was only warm skin beneath her caressing fingers. Her fingers rubbed beneath the legs of his jeans, easing upward until his calves flexed against her palms. As hard as ebony, hotter than sunlight, the clenched power of his muscles both surprised and excited her.

Slowly she worked her fingers back down to his ankles once more, pricking his skin lightly with her nails, smiling when she felt his response. She rubbed her palms up the outside of his jeans, slowly savoring the power of his thighs, hesitating, then sweeping up past the hard evidence of his desire without touching it. He stifled a groan of protest and need and pleading, for he wanted only those caresses that were freely given to him, and she had been so very innocent when she first had come to his meadow.

This time there was no hesitation when Lisa touched Rye's belt buckle. She undid the clasp, reached for the row of steel buttons that fastened the fly, then paused, trying to control the shaking of her hands.

"You don't have to," Rye said softly. "You're still so innocent in many ways. I understand."

"Do you?" asked Lisa, shivering. "I want you, Rye. I want everything with you. I want it tonight. I want it...now."

Rye's indrawn breath made a ragged sound as Lisa's fingers slid into the openings between the warm steel buttons. He twisted slowly beneath her and then shuddered heavily at the first touch of her fingertips on his hard, naked flesh. When she realized how intensely he enjoyed her caresses, her own body quivered within the grip of the same fever that made him hot to her touch. The last of her hesitation vanished as heat shimmered and burst within her, transforming her. She unfastened each steel button with growing anticipation, freeing him for her soft hands and even softer cries of discovery.

"You make me feel like a present on Christmas morning," Rye said thickly, wanting to laugh and to groan with pleasure at the same time.

"You are a present," Lisa murmured, stroking the length of him with her fingertips. "You're wonderful...but still much too well wrapped," she added, smiling and plucking at his jeans.

"Finish the job," Rye offered, his voice breaking between laughter and a need so great that it was tearing him apart.

Lisa had no hesitation about undressing Rye this time, but she was reluctant to give up what she had already unwrapped, even if only for a few moments. Rye was just as reluctant to lose the exciting heat of Lisa's fingers. Slowly, with many heated distractions, the rest of his wrappings slid down his legs. Without looking away from him, she threw his clothes into the darkness that lay beyond the shaft of moonlight pouring through the open cabin door.

Then Lisa stepped into the darkness, vanishing. When she reappeared moments later, drenched in moonlight, she was as naked as Rye. As he looked at the hardened tips of her breasts and the pale triangle at the apex of her thighs, his breath came in with a harsh sound and went out as a husky sigh. The sounds were like a cat's tongue stroking her, hot and raspy at once.

"Where were we?" Lisa teased, but her glance was already traveling down the length of Rye's lean, powerful body stretched out on the blankets. "Yes, I remember now," she said, her voice catching. She knelt, letting her hair sweep over his nakedness in a caressing veil. "It was summer and the meadow was a clear golden bell that trembled when we did, ringing with our cries. There was no yesterday, no tomorrow, no you, no me, just sunlight and...this." She caught up a handful of her hair and leaned down to him, brushing his hot flesh with the cool silken strands, following each slow stroke with the even greater softness of her tongue. "Do you remember?"

Rye started to answer, but could not. Delicious pleasure racked him, stripping him of all but a need so fierce that his breath unraveled into broken groans. Each sound sent another rush of heat through Lisa, shaking her. Her fingers flexed into his buttocks and stroked his thighs, glorying in the depth and power of his clenched muscles, the fiery heat of his skin and the intense intimacy of exploring him so completely, hearing his response, feeling it, tasting it.

"Baby," he said thickly, "I don't know how much of this I can take before..."

The last word splintered into a hoarse sound of pleasure. The dry, cool caress of Lisa's hair sliding across his loins was a violent contrast to the moist heat of her mouth savoring him. He tried to speak again and could not, for he had no voice, he remembered no words, nothing existed but the ecstasy she brought to him. He abandoned himself to her hot, generous loving until he knew he must be inside her soon or die. He reached for her, only to be shaken by a wild surge of pleasure when he looked down and saw her pale hair veiling his body and simultaneously felt the heat of her intimate caress.

"Come here," Rye whispered. "Come here, baby. Let me love you."

Lisa heard the words and felt Rye's need in every hard fiber of his body. With a reluctance that nearly undid the last measure of his control, she released him from the sensual prison of her mouth. When his hands captured her nipples, she moaned softly. She hadn't known until that instant how much she needed his touch.

"Closer," Rye coaxed, caressing Lisa's breasts, urging her to slide up his body. "Yes, that's it, closer. Come to me. Closer. Come closer, baby. I want you," he said, slowly biting her inner thigh, kissing away the mark, glorying in the violent sensual shudder that went through her when he caressed her soft, incredibly sensitive flesh. "Yes, that's what I want," he said thickly. "I love the heat of you...the velvet fever.... Closer, baby. Closer, come closer...*yes*."

Lisa swayed and bit her lip against the force of the sensations ravishing her body. A low moan was ripped from her, but she didn't hear it. She was deep within an ecstasy that devoured her so sweetly, so fiercely, that she could not say when it began or whether it would ever end. Suspended within the hot triangle of his hands and his mouth, she wept and called his name while he repaid her sensual generosity many times over, sharing her pleasure even as she had shared his, until she could bear no more and begged to feel him inside her again.

Slowly, with a sensuous anticipation that made his eyes blaze, Rye lifted Lisa, easing her down his body until she could feel the hard length of his arousal seeking her. At the first touch of him parting her soft flesh, fever radiated out from the pit of her stomach, drenching her with rhythmic pulses of heat and pleasure. When he slid into her, she made a hoarse sound and moved her hips over him very slowly, abandoning herself to him and to the waves of ecstasy sweeping through her. He tried to hold back, but the feel of her satin convulsions was too exciting. His hands tightened on her waist as he buried himself fully within her, sinking deeply into the velvet fever, giving of himself again and again until finally the last, lingering pulse of ecstasy had been spent. Even then he held on to her, staying deep inside her, savoring every shift and hidden warmth of her body stretched out on his chest.

After a long time Lisa lifted her head. He made an inarticulate sound of protest and snuggled her close once more. She kissed the swell of his biceps, then licked the mist of sweat from his skin with languid deliberation. When she turned her head and nuzzled through chest hair to the flat nipple beneath, she felt him tighten inside her. The sensation was indescribable, as though whole networks of nerves were being brushed with gentle electricity.

Rye smiled when he felt the telltale softening of her body, as though she were trying to sink into him as deeply as he was in her.

"Look at me, baby."

Lisa looked up. The movement tightened her body as Rye had known it would. He smiled even as he felt his own body tightening in anticipation. He kissed her lips, felt the racing of her heart against his chest and saw the sudden, heavy-lidded intensity of her eyes as she felt the growing tension of his body.

"This time we'll take it slow," Rye said, his voice husky with the renewed thickening of his blood, "so slow you'll think you're dying."

She started to say something, but he was moving within her and nothing else was real to her. She clung to him, following him, holding the end of summer at bay with every touch, every soft cry, every dizzying race of ecstasy. Each shift of body against body, each caress given and doubly returned, each sensation shared and enjoyed, each one was a brilliant aspen leaf shimmering against an autumn sky. Moonlight and midnight blurred together until time was suspended, all beginnings and endings swept aside and forgotten, leaving only man and woman intertwined, neither knowing nor wanting to know where one ended and the other began.

Lisa awoke at the first brush of dawn on the high peaks. She memorized Rye's peaceful expression before she eased from the tangle of blankets and dressed without waking him. She put a few final items in the backpack, shrugged into it and silently walked out into the white dawn. Frost lay everywhere, glittering doubly through her tears, a chill so deep that even the midday sun would not be able to deny the changing of the seasons. Leaving shadow footprints in the white, she saddled the patient gelding and urged him out over the lip of the high meadow into the world beyond.

The raucous call of a whiskey jack pulled Rye from sleep. Eyes closed, he reached for Lisa and found only empty blankets. He went to the door, opened it and looked toward the campfire. The world was still white, frost scintillating with each shift of the breeze. There was no sign of Lisa, no smoke rising from the direction of the campfire, no invisible twists of flame warming the chilly air. He stared for a moment longer, feeling as though something about the camp had changed, deciding finally that it was just the different perspective that came from the mantle of frost.

"Lisa?"

No answering voice came lilting back to him through the meadow's silence.

"Lisa!"

Rye's call echoed and then silence returned, broken only by the empty rasping of a whiskey jack flying over the ice-rimmed meadow.

"Lisa!"

The meadow's chill penetrated, making Rye realize that he was naked and shivering. He turned back to the room and pulled on his clothes as hurriedly as they had been removed the night before, telling himself the whole time that nothing was wrong, Lisa was simply out in the meadow checking on the plants and she hadn't heard him, that was all.

"Damn," he muttered as he yanked on his boots, "I'm real tired of turning around and finding her gone. Once I get my hands on her again, she's going to find herself wearing a short leash. The meadow doesn't need her attention half as much as I do."

The memory of the previous night returned to Rye with a vividness that sent heat snaking through him, changing the fit of his jeans within the space of a few breaths. He cursed his unruly body even as he remembered the caressing heat of Lisa's mouth. He had never known a woman so sweet and yet so abandoned, wanting only him, taking nothing from him, asking nothing of him.

And he had given her just that. Nothing. Yet still she had run to him through the darkness, wanting him. Just him. A man called Rye.

Rye froze in the act of grabbing his jacket from the floor. The uneasiness that he had been trying to ignore since he had awakened without Lisa stabbed through him, and in its wake came questions he could no longer evade.

She wanted just a man called Rye. But I'm not just Rye. I'm Boss Mac, too, and Edward Ryan McCall III.

He wondered if that was why Lisa had cried last night—had she expected something from him? Yet she had asked for nothing. Not once. And when her tears had been spent, she had made love to him as though he had poured a river of diamonds into her hands.

Restlessly Rye went to the cabin door and looked out over the white expanse of meadow, seeking any sign that Lisa was out there. Only the aspens seemed alive, their yellow leaves more brilliant than a thousand smiles. Memory tantalized him, something that Lisa had said last night, something that he hadn't understood then and couldn't quite remember now, something about aspens and smiles. He raked the meadow with his narrow glance once more, then turned back to the cabin, trying to shake the apprehension that was seeping through him as surely as the cold.

"Might as well make coffee," he muttered to himself. "Whatever she's doing, she won't be long. It's cold out there and she doesn't have a decent jacket. Hell, she should have had the sense to take mine."

Even as Rye said it, he knew that Lisa would never have taken his jacket or even have thought of taking it. She was too accustomed to making do or doing without things that most people took for granted. Suddenly the idea of giving her a soft, warm jacket made him stop pacing and smile. The gift would be unexpected and all the more cherished for it. He would buy a jacket that matched her eyes, and laugh with her as he zipped her into it, making her snug and warm and protected against the worst cold that winter could deliver.

Still smiling, Rye went out to the campfire. Halfway there he stopped walking, feeling uneasiness crystallize like frost in his blood.

There was no fire ring beneath the frost, no grate, no soot-blackened pot, no tools laid out for quick use. It was as though Lisa had never built a campfire there, never warmed her hands there, never fed hungry men freshly made bread and strong coffee.

Rye spun and looked at the meadow, realizing too late what had been bothering him. There were no tracks in the pristine frost, no sign that Lisa had slipped through the fence to check on the plants without awakening him. He opened his mouth, trying to call Lisa's name, but nothing came out except a low sound of disbelief and denial.

She was gone.

Rye ran into the cabin, telling himself that he was wrong, she couldn't have left. He flung open the closet door—and saw not a single piece of clothing. Nothing remained of Lisa's. No backpack. No camera. No film. No log or seed packets. Nothing but a creased brown paper bag that had been put on the farthest corner of the highest shelf and forgotten.

He stared at the bag for a long moment, remembering the last time he had seen it, remembering the hurt in Lisa's eyes when she had discovered his identity; and then she had taken the bag from his hands, telling him that it had been for a man called Rye, not for Boss Mac, who had no need of her gift.

Slowly Rye brought the abandoned gift out of the closet. He opened the worn bag, reached in and touched a fabric so fine that at first he thought it must be silk. He upended the sack, letting its contents slide into his hands.

Luminous gray cloth spilled over his skin in a cool caress. Tiny glints of blue and secret hints of green gleamed from the fabric with each shift of his fingers. He walked slowly to the sunlight streaming through the open cabin door and shook the cloth out. It became a man's shirt, which shimmered in his hands as though alive, a gray that held elusive hints of all colors, all tints, all moods. The fabric itself was such a fine weave that he could barely accept what his sense of touch told him; he was holding linen of unbelievably high quality.

He stroked the fabric very gently, as though it were smoke that would vanish at the least disturbance. The surface of a button slid beneath his fingertip. The satin texture caught his attention, as did the subtle patterns within the button itself. Slowly he realized that he was looking at ivory or antler cut very carefully so as to use only the cream-colored parts. The same care was obvious in the collar, which had no puckering at the tips and whose stitches were almost invisibly small.

"Where on earth did she get this?" he whispered. "And how in hell did she afford it?"

Rye looked on the inner side of the neck where most shirts carried a label. There was none, but the workmanship was superior to anything he had ever seen. He opened the shirt and searched in the side seams, where the most exclusive designers often left their labels. Again, there was nothing to be seen but the incredible care with which the shirt had been made. Every seam was finished so that no cut edges were visible anywhere. The seams were smooth, flawless, ensuring that the fine cloth would hang perfectly.

Unbelieving, he went over each seam again, running his fingertips over the myriad stitches, telling himself that it couldn't be true, she couldn't have made this for him with nothing more than the few tools she carried in her backpack. She couldn't have cut buttons from antler and polished them with her own hands until each button felt like satin beneath his fingertip. She couldn't have spent hour after hour sitting cross-legged on the cabin floor, taking tiny stitches, smoothing the cloth, taking more stitches and then more until the light failed and she had to put the shirt away until the coming of tomorrow's sun. She simply couldn't have…and yet she had. And then she had found out who he was, and ridden off without even mentioning the gift that had taken so much care to create.

What's in the bag?

Nothing you need.

Rye closed his eyes for a moment, unable to endure the pain of the truth that he held in his hands, all questions answered except one, and that one was tearing him apart.

I was going to be like the aspens. They smile so brightly no matter what.

But she had wept…and then she had followed summer, leaving him alone.

Why did you leave?

I don't belong down there. I belong in a summer meadow with a man called Rye.

Last night he hadn't asked her what the words meant. This morning he was suddenly afraid that he knew. Summer was over, and she had discovered that the man called Rye had never existed outside of the timeless meadow.

The shirt slid caressingly over his hands, tangible proof of what he had been too blind to see. He had been protecting himself so fiercely that he had wounded her unbearably, and he hadn't known that, either. Until now.

What's in the bag?

Nothing you need.

Rye stared at the shirt until it was blurred by the wetness that ran down his cheeks in scalding silver streams. Slowly he removed his jacket and faded work shirt and put on the gift that Lisa had made for a penniless cowhand called Rye.

It fit him as she had. Perfectly.

Lisa reined the gelding onto the trail that led away from the wagon road. The trail led over High Pass and to the neighboring Leighton ranch. Nosy immediately decreased his pace to a kind of slow-motion walk. Lisa urged him with her voice and finally with her heels. Grudgingly the horse speeded up. The instant she relaxed, Nosy's feet slowly became glued to the ground again. He wanted to go back to the Rocking M's barn and he wasn't prepared to be gracious about going in any other direction. He shied at every shadow, dug in at every blind turn in the twisting trail and kept his ears back in a way that announced his bad temper to anyone with eyes.

"Look," Lisa said, glaring at the stubborn animal's flattened ears as Nosy balked again. "I know this isn't the way back to the ranch, but it's the trail I want to take."

"You sure about that?"

Her head snapped up. She stared in disbelief at the trail in front of her. Rye was sitting on Devil, watching her. The horse's black coat was gleaming with sweat and his nostrils were wide as he drank in great gulps of air. Bits of evergreen and aspen clung to unlikely parts of the bridle and saddle.

"How did you...?" Lisa's voice faded.

"Shortcut," Rye said succinctly.

"You shouldn't have come," she said, fighting not to cry. "I wanted you to remember me smiling...."

"I had to come. You left something important behind."

She watched helplessly as he unbuttoned his jacket. When she saw the luminous shirt she went pale.

"You d-don't understand," Lisa said painfully, giving up the uneven battle against tears. "I made th-that for a cowhand called Rye. B-but he doesn't exist outside the summer meadow. And neither do I."

"You're wrong. I'm very, very real, and so are you. Come here, little love."

The soft command made Lisa tremble. "I don't think..."

"Let me do the thinking," Rye said, his voice husky, coaxing. "Come closer, baby. Closer."

With an anguished sound she shut her eyes, unable to bear looking at him without touching him. He was so close, but he was forever beyond her reach.

With no warning he spurred Devil forward, leaned over and lifted Lisa from the saddle into his arms. He buried his face in her hair, making no attempt to conceal the tremors of emotion that ripped through him when her arms slowly came around his neck to hold him as tightly as he was holding her.

"Meadow or ranch house, summer or winter," he said, "Rye or Boss Mac or Edward Ryan McCall III, it doesn't matter. They all love you. I love you. I love you so much that I can't begin to tell you."

Rye kissed Lisa slowly, wanting to tell her how much he loved her, needed her, cherished her, but he had no words, only the warmth of his body and the tenderness of his kisses. He felt the sudden, hot glide of her tears over his lips and heard her love for him told in broken whispers. He held her close, knowing that he would never awaken alone in the meadow again.

They were married in the meadow, surrounded by the aspens' brilliant smiles. He wore the gift of her love that day, and on that same day of every year thereafter. Seasons came and went within the meadow, cycles of renewal and change, growth and harvest, the elemental rhythm of tribal time. The golden bell of the meadow rang with the laughter of their children and their children's children, and each of them discovered in the fullness of their lives what the aspens had always known.

The velvet fever known as love is bounded neither by seasons nor by place nor by time.

*   *   *   *   *

EYE OF THE TIGER
by Diana Palmer

One

Eleanor Whitman saw the red Porsche sitting in the driveway and deliberately accelerated past the small shotgun house on the mammoth K.G. Taber farm outside Lexington, Kentucky. She knew the car too well to mistake it, and she knew who would be driving it. Her heart quickened despite all her efforts at control, although she had every reason in the world to hate the car's owner.

Her slender hands tightened on the steering wheel and she took slow, deep breaths until they stopped trembling, until the apprehension left her huge dark eyes.

She had no idea where she was going as she turned onto a long, calm avenue with big, graceful shade trees down the median. Lexington was like a series of small communities, each with its own personality and neighbors who were like family. Eleanor often wished that she and her father could live in town, instead of on the farm. But the house was theirs rent free as long as her father lived, a kind of fringe benefit for employees of the elder Taber. Dozens of employees lived on the mammoth farm: carpenters, mechanics, farm laborers, a veterinarian and his assistants, a trainer and his assistants, a black smith...the list went on and on. The farm had two champion race-horses, one a Triple Crown winner, and a prime collection of purebred black Angus bulls as well. It was a diversified, self-contained property, and the Tabers had money to burn.

Eleanor's father was a carpenter, a good one, and he alternated between repairing existing buildings and helping put up new ones. He'd had a bad fall and broken his hip three months ago, an accident from which he was only just now recovering after extensive physical therapy. And the Tabers had been keeping him on, paying his insurance and all his utilities despite Eleanor's proud efforts to stop them. They were holding his job open and looking after him like family until he could work again, which the doctors said would be soon. Meanwhile, Eleanor took care of him and petted him and was grateful that the fall hadn't killed him. He was all she had.

In her teens, Eleanor had loved the big white house with its long, open porches and wide, elegant columns. Most of all, she'd loved Keegan Taber. That had been her downfall. Four years of nursing school in Louisville had matured her, however, and her decision to accept a position at a private hospital in Lexington was a measure of that maturity. Four years ago, she'd succumbed to Keegan's charm and accepted one tragic date with him, not knowing the real reason he'd asked her out. She'd hated him ever since. She spoke to him only when he was impossible to avoid, and she never went near him. It had taken her a long time to get over what had happened, and she was only now starting to live again.

What puzzled her was that Keegan had been acting oddly ever since her return. He didn't seem to mind her venomous looks, her dislike. And it didn't stop him from visiting her father at the house, either. The two men had become close, and Eleanor wondered at the amount of time Keegan had been spending with her father lately. Keegan seemed to have plenty to spare, and that was odd because his business interests were diverse and made many demands on him. Now that his father, Gene Taber, was feeling his age, Keegan had assumed most of the responsibility for the farm. Keegan was an only child, and his mother had died many years before, so there were only the two men at Flintlock, the huge estate with its graceful meadows and white-fenced lushness.

Flintlock had been the site of a miraculous occurrence during the settlement of Kentucky. During a fight between pioneers and Indians, the settlers ran out of water. In a daring act, a pioneer's wife—some legends said Becky Boone herself, wife of Daniel—led the womenfolk of the encampment down to a bubbling stream to fetch water in their buckets. And, miracle of miracles, the Indians actually held their fire until the women were safely back with their menfolk. There was a historic marker at the site now; it was in the middle of a cattle pasture. Tourists still braved the bulls to read it.

Eleanor drove past that pasture now and remembered going to see it with Keegan long ago. How naive she'd been, how infatuated with him. Well, she was over it now; Keegan had given her the cure. But the experience had almost killed her. Certainly she'd been dead inside for a long, long time. Thanks to Wade, however, she was beginning to feel alive again.

Wade had been invited to the house tonight for the first time to meet her father. Eleanor hoped that Keegan didn't have any standing plans to visit with Barnett Whitman that evening to play their regular game of chess; she wanted her father and Wade to get to know each other. Keegan, she thought with a flash of irritation, would only be in the way.

Wade Granger had become someone special in her life, she mused, smiling as she recalled their first few meetings. He'd been a patient and had formed an attachment to her, as patients sometimes did to their nurses. She'd laughed off his invitations, thinking he'd get over it when he left the hospital. But he hadn't. First he'd sent flowers, then candy. And she'd been so shocked at the royal treatment, because he was as wealthy as Keegan, that she'd dropped her guard. And he'd pounced, grinning like a cartoon cat, his dark hair and eyes sparkling with amusement at her astonishment.

"What's wrong with me?" he'd asked plaintively. "I'm only six years older than you are, eligible, rich, sexy. What more do you want? So I'm a little heavy, so what?"

She'd sighed and tried to explain to him that she and her father weren't wealthy, that she didn't think getting involved with him would be a good idea.

"Poppycock," he'd muttered dryly. "I'm not proposing marriage. I just want you to go out with me."

She'd given in, but she'd invited him home for a meal instead of accepting his invitation to go nightclubbing. She thought if he saw how she lived, and where, it might cool him off.

He was a nice man, and she liked him. But she didn't want to get involved. Keegan had cured her of being romantic. Now she knew all too well the consequences of giving her heart, of trusting a man to return her love. She knew how cold the ashes of a love affair could be.

Her father had no idea of the relationship she'd had with Keegan, and she wanted it to stay that way. It had only been one date anyway, one magical night when she'd believed in fairies. What a pity she hadn't been levelheaded. But she'd been flattered by Keegan's sudden interest, and she hadn't questioned it at all. She certainly hadn't suspected that Keegan was only using her to get back at the woman he really loved. She often wondered what had become of Lorraine Meadows. Petite, blond Lorraine with her Park Avenue tastes and no-expense-spared upbringing. Keegan had announced his engagement to Lorraine the morning after his date with Eleanor. She remembered hearing it and bursting into tears. Keegan had tried to talk to her, and she'd refused to come out of her room. What was there to say, anyway? He'd gotten what he wanted.

But although the engagement made social headlines, less than two months later the couple quietly dropped their marriage plans and went their separate ways. It was incredible to Eleanor, who was in nursing school in Louisville by then. She felt Lorraine would have been the perfect mistress for Flintlock. These days, of course, Lorraine Meadows was never mentioned. Keegan was apparently playing the field now, according to local gossip.

Eleanor drove around for half an hour or so and then went home, thinking Keegan had had plenty of time to finish his business with her father. But he was still there. And she didn't have the time to avoid him any longer, not with Wade coming at six-thirty. It was four now.

She pulled up at the front steps, behind the classy Porsche, and cut the engine. Nurse's cap in hand, she walked wearily in the front door and fought down the rush of excitement that seeing Keegan never failed to create.

He was in the living room, sitting across from her father and looking out of place in the worn, faded armchair. He rose as she entered the room, all lean muscle and towering masculinity. There was an inborn arrogance about him that actually rippled the hair at her nape, and he had a way of looking at her with narrowed eyes and a faint smile that brought the blood to her cheeks. His flaming red hair had a slight wave in it, and his eyes were as blue as a summer sky. His cheekbones were high, his features sharp and cutting, his mouth thin and cruel and oddly sensuous. He looked lithe and rangy, but she knew the strength in that slender body. She'd seen farmhands underestimate it, to their cost. She'd underestimated it herself, once. But never again.

"Hello, Keegan," she said in greeting, her voice calm, confident. She even smiled at him as she bent to kiss her father on the forehead. "Hello, darling, had a nice day?"

"Very nice." Her father chuckled. "Keegan drove me into Lexington to the therapist. She says in another month I'll be back on the job."

"Lovely!" Eleanor laughed.

Keegan was watching her closely, as usual. He got lazily to his feet. "I've got to run. Eleanor, your father and I can't find that last cost estimate he did on building my new barn. Do you know where it is?"

So that was why he'd been here so long. She smiled at her own wild thoughts. "Surely. I'll get it for you."

She went into her father's small study and reached up on a high shelf for the box where he filed his bills and important papers. Her breath caught when she got down to find Keegan lounging in the doorway, his blue eyes narrow and intent on her slender body in its neat white uniform.

"Did I shock you?" he asked with a taunting smile. "It's been some years since I've managed that, hasn't it, Ellie?"

"I don't like that nickname," she said coolly. She avoided his gaze and sat down behind the desk, riffling through her father's papers until she found the estimate. She pulled it out and extended it toward Keegan.

He jerked away from the doorframe and took it from her. "How long do you plan to hold this grudge against me?" he asked softly. "It's been years."

"I have nothing against you, Mr. Taber," she said innocently.

"Don't call me that," he said curtly. "I don't like it."

"Why not?" she asked with a bland expression. "You're the big boss, aren't you? We live in your house, provide you with entertainment—of all sorts," she added bitterly, meaningfully.

His thin lips compressed. He rolled the paper in his hands, making a tube of it. He stared at it, then at her. "You came back. Why?"

"Why not?" she asked, lifting her eyebrows mockingly. "Did you expect me to stay away for the rest of my life to spare you embarrassment?"

"You don't embarrass me," he said shortly.

"Well, you embarrass me," she returned, and her brown eyes glared at him. "I hate the memory, and I hate you. Why do you come here?"

"I like your father," he replied. His chin lifted slightly as he studied her. "He was injured on the job. I've been keeping an eye on him since you couldn't."

"I know that, and I'm grateful. But he's almost healed...."

"He plays a good game of chess," he said. "I like chess," he added through pursed lips, smiling thoughtfully, and his gaze was thorough and bold.

"You like strategy," she returned. "I remember all too well what a wonderful manipulator you are, Keegan. You're great at getting people to do what you want. But not me. Not anymore."

"You just can't give me credit for an unselfish motive, can you?"

"Ah, you forget," she said silkily. "I know all about your motives, don't I?"

His blue eyes glittered at her like sun-touched sapphires, and his face tautened. "My God, haven't you ever made a mistake in your unblemished life?"

"Sure. With you, that night," she replied heatedly. "And the irony of it is that I didn't even get any pleasure out of it!"

He seemed to go rigid with that accusation, and his face actually colored. "Damn you," he breathed furiously, crushing the tube in his lean hand.

"Does that rankle? Forgive me for trampling on your vulnerable male pride, but it's the truth." She pushed back a wayward lock of her soft, brown hair. "I gave you what I'd been saving all my life for a man I loved, only to find out when it was too late that it was a ruse to make Lorraine jealous, to get her to marry you! Did you ever tell her just how far it went, Keegan Taber?'' she demanded, burning up with the years of bitter anguish. ''Did you?''

''Lower your voice,'' he growled. ''Or do you want your father to hear it all?''

''Wouldn't he have a sterling opinion of you then?'' She laughed wildly. ''His chess buddy, his idol. He doesn't know you at all!''

''Neither do you,'' he said shortly. ''I tried to explain it to you then, and you wouldn't listen. I've tried since, several times. I even wrote you a letter because you wouldn't talk to me.''

''I burned it, unread,'' she replied triumphantly. ''What could you have told me that I didn't already know? Lorraine called me herself. She was delighted to tell me all the details....'' Her voice broke and she turned away, biting her tongue to keep from crying out, the pain was so fresh. She took a steadying breath and rubbed the back of her neck. ''Anyway, as you said, it was all over a long time ago. I'll even forget it one of these days.'' She glanced at his rigid figure. ''Wouldn't you like to go and manage your farm or something? I've had a long day, and I still have to cook supper.''

He was silent. She heard him light a cigarette, heard the snap of his lighter as he pocketed it. She thought he'd stopped smoking, but apparently her father hadn't known that he'd started again.

His voice sounded bleak when he spoke again. ''I didn't realize until afterward how much you cared about me. And by then it was too late to undo the damage.''

''I hope I wore your conscience thin,'' she replied. ''You can't imagine what you did to my pride. But at least I didn't get pregnant.'' She managed a laugh, folding her arms over her breasts. ''Whatever happened to your intended, by the way? I expected you to drag her to the altar the minute she opened her mouth and said yes.''

''I don't want to discuss Lorraine!''

Of course he didn't; he'd loved the socialite to distraction, despite her wearing ways. She shrugged, as if it didn't matter, and went to the doorway.

''If those papers are all you needed, I'll excuse myself. I have to get my man a decent supper.''

He stared at her, his eyes searching and curious. ''Your man?''

Her dark eyes widened. ''Shocked? I do realize you think you're a tough act to follow, but I can't believe you expected me to moon over you for the rest of my life. Yes, I have a man,'' she lied. Well, Wade was a man, and he might be hers someday. "He's gorgeous and sexy and rich as sin.''

"Rich?'' he returned.

"You probably even know him. Wade Granger?''

His face flooded with angry color. "You little fool! He's what's known as the crowd Romeo! The only way he hasn't been caught doing it is hanging from a limb!''

"How erotic!'' she murmured, smiling sweetly. "I can hardly wait!''

"Damn you, will you listen to me? He's just out for a good time!''

"So were you.'' Eleanor folded her arms across her breasts. "Go ahead, boss, warn me about the consequences. Lecture me on rich men who look upon less wealthy women as fair game for their unsatisfied desires. You sure ought to know what you're talking about.''

He looked as if he might blow up any minute, a redheaded stick of dynamite looking for a match. Even his freckles seemed to expand.

"Eleanor…!''

She knew the tone, but it didn't intimidate her anymore. "Now, don't get all worked up,'' she advised, smiling. "We don't want your blood pressure shooting up, do we, you poor old thing?''

"I am not old,'' he replied through clenched teeth. "I'm barely thirty-five!''

"Oh, but you're thirteen years older than I am,'' she reminded him. "Definitely a different generation,'' she added on a sigh, studying him. "Too bad I was too smitten with you four years ago to notice. But I'm all better now. You'll be relieved to know that I don't have any inclination to chase after you these days. Doesn't that make you feel better?''

He didn't look confident, or enthusiastic or particularly happy. He stared at her for a long time. Then, "Wade is two years older than I am,'' he pointed out in a strained tone of voice.

She shrugged. "Yes, but he has a young mind.'' She grinned. "And not a bad body, to boot.'' She pursed her lips thoughtfully. "A Romeo, you said? How fascinating. I can't wait to see how good he is.…''

He whirled on his heel and stormed out the door without another word. Eleanor had to smother a giggle. Well, so much for his over-bearing arrogance, she thought with a trace of cold pride. At least she could handle herself now; she could protect herself. And she might need that ability, because he had a slightly possessive attitude toward her. She didn't want that; she didn't want the risk of running headlong into him again. Part of her remembered too well the vulnerability of loving him. She wouldn't be that stupid again. And why should he be worried about Wade? It probably irritated him that she might wind up in bed with someone else.

Good, she thought as she went to her room to change. Let him worry. It would be small compensation for the anguish he'd caused her with his manipulations!

She got ready for dinner, dressing in a pair of lavender slacks, a striped crinkle-cloth blouse and sandals. She peeked in the living room on her way to the kitchen.

"Wade's coming to supper," she announced, grinning.

"Is he?" her father asked mildly, studying her. He grinned back. "So I finally get to meet him, do I?"

"He won't take no for an answer." She laughed. "I gave up."

"Just as well, the flowers were taking over the house." He frowned, looking so much like a mirror image of Eleanor except for his silver hair and wrinkles that she smiled. "Did you and Keegan have words?"

Her eyebrows arched. "Why do you ask?"

"He came out looking like a thunderhead, muttered something about a meeting and dashed out. It's our chess night, you know."

"Oh, I forgot," she replied honestly. "I didn't remember."

"You don't pay a lot of attention to him these days, do you? Used to be wild about him, too. I remember how you cried when he got engaged. You went rushing off to nurse's training in Louisville that same week." He started to fill his pipe, aware of her sudden color. "I don't think it's just to see me that he's starting hanging around here so much, Eleanor."

"Well, don't make the mistake of thinking he's mad about me," she replied. "I know better."

He met her gaze. "He's been hanging around here longer than you realize," he replied. "You haven't noticed."

"I don't want to notice. Please don't play Cupid, darling. Keegan doesn't interest me that way. Not anymore. Now, Wade," she murmured dryly, "is another matter."

"Do you think he'll keep coming when he sees where we live?" he asked bluntly.

"Of course," she said with a grin. "He's no snob."

He shifted in his rocking chair and set it into motion as he lit his pipe. "I'll wait and find out for myself, if you don't mind."

"If you think we need improvements, ask your friend the farm tycoon," she told him. "Use your influence."

"I wouldn't dream of it!" he sputtered, glowering at her. "And you might remember that his daddy made his money the hard way. He wasn't born into money, he earned it. The Taber farm is... Where are you going?"

"I've heard this sermon before." She sighed. "I know all about the Tabers. More than I want to know. I have to get dinner."

He studied her stiff back. "You could be a little more hospitable to my chess partner," he told her.

"Oh, I'll strain a muscle being hospitable, you just watch. I'll even curtsy when he walks in the door."

"Don't get smart," he grumbled.

"Okay," she promised. "I'll treat him with all the respect due his age. After all, I am a mere child by comparison." She turned and went into the kitchen. "I'm making spaghetti tonight, if that suits you."

"Suits me fine. Will it suit the snooty dinner guest?"

She glowered at him from the kitchen doorway. "Shame on you. Just because he has money doesn't make him a snob."

"Yes, I could say the same thing about Keegan, if you'd listen."

She stuck her tongue out at him.

"Why do you dislike him so?" he asked unexpectedly, his eyes narrowed.

What could she say to that? Telling him the truth was out of the question, and nothing short of it would convince him. She leaned forward with a conspiratorial smile. "He has freckles," she whispered. "I hate freckles."

And while he was laughing at her cheek, she vanished into the kitchen.

Two

Wade was right on time, and Eleanor met him at the door with a bright smile. She had expected to find him wearing slacks and a shirt, as Keegan frequently did when he visited them. But Wade was wearing a very trendy navy-blue blazer with white slacks and a white shirt and tie, and he looked taken aback by Eleanor's neat slacks and blouse.

"Sorry, love, am I overdressed?" he asked apologetically, looking briefly uncomfortable, then even more so as his gaze wandered around the hall, taking in its far-from-recent paint job, worn linoleum and single light bulb hanging bare from the ceiling.

"We're a little primitive around here," she said with a faint smile. "The house was given to us rent free by the Tabers due to the length of my father's employment here. We tend to forget how it looks, but there's never been any reason to update it, you see...."

"Was I criticizing?" he said quickly, and smiled to soften the words. "My world is a bit different, but that doesn't make it better, now does it?" He chuckled.

"No," she said with a laugh. "You're a nice man."

"That's what I've been trying to tell you." He sighed.

She stood back to invite him in, feeling underdressed and underprivileged, even though she knew he hadn't meant to make her feel that way. "Won't you come into the living room and meet my father?"

She led him there, swallowing her embarrassment at the shabbiness of their furniture. The living room needed painting, too—why hadn't she noticed that before now? And the rug—oh, Lord, it was in rags! She hadn't paid the slightest attention to the condition of the house since she'd been back. Helping her father since his accident and holding down a full-time job of her own left her just enough time to keep the house clean and neat. And there hadn't been any company to speak of, except other farm employees who were friends of her father…and Keegan, who never seemed to notice where he was, making himself right at home in castle or hovel alike.

Her father would be wearing that sweater with the hole in the sleeve, she reflected, groaning inwardly. He had better ones, but that was his favorite. Smiling, Barnett Whitman extended his hand to Wade, not seeming to notice that he looked positively ragged in his old baggy trousers, faded print shirt and slippers.

"Nice to meet you, Mr. Granger," he said easily. "Sorry I'm not getting up, but I've had some trouble with my hip and sitting down feels better."

"Yes, your daughter was telling me about your fall," Wade replied. "I hope it's better."

"I'll be able to go back to work next month," her father assured him. "The Tabers have been wonderful to me, to us."

"I know the Tabers," Wade said. "Keegan's a character, isn't he?" he added conversationally. "Quite a guy."

Her father immediately brightened. Anyone who liked Keegan was instantly a friend, Eleanor thought with bitter irony.

"Keegan often plays chess with me," Barnett Whitman said proudly.

Wade raised an eyebrow and grinned. "I can't imagine him sitting still that long. He always seems to be on the run, doesn't he?"

"In a dead heat," Barnett agreed with a smile. "But he's a good chess player, for all that."

Quickly Eleanor took Wade's arm and said, "Shall we go into the dining room?" to prevent her father from further extolling the virtues of the one man she wanted to forget. "I hope you like spaghetti, Wade. I was on seven-to-three today, and I didn't have a lot of time to prepare."

"Spaghetti is fine," Wade told her. "I should have brought a bottle of Chianti to go with it. Or a nice rosé. What do you have?"

Eleanor stared at him. "I beg your pardon?"

"Wine, darling," he said.

"Oh!" She felt her cheeks grow hot. "I'm sorry, we don't drink."

"I'll have to take you in hand and corrupt you, you innocent little thing. Shhh, we don't want your father to think I'm a rake," he added in a stage whisper.

Her father, liking this obvious attention, grinned as he sat down. Eleanor smiled as Wade seated her, but she felt oddly uncomfortable, as if her social graces were nonexistent. Without meaning to, Wade made her feel like a country mouse.

It wasn't the most successful evening Eleanor had ever had. She felt uncomfortable, although her father did his best to liven things up. By the time dinner was over and Eleanor had served up her special home-made apple pie with ice cream, she was more than willing to show Wade to the door.

He shook hands with her father and walked out onto the porch with Eleanor.

"Not a wild success, was it?" he asked with a rueful smile. "I'm sorry, darling, did I hurt your feelings?"

"Yes, you did," she said, surprised at his perception. "But it's not your fault. It's just...I guess I felt the difference in our situations...."

"You little snob," he accused her lightly.

She blushed furiously. "I am not!"

"I think you're charming, Eleanor Whitman," he said with an intent stare. "A nice person as well as a sexy lady, and I like you. I really didn't come to appraise the furniture," he added with a grin.

"Sorry," she murmured with downcast eyes. "I guess I'm a little uneasy about it, that's all."

"Stop worrying about the differences, and let's concentrate on the things we have in common. Over dinner. Tomorrow night."

She hestitated.

"Come on, sweet thing, you know you want to," he teased, bending to kiss her soft mouth gently. "Come on, go out with me, Ellie."

He made the hated nickname sound special and sweet, and she

smiled dreamily up at him. He was handsome, she thought. A nice, lovely, ordinary man, despite his wealth and prominence.

"All right," she agreed.

"Good girl." He cupped her face in his hands and kissed her again, breaking the line of her lips this time. He was adept at lovemaking— it showed in the sensuous deliberation of his warm mouth. And if some spark was missing, Eleanor ignored it. It was very pleasant to kiss him. She relaxed and gave him her mouth, smiling when he finally drew back.

"Whew!" he whistled, looking breathless. "Sweetheart, you're delicious."

She laughed at the warmth in his eyes. He made her feel special, womanly.

"So innocent," he murmured. He drew her closer, nuzzling his chin against her forehead. "I like that, I like being with an innocent woman for a change. It's exciting."

He thought her inexperienced, and in a sense she was. But he was obviously making assumptions about her innocence that were false, and she didn't know how to correct him. She drew back, looking up at him, and her eyes were worried.

"Such a frown," he murmured. "Don't. I'm not that much a wolf, Little Red Riding Hood. I'll take care of you. I'll give you plenty of time. Now go back inside, it's chilly out here. I'll call you tomorrow, all right?"

She beamed. "All right."

"I enjoyed dinner," he murmured. "But dessert was the best course." Bending, he drew her completely against him and kissed her hungrily.

She should have told him. But there would be time for that, later. And she might never have to tell him. She wasn't planning on having an affair with him, and she was sure that wasn't what he had in mind, either. He seemed to be serious. That would make a nice change. She might enjoy letting him be serious about her. She kissed him back, sighing when he released her. If only she could forget how it had felt when Keegan had kissed her....

"Good night, darling," he said in a shaky whisper, and ran down the steps to his Mercedes convertible. He started up the engine and waved, his dark hair ruffling in the night breeze as he turned the car and sped away.

Eleanor drifted back inside, feeling a little removed from reality. It hadn't been a total loss, this evening. Something wonderful might come of it.

"He's a nice man," her father said kindly. "Is it serious?"

"Serious!" she burst out, throwing up her hands. "One date, and you're wording wedding invitations!"

"So I'm anxious to see you happily settled," he grumbled, and glared at her. "Get married. Have children! I'm not getting any younger!"

"At the rate you're going, you'll outlive me!" she threw back.

He made a rough sound under his breath, got out his copy of Thucydides and began reading, deliberately ignoring her. She laughed as she went into the kitchen to wash up.

She was off the next day, having worked nine days in a row to compensate for a personnel shortage following a viral outbreak. Wade called early and had to break their dinner date because of business. He was going to be busy until the weekend, he said, but could she go to a party with him Saturday night at a nearby estate?

Eleanor held her breath, trying to figure out whom she could swap duty with to make it. Yes, she said finally, she'd work it out somehow. He told her when to expect him and rang off.

Immediately, Eleanor dialed her friend Darcy at the hospital. Darcy would take over for her, she knew, if she agreed to work Friday for Darcy.

"Can you cover for me Saturday night if I cover for you Friday night?" she asked breathlessly when her friend answered the phone. "I've got this really hot date."

"You, with a hot date?" Darcy gasped. "My gosh, I'd get up off my deathbed to cover for you if you're really going out with a man! It is a man?" she asked. "Not some sweet old gentleman you're taking pity on?"

"It is a man. It's Wade." She sighed.

Darcy paused. "Honey, I hope you know what you're doing. That isn't a man, it's a ladykiller."

"I'm a big girl now."

"A babe in the woods."

"Not quite," Eleanor said gently. "Not at all anymore."

Darcy sighed. "Well, I should be shot for agreeing, but I will. Where are you going?"

"To a cocktail party at the Blake estate."

"The Blakes own half of Fayette County!"

"Yes, I know. I'm so nervous. I thought I'd wear that little black cocktail dress I wore to our Christmas party...."

"You will not! It's three years old! I have a strappy little gray silk number, you'll wear that. It will just fit you. And I have an evening bag and shoes to match. No arguments. I'm not sending you to the Blakes' looking like something out of a Salvation Army charity store!"

That cut, because it was how Wade had made her feel. She hesitated, then gave in gracefully. She really did want to go to the party with Wade, to get a taste of that luxurious other world. And her little black dress would only embarrass him.

"Okay," she told Darcy. "You're a pal. I wish I could do something for you."

"You are," came the smug reply. "You're filling in for me Friday so that I can see that new picture with Arnold. Come over Saturday morning and we'll fix you up."

"I'll be there at nine, with coffee and biscuits from the Red Barn, how's that for true friendship?" She laughed.

"That's true friendship," Darcy agreed. "See you then."

Eleanor excitedly told her father about her plans for Saturday, then went back into the kitchen to wash the breakfast dishes, frowning when she heard a car drive up in front. She peeked into the living room, and her heart leaped as Keegan walked into it, frowning and looking worried. He sat down and started talking to her father, fortunately not glancing toward the kitchen. She quickly drew back inside.

She was too far away to hear what was being said, but she had a terrible feeling it had something to do with her. Well, let them talk, it wouldn't stop her. She liked Wade, she'd been in a state of hibernation for over a year, and she was tired of her own company. She wanted to get out and live a little before she turned into a vegetable or an old maid. And if Keegan didn't like it, that was too bad. She didn't care about his opinion. She didn't care about him, either.

The kitchen door opened, and the object of her dark thoughts came into the room, hands rammed into the pockets of his pale slacks. She glanced at him and then concentrated on her dishes.

"Can I help you?" she asked carelessly.

"Your father says you're going to a party at the Blakes' with your new boyfriend."

"So what if I am?" she asked coldly.

"You're going to be out of your league, little girl," he said bluntly. "They'll eat you up."

Her cheeks reddened with anger. She put the dishcloth down slowly and turned to face him, her dark eyes narrow and icy. "You don't think I can behave like a lady, is that it?" she asked, glaring up at him. "Well, don't worry, Mr. Taber, you won't have to suffer my embarrassing presence. And I think the Blakes will manage not to laugh at me."

"I didn't mean... Damn it, girl, will you stop putting words in my mouth? I'm talking about Granger. I've already told you he's a wolf! A rich, sleek, well-fed wolf with a big wallet, just fishing for a naive little girl like you to warm his bed!"

She turned and stared at him. "Just like you," she agreed, and watched him explode, then turned back to her dishes. "Why are you worried about my morals? If I want to be corrupted by someone else, that's my business. Besides, I've always wanted to make love suspended from a tree limb," she added dryly.

"That's what I'm afraid," he murmured, studying her. "Eleanor, you're trying to fit into a world that has nothing of value to offer you."

"Like yours?" she asked politely.

"I'm talking about you and Wade Granger! Aren't you experienced enough to realize why he's sniffing around you?"

He made it sound so cheap and vulgar! "I am not a tramp," she replied through clenched teeth, "despite your efforts to make me feel like one."

"When did I ever do that, Eleanor?" he asked in a deep, poignant tone, his eyes searching hers.

She didn't want to remember that night. "If you want to stay to lunch, I'm making ham sandwiches," she said abruptly, washing a plate hard enough to scrub half the pattern off.

He came up behind her, smelling of tangy cologne. She remembered the scent of it: it had clung to her body that night. It had been on her pillow when she awoke the next morning. It was a graphic reminder of her one lapse in a lifetime of sanity. The warmth of his body radiated toward her, warming her back, threatening her.

"I was careful with you that night," he said, his voice velvety rough, warm. "More careful than I've ever been with a woman, before or since. Even afterward, I was tender. I've never been able to forget it, the way you wanted me at first, the wild little shudders, the sweet cries that pulsed out of you until I hurt you."

"Please," she whispered, closing her eyes. "I don't want to remember!"

"You cried," he murmured. His lean hands smoothed her waist, drew her back so that she rested against his powerful body. "You cried when I took you, looking straight into my eyes, watching...and I felt that you were a virgin, and I tried to stop, but I was so far gone..."

"No!" She wept, lowering her face.

His lips touched her hair, and his hands trembled. "You were fire and honey in my arms," he whispered, "and I remember crying out because the pleasure was an agony."

She tore out of his arms and retreated behind the table, looking across at him with dark, wounded eyes. "Go away!"

His eyes were dark blue with remembered desire, his face shadowed by the flash of light behind him through the curtains. "I will, but the memory won't," he said huskily.

"You used me," she whispered brokenly, involuntarily, letting the hurt show, seeing how his face hardened. "You had a fight with your sophisticated girlfriend, and you took me out to spite her. And like a fool, I thought you'd asked me because you cared about me. It wasn't until...until it was all over, until it was too late, that you told me the truth. I hated you then and I hate you now. I'll hate you until I die, Keegan Taber!"

His eyes shifted to his boots, to the worn linoleum. "Yes, I know," he said quietly.

"Will you please go?" she said in a defeated tone, refusing to look at him again. "My life is none of your business now. Nothing I do concerns you."

"Do you want him?" he asked.

She went and opened the kitchen door. "Goodbye. Sorry you have to leave so suddenly," she said with a bright, empty smile.

"I thought I was invited to lunch."

"Do you really like arsenic?" she asked with raised eyebrows. "Because I've never been more tempted in my life."

"Neither have I," he agreed, but he was studying her slender, pretty figure with narrowed, blue-black eyes. "You're exquisite, Eleanor. You always were, but maturity has done amazing things to your body."

"I am more than a body," she said curtly. "I'm a human being with thoughts and feelings and a few minor talents."

"I know that, too.... Do you fancy a guardian angel, Eleanor?"

She blinked. "I don't understand."

"You will," he said with a grim smile. "At least keep away from his apartment, can't you? I hear he has a bed that begins at the doorway."

She had to bite her tongue to keep from laughing, and his twinkling eyes very nearly threw her off balance.

"Well, that surely beats the back seat of a luxury car, wouldn't you think...?" she asked with blatant mockery.

He sighed. "You won't quit, will you? I don't suppose you'd believe me if I told you I was so out of my head at the time that I wasn't even thinking about anyone but you?"

"Right the first time," she said, grinning carelessly. "Do you want a ham sandwich or don't you?"

He pulled a cigarette out of his pocket and took his time lighting it. "I'm going to get around that wall you've built, one way or the other. You can make change on that."

"Better buy a rocket launcher and a couple of grenades," she told him. "You're going to need them."

"You may, if Romeo gets a foot in the door," he said grimly. "Don't worry your father, will you? He broods."

"He'll have to give me up one day," she remarked.

"You aren't thinking that Granger might propose, for God's sake?" he burst out, laughing coldly. "Marry a sweet little nobody like you? Fat chance, honey."

"I'm not your honey," she shot back.

"You were," he said, his voice rough and soft all at once, his eyes intent. "You were the sweetest honey I ever tasted."

"The beehive is out of order," she replied stiffly. "You'll have to appease your appetite elsewhere."

"There isn't anywhere else," he said absently, watching her as the cigarette smoldered in his hand, its glowing tip as red as his waving hair. "There hasn't been for a long time."

"I don't believe in fairy tales," she said. "If you're quite through, I have things to do."

He shrugged. "Turned out into the cold," he said, watching her. "Heartless woman."

"It's spring, and it isn't cold. And you're one to be accusing someone of not having a heart."

"You don't think I have one, Eleanor?" He laughed. "You might be surprised at the bruises on it."

"I would, if there were any."

"Nurses are supposed to have compassion," he reminded her.

"I have, for those who deserve it. I have dishes to wash, sandwiches to make...."

"Wash your damned dishes, and forget making any sandwiches for me," he muttered, turning to go. "The way my luck's running lately, you'd probably make mine with a live pig."

She heard the door close and went back to her soapy water. It took a long time for her heart to calm down, and she thanked providence for removing his disturbing presence. She didn't want to remember that night. Why couldn't he go away and let her forget it? Just the sight of him was a constant reminder, an eternal opening of the wound. She closed her eyes and went quickly about her tasks.

Three
___

Early Saturday morning, Eleanor left her father sleeping soundly and drove to the Red Barn to get biscuits and coffee for herself and Darcy. The older nurse with whom she worked was still in her housecoat when Eleanor reached her small efficiency apartment downtown.

Darcy blinked, yawning, her pale brown eyes bloodshot, her round face blank. "Coffee and biscuits," she murmured dreamily, closing her eyes to smell. "Wonderful!"

Eleanor laughed, following her friend into the apartment. The furniture was in about the same shape as that in Eleanor's house, and she felt comfortable here. Not that Darcy would ever have put on airs, even if she'd had gobs of money. The two of them had become friends years before in high school. Darcy had done her nurse's training in Lexington, while Eleanor had gone to Louisville. But now they found themselves working at the same hospital, and it was as if the four-year absence had never been. They were as much alike as ever and had fallen back into their easy, close relationship with no trouble at all. Only Darcy had known just how deeply in love Eleanor had been with Keegan, although Eleanor hadn't told even her best friend the full extent of her stupidity. But Darcy knew why Eleanor had left town when Keegan announced his engagement because Eleanor had cried on her shoulder for hours afterward.

They sat at Darcy's small white kitchen table and ate the fluffy sausage biscuits, washing them down with coffee. It was just after nine, and the city hadn't started to buzz yet. Soon, however, the downtown traffic would be murder.

"I needed that. Thanks!" Darcy smiled.

"Oh, anytime." Eleanor grinned. "Now, about that dress…"

Darcy burst out laughing. "You shrewd operator! Okay, come on in here and let's look it over."

It was a dream of a dress, silk chiffon that fell in soft folds around Eleanor's slender body, a pale gray that emphasized her dark eyes and soft brown hair. She smiled at her reflection, liking the demure rounded neckline and the transparent sleeves that gathered at the cuff.

"It's heavenly." She sighed. "You're sure you want to risk this with me?"

"I got it at a nearly-new shop. It's a designer model, only worn twice. Here are the shoes and bag."

The shoes had small Queen Anne heels and straps around the ankles. They were elegant, like the tiny gray leather purse that finished the outfit.

"Wow, is that me?" Eleanor laughed at her reflection.

"Well, almost," Darcy murmured. "Sweet, your hair is dreadful. I have to get a cut today; suppose you come with me?"

Eleanor looked at the soft waves falling around her shoulders and tugged at a strand of hair that seemed more like wire. "Dreadful is definitely the word all right. Can we get an appointment for me at such short notice?"

"They take walk-ins anytime," Darcy assured her. "And some new makeup. And for God's sake, honey, a bra that has a little support."

Eleanor sighed, nodding. "I never buy under things until the old ones lose their elastic and have holes."

"You need taking in hand." Darcy shook her head. "Pretty lacy under things give you confidence. You could use a little of that!"

"I guess I could, at that. Okay. Let's renovate me."

The two of them walked to the hairdressing parlor, and the operator gave Eleanor a cut that suited her face: softly waved and very short. She looked different already, and when they went into a department store where Eleanor was shown how to apply new makeup, the transformation was complete.

"Mmmmm," Eleanor said with a smile, looking at her face in the fluorescent mirror. "Is that me?"

"It sure is, honey." Darcy laughed. "I've been wanting to do that for months. You used to be so particular about your appearance, but lately you've just let yourself go."

"I guess I have," she agreed. She touched her hair. "What a difference. Wade is going to love this."

Darcy pursed her lips. "That party's really got you perking, hasn't it?"

"Yes, it has," she admitted as they went through the women's department browsing through the latest styles. "Not that I'm trying to break into high society. That would be ridiculous. I just want to do something different, you know? My life is deadly dull. I feel like I'm growing old second by second."

"That's a laugh. You're the youngest person I know at heart. Just like your dad. How is he, by the way?"

"Getting back in shape slowly but surely, and trying to get me married off."

"Same old Dad." Darcy laughed.

"Amen."

"Wouldn't he settle for letting you have a wild, passionate affair?"

Eleanor sighed. "He couldn't get grandkids that way," she reminded her friend. "Anyway, I'm not sure I want to have an affair with anyone. Wade's wonderfully nice, and I like him a lot. But he doesn't start any fires just yet. I think that has to accompany emotional involvement, for me, at least."

"Well, personally speaking, if I were looking for a blazing affair, I know which direction I'd be staring. My gosh, I'll bet Keegan Taber is just plain dynamite in bed!"

"Oh, goodness!" Eleanor cried as her hand tore down half a dozen gowns from the rack. She colored furiously as she bent to pick them up.

"Sorry," Darcy murmured as her friend fumbled gowns back onto hangers. "I guess I shouldn't have said that, considering... But he is gorgeous, honey." She eyed her friend thoughtfully. "I bet he'll be at that party. His family and the Blakes are real friendly, aren't they?"

"Isn't this pretty?" Eleanor enthused over a pale green silk gown.

Darcy got the hint and said nothing more about Keegan. But the look in her eyes was more eloquent than words.

For the rest of the day, after she and Darcy parted company, Eleanor worried about the party. Keegan wouldn't be there...would he? She didn't want him to spoil her fun, to intrude into her life anymore. She found things to do, to keep busy. She couldn't bear thinking about it. Anyway, Wade would be with her. He'd protect her.

She got dressed early and went into her father's study, where he'd been holed up all day, to show him her borrowed outfit and her new look.

He stared and nodded solemnly. "You look just like your mother, darling," he said, smiling wistfully. "So beautiful."

"Not me. Wrong girl." She laughed. "But if you think I'll do, that's fine."

"You'll do all right. You may need a stick to beat off the boys." He lit his pipe. "Watch yourself."

"Everybody tells me that." She sighed.

"Then I'd listen if I were you." He studied her with shrewd eyes. "Remember that it's a long way from the presidential suite to the economy-class rooms, will you?"

"We're not servants," she said haughtily.

"Yes, I know that. But we're not high society, either. See that you remember it."

"Yes, Your Worship," she said, and curtsied.

"Away with you! And don't drink. You know what it does to you."

She did indeed, remembering that one date with Keegan. Her face colored, and she bent, pretending to fix her shoe strap.

"I'll remember."

"And have a good time," her father added.

"Oh, I expect to."

"And say hello to Keegan for me," he added with a twinkle in his eyes. "Didn't you know he was invited, too?"

She glared at the knowing look in his eyes, then turned as she heard a car pull into the driveway. "Well, I'm off. I'll see you when I get back. Don't be up too late, now."

He made a face at her and she closed the door on it.

The Blakes lived in a house just a little less palatial than Flintlock. It was redbrick, very old, and stood on the banks of a private lake overlooking one of the most beautiful plains near Lexington. There was rolling farmland around it, and Thoroughbreds pranced jauntily in the confines of white fences.

"Nice little place, isn't it?" Wade asked as they stopped in the driveway where a liveried chauffeur waited to drive them from the parking spaces up to the house.

"Little," she scoffed, getting into the back of the Rolls-Royce limousine. She tried to memorize every inch of the leather luxury so that she could tell her father and Darcy. It was a little like being Cinderella.

"Little compared to some," Wade replied with a laugh. Riding around in Rolls-Royces was probably nothing unusual for him. He leaned back, scanning Eleanor's ensemble. "I like your dress, darling. Silk wears well, doesn't it?"

"Uh, yes, it does," she returned. Odd that he could recognize silk; he probably wore silk shirts. Most rich men did. She remembered that Keegan had worn a white silk shirt that night....

"I like the new haircut, too," he said. "You pay for dressing, Eleanor. I like the way you look."

"I'm glad."

"Nervous?" he asked as the driver pulled up in front of the house, which was blazing with light. Exquisitely gowned women and men in black evening wear strode elegantly along the cobblestone walkway, and Eleanor did feel uneasy.

"Just a bit," she confessed.

"Just stick with me, kid, I'll take care of you," he said with a wink.

She glanced at him. Was he afraid she might slurp her soup and try to butter her bread with her spoon? She frowned. Was it a dinner party? She asked him. "No, darling," he replied, guiding her to the front door. "It's a champagne buffet."

"With different kinds of champagne?"

"Not quite," he chuckled, pressing her hand closer. Tall, dark, good-looking, he attracted attention, even with his slightly overweight frame. And Eleanor seemed to be doing that as well. And not because she was out of place. "Champagne and hors d'oeuvres," he whispered. "Conversation and dancing. There's even a pool, if you fancy swimming."

"Well, not in my gown," she murmured demurely.

"They keep bathing suits on hand," he said, laughing. "Sometimes, they actually fit."

"I'll pass, thank you," she said with a smile.

She was introduced to her host and hostess. Mr. Blake was sixtyish, heavyset and pleasant. His wife—his third wife—was barely forty, vivacious and dripping diamonds. Their daughter was in her early twenties but already married. Her husband, an executive type, was beside her, helping to receive guests.

Fortunately no one asked if Eleanor was related to the Cape Cod Whitmans or the Palm Beach Whitmans, and she didn't have to confess that her father was a carpenter on the Taber farm. That would have humiliated her beyond bearing. She hated being an outsider. But these people and their elegant furnishings graphically reminded her of what she would be going home to. They pointed up the difference between living and surviving. And she wondered if she hadn't been better off not knowing that some people could afford trinkets like original oil paintings and velvet sofas and leather chairs and Oriental carpets and crystal chandeliers.

She had only one glass of champagne, standing rigid beside Wade while he discussed money matters with acquaintances. Conversation seemed to center around good stocks, municipal bonds, money markets, income taxes and new investment opportunities. The only investments Eleanor knew about were the ones she made on her car and groceries. She smiled into her champagne and nibbled on a delicate little puff pastry filled with chicken.

"Well, look who's arrived," murmured the older man beside Wade, glancing toward the door.

Eleanor followed his amused stare and found Keegan, in a black tuxedo, just entering the house with an elegant little black-clad brunette on his arm.

Eleanor's heart skipped a beat just looking at him. He was devastating in evening clothes, his red hair neatly combed, his patrician features alarmingly handsome. Lucky, lucky girl who had his whole attention, she thought miserably, then chided herself for the thought. After all, she was long over him.

"Isn't that the O'Clancy girl, the one who's visiting them from Ireland?"

"Yes, I think it is. Lovely, isn't she? She and her parents are hoping to work a deal with Taber, or so we hear, on a Thoroughbred of theirs," Wade murmured with a smile. "Trust Taber to come up with an escort like that. But what's he doing here?"

"He's after that new colt of Blake's—the Arabian out of Dane's Grace by Treadway. Probably Blake decided they could discuss business here as well as at the golf course." He chuckled.

Watching Keegan with the brunette, Eleanor couldn't help but wonder how many women he'd gone through since the night he'd seduced her. The thought made her go hot all over.

"Why the long face?" Wade teased, whispering in her ear.

"I don't like him," she blurted out.

His eyebrows arched. "Why not?" he exclaimed.

"He has freckles," she muttered, glowering at the redheaded man, who seemed to feel her cold scrutiny and turned abruptly. He caught her eyes across the room, and she stood there dying of old wounds, feeling the floor lurch under her feet. Her body ached; it took her last ounce of willpower to jerk her gaze back to Wade and calm her wildly beating heart. "Don't you think freckles are just horribly blatant?" she asked matter-of-factly. "I can't think why anyone would want to have them."

He laughed helplessly. "I don't suppose he can get rid of them, darling," he said.

"A likely story," she returned.

He laughed even harder and pulled her close against his side. "You bubbly little thing. I'd rather have you around than a magnum of champagne."

She knew. Oh, how she knew. She smiled up at him just as Keegan looked her way, intercepting her smile. He seemed to grow two feet and his eyes were suddenly darker, possessive. He let his gaze rove over her from head to toe, and even at a distance the look was powerfully narcotic. She avoided it this time, in self-defense.

"Shall we dance?" Wade asked. He put their glasses aside and moved her into the ballroom, where a small orchestra was playing Strauss waltzes. She moved across the floor with him like thistledown, and he grinned.

"You dance gloriously!" he said.

"Not what you expected of a nurse?" she teased. "Actually, I took dancing for three years. Ballroom dancing was part of the course. I do love a waltz."

"Then let's show them how a waltz should be performed," he murmured, and drew her around and around in the center of the floor.

Soon people were standing back to watch, because they moved as one person. He was an excellent dancer, and she followed him without a single missed step. She laughed up into his face, loving the music, feeling young again, full of life. It had been a long, bleak year, and now she was coming to life again. She closed her eyes and drifted, giving herself up to the joyous, seductive rhythm. It would have been perfect, she thought dreamily, if the arms holding her were wiry and strong, if the body against hers were lithe and lean and hard-muscled. And if the face above hers were surrounded by red hair, and if there were horrible freckles all over it....

She bit her lip. If. How long did it take a dream to die? she wondered sadly. Hers had lasted too long already.

Eleanor returned to the reality of applause all around as Wade bowed to her and led her off the dance floor. She held tight to his hand, vaguely aware of Keegan's blue eyes watching. Always watching. Why did he stare at her so? she wondered. Was it guilt?

"That was nice," she told Wade.

"I thought so, too. You're magic." He bent and brushed a kiss across her forehead. Across the room, a redheaded man clenched his fists and looked as if he could do murder.

When some of the other guests discovered that Eleanor was a nurse, she found herself much in demand to answer medical questions, none of which she felt qualified to address. She learned to excuse herself before things got too complex, and she never lacked for partners. But inevitably Keegan claimed her for a dance, and the evening turned dark.

"Having fun?" he asked dryly. "You do seem to be the center of attention."

"I'm having a lovely time," she replied. "Are you?" she added with a glance at his young partner, who was dancing with an older man and smiling at him radiantly.

"Yes, I am, as a matter of fact," he replied. "She's a sweet girl. Generous and kind and beautiful."

"Not your usual choice, but we all like a change, don't we?" she taunted.

He looked down at her possessively, his eyes charming hers as he pulled her closer, letting her feel his strength as he turned her expertly to a slow box step. "What do you know about my usual choices?" he asked. "You make a science out of trying to avoid me."

"Do I?" she asked with a carefully blank expression. "I hadn't noticed."

His eyes searched her body possessively, and the strong hand holding hers contracted a little; subtly his fingers eased between hers so that his palm meshed with her own. Her heart jumped, and his other hand felt it because it had snaked around her waist and was resting just underneath her breast.

"Not quite immune yet, Eleanor?" he asked, searching her dark eyes, her parted lips.

"I've been dancing, haven't you noticed?" she hedged.

"I've noticed you all night, and you know it. This dress is pure witchery. Where did you get it?"

She smiled. "From the Salvation Army. Isn't it nice?"

He drew in an irritated breath and turned her quickly, so she almost lost her balance. She felt his body intimately in the turn and put a little distance between them.

"Stop fighting me," he muttered.

"Am I?" She looked up into his eyes lazily. "I thought you were reminding me of my place. Do you think this scene is a little too grand for your carpenter's daughter, Mr. Taber, sir?"

"Have you been drinking?" he demanded.

"Just an itty-bitty glass of champagne, boss. Not to worry," she mocked.

"I do worry," he said beneath his breath. He studied her face quietly as the music flowed around them. "Wade isn't the marrying kind, and you are."

"What difference does that make?" she asked, shrugging. "You know yourself that men only sleep with the carpenter's daughter, they don't marry her...."

"Eleanor, hush!" he hissed, glancing around to make sure no one had heard her.

"Why?" she asked. "Are you worried that someone might suspect you of playing around with the hired help?" she whispered conspiratorially. "God forbid!"

"Eleanor...!"

"I never knew until then that I had so much in common with the downstairs maid. Isn't that whom the master of the house usually seduces?" she asked, wide-eyed.

"Oh, for God's sake!" he burst out in helpless frustration. "Can't we have a normal conversation without sex coming into it?"

"Look who's talking!" she returned, stopping in the middle of the dance floor. "And I don't want to have any normal conversations with you. You're the only man I know who could probably talk a woman pregnant!"

He chuckled softly as he gazed at her, his eyes so warm they took the chill of the room off her. "We could try that, I suppose. How about coming with me on a picnic tomorrow?"

The invitation shocked her, but she kept it from showing. So he was trying to help history repeat itself, was he? Well, he wasn't manipulating her into any tight corners again.

She smiled and shook her head. "Thanks, but Wade and I are going sailing tomorrow. He has a sailboat."

The hand holding hers contracted. "He's on the make, you little fool; can't you see it? He doesn't give a damn for you or your feelings. He only wants to get you into bed!"

"Just like you did?" she probed.

He glared back at her. "You're not in his class," he began.

Her eyes widened and she smiled coldly. "Thanks a lot for reminding me. I'm not in yours, either, though, am I? Isn't it beneath you, asking the carpenter's daughter on picnics?"

He looked suddenly dangerous, those blue eyes glittering down at her through narrowed lids. Sensing explosions, she pulled out of his arms, regardless of the puzzled glances it brought, and went back to Wade as fast as she could walk. He was waiting, a faint smile on his dark face.

"Have a problem?" he asked amusedly, glancing past her to a glowering, blazing Keegan Taber.

"Not anymore, thanks," she replied. She smiled up at him dazzlingly. "Would you like to dance with me?"

"Honey chile, I'd love to," he drawled, and drew her lazily into his arms. "But do you think it's quite safe?" he added, nodding toward Keegan.

"Mr. Taber and I just had a minor difference of opinion," she said sweetly.

"It looks like he just got punched in the ego to me," Wade said conversationally. "You really don't like him, do you?"

"I like flies better than I like him," she muttered, glaring at Keegan. "Conceited ape!"

Keegan must have read her lips, because he turned suddenly and went back to the Irish girl, appropriating her from her current partner with noticeable flair.

"Just look at him," Eleanor glowered, "taking women away from other men, making passes at everything in skirts...."

"He's quite popular with the ladies," Wade observed. "I'm surprised you're able to resist his charm so easily."

If only he knew! "I've known him for years," she said shortly. "He's always around the house these days, talking to my father."

"And playing chess?" Wade ventured. He cocked his head and studied her while they danced. "Does he really come to play chess, or to chance his arm with you?"

"He'd get his arm broken for him if he tried to put it around me," she returned curtly. "And can we talk about something else? You're ruining my appetite."

"Oh, gladly," he murmured, and whirled her around the floor with a smug expression that wasn't lost on the tall, handsome redhead with the stunning brunette in his arms.

Four

Wade kept his sailboat in a slip at the marina on Cave Run Lake. It was a beautiful area, in the Daniel Boone National Forest, and there were hiking trails and a skylift in the forest area. It was late spring, almost summer, and the woods were filled with picnickers and fishermen and hikers. Eleanor stared after them a little wistfully as Wade led the way to his slip at the sprawling marina. She liked boats but knew little about them. Her tastes leaned much more toward fishing and walking in the woods than toward water sports. It was another of the big differences between Wade's life-style and her own, but perhaps she could adjust.

He looked handsome in his white slacks and navy pullover shirt, not a bad-looking man at all. She glanced ruefully at her jeans and multicolored knit shirt. She hoped she was properly dressed for sailing. She'd remembered the tennis shoes he told her to wear, but he hadn't specified what kind of clothes to wear. She sincerely hoped he didn't have any ideas about taking her to an exclusive restaurant dressed like this.

"We have a budding sailing fraternity here," he was telling her, glancing over his shoulder with a smile. "In October we have the Grand Annual Regatta. You'll have to come with me this year," he added, taking it for granted that theirs was going to be a long-term relationship. Eleanor beamed.

"Is it all sailing?" she asked innocently.

"Mostly," he replied. "It's the first weekend in October, and starts out with around-the-course racing the first day, with a big dinner that night and another race the second day. There's an open regatta for all classes."

"Do a lot of people from Lexington race in it?" she asked.

He grinned at her. "Darling, it's only a short drive from the city. Even shorter from where we live, outside the city. In fact, the Tabers have a slip here, and Keegan and Gene won their class in the regatta last October."

Her face colored. She knew that Keegan loved sailing, but she hadn't remembered that he kept his sailboat here, or that his father raced with him. It was the kind of thing that Gene Taber would do, though. Like his son, he had a reckless streak. It was one of the first things she'd admired about Keegan, that recklessness.

"Speak of the devil," Wade muttered, staring past her just as they reached his slip.

She half turned and found Keegan Taber walking casually along the marina, as if he spent every day there and was right at home.

"Hello, Wade!" he called with a friendly wave. "You have a call at the desk. I told them I'd relay it, since I was on my way to my own slip."

Wade sighed. "I might have known. You can't ever get away from work, not as long as there are telephones anywhere on the planet."

"Wait until the cellular phones catch on," Keegan said with a grin.

"God forbid! Be right back, darling. Thanks, Keegan."

"Sure." Keegan stuck his hands in his pockets. "I'll watch out for Eleanor until you get back."

Eleanor glared at Keegan as Wade disappeared into the marina office. He looked as casual as she did, in jeans and a yellow knit shirt, and in deck shoes he didn't tower over her as much as usual. The boots he wore around the farm gave him even more height. The wind was blowing his red hair around, disrupting its slightly wavy perfection, and against his deep tan the white flash of his teeth was even more attractive. The wind was behind him, blowing the heady scent of his after-shave into her nostrils, drowning her in its masculine lure.

"What are you doing here?" she asked.

"The same as you. Enjoying myself."

"Aren't you a little far from home and your houseguest?"

His eyebrows lifted. "Which houseguest?"

"The one with the figure," she returned, smiling coolly.

"The one with the figure is on a tour of local farms with my father and her father," he replied.

"And you didn't want to go, too?"

His blue eyes twinkled at her. "I work hard enough during the week that I like having Sundays off." He chuckled.

She lowered her eyes to his throat, where fine red hairs peeked out. She remembered that his chest was covered with that softly abrasive hair, and her face colored because of the intimacy that memory involved. She wrapped her arms around herself protectively and stared toward the marina office.

"He won't save you, you know," he remarked. He pulled out a cigarette and lit it. "That sounded like his housekeeper Mildred to me. And she'd never bother him on a date unless it was an emergency."

"He won't go home," she said. "We're going sailing."

"Want to bet?"

She looked up at him, her eyes narrowed. "Not with a renegade like you," she replied. "You stack the deck."

He smiled, and little thrills raced through her body. She was still vulnerable, and she hated it. Four years should have given her some immunity. In fact, it had only fanned the flame, made her hungry for the sight of him.

Her eyes met his, and she felt her toes curling under at the pleasure of the exchange. The hand holding his cigarette froze in midair, and suddenly his smile was gone. She sensed his abrupt rigidity and felt it reflected in her own posture. At that moment she wanted nothing quite so desperately as to reach up and kiss that warm, hard mouth.

"Dangerous, baby, looking at me like that in public," Keegan said in a tone she'd never heard him use. He smiled faintly, but it did nothing to disguise the flare of hunger in his eyes.

Before she could answer him, and while she was still trying to get her heart to stop racing, Wade rejoined them. He was frowning, his mind already on business.

"I'm sorry as hell, but I've got a European businessman sitting on my front porch drinking my best bourbon and just dying to give me gobs of money for a foal." He sighed. He grinned at Eleanor and Keegan, ignoring the tension. "I'm sorry, darling, but I'm so mercenary…"

She burst out laughing. "It's all right. If you'll drop me off…"

"I'll let her ride home with me," Keegan interrupted, lifting the cigarette to his lips. "Then you won't have to go out of your way."

Wade and Eleanor both started to protest, but they weren't as quick as Keegan. He took Eleanor firmly by the arm.

"Come on, I have to pick up some papers from the boat first. See you, Wade!"

Wade faltered. "Well…Eleanor, I'll call you tonight!"

"Yes…do!" she called over her shoulder, half running to keep up with Keegan's long strides. She scowled up at him as he propelled her down the marina. "No wonder you have your own boat; you're a pirate! You can't just appropriate unwilling passengers!"

"You're willing," he replied without looking at her. "At least you will be when I show you what I've got in the boat."

She sighed. "Does it bite?"

"It used to," he murmured, grinning. He helped her onto the polished deck of the big sailboat, its huge sails neatly wrapped and tied, and went below for a minute. He was back almost before she missed him, with a picnic basket in hand.

"How…what…?" she stammered.

"I had Mary June pack it this morning for us," he said. He helped her back off the boat. "We can drive down to the picnic area and gorge ourselves. I didn't have breakfast. I'm starving."

Her mind was whirling. "You couldn't have known Wade was going to have company."

"Sure I did. I sent it over, as a matter of fact," he said imperturbably, herding her right along.

Her jaw dropped. "Your Irish guests!"

"Dead straight," he agreed, grinning broadly. "And he'd better hurry home, too, or O'Clancy will have persuaded Mildred to go home with him to Ireland. That man could get funding from Congress for a fruitfly-mating program. I've never seen the beat.''

"You set me up!'' she groaned.

"It's your own fault,'' he replied. He led her to his bright-red Porsche and put her in on the passenger side. "You wouldn't come with me when I invited you.''

"I didn't want to! I still don't!''

He got in beside her and, flashing a dazzling smile, started up the little convertible. "Mary June's got roast beef and potato salad and homemade yeast rolls in the basket,'' he coaxed. "And she made fried apple pies for dessert.''

She glanced at him mutinously. "I'll get fat.''

"Is there hope?'' he asked wide-eyed. "You've lost ten pounds since you came back home, and you were never heavy to start with.''

"I like me the way I am,'' she fired back.

"I'll like you better twenty pounds heavier,'' he replied. "There. That looks like a nice, private spot.'' He pulled into a parking space in the deserted picnic area and cut off the engine. "Nice view. No people.'' He stared at her musingly. "You could make love to me if you wanted to.''

The unexpected remark made her grow hot all over. She practically dived out of the car, avoiding his eyes.

He brought the picnic basket and bypassed the tables. "This looks good,'' he remarked, scanning the area. He put the basket down under a huge oak tree overlooking the lake. Far away, the white and multicolored sails spread like tiny map indicators over the blue, blue water. "We can eat and watch the competition all at once.''

She sat down reluctantly in the pleasant shade, watching him spread the cloth and lay out the food. It did look delicious, and she knew Mary June's reputation as a cook. She and her father had been invited to barbecues and other special events that the Tabers hosted annually for their employees on the farm, and she'd tasted the housekeeper's cooking many times. Mary June was something of a family institution. Like her father, a treasured employee. The thought made her feel bitter, and she sighed, staring down at her hands in her lap.

"Don't curdle the dessert by glaring at it,'' he teased. "Eat something!''

He handed her a plate and busied himself pouring sweetened iced tea into plastic glasses from a huge jug that contained crushed ice.

She held out her hand for it and sipped the cool liquid with a dreamy smile. "How delicious!"

"I'm partial to it myself." He filled a plate for her, handing it over and ignoring her dubious expression as he filled another for himself. "Nothing like a picnic to make you hungry, I always say. Eat, for God's sake, Eleanor!"

Her dark eyes pinned him. "Must you always sling out orders? Can't you ever just ask?"

"Not my nature," he said between bites of beef. He sipped tea and watched her for a minute as she began to eat.

"No, that's true," she said after she cleared her plate. "You're a born manipulator. You're only happy when you get your own way."

"Aren't most people?" he asked. He put the plates aside and refilled her glass and his own with iced tea. Then he sprawled back comfortably against the huge tree trunk and crossed his long legs with a sigh. He looked as at ease here as he did at a formal party. Keegan never put on airs or lorded it over anyone. He seemed at home anywhere.

Eleanor sipped her tea, looking out over the lake. "I've never been here before," she remarked. "Dad and I drove past it on our way to see one of my great-aunts once, but we never stopped. We always go fishing on the river."

"There's a lot of bass and crappie in this lake," he replied, smiling. "So you like to fish, do you?"

"Dad does. I go along for the ride, and the peace and quiet. You don't get much of that in a hospital."

"What made you choose nursing?" he asked unexpectedly.

She held the cool, frosty cup in both hands and smiled faintly. "Oh, I don't know. I guess I always liked patching people up when they were hurt. I still do. I feel as if I'm giving something back to the world, paying my way as I go."

"Is that a dig at me?" he asked conversationally, but his blue eyes were serious.

"You work every bit as hard as I do," she said honestly. "I didn't mean it as an insult. I was explaining my own philosophy, not condemning your life-style."

His broad chest rose and fell heavily. "Maybe I feel like condemning it," he said broodingly. He ran a lean finger around the rim of his glass absently, watching its path. "My father built the farm up from bankruptcy when he was a young man. He worked hard all his life so that he'd have something to pass on to me, so that I wouldn't have to break my back for a living. Well, I didn't have to work, and it affected me. In consequence, I spent the first twenty-five years of my own life giving my father hell and expecting something for nothing. No matter how well meant, you can give a child too much." He looked up into her eyes. "I won't make that mistake with my sons."

"Sons?" she echoed. "Do you already have names picked out for them, too?"

"Sure," he said, grinning as the atmosphere changed between them. "Well, for the tenth one, anyway. I'll call him Quits."

She smiled, radiant. How odd, to sit and talk, really talk, to him. That was a first. She didn't want to enjoy it, but she couldn't help herself.

"How about you?" he asked with apparent carelessness. "Do you want kids?"

"Of course," she said. "I'd like a daughter, though."

"A daughter wouldn't be bad, although boys run in my family. The father determines sex, you know."

"No!" she asked in mock astonishment. "And here I thought the cabbage fairy did all that!"

"Stop it, you idiot," he muttered, chuckling. "I keep forgetting you went through nurse's training. I expect you know more than I do about reproduction."

"About some of it, maybe," she said tightly. She finished her tea and got up to put her cup and the plates in a nearby garbage can. When she came back, Keegan hadn't moved. He was still watching her, his eyes narrow and calculating.

"How about putting my cup in there, too?" He drained it and handed it to her, but just as she reached down to take it, he caught her wrist and propelled her into his hard body, cushioning the impact with his arms.

"Keegan!" she protested, struggling.

He only held her closer, positioning her across his legs, with her head captured in the crook of his elbow. He looked down at her, watching her struggles, feeling the touch of her hands on his chest as she pushed at it, and the blood rushed like lava through his veins.

"I'm not...on the menu," she said, panting.

"You should be," he murmured. His blue eyes scanned her delicate features, her full mouth and big brown eyes in a frame of blondish-brown hair. "I like what you've done to your hair, Eleanor. I like the new makeup, too."

She hadn't thought he'd even noticed it. Her eyes, steady and curious on his hardening face, reflected her puzzlement.

"You were sixteen the first time I kissed you," he said abruptly, watching her mouth. "It was at the annual Christmas party, up at Flintlock, and you stood under the mistletoe with the damnedest lost look on your face. I bent and kissed you, so gently, and you went beet red and ran away."

"I wasn't expecting it," she muttered, renewing her struggles.

He felt his body going rigid, and he stilled her with a firm hand on her hip. "No," he said softly. "Lie still. You're hurting me."

She froze, because even as he said it she could feel it. Her eyes levered back up to his and were captured by the mixture of hunger and pain she read in them.

"I'm sorry," she said, lying quietly. "But if you'd just let me go..."

"I don't want to," he replied. His possessive gaze traveled boldly from her face to the soft curve of her breasts in the revealing knit shirt, to her slender waist and her long, elegant legs in their tight blue-jean casing. "I'm sorry I hurt you that night," he remarked in a deep, velvet-soft tone. "I'm even sorrier that I didn't make up for it. By then, the risk would have been no worse. I left you with scars, didn't I?"

"Enough...that I don't want any more of them! Will you let me go?" she said, panting.

His voice was tender, the slow movements of his hand on her hip maddening. "It must have gone against everything you believed in to give yourself to me. I wasn't thinking about your upbringing; I was so drunk on the taste and feel of you that I couldn't think. I remember the scent of your body, the sound of your voice in my ear whispering that you loved me...."

"Stop it!" she cried, hiding her red face against him. Her hands clenched into fists against his chest. "Stop it, Keegan, for heaven's sake! I was a teenage girl with a furious crush, and you were an experienced man out to revenge yourself on the girl you really loved. That's all it was!"

"Are you sure?" He tilted her face up to his quiet, solemn eyes. "I'll admit that I'd had too much to drink and had fought with Lorraine, and you looked..." His mind went back to the way she'd looked in blue satin with her long hair curving around her shoulders and her full, lovely breasts provocatively displayed in the strapless gown. "You looked like Venus walking. I only meant to show you a good time, kiss you a little. But when you moaned and started kissing me back so hungrily, I forgot everything."

It had been explosive, she remembered, the bare touch of his mouth enough to trigger unexpected longings. She'd wanted it for so many years, hungered for it, ached to know his lovemaking, his possession. She'd had a few drinks of her own, and when he'd started undressing her, she'd gone wild at the touch of his skillful hands on her bare flesh.

He saw those memories in her eyes and felt his body going tense. The soft warmth and weight of her in his arms was making him ache. She smelled of gardenia, and his mind wouldn't let go of the picture it carried of her that night in the moonlit darkness, writhing under his touch while the car stereo played an exotic, sultry tune that could still bring his blood up four years later.

"Don't you dare touch me there!" she burst out as his fingers went down to her knit blouse and edged under it to the bottom of her bra.

But his hand kept moving, and she could feel his warm breath at her ear, whispering things she didn't hear. She struggled again, until his strength subdued her. The silence around them was tense, broken by bird songs, the lap of the water on the shore and the rustle of windblown leaves. Eleanor could hardly hear them above the beat of her heart. She could even hear his, and she marveled at the electricity they created together. It seemed even more potent than it had four years ago, perhaps because she was a woman now.

"Hush, Ellie," he whispered, ignoring the hand tugging at his wrist. "Shhhhh. Lie still for me...."

She had to bite her lip to keep from crying out. He had her wrapped up so tightly that she couldn't even squirm. She didn't want his hands on her; she couldn't bear the remembered pleasure of it. She moaned sharply, hating the vulnerability that he could hear now as he found the front clip of the garment and gently unhooked it. She could feel herself swelling, and he wasn't even touching her yet. His fingers rested on the clip as the bra parted in front and began to peel away.

He lifted his head, finding her eyes, paralyzing her with the sweet warmth of that possessive gaze, while his fingers tortured her with slow, expert movements.

"All I want is to touch you, stroke you a little," he said in a voice as lazy and sultry as a summer night.

"Don't!" she cried, biting her lip hard as his free hand began to move the bra away from soft flesh. "Please don't do this to me, Keegan!"

"Why are you so afraid of it?" he asked gently, searching her wild eyes. "You're a woman now, not a child. Four years older, wiser, experienced yourself. This is just an interlude. Share a little pleasure with me, Ellie. Let me bring back the memories."

"They were terrible memories," she reminded him on a caught breath. "You hurt me!"

"I know, baby," he said softly, and his eyes for an instant were haunted. He bent and brushed his mouth gently over her forehead. "Once, but never again, never. Lie still, baby, and let me touch you."

She wanted to stop him. To cry out, to protest. He'd hurt her pride so desperately, and he was only playing with her. But he was calling her "baby," just as he had on that night, and she remembered the feel of his hair-roughened chest against her taut breasts, the smooth, hard muscles of his bare legs against her own, the unexpected steely strength of his body as he held her down and overwhelmed her in the moonlit darkness....

How could she want this, after the way he'd hurt her? But she did; she wanted it, her body was gently arching, and his hand was tracing her rib cage, taunting her, teasing her. "Shhhh," he whispered again.

The arm supporting her lifted her a little closer to his chest, turning her so that her hot face could fall against his neck.

She shuddered helplessly and raised her hands, tangling them gently in the slightly curly hair at the nape of his strong neck. She couldn't breathe properly, and she couldn't hide it. She moaned again, a breath of sound that barely reached his ear.

His cheek brushed against hers. His mouth touched her ear, her cheek, her nose. "Ellie," he whispered, and his lips found hers, probing them delicately apart, biting at them.

It was just like that night. Explosive. Blazing. Frightening, a brush-fire that hardly needed its own spark to ignite.

"Keegan," she moaned against his lips, shaking all over. Her eyes opened, anguished, and found a matching torment in the blue depths.

"Nothing's changed," he whispered, his deep voice a little husky with emotion. "Touching you excites me so. This, with you, is as satisfying as lovemaking. You make such sweet noises when I do this...."

"This" was an achingly slow tracing around her breast until his fingers brushed the taut hardness and made it throb with pleasure. Her body jerked and she moaned against his mouth. He reveled in the trembling hunger he could feel in her. Lost, burning up with remembered passion, he opened his mouth and gently thrust his tongue into her mouth. It was surprising, the way she tensed, as if she weren't used to this kind of kissing. Surprising, and wildly arousing.

His hands teased her body until he felt her fingers at his wrist, pleading, guiding. Surges of pleasure shot through him like fire as his hand found her, so gently, and she froze in the tender embrace, her breath catching as he took the delicate weight and found the hardness with his thumb. She jerked at that brushing contact, shuddering with obvious pleasure.

"Do you like it like that?" he whispered. "Does it please you when I touch them this way? Or is it better like this?"

His thumb and forefinger contracted, and she arched back, groaning, abandoned. And he went crazy.

She felt her body being forced down against the hard ground, felt the weight of his body as he kissed her fiercely, and was powerless to stop him. She was caught in the power of what they were sharing, in the sweet, warm beauty of it. Her mouth felt bruised when he finally lifted his head, and her eyes opened lazily to look up at the passion-hard face of the man above her. "I'm going to look at you," he whispered, catching the hem of her blouse while she lay helpless under his body. "I'm going to get drunk on you, and then I'm going to eat you like candy."

She moaned, beyond pride, beyond protest, wanting the breeze on her bare skin, his eyes, his mouth there. She trembled a little as she felt her rib cage being stroked by his lean, strong hands and the wind.

His face was dark with passion, his eyes glittering with it, as he looked down at her body, his hands just the least bit unsteady. Her arms lifted above her head as he raised the hem of the blouse just to the lacy bottom of her bra. Then, as he started to bare her breasts to his eyes, the sound of an approaching automobile penetrated their passion-hazed cocoon.

Keegan froze, shuddering. "No!" he whispered in anguish. He glanced up. "Oh, God, go away!"

But the car, loaded with children and a dog with a tongue half the length of his body, pulled into a parking spot right beside the Porsche.

Keegan dragged his eyes from Eleanor's shaking body and got to his feet with a rough curse, ramming his hands in his pockets and actually shuddering with frustrated passion.

Eleanor dragged herself into a sitting position, shocked to find that she wasn't even very disheveled except that her bra was unclipped. She fastened it unobtrusively as the family talked merrily and slammed things around getting out of the car. Eleanor had a glimpse of Keegan's obviously aroused body before he turned away and walked down to the water's edge. With a shaky sigh, she began to get the picnic items together.

She lifted her head and managed a smile at the group of picnickers as they rushed past to a table a few hundred yards away. She'd had a narrow escape; now she wanted to go home and mentally flay herself for the way she'd given in. She wondered if she might be a nymphomaniac or something. She certainly seemed wanton with Keegan.

He came back minutes later, still pale and rigid. He lifted the basket for her and carried it up to the Porsche, sticking it in the trunk with little respect for its age.

He held the door for Eleanor with a face hard enough to make her uncomfortable. She knew a little more about men now than she had four years ago, and she didn't have to ask what was wrong with him.

As they drove back toward her home, he lit a cigarette and smoked it silently, his red hair blowing in the wind with the top down. Eleanor kept her silence, too, ashamed of her behavior, ashamed of letting him see that she was still vulnerable.

He pulled up in front of her house and cut the engine. "I didn't mean for that to happen," he said unexpectedly. He leaned back against his door, watching her with an expression that didn't quite register.

"You never did," she replied curtly. "Well, if you're expecting me to be available for fun and games, you can forget it. I had one dose of you, and one was enough. I'm over you."

His thin lips moved up slightly as he read the fear so plain in her big, dark eyes and controlled the automatic urge to retaliate. He stared down at his cigarette. "I came on too strong, I guess," he said quietly. "I expected you to be experienced by now, Ellie."

"And what makes you think I'm not?" she demanded.

He looked up into her eyes, and the expression in them caused her to flush. She opened the door and got out, so quickly that she almost fell.

She was almost to the house when he caught her up with his long, easy stride.

"I won't flatter myself by thinking that no other man measured up, if that's what caused the scarlet blush," he told her, turning her at the front door. "Did I leave such deep scars that you can't give yourself again, Ellie, is that what happened?"

"Now you are flattering yourself," she said tightly.

He touched her hair, hating the tiny flinch of her eyelids that told him how very vulnerable she was, how frightened. "Don't," he said softly, tenderly. "I don't think I could bear it if you pushed me away."

Her eyes widened, shocked as she searched the blue depths of his gaze.

"Can't you see how hard this is for me?" he asked quietly. "I know how badly I hurt you, what I did to your pride."

"And what are you trying to do now, make it up to me with a little light lovemaking between women?'' she accused angrily. ''No, thanks! You caught me off guard today; some old memories got in my way and I lost my head. But that won't happen twice, Keegan Taber. I'd rather throw myself at a shark than at you.''

He forced himself to smile, as if it didn't matter. ''Would you? The shark might take off a leg. The worst I could take is something you once gave me.''

''Something I can never give again, thanks to you,'' she returned. Her dark eyes flashed as she dragged them away. ''Dad likes you, so feel free to visit him whenever you like. But I'm not at home to you anymore.''

''Suppose...I didn't rush you.'' He sounded oddly hesitant, even hopeful. He looked at his deck shoes, not at her. ''Suppose we got to know each other again—''

''In whose bed, yours or mine?'' she interrupted, her voice chill and distant.

He sighed impatiently, and the iron control faltered. ''For God's sake, I'm not trying to seduce you!''

''What an interesting denial, after what happened by the lake!''

He inhaled and seemed to grow two inches. ''You weren't fighting very damned hard!''

Her lower lip trembled, and he cursed himself inwardly for that blow to her pride. It was the worst thing he could have said, justified or not.

''Ellie...'' he began.

''Never mind,'' she told him, reaching for the doorknob. ''No, I wasn't fighting, you're very good at seduction. I should have tried to remember how good, shouldn't I? Just leave me alone, Keegan!''

She rushed into the house without another word, hurt and humiliated all over again. She was horrified at what she'd done. Stupid, she told herself. He was the kind of man to take advantage of any lapse. If she wasn't careful, she'd wind up back in the same shape she'd been four years ago. It was very likely he was pulling the same stunt again, this time with the pretty Irish girl as the prize. Well, he wasn't going to pull the wool over her eyes a second time, no, sir. This time she knew exactly what she was doing.

As long as she kept five feet away from him, she amended with a wistful sigh. Her body still tingled from his hands; she could taste him on her mouth. She closed her eyes and tried to picture Wade. But the only man she saw in her mind had red hair and freckles, and he sat in the living room with her father for what seemed like forever until finally he gave up and left.

Five

Eleanor stayed in her room until she was sure Keegan had gone. She didn't want to see him again while her emotions were still in turmoil. Who would have thought she'd be so vulnerable with him after what he'd done to her four years ago? She hadn't realized that she'd be quite so easy to seduce, but now she was forewarned. It would be a cold day in hell before she let him get that close again. Just remembering it made her go hot. To make matters worse, she knew it would take days to get over what they'd done together.

What bothered her most was why he'd done it. He hadn't seemed quite in control at the last, as if he'd been as crazed by passion as she. Well, he wanted her—she knew that. He'd never made any secret of it, either. But it didn't make things any easier. The hardest thing to take was his accusation that she'd wanted it just as much as he had. That was true, but she didn't want him knowing it. She had to remember what had happened before, had to remember that she couldn't trust him. Otherwise, she was going to find herself in another big mess.

Finally Eleanor joined her father in the living room. She'd reapplied her makeup, and except for the slight swelling of her lips where Keegan's hungry mouth had bruised them, she looked quite normal.

But her father's keen eyes didn't miss the swollen mouth, and he had an unbearably smug look on his face as well.

"How is it that you left with Wade and came home with Keegan?" he asked.

She cleared her throat. "Actually, Keegan sent his Irish guests over to buy one of Wade's horses, and then kidnapped me before Wade could offer to drive me home. We went on a picnic."

"Kidnapped you, did he?" He grinned broadly. "A man after my own heart."

"Well, it was underhanded, all the same." She tried to sound indignant. "I was looking forward to going sailing with Wade."

"Keegan has a boat. I'll bet he'd take you sailing if you asked him."

"He'd love that," she grumbled, "having me beg him to take me places."

"I doubt you'd even have to ask," he said quietly. "Easy to see he's got a case on you. I think he always did."

Fathers, she thought fiercely, glaring down at him. "Cupid Whitman," she accused. "Where's your little bow and arrow?"

"You might give him a chance, before you wind up with that Wade fellow."

"I gave him a chance," she said coldly, "four years ago. And he got engaged to Lorraine, remember? He's not putting my neck in a guillotine twice in one lifetime, oh, no. I'm older and wiser now, and I won't be manipulated anymore by your chess-playing hero."

He lifted an eyebrow and stared pointedly at her lower lip. "Looks like that statement comes a bit late, doesn't it?" he remarked carelessly.

She started to speak, threw up her hands and left the room. What was the use in arguing? Keegan had a ready and waiting ally, right here in her own house. If only she could tell her father the whole truth, he might not be so eager to push her into Keegan's waiting arms. But that was a secret she'd have to keep.

At times like these, she wished her mother were alive. Geraldine Whitman was little more than a soft memory now, the accident that had taken her life just a nightmare. She'd been only ten when it happened, and her father had been her whole life in the years since. Eleanor wondered how it would have been to have someone to talk to. She had Darcy, of course, but a mother would have been different.

She didn't see Keegan again in the next few days, and she was grateful for the breather. She went to work and on Tuesday afternoon rushed home to get ready for her date with Wade.

Her father looked depressed when she returned to the living room; he was sitting huddled in his chair with a scowl on his face.

"What's your trouble?" she asked him mischievously.

"You've run off my chess partner," he grumbled, and her heart leaped at the reference to Keegan.

"He's gone away? Oh, goody!" she said gleefully.

He glared at her. "No, he hasn't gone away. He just can't come down for chess. He's taking that Irish girl to a party."

She couldn't camouflage the pain in her eyes fast enough, although she turned away quickly. "Is he?"

"If you'd warm toward him a little... For God's sake, girl, he's going to wind up with another one of those heartless, self-centered little idiots, and it will be all your fault!"

"On the contrary," she said, forcing a smile, "if that's the kind of woman he likes, nothing I do will reform him. Dad, I don't want Keegan. I'm sorry, you'll just have to accept it."

He looked as if he'd lost his last friend. "Yes, I suppose so. Well, have a good time." He glanced up, approving of her full blue-plaid skirt, pale-blue blouse and high heels. "You look very nice."

She curtsied. "Thank you. Can I bring you back anything?"

He shook his head with a sigh. "No, I'll watch a little television, I guess, and go to bed. Maybe I can get back to work next week. I'm sure tired of sitting around here like a stick of furniture."

She bent and kissed his bald head. "I can imagine. Have a nice evening, Dad. I won't be late."

"Have fun," he called as Wade's car drove up.

Wade helped her into the Mercedes with a flourish. He looked debonair in a navy-blue blazer and white slacks with a white shirt and ascot. With his natural darkness, the contrast gave him a rakish look.

"And here we are again." He grinned. "Sorry about Sunday, but I managed to sell O'Clancy two colts. Forgive me for stranding you with Keegan."

"You apologized Sunday night," she reminded him, "and I accepted. It wasn't so bad. He brought me home in one piece."

"Odd, him being at the marina on a Sunday," he said carelessly.

"He doesn't usually go near the place except with his father. I suppose it was those papers he had to get."

She didn't mention that she hadn't seen him get any papers. She didn't want to remember what had happened Sunday at all.

"I missed you," she said with a mischievous smile.

"I missed you, too," he murmured dryly. "Not that the Irish girl wasn't a dish. Very, very nice. Pretty face, good manners…a little mercenary, but nobody's perfect."

"Dad's miffed at her for costing him his chess partner," she mentioned. "He said that Keegan's taking her out tonight."

"Lucky stiff," he said with feeling. He glanced sideways. "Not that you aren't a dish, darling. How do you feel about feverish affairs, by the way?"

He might have been kidding, but she didn't think so. And it was better to have it all out in the open, anyway. "I don't care for feverish affairs, in all honesty," she told him with a quiet smile. "I'm sorry, but I'm the product of a strict upbringing."

"No need to apologize," he said, and for once he dropped the façade of devil-may-care charm. "It's rather refreshing, in fact. I think I might enjoy really talking to a woman for a change. This playboy mask is wearing a bit thin, the older I get."

Suddenly he was another person, something besides the surface bubbling charm. He slowed down as they approached the restaurant. His dark eyes cut sideways and he smiled, but it was a different kind of smile. "Are you always so honest?"

"Most of the time." She sighed wearily. "I'm hoping to outgrow it eventually." She half turned in her seat when he stopped the car. "Why did you start taking me out, if a quick affair was what you had in mind? Surely you heard about me through the grapevine?"

"Sure. That was part of the appeal." He sighed and smiled, a genuine smile this time. "I guess the reverse is true as well. What did they say about me?"

She remembered what Keegan had said. "That you'd been caught doing it every way except hanging from a limb of a tree," she said flatly.

He burst out laughing. "Oh, that's good. That's really good." He took her hand in his and lifted it to his lips. "In fact, there is a bit of truth in that rumor. But a lot of my reputation is inflated. I'm not really the big, bad wolf.''

"You're a nice man,'' she told him, and smiled back. "I like doing things with you.''

"I like being with you, too,'' he said, then searched her dark eyes. "Suppose we give it a chance. I won't try to seduce you, if you won't try to seduce me. How's that for fair?''

She grinned up at him. "That's fair enough.''

He kissed her fingertips and got out to open the door for her.

Dinner was exquisite. She ate things she could barely pronounce, and Wade introduced her to a white wine that convinced her "bouquet'' could mean something besides flowers. He taught her how to pronounce the gourmet dishes they ate and seemed to enjoy tutoring her.

"I'm so backward,'' she grumbled as she stumbled over a name.

"No,'' he said, and meant it. "You're a refreshing change. I like you, Eleanor Whitman. You may take that as a compliment, because I don't like many people, male or female. I've learned in my life that most people are out for what they can get. And a rich man quickly becomes a target.''

She'd heard Keegan say something similar, years before, about not knowing if he was liked for himself or what he could provide.

"I'd like you if you didn't have a dime,'' she told Wade. "You're pretty refreshing yourself. For someone who's filthy rich, that is,'' she said.

He smiled at her over his wineglass. "Having fun?''

"Yes. Are you?''

"Oh, this could definitely become a habit,'' he said, lifting the glass to his lips. "How about dessert?''

She smiled back. He had a nice face. Very dark. No freckles....

Just as that registered, Keegan walked through the door of the restaurant with the Irish girl on his arm, and Eleanor wanted to go through the floor.

Wade glanced up, chuckling. "I'll be damned. You'd think he was following us around, wouldn't you? Hey, Keegan!'' he called.

Keegan spotted him with Eleanor and smiled easily, drawing the Irish girl along with him.

"Well, what a coincidence," Keegan said. "Wade, Eleanor, I'd like you to meet my houseguest, Maureen O'Clancy. Maureen, Wade Granger and Eleanor Whitman."

Wade rose, smiling as he took Maureen's dainty hand. "How lovely to see you again," he murmured with his most wicked smile as he lifted her hand to his lips.

"How nice to see you again, too," the Irish girl replied in her delicately accented tones. "We enjoyed our visit to your farm." Her blue eyes smiled at Wade, and then she seemed to notice Eleanor. "Haven't we met before?" she asked.

"At the Blakes' party," Keegan prompted.

"Ah, yes." Maureen made the connection and smiled cattily. "Your father is one of Keegan's carpenters, I believe?"

"How kind of you to remember," Eleanor returned without blinking. "Isn't it wonderful how democratic Lexington society is? I mean, letting the hired help attend social functions—"

"Let's sit down, Maureen," Keegan interrupted quickly, recognizing too easily the set of Eleanor's proud head and the tone of her voice. "Nice to see you both."

He all but dragged Maureen away whle Wade tried but failed to smother a grin.

"Hellcat," Wade accused as he sat back down. "That was nasty."

"Do you really think so?" Eleanor asked, her bright eyes smiling at him. "Thank you!"

He shook his head. "I can see real possibilities in you, Eleanor," he mused. "You'd be the ideal wife for a businessman; you can hold your own with the cats."

"I came up hard," she told him. "You sprout claws or get buried. She's interesting, though," she added, glancing at the corner table where Keegan and Maureen were just being seated. "Imagine how many years of training it must have taken to get her nose at just that exalted angle...."

"Shame on you!" he chided. "Here, eat your trifle and let's go. I want to get home in time to play your father a game of chess."

She gaped at him as he pushed the delicate pudding in front of her.

"Well, he likes chess, doesn't he?" he asked innocently. "I'll even let him win," he added, rubbing his hands together.

"He beats Keegan," she volunteered. "And Keegan tries."

He whistled. "Keegan beats everybody."

"Not this time," she said under her breath, and glancing toward the corner table, she smiled through a wave of pain. Old times and old tactics, she thought. Keegan, playing women off against each other, and the Irish girl didn't even know it. Perhaps she didn't care, either. But Eleanor did. She felt as though Keegan had always belonged to her, and it was hard seeing him with someone else.

It was understandable that she might feel that way, she told herself. After all, Keegan had been her first man. She only wished that it didn't hurt quite so much. She didn't dare let him see that it bothered her, either. He already thought, with some good reason, that she was vulnerable to him. It wouldn't do to let him know exactly how vulnerable.

So when he looked up from the Irish girl's face and caught Eleanor's eyes, she actually raised her wineglass and inclined her head gracefully. Then she turned back to Wade with magnificent disdain.

"What was that all about?" he asked with a faint smile.

"That was a congratulatory toast," she replied innocently. "He's bagged another one."

He chuckled. "You make him sound like a headhunter."

"Why not? His reputation's worse than yours," she replied.

He lifted both eyebrows. "Do you suppose he's ever done it suspended from a tree limb?"

She burst out laughing, almost choking on her wine. Across the room, a pair of deep blue eyes saw and darkened with an odd kind of pain. But Eleanor didn't see them.

Six

It was just past midnight when Wade took her home, and she was still a little shaken from trying to eat with Keegan watching her. Had he really gone there by coincidence, or had her father told him where Wade was taking her? She had to know.

"I had a great time," she told Wade as he cut the engine of the Mercedes at her front door. "Thanks for the meal."

"My pleasure," he said sincerely. He leaned toward her, giving her plenty of time to draw away.

But she didn't. She liked Wade. Tonight he'd been there when she'd needed a buffer against Keegan. She owed him this, if nothing more. She smiled against his warm mouth and closed her eyes.

It was pleasant kissing him. Not threatening or explosive as it was with Keegan. Keegan. She drew back against her will with a tiny sigh. What was the use in pretending? No one would ever move her as Keegan did. She couldn't hurt Wade by letting him believe she felt something that she truly didn't.

He touched her face and shrugged. Then he smiled, without anger. "You're a nice kid," he said. "Hang around with me, anyway. I'll teach you all kinds of useless information and leave you panting with my expertise as a local tour guide."

She burst out laughing. "You crazy man!"

His white teeth showed brilliantly against his dark tan as he returned the smile. "It beats sanity, from what I've seen." He took her hand and lifted it to his lips. "Just don't let the rabid redhead see that lost look in your eyes, darling," he cautioned solemnly, nodding when her eyelids flinched. "Oh, yes, you're very transparent sometimes, innocent lady. I don't think he noticed, but you'd be a basket case if he did. Keegan doesn't play around."

She knew that far better than he did. She straightened proudly. "You're wrong," she replied firmly. "I had a crush on him when I was eighteen, but I outgrew it. I don't feel that way anymore."

"Of course you don't," he said, humoring her. He leaned forward and brushed a kiss across her forehead. "Be careful, all the same. I wouldn't like to see him hurt you. I've gotten very fond of you, miss nurse."

"You're nice people," she murmured.

"I try, I try," he replied, dark eyes sparkling with humor. "We're having a garden party Saturday. You're invited. I'll pick you up about ten o'clock, and don't argue," he said when she opened her mouth. "Consider it private tuition," he added wickedly.

"And how will your family feel about having the Tabers' hired help to entertain?" she asked hesitantly.

He actually glowered at her. "For heaven's sake, don't start that. All you have to worry about is keeping your head while you fend off my mother and sister. My dad will be a pushover." He chuckled. "He likes pretty girls."

"Well—" she sighed "—if you're willing, I'm willing. I don't want to embarrass you, though, and I have a quick tongue."

"Do you?" he asked eagerly. "Show me!"

She hit him. "You stop that, you animal," she teased.

He stretched lazily, still smiling. "Well, it's too late for a game of chess with your father, so I guess I'll go home to my lonely bed and try to sleep." He glanced sideways at her as she reached for the door handle. "Sure you won't go home and share my pillow, Eleanor? You can use half my toothbrush, and I'll even share the cover with you."

"Thanks, but my father has this enormous shotgun...."

"I withdraw the invitation," he said hastily. "I'm allergic to shotgun blasts."

She leaned over and kissed his tanned cheek. "You're a lovely man. I wish I'd met you five years ago."

"Yes. So do I," he replied quietly. Then he winked. "Night, love. I'll see you Saturday morning. Ten sharp."

"Wait! What should I wear?"

"Something wispy and feminine."

She watched him drive off, wondering what would qualify as wispy. A cocktail dress? She grinned wickedly as she went into the house. A nightgown...?

Her father had already gone to bed. She had to wait until the next morning at breakfast to ask him if he'd told Keegan where she was going with Wade. So it came as a shock, when she got downstairs, to find Keegan sitting at the kitchen table with her father, drinking coffee.

"Well, it's about time," Keegan muttered, glaring at her. "This is a fine way to treat an injured man, making him go hungry while you sleep off your hot date!"

It was barely six in the morning. She was half-asleep and, worse, wearing her old worn green quilted robe with only a flimsy peekaboo nightie under it. Her hair was disheveled, and she had no makeup on.

"What injured man?" she demanded, glaring at Keegan. "And what are you doing here?"

"Your father," he reminded her. "Just look at the poor man. He's so weak from hunger he can hardly sit up at all."

Her father was enjoying himself, all wide grins and flushed pleasure, Cupid in the flesh. His daughter glared at him, too.

"Weak from hunger, my foot, and who appointed you his guardian?"

"Well, somebody has to protect him from his heartless offspring," Keegan returned doggedly. His blue eyes flowed over her like the warmth of the sun, and that arrogant smile tugged at his thin lips. "Do you always sleep like that?"

He of all people would have to ask that question. She blushed furiously and turned away to start cooking breakfast before anyone could see.

"Are you here to criticize or eat?" she demanded as she started frying bacon in the big iron skillet.

"Eat," Keegan replied. "I'm starving to death. Mary June turned her ankle and can't get up, and Maureen doesn't wake up until eleven o'clock.''

"Well, where's your father?'' she asked.

"He went to the Red Barn for breakfast,'' he replied.

"Really? I'm astonished that you didn't bring him with you,'' she muttered.

"I invited him.'' Keegan sighed. "But he didn't want to impose.''

She could have thrown something at him. And her father just sat there sipping coffee, enjoying himself. Men!

"I like my eggs sunny-side up,'' Keegan remarked as she started to mix some in a bowl to scramble.

"Do you?'' She gave him a sunny smile. "How nice.'' She went back to breaking eggs into the bowl.

"Is she always such a bear in the mornings?'' he asked her father.

"Oh, not at all,'' Barnett replied. "She's disgustingly sunny as a rule.''

"Then it must be me,'' the younger man said with a sigh. He stared at Eleanor quietly as she moved around pots and pans, smiling at her stiff back. He was wearing work clothes this morning—jeans and a chambray shirt that probably cost the earth, she thought irritably. It wasn't completely buttoned, and she wished he would at least cover up his chest so that she didn't get sidetracked while trying to make biscuits. The sight brought back some very disturbing memories.

"Biscuits,'' Keegan sighed, leaning his forearms on the table. "Nobody makes them like you do, Ellie.''

"How would you know?'' she demanded, glancing over her shoulder as she cut the biscuits and put them into a pan.

"I usually come over for coffee with your father,'' he said. "After you're gone, of course, but there are usually biscuits left over. I love the way you make them.''

Disgusting, the way that pleased her. She bit back a smile. "I make sourdough biscuits,'' she said. She glanced at him. "Go ahead, make a comment.''

"I wouldn't dare. At least, not until you take up the eggs.'' He grinned.

She turned back to her chores. Keegan and her father started talking, and she got busy setting the table and getting everything cooked.

When she was through, she put the food on the table and started to leave.

"Where are you going?" Keegan asked with his fork poised over the bacon platter.

"To...to get dressed," she faltered.

"It will be cold by then," her father chided. "Sit down, for heaven's sake; you're decently covered, after all."

"My thoughts exactly," Keegan seconded. "Sit, girl, you won't inflame me with passion. I have willpower."

She made the mistake of staring into his eyes at that instant, with the memory of that Sunday afternoon picnic in her face. The look she shared with him made her tingle all over, and thank heaven her father was buttering a biscuit. She averted her eyes and quickly sat down across from Keegan, her hands trembling as she tried to pour coffee from the carafe into thick white mugs.

"Here," Keegan said softly, putting his hand over hers to help her.

She looked up, and all the years fell away; it was painful for her, so painful to feel that way about him and know that he didn't share it, that he had nothing to give her.

His fingers caressed hers as he helped her steady the carafe, and his blue eyes searched her face. "Did you enjoy yourself last night?" he asked in a tone like velvet.

"The food was delicious," she returned. "Didn't you think so?"

"Yes." He didn't release her hand when she finished pouring. He let his eyes brush over it, then reluctantly he let her move away.

"How did Miss O'Clancy like it?" she forced herself to ask.

He shifted restlessly in his chair. "She found it a bit trying, I think," he replied. "She doesn't like French cuisine."

"Then why take her to a French restaurant?" she burst out, wide-eyed.

"She didn't tell me until it was too late," he replied.

She wanted to ask if he'd known that she and Wade were going to be there, but her courage failed her. She concentrated instead on eating her breakfast, leaving the conversation to the men, who seemed intent on discussing farm business anyway.

When they were through, she got up to clear the table and put the dishes in to soak until she dressed.

"I have to run," she remarked, drying her hands. "I go on duty at seven."

"Will the world end if you're a few minutes late?" Keegan grumbled, almost as if he didn't want her to leave.

"No, but my job might," she replied. "Unlike you, Mr. Taber, sir, I have to earn my living."

"Eleanor!" Barnett burst out, shocked.

"It's all right," Keegan soothed him. "Eleanor and I have been sparring for years. Haven't you noticed?"

"Yes," her father replied, and there was a world of meaning in the word.

Keegan sipped his coffee quietly. "Feel like going sailing with me Saturday?" he asked unexpectedly.

She gaped at him. "Me? My goodness, you're courting the angels these days, aren't you, being so good to the hired help!"

"Oh, Eleanor," her father groaned, burying his face in his hands.

"I like the hired help," Keegan shot back at her. "And will you please stop embarrassing your father?"

"He's my father after all; I can embarrass him if I want to!" she flared, dark eyes angry and cold.

"Will you come sailing or not?" he demanded.

"I don't like sailing."

"You were going with Wade!"

"I like Wade," she returned. "I'd rather go fishing or walking, if you want to know, but I was willing to go sailing with him because I like his company. I do not like yours," she continued relentlessly, "and you know why!"

He stared at her unblinking while Barnett watched them curiously.

"Besides," she muttered, dropping her eyes, "Wade's already invited me to a garden party at his home Saturday."

"At his home?" he asked silkily.

She glared at him. "His mother and sister will be there, as well as a number of guests. And before you ask, no, he doesn't do it hanging from tree limbs because I asked him and he told me so!"

"Oh, God." Barnett covered his face again, shaking his head. "Where did I fail her?"

"Will you hush?" Eleanor said to her father, then slid her angry gaze back to Keegan. "See what you've done now?"

"How could you ask him a question like that?" he demanded. "You'll put ideas into his head!"

"Dad's?" she asked innocently.

"Wade's! As you damned well know!" Keegan looked furious. Even his face seemed red, like his hair. He stuck his hands on his lean hips and glared at her. "Did he try anything last night?"

"Did you?" she shot back.

He was looking more furious by the minute. "Listen, Eleanor, you're going to get in trouble if you keep hanging out with that playboy."

"Dad, why don't you tell him that you're my father and that he has no right to grill me like this?" Eleanor moaned.

Barnett grinned. "But he's doing such a good job, darling."

She threw up her hands. "I'm going to work!"

"Running away?" Keegan taunted.

"You bet!" she replied without turning. She continued on to her room to get into her nurse's uniform and put on her makeup.

But if she'd expected that Keegan would be gone when she returned to the kitchen, cap in hand, she was disappointed. He was still sitting there.

His blue eyes gazed approvingly at the neat fit of her crisp white uniform with its metal nameplate. "Nice," he said with a slow smile. "You do look like an angel of mercy, baby."

Did he have to use that particular endearment? It made her grind her teeth, and the blush that covered her cheeks certainly aroused her father's curiosity.

"I'll be late if I don't hurry," she muttered, bending to kiss her father's cheek. "See you later."

"Don't I get a kiss, too?" Keegan asked.

She glared at him. "I only kiss family."

"How about long-lost cousins?" he asked. "I'll run right out and have a family history done."

She stuck her tongue out at him. "Beast."

"Have a nice day, darling," Barnett told his daughter as she went out the door.

She returned that, without looking at Keegan, and made a dash for her car. He probably wouldn't have come after her, but she wasn't taking any chances.

It was a long day. She couldn't seem to finish anything. There was one emergency after another, and by quitting time she was a frazzled wreck. Wade called that night, and she was barely able to talk to him for plain weariness. The rest of the week was equally rushed. In a way it was a blessing, because she didn't have time to brood over Keegan, who'd missed his Thursday night chess game with her father because of some business meeting. Eleanor was looking forward to an uncluttered weekend.

Darcy went with her Friday afternoon to shop for a wispy something to wear to the garden party at Wade's home.

"This is getting to be a Saturday ritual," Darcy laughed as they walked through the huge store's dress department.

"Yes, I know." Eleanor sighed. "I just hope I don't run out of money before Wade runs out of places to take me. I'm not too keen on this garden party, you know. I won't even know the people."

"You're every bit as good as anyone else," Darcy reminded her gently. "Just keep that in mind."

"I try. If I didn't like Wade so much, I'd break it off. He's a lovely man, but it's never going to amount to anything serious. Bells don't ring."

"Bells are noisy," Darcy said firmly. "Settle for security. You can buy bells, for goodness' sake!"

Eleanor burst out laughing at her friend's down-to-earth practicality. "Oh, you doll, you." She sighed. "What in the world would I do without you?"

"Let's not try to find out. Now this is a nice little outfit," she said, steering her friend toward a heavenly little purple-and-white cotton frock with lots of ruffles. Sure enough, when Eleanor tried it on, it was perfect. It emphasized her long, pretty legs and her nicely tanned arms and face, and gave her the appearance of an ingenue.

"That's the very thing," Darcy said firmly. "Now, quick, get it to the cash register before you look at the price tag, okay?"

It was a good thing Eleanor did, because it was half a week's salary. But then she could always wear it to barbecues and coffees and other high-society occasions, like being introduced to the Queen if she ever came to Lexington.

She told Darcy that and watched the older woman's face crumble into laughter.

"You can wear it to church, can't you?" Darcy asked. "Besides, just imagine how many heads will turn when you walk out wearing that!"

Eleanor sighed. The only head that came to mind was a red one, and she tried to imagine having Keegan pass out with frustrated passion just by looking at her. That was some joke, and she just shook her head. No, by now the Irish girl probably had him halfway to the altar. That depressed her, so she invited Darcy into the nearest ice cream shop and treated them both to enormous banana splits.

Wade came by to pick her up at ten the next morning, and she felt so nervous that she almost backed out.

"It'll be all right," he assured her. "You look gorgeous, you silly woman, and I'll be right with you every minute. Okay?"

She gave in. "Okay. Just, please, don't strand me, will you?"

"I won't strand you," he promised. "Now, come on."

Her father had vanished earlier; she hadn't even seen him since she'd gotten up. She left him a note and allowed Wade to herd her out the door.

Wade's home was beautiful. It was almost as big as Flintlock, set in the middle of a wide stretch of pasture surrounded by white fences and racehorses. One of the Granger stable had come in third at the Kentucky Derby last month, at the same time the Tabers' entry had finished second. There was great rivalry among stable owners, although Eleanor wasn't close enough to that society to encounter much of it.

"Like it?" Wade asked as he parked behind a Rolls in the driveway, near the huge brick house.

"It's lovely, especially the gardens," she replied, sighing.

"Wait until you see the backyard," he murmured dryly, and escorted her there.

Whatever she'd expected to see, the reality was a shock. There were tented pavilions everywhere, with ladies in wispy dresses and picture hats being escorted by nattily dressed gentlemen in ridiculously expensive leisure wear, with a huge Olympic-size swimming pool in the background. Everyone looked pleasant enough, and Eleanor's entrance didn't cause any riots. The guests didn't all rush together in panic and point fingers and speak in shocked whispers about the carpenter's daughter being included on the guest list.

"See?" Wade teased, taking her hand in his. "Now, they're just people, aren't they?"

"I guess so," she said hesitantly, her worried dark eyes glancing around. They came to a young dark-haired woman and a silver-haired matron, both exquisitely dressed, who were suddenly staring daggers at her. She sighed, expecting to do battle, because she knew whom they both favored. "Wade, would that be your mother and sister?" she added, nodding toward the hostile-looking pair.

He turned his head and grimaced. His hand, holding hers, contracted. "Oh, boy. Well, just ignore them, Eleanor," he said with an irritated expression. "They never like anyone I bring home, so don't take it personally. They're terrified that I'll get married and they'll lose control of the household."

"Let's go and meet them," she suggested, her eyes sparkling at the prospect of battle. "I love war movies, don't you?"

He laughed, surprised. "You little Amazon, you. All right, we'll get it over with."

She was dreading it, to tell the truth, but she wasn't about to spend the entire morning letting them make her uncomfortable. After all, the worst they could do was embarrass her, and maybe when they were through, they'd find someone else to victimize. During her four years of nursing, Eleanor had learned a lot about managing people. Buckling under, she knew, was a one-way road to misery. She hadn't let herself be walked on since she'd graduated from nurse's training, and she was now assistant floor nurse.

She smiled broadly at the two women, inwardly amused at the slight surprise that registered on their exquisitely made-up faces.

"This is your guest?" Mrs. Granger asked her son with a snooty look at Eleanor's dress. She lifted her chin. "Don't I know you, my dear?" she added with a faintly malicious smile while her daughter watched with a matching glint in her eyes. "You're the daughter of the Tabers' carpenter, I believe...."

"Why, that's right," Eleanor drawled. "You must be Wade's family," she gushed, reaching forward to drag his mother's white hand into her own and shaking it firmly. "How delightful to meet you both! I just can't tell you how astonished I was when Wade invited me. Imagine, little old me in a fancy place like this! I'll just do my dead level best not to slurp my coffee or wipe my mouth on my sleeve. Hot dang, is that a real swimming pool? You people must be just filthy rich!"

Mrs. Granger was openly gaping. So was her daughter. Wade was doubled over with laughter, no help whatsoever.

"I do love parties!" Eleanor continued, unabashed. "Say, is it okay if I strip off and go swimming in my undies? I didn't pack a bathing suit, you know."

Mrs. Granger cleared her throat and got a death grip on her glass of red punch. "I...uh..." she began, glancing irritably at her son. "Wade?"

He straightened, tears of amusement in his eyes. "Mother, you're out of your league with Eleanor," he said, wiping the tears away. "You've heard me speak of her—and please don't mind her atrocious manners," he added, tugging sharply on Eleanor's short hair. "She's had too much fresh air this morning, and it's affected her brain. Eleanor, darling, this is Mother and my sister, Sandra."

"I can apologize for my own atrocious manners, if you don't mind," Eleanor told him firmly. She nodded at the two women and smiled mischievously. "I'm very glad to meet you both. And you don't have to worry about having me cavort around the pool in my underwear. Actually, I don't swim at all."

Mrs. Granger was actually flapping, her face pale and her eyes startled. Her daughter was only a little less baffled and actually seemed to be amused.

"I'm glad to meet you, Eleanor Whitman," Sandra said with a grin. "Congratulations, you just passed the acid test. Right, mother hydrochloric?"

Eleanor laughed, delighted, and extended her own hand to meet Sandra's. "I'm sorry if I came on strong," she apologized. "It's been a wickedly long week, and it's telling on me, I'm afraid."

"Eleanor is a nurse, you know," Wade informed them proudly,

drawing her close to his side. "She's an assistant floor nurse at Peterson Memorial."

"I'm impressed," Mrs. Granger said, and actually seemed to mean it. "Go away, Wade, and let me talk to Miss Whitman."

"No intimidation," he warned his mother. "I like this one."

"I never intimidate people," came the gruff, indignant reply. "Scat!"

Wade brushed a kiss against Eleanor's cheek and went off with his hands in his pockets to join a group of businessmen.

"Sit down, dear," said Mrs. Granger, guiding Eleanor to a shady umbrella near the pool. A waiter was just passing with glasses of ice-cold lemonade, and she appropriated three of them for herself and her companions, then sat heavily down in the shade, fanning her full face with her hand.

"It's so hot," she complained. "I wanted to be in St. Croix this week, but Sandra had to have help organizing this little social thing."

"So Mother always says." Sandra grinned. She looked very much like her brother and was about the same age, with dark eyes and very white teeth.

"St. Croix is in the Caribbean, isn't it?" Eleanor sighed as she sipped her lemonade. "We had a patient who'd just returned from there. It must be lovely, being able to travel."

"It gets boring after a time," Mrs. Granger said kindly. "Anything does. I enjoyed it much more when I was younger than I do now, although I confess I'm partial to the West Indies. The pace is much slower down there. I can relax."

"Are you going to marry Wade?" Sandra asked bluntly.

Eleanor smiled. "No."

"I see," Sandra murmured with a mischievous smile.

"No, I don't think you do," Eleanor replied. "I don't have wild affairs, even with fabulously wealthy men. I like your brother very much, but like is as far as it goes. I have a career in mind, not marriage."

"Well, I never." Mrs. Granger grimaced. "Just when we find a really suitable candidate, she turns out to be a career girl. What's wrong with my son? Isn't he good enough for you?" she demanded.

"He's wonderful," Eleanor said genuinely. "And I wish I'd met him years ago. But he deserves a woman who can love him to pieces, and I can't."

"It's all your fault," Sandra told her mother. "If you hadn't attacked her the minute she walked onto the property..."

Mrs. Granger actually blushed. "It's the kind of women he usually brings here," she confessed miserably. "And, well, there were some rumors about you a few years ago...." She blushed even more.

Eleanor had to bite her tongue to keep from responding defensively. "What kind of rumors?" she asked as politely as she could.

"About you and Keegan Taber," Sandra said quietly. "Lorraine was putting it around that you were the reason she broke her engagement to Keegan. She accused him of having an affair with you."

"But that's not true!" Eleanor exclaimed. And it wasn't. Yes, she'd been tricked into his bed, but one indiscretion hardly constituted an affair. "Keegan took me out one time to make her jealous. It worked; they got engaged the next day, and I left for nurse's training in Louisville that same week. That's all there was to it."

Mrs. Granger smiled sadly. "I'm very sorry. I don't know you, you see, or I wouldn't have believed the rumor. Mothers are very protective about their sons. Perhaps too protective in my case. Wade has very poor insight into character as a rule. Although," she added, "I'll be the first to admit that I have no quarrel with his choice this time." She offered Eleanor a platter of cheese appetizers. "Do have some. And wouldn't you really like to marry my son?"

"We'll arrange everything," Sandra added with a grin. "All you'll have to do is stand in church and say two words. We'll take care of the rest."

Eleanor laughed softly. Talk about wrong first impressions, she thought. Gradually, as the conversation eased to other topics, she got to know Wade's family. And what a delightful duo they were, nothing like they'd seemed at first. By the time Wade returned, she felt as if she'd known them for years.

"Is your scalp still in place, darling?" Wade teased Eleanor.

"Not a hair disturbed," she responded gaily. "These two are pretty nice, for rich people, that is," she added with a mischievous grin at the pair sitting with her.

"And she's not half bad—for a career girl, that is," Sandra declared.

"We're trying to talk her into marrying you and taking you off our hands."

Wade actually flushed. "Now, see here...!" he began hotly.

"Oh, it's all right. I refused," Eleanor assured him. "You're perfectly safe."

"Whew!" He wiped a hand across his forehead. "And there I was, fearing for my freedom!" He smiled back at her. "Actually, I wouldn't mind marrying you, you know."

"Yes, you would. I snore and I can't bake cakes."

"You could hire a cook," Mrs. Granger interjected, shaking a finger at her son. "Don't take no for an answer, boy!"

"Yes, ma'am," he replied, helping Eleanor to her feet. "Now you've got to marry me," he told her. "Mother has spoken."

"Mother will be yelling shortly if we don't circulate," Sandra sighed, rising gracefully. "Can I bring you a fan, darling?" she asked her mother.

"Some ice would be lovely," came the reply. "Wade, introduce Eleanor to that Arab prince, she can't miss that!"

"Yes, dear."

"See you later," Eleanor called over her shoulder as Wade took her hand and guided her toward the punch bowl. "I like your mother and sister," she said after a minute.

"I'm glad, especially after the way Mother came on at first." He shuddered. "I could have dropped through the ground. She isn't a snob, you know, not really. She just..."

"She explained it to me," she replied quietly, cringing inwardly at the reason Mrs. Granger had given for her behavior. She'd never known about the rumors; her father had never said anything. Of course, he didn't travel in these circles, either....

How terrible for Keegan, that his attempt to make Lorraine jealous should have ended in such a way. But why had she waited two months to break the engagement and then accuse Eleanor of having an affair with Keegan? That didn't make sense. Most of all, why didn't Keegan bear a grudge? He had good reason to, even though he'd started it all. Losing Lorraine must have hurt him deeply, especially since his date with Eleanor had apparently been the cause of his broken engagement.

Poor Keegan. His manipulations had damaged two lives—his own as well as Eleanor's.

"She told you about the rumor, I gather," he said without looking at her.

Her eyes darted up to his set features. "You know?"

He looked down at her. "Yes. It was all over Lexington, thanks to Lorraine. She was rabid about losing him."

"But she broke the engagement," she faltered.

"Yes, that's what people think. But I know Keegan, and I knew Lorraine. And I promise you, she didn't do the casting off. He did."

That was a shock, but then, it had been a day for them. She bit her lower lip thoughtfully as they walked. "Why?"

He locked her fingers in his. "Maybe his conscience was bothering him, Eleanor," he said gently. "He treated you pretty shabbily."

She shifted in his grip. "You seem to know a lot about it."

"You don't remember, but I was at the Crescent Club the night Keegan took you there," he said. "I'd seen him in action before, and I saw the way you looked at him." He studied her fingers while she trembled inwardly. "At a guess, darling, I'd say he seduced you that night."

Her face went paper white, and when he saw it all the puzzle pieces fell into place.

He said something under his breath, and his dark eyes grew stormy. "So I guessed, did I? And it backfired, for all his manipulations. He got what he thought he wanted, only to find that Lorraine was as brittle as glass and just as cutting. She wanted his wealth, not him. Everyone knew, except Keegan. He was blinded by what he felt for her. But it didn't take him long to sort her out, and I'd bet it was what he did to you that opened his eyes. He never quite got over it. He's hardly even dated in the years since then. He has something of a reputation these days for leading a quiet life. The old playboy image is well and truly gone."

Keegan himself had mentioned something like that, but she'd only half heard him. She couldn't look at Wade. It was too embarrassing to have him guess what had happened.

He seemed to sense that. He touched her cheek lightly and coaxed her eyes up to his. "Don't worry. It's our secret. I'd never tell another soul."

She relaxed a little. "It was all over a long time ago," she said. "I have a few emotional scars, but I'm not carrying any torches."

"So you keep saying. But when you look at him, there's such a hunger in your eyes, Eleanor. You look at him as if you'd die to have him." He smiled gently. "And if he ever catches that look, darling, you're dead. Because he's doing some looking of his own."

"Conscience," she said tightly.

"Perhaps. Perhaps not." He pursed his lips, studying her flushed face. "Keegan's spent most of his life manipulating people. So suppose we manipulate him for a change?"

She stared at him blankly. "What?"

"Let's manipulate him. I'll take you in hand and teach you how to be a society belle. We'll go everywhere together, become what's known as 'an item.' We'll haunt his favorite restaurant, be seen at the marina, we'll do everything but announce future plans, and watch him sweat."

"He won't..." she began.

"I'll bet you a tuna fish casserole that he will," he returned.

"Tuna fish casserole?" She groaned. "Ugh! I hate them!"

"So do I, and the loser has to eat the horrible thing," he declared. "Is it a deal?"

She hesitated. "Why do you want to do this for me?"

"Because I like you, darling," he said gently, and smiled at her. "I'd love to marry you and take care of you all my life, but since you haven't a heart to offer me, I'll help you find what you want."

"And what do I want?" she mused.

"Oh, revenge," he said absently. "Maybe a little fulfillment. Whatever. Come on, Ellie. Let's give it a shot. Mother and Sandra will help. Look upon it as a project."

"Well..." She hesitated. It did have possibilities, however, and it could be fun. She smiled. "Okay."

"Good girl." He kissed her cheek. "Come and meet the Arab prince, and then we'll explore some of the more wearing social graces."

"Lead on," she said. "I'll follow." She only hoped she wasn't following him into quicksand. It might be fun to manipulate Keegan a little, but she didn't want to get caught in the middle. Once was enough.

Seven

"Well, well, look who's visiting," Wade chuckled as he pulled up in front of Eleanor's door late that afternoon.

Eleanor glanced at the red Porsche, a sinking feeling in her stomach. "Oh, for heaven's sake," she grumbled.

"And he wasn't interested, I believe you said?" he teased. "Funny, I'd call this hot pursuit, myself."

"Care to come in and have coffee?" she asked hopefully.

"I'd love to," he sighed, "but my dad is flying in from Greece. I have to meet him at the airport at five, which it almost is now. I'm sorry he didn't get to meet you. We hoped he'd make it home in time for the party."

"Some other time," she replied, and grimaced. "I don't want to go in there," she moaned.

"Chin up, girl," he said. "Remember—he's the victim this time, not you. Now get in there and tell him what a wonderful person I am, and how much you love my family, and how close I came to proposing! Lay it on thick. Spread it like butter."

She studied him. "Ever think of coaching a professional football team?" she asked.

"I sure have, but I'll settle for you right now. Come here, I see the curtains fluttering," he murmured with a grin. He pulled her close and kissed her warmly, smiling against her lips. "Nice." He laughed. "Like eating cotton candy. Now get in there and give him a taste of his own medicine."

"Yes, sir." She kissed him back, lightly, and got out of the car. "Do I look disheveled enough?"

"You look delicious," he said wistfully. "Oh, well, I'll go back to my cinders and ashes."

"Have you ever thought about having a glass boot made?" she asked. "You could give a party, and drop it...."

"I am leaving," he returned with mock indignation.

"A few white mice and a pumpkin might be a good idea, too," she added as he put the car in gear.

"I'll show you white mice and pumpkins, just wait," he threatened. He held up his hand. "Call you tomorrow."

"Good night. Thanks for inviting me, I enjoyed it."

"Me, too, honey. Bye!"

She watched him drive away, feeling wistful. He was such a nice man. It was too bad her heart belonged to that freckled redhead waiting in her house.

She turned, purse in hand, and went inside. Her father and Keegan were sitting in the living room, apparently just talking. Keegan was still wearing work clothes, and he looked as if he'd been out with his horses. He liked to work with the trainer occasionally, and in his younger days he'd participated in show jumping and polo. He was an expert rider.

"Hello, dear, how was the party?" Barnett asked, smiling as his daughter came into the room.

"Just lovely," she said with an exaggerated sigh. "I love Wade's mother and sister. They're so sweet."

Keegan cocked his unruly red head at her. "You do mean Gladys the gladiator and Sandra the snake?" he asked.

"Shame on you for calling them names," she chided. "They're terrific people."

Keegan leaned back against the seat. "Wade must have threatened to write his life story," he murmured. His deep blue eyes traveled over her slender body in the becoming white-and-purple dress. "I like that," he remarked. "The style is very becoming."

"Wade thought so, too," she said with a demure smile. "I'll get changed and start dinner, Dad." She glanced at Keegan. "Are you staying?"

"Are you inviting me?" he countered, his voice velvety and deep.

"You're the boss," she reminded him, watching his expression change. "I can hardly order you out of a house you own, can I?"

"Eleanor," Barnett groaned.

"Will you stop that?" Keegan growled.

"Okay. You're welcome to stay for dinner, Keegan, dear," she said with a faint smile. "I do hope you like broccoli and liver, because that's what I'm fixing."

"Darling, you know Keegan hates broccoli and liver," Barnett protested.

"I'm reforming," Keegan said through clenched teeth. "I love liver and broccoli."

Eleanor went down the hall to her room with revenge in her heart and a smile on her lips.

She changed into worn jeans and a loose patterned blouse that had seen better days. She didn't bother to brush her hair or fix her makeup, and she left her shoes off. That would show Keegan Taber that she didn't care what he thought of her appearance.

Bypassing the living room where the men were talking, she went straight to the kitchen and busied herself with getting the meal together. Odd, she thought, how much time Keegan seemed to be spending here lately. Whatever did he and her father find to talk about?

It only took about half an hour to get dinner ready. Eleanor called the men and poured tall glasses of iced tea for the three of them.

Keegan was quiet at the table, very reserved. But his blue eyes followed Eleanor as she moved around the kitchen between courses, pouring more tea, bringing dessert, moving serving dishes to the sink. His intent scrutiny began to wear on her nerves after a while, and she was glad when it was over and the men returned to the living room to play chess.

She washed the dishes, then slipped on an old pair of loafers to go walking behind the house. Their small yard overlooked the vast acreage of the farm, and from the wooden fence under the oak trees out back, she could watch silky racehorses prance around arrogantly in their paddocks. She loved to watch them move: they were so graceful, so much a part of her childhood. Like this house where she was born, where her mother and father had lived all her life. Like…Keegan.

She was barely aware of the footsteps behind her. She didn't turn, because she knew his steps as well as she knew her own. She didn't have to look to know that it was Keegan.

He came close behind her and stopped. "Why are you hiding out here?" he asked softly.

She shrugged, folding her arms over her breasts and smiling faintly. "Was I hiding?"

His heavy sigh was audible. He moved beside her, one hand tucked into his belt, the other holding a smoking cigarette. "It seems like it sometimes," he said absently.

"I thought you'd given that up." She nodded toward the cigarette.

He shrugged. "I keep trying." He lifted it to his thin lips. "How did you like the garden party?"

"It was very nice," she said. "Lots of people and food and even a band."

"Gladys likes to give parties," he said. He studied her body in the floppy ensemble. "Is that for my benefit?" he asked quietly.

"My ensemble?" she asked innocently, spreading her arms. "Actually, I thought it might inflame your passion…Keegan!"

He caught her with one lean arm, jerking her against the length of his hard body so quickly that she couldn't dodge in time.

"You inflame me all right," he said curtly. He was so close that she could feel his breath on her lips as he bent toward her. "Shall I let you feel how much?"

"Will you stop!" she protested. Her heart was beating out of control; he had to be able to feel it as close as he was. Her breasts were crushed against his hard chest in the rough embrace.

"Make me believe you want me to stop, Eleanor," he said tautly. His eyes darkened as they searched hers. Around them, the sun sprinkled dark leaf patterns on the ground and the breeze ruffled her silky hair. A horse neighed somewhere nearby. And in all that normalcy was this—Keegan holding her with his arm and his eyes, and the rough beat of his heart keeping time with her own.

"I'm off the market; haven't you heard?" she asked belligerently.

"I heard," he replied. "I just don't believe it. Kiss me."

She averted her face as his descended, and his mouth followed hers. His free hand dropped the cigarette and came up to tangle in her hair and hold her face where he wanted it.

"Now, fight..." His voice muffled against her lips as he took her mouth with his in a kiss that made her body throb with helpless longing. He knew so well how to do this, how to awaken her deepest hungers.

She pushed against his chest, but he only tightened his arm.

"Don't fight me, baby," he whispered as he lifted his head slightly and teased her full lips. "What can I do to you here, with your father right inside the house, hmmm?"

"I don't want this," she whispered brokenly.

"Don't you?" His fingers moved to caress her breast, then pressed it gently so that he could feel the beating of her heart. "Your heart's going wild, little Ellie. Just like mine. Here. Feel."

He took her hand and slid it into the open front of his shirt, hearing her sudden intake of breath, feeling the clenching of her fingers against his flesh.

"Here." He spread her fingers and moved them into the thick thatch of reddish-blond hair, watching her face as he felt the slow, involuntary movements of her long fingers. His heart ached with its hard beating. She aroused him as no other woman ever had.

"Ellie," he breathed. He brushed his mouth over her forehead, trying to catch his breath while her hands made him shudder. She didn't quite know what to do, he realized, but even that hesitant touching made his knees weak.

After a moment she put both hands against his chest. The weakness was growing: she could hardly stand up, and she wanted very much to move her legs closer to his. But she knew what would happen if she did, and despite her doubts and suspicion, she didn't want to hurt him.

He felt so solid and muscular, his skin cool under her searching hands, the thick growth of hair tangling in her fingers. She remembered much too well how that hair had felt against her bare breasts the night he'd made love to her. The memories were so intimate that she could hardly bear them. Even now, his heart was shaking him with its beat, and she remembered that it had been like that the night he'd taken her out.

"Keegan..." she began to protest.

"Shhh," he whispered. His mouth moved tenderly across her eyebrows, her closed eyelids. "Don't think. Touch me some more."

He guided her hands down to his rib cage, his flat stomach. He shuddered a little as her hands caressed him there. But she hesitated as he tried to move them lower, until he put his mouth over hers again and probed delicately with his tongue.

"It's all right," he whispered. "It's all right, baby, don't be embarrassed...."

She let him move her hands again, and he shuddered, moaning as she touched him. Immediately she drew back, shocked at her own boldness, at his groan.

"I can't!" she exclaimed.

"All right," he murmured. He drew her completely into his arms and wrapped her up against him, letting her keep a discreet distance from his legs as he rocked her in his warm embrace. "You're still very innocent in some ways, little one. It's nothing to be ashamed of. I like you just the way you are."

"You mustn't do things like that," she said firmly. Her voice was trembling, which robbed the little speech of its force.

"Aren't you curious about my body?" he asked quietly. "I am about yours."

"You already know all there is to know," she said tautly.

"No. I know a little." He lifted his head and searched her shy, soft eyes. "I'd like to know you in passion, Ellie. I'd like to see you the way you saw me that night, burning up with fulfillment."

Her face colored and she tried to tear out of his arms, but still he held her.

"I cheated you that night," he said, searching her face. "I want to make it up to you."

"I won't sleep with you again," she said shortly.

His eyes were calculating, watchful. He framed her face in his lean hands and made her look into his eyes. "I want to make love to you. That isn't the same thing as sex."

"It is with you," she burst out. "You just want to get me under your thumb again, Keegan Taber. You don't really want me, you just don't want Wade to have me. You see, I know you now," she continued coldly. "I know how your mind works. And what you have to offer me, I don't want, is that clear enough? Now let me go!"

The fear was still there, behind the harsh words. He saw it, and hated it. He let her go because this wasn't accomplishing anything.

"I have work to do," she muttered, embarrassed. She turned and walked away. Later, she knew, she was going to be very angry with herself for this show of weakness. She could hardly bear the thought of having let him see it again. Why couldn't she fight him off? Didn't she have a single instinct for survival left in her body? She wondered if she was ever going to rid herself of the hopeless attraction she felt for him.

"Why won't you listen to me?" he called gruffly. "You always assume you know exactly what I'm feeling, what I want. But I can't begin to explain it to you, because you won't hear what I'm saying!"

She turned to glare at him. "If I listen, I'll just wind up in the same shape I was in four years ago," she replied. "I'm not stupid anymore, Keegan."

"No," he agreed, "just deaf and blind." Frustrated, he stuck his hands in his belt and drew in a deep, slow breath. "Well, you may be stubborn, honey, but so am I. And despite all those fine words about how you feel and how you don't feel, all I have to do is touch you and watch you melt."

Her face colored, but she didn't look away. "You have that effect on other women, I'm sure."

"I don't care how I affect other women. Only you." He let his eyes run over her slowly, absorbed. "Suppose we go off someplace alone and talk for a few hours? I'll tell you exactly how I feel."

Showing her exactly how he felt was more likely, and she knew it. She managed a smile, then shrugged. "Sorry, boss man. I have a great instinct for self-preservation. You just stand back and watch me exercise it!" She cast him a defiant glare, then turned and stormed back toward the house.

Watching her, Keegan felt as if the world had swallowed him up. It was always like this. He could only get close by forcing her to yield, and he disliked the tactic. But she didn't trust him. Perhaps she never would again, and he had only himself to blame. If only he could tell her how he regretted that night four years ago, how he'd cursed his own behavior. Lorraine had left a bitter taste in his mouth, all because of Eleanor, because she'd bewitched him with her innocent body and her ardent eagerness to do whatever he wanted of her.

Eleanor had loved him. That hurt most of all, that he'd been so careless of her young emotions and so callously indifferent to her feelings for him. Now he'd give anything to have her throw herself at him and whisper that she loved him. And now she never would. He'd robbed her of self-respect, of confidence. He'd paid for it in double measure, but he couldn't tell her that because she didn't care anymore. She was crazy about Wade, emotionally at least, and the pain of that knowledge cut deep inside him. All he could do was watch and hope that Wade didn't put a ring on her finger before he could win her back. If he could win her back.

He, who had always been bristling with confidence, suddenly had none. All he could do was play a waiting game. And even then, it might be too late.

He sighed and followed her into the house. Well, she still wanted him. That was something. And he hadn't expected her to capitulate without a fight. She had to save her pride; after all, she couldn't make it too easy for him. He smiled ruefully. He was just going to have to think up some way to cut Wade Granger out.

Blissfully unaware of the train of his thoughts, Eleanor stomped back into the kitchen and slammed dishes around angrily.

He came in behind her, closing the door gently.

She glared at him. "Don't you have something to do?"

"I'm going to play your father another game of chess in a few minutes," he said. "He's on the phone right now with old man Jenkins."

"Oh." So that was why she wasn't being deprived of Keegan's company.

"Why won't you come out with me?" he asked unexpectedly.

"You know very well why."

He pulled out a kitchen chair and straddled it, then lit another cigarette. "We talked last Sunday," he reminded her. "Really talked, I mean. I liked that."

She had, also, but being alone with him, talking and growing close, was too risky. She'd just had proof of her own vulnerability.

"You still want me, Ellie," he observed quietly. "Yes, I know, you don't like having me know that," he added when she jerked around to deny it. "But it's true. And I feel the same way."

"I won't have an affair with you," she said, turning to stare at him with dark eyes. She seemed to be making a life's work of telling this to men, she thought with a flash of humor.

"I'm glad. An affair isn't what I want," he replied.

"You're more in the mood for a one-night stand, I gather?" she asked, smiling coolly.

"If you want the truth..."

But before he could continue, her father ambled into the room, grinning from ear to ear.

"Old man Jenkins is finally willing to sell me that bench press I wanted for my woodworking shop," he said gleefully. "He's decided that his arthritis is just too bad to do that kind of work anymore. Now I can throw out that piece of junk I'm using and do some decent work."

"When can you pick it up? I'll drive you over," Keegan offered.

"You wouldn't mind?" asked Barnett. "Then can we go now, before the old goat changes his mind?"

"What a way to talk about your best friend," Eleanor chided.

He grinned at her. "Why not? You ought to hear what he called me when I won that bet on the World Series."

She threw up her hands. "I quit."

"Only after the tenth one," Keegan said as her father left. He grinned at her expression. "The tenth son, remember? We'll call him Quits."

She flushed as she met his level blue gaze. "We?"

He let his eyes run slowly down her body, and the faint smile on his lips made her uneasy. "My wife and I, of course," he said smoothly.

Wife?...Was the Irish girl getting to him? She searched his face, confused.

"I'll be back, so don't go off with Romeo," he told her.

"As if I care whether or not you'll be back," she replied defiantly, her gaze averted.

"I'll make you care, somehow," he said. When she glanced up, however, he was gone.

It only took the two men an hour to get the bench press and return home, and then they spent another hour or two in the workshop behind the house setting it up and working with it.

Eleanor hadn't known that Keegan liked woodworking, but she should have realized that he and her father couldn't talk about chess and work all the time. She went out to see the bench press and watched Keegan run up a table leg on the lathe with quick, precise movements of his deft hands. He was good at it.

He was good at anything, she thought. Except maybe one thing...and even then, it had been her body's response that had caused her discomfort. It would have been uncomfortable with any man, but her headlong ardor had probably caused Keegan to be less gentle than he intended. And he hadn't known that she was a virgin, either.

She didn't like remembering. Leaving the men to their work and their talk, she went back into the house, set a carafe of coffee on the warmer and a plate of wrapped cake slices on the table with a note, and went to bed. She couldn't take one more minute of Keegan tonight. She'd had enough.

Eight

Eleanor got up an hour earlier the next morning, even though sleep had been long in coming. Wade had called after she'd gone to bed. Her father had knocked on her door to tell her Wade was on the phone, but she hadn't wanted to see Keegan again, so she'd had him tell Wade to call her the next day. She'd hated to do it, but Keegan was getting to her.

She was making biscuits when the phone rang. Her father was still in bed, so she dusted off her hands and answered it.

"Eleanor?"

The voice was male and familiar, but she couldn't place it. "Yes?"

"This is Gene Taber," he replied, sounding a little frantic. "Eleanor, I hate to ask, but could you come up to the house? Something's wrong with Keegan...."

Her heart gave a sickening lurch. "What's the matter?" she asked, gripping the receiver tightly.

"Nausea, diarrhea...he's in a bad way."

She took a deep breath. Be calm. Above all, be calm. She was no use to him hysterical. "When did it start?"

"About three hours ago," he groaned. "I thought it would quit eventually, but it hasn't. He can't lift his head, and he's having damned bad stomach cramps. I tried to give him something for it, but he can't keep it in his stomach. What should I do?''

"Call an ambulance," she said immediately. "I'll come right up. See you in five minutes."

What good she could possibly do she wasn't sure, but she had to go. It could be anything from simple food poisoning to a rupturing appendix; only a doctor would know for sure.

She dressed in a feverish rush, telling herself that it would be all right, that Keegan wouldn't die. But she kept thinking back to the day before, to what she'd said to him, the way she'd avoided him, and she felt guilty. He couldn't help being himself; he was just a playboy. She shouldn't keep blaming him for the past. And now he was desperately ill.... She had to fight the tears. Keegan was indestructible. He was never sick. But for Gene to get upset, it had to be bad. Gene wasn't one to panic.

She got into her uniform and didn't stop to fix her face. Two minutes later she was pounding on her father's door.

"Keegan's sick," she said without preamble when he called for her to come in. "I'm on my way up to the house. I'll phone you later."

"Keegan?" He sat up. "What is it?"

"I don't know," she said, worry showing in her face. She ran down the hall and out to her car. Even as she cranked it, she was hoping the ambulance would be right behind her. Dehydration, whatever its cause, could be fatal.

When Eleanor drove up at Flintlock, the front lights were on. She rushed up the steps onto the long porch, and Gene met her at the door in his robe. Except for some graying hair and the lines in his face, he was very much like his son, redheaded and tall.

"The ambulance?" she asked.

"On its way. He's in his room."

He led the way upstairs, filling her in as best he could. "He cooked himself some chicken for lunch yesterday. Mary June's been laid up with an ankle; she's just now able to hobble around a bit. I don't know if the chicken could have done it...."

Eleanor added it all up in her mind. The incubation period would be just about right for salmonella. Especially if he'd laid the cooked chicken in the same plate where he'd had the raw chicken, something a man not used to cooking might do.

Gene led her into a huge room done in greens and whites with a king-size bed in which Keegan lay moaning, half-unconscious. She went to his side, shocked at his weakness and pallor. He didn't stir when she took his pulse. His eyes didn't open. And even as she put his wrist down, he was sick again.

There was a pan beside the bed, obviously put there by Gene, and a wet washcloth in a bowl on the table. She grabbed at the pan and got it under his mouth just in the nick of time. She mopped his brow with the cloth and soothed him until the bout was over, and then she eased him back onto the pillows. He was very nearly unconscious. Probably half-dead of nausea, too, she thought pityingly. Poor, poor man. She touched his red hair with a tender hand, pushing it away from his pale brow. She couldn't remember a time in their turbulent relationship when he'd been helpless. She cradled his head in her hands and bit her lip to keep from crying. He was sick all right, and he was going to need some intravenous fluid and bed rest in a hospital at the very least.

"Will he be all right?" Gene asked nervously as he paced the floor.

"Yes," she said, smiling reassuringly. "Of course he will. But I'm pretty certain that they'll admit him. He'll need to be given fluids."

"What do you think it is?" he persisted.

"I don't know," Eleanor replied. She wasn't allowed to give medical opinions: it wasn't ethical. "Don't worry," she added gently, "we'll have him better before you know it. After all, he's a Taber, isn't he? Tough."

He managed a weak smile. "Yes. I suppose so. Where the hell is that ambu— Ah! There it is!"

The siren was unmistakable, and through the pale green curtains Eleanor could see the red flashing lights coming up the long, winding paved driveway.

"I'll run down and show them where to bring the stretcher," Gene volunteered. "Are you going with the ambulance?" he asked over his shoulder.

"Of course," she replied without thinking.

"Give me your car keys," he said, holding out his hand. "I'll drive your car to the hospital and meet you there."

She handed him the keys from her pocket without protest. It would have been unthinkable to refuse to ride with Keegan, she told herself in justification. She looked worriedly at Keegan's face as he groaned, and clenched her teeth. It bothered her, seeing him like this. Keegan was so vital, so full of life. She was just realizing that he wasn't invulnerable, that he was just a man after all. Her fingers touched the red, red hair and smoothed it back gently.

"It's all right," she whispered as he grimaced and moaned roughly. "It's all right, you'll be well in no time."

It seemed to take forever, though, for the paramedics to get upstairs with the stretcher. She stood back, giving them the vital signs as they loaded him on the stretcher and strapped him down. Fortunately they were both big men, because Keegan for all his slimness was no light-weight.

Eleanor said goodbye to Gene as she followed the stretcher toward the winding staircase.

"Whatever is all the racket?" Maureen O'Clancy groaned, opening her door. She stood stock-still when she saw Keegan on the stretcher. "Oh, my God! Is he dead?" she burst out, putting a hand to her mouth.

"No," Eleanor said. "Just very sick. We're taking him to the hospital."

"Poor, poor man," the Irish girl wailed. She was beautiful even without makeup, her black hair around her slender shoulders in a pale blue silk robe, her blue eyes wide and concerned. "Do take good care of him, now," she told Eleanor. "I'll be down directly to see him."

"I'm sure he'll appreciate that," Eleanor mumbled, dashing after the attendants. Behind her, she heard Maureen's father ask a question, which Maureen answered, but Eleanor didn't catch the words.

Gene opened the front door for them, frowning worriedly as they filed out. Eleanor stopped long enough to touch his shoulder reassuringly.

"It will be all right," she said firmly. "Don't wreck the car getting there, please."

"I'll be careful. Eleanor, he's all I've got," he blurted out, the blue eyes that were so like Keegan's narrowed on his son's pale, writhing body.

"I know. He'll be fine," she said gently, and forced a smile. Then she ran down the steps to climb in the back of the ambulance with Keegan. She took his hand in hers and held it every mile of the way to Peterson Memorial.

Dr. Stan Welder was on duty in the emergency room when they brought Keegan in. She filled him in on the background and stood quietly by as the duty nurse assisted. Dr. Welder did a thorough examination, ordered an antibiotic and fluids and asked Eleanor to take Gene Taber down to admissions as soon as he arrived.

"I'll go with him," Eleanor said. "I'm not on duty for another half hour."

Dr. Welder nodded, his bald head shining in the overhead light. "Friend of yours?" he asked, noting her own pallor and the lines of worry in her face.

"Yes," she said without hesitation. "Will he be all right?"

He nodded. "Salmonella, most likely," he added. "We'll know when we get a blood workup. We'll get him into a room and give him something to stop the dysentery and nausea, and build him back up with fluids. Send his father down to talk to me when he's through answering questions for Lettie."

Lettie was Leticia Balew, the night admissions nurse, a capable and dedicated technician, well liked by Eleanor and most of the other staff. It was a good hospital, with some excellent health-care professionals. Eleanor felt fortunate to work with them, and more grateful than ever now for their expertise. Keegan was still important to her; tonight had brought that fact home with a vengeance. She couldn't bear the thought of losing him.

Dr. Welder noticed her uncharacteristic hesitation. "He'll be all right. I promise," he added with a faint grin. "Now go find his father, will you?"

"Yes, Doctor," she said automatically.

She cast a last, lingering look at Keegan's still form and grimaced as she turned and went down the long hall. Gene Taber met her halfway, pale and looking as if he expected to hear the worst.

"Salmonella," she said, quoting the doctor. "They're giving him something to stop the nausea and dysentery. They'll keep him, I'm sure, until they get some fluids back into him. He'll be fine now."

"Can I see him?" he asked.

"Yes. First, though, we have to give Lettie some information," she added, drawing her arm through his. "Meanwhile, they'll draw blood for testing and get him into a room and settled. By the time you see him, he'll be much better."

He didn't argue, but he looked as if he wanted to. "I should have stopped him," he murmured as they walked. "I was going to go out and get us something to eat, but O'Clancy wanted to see some videotapes of my new colts, and Maureen doesn't cook, you know. Keegan had a terrible appetite. Mary June will be sick herself when she hears about this."

"Salmonella isn't a killer, if it's caught in time. And you did the right thing," she said. She smiled up at him. "Now, come on, nervous dad, and I'll give you some coffee while you answer all Lettie's questions, okay?"

"You're a nice girl," he said sincerely, smiling wearily at her. "I was scared to death when I called you. Thank you for coming."

"I like him, too," she confessed ruefully.

"Only like, Eleanor?" he asked delicately.

She turned down a hallway. "Here's Lettie's office," she said cheerfully, ignoring the question.

She introduced him to the elderly nurse, then went down to the canteen to get coffee from the machine. When she took it to him, she sat quietly by his side while he answered the necessary questions. By the time he finished, Keegan was installed in a private room and sleeping peacefully, an IV in one muscular arm and the night nurse buzzing around taking vitals when they entered.

"Thank goodness it's almost your shift," Vicky Tanner said, grinning at her coworker as she jotted down the information on Keegan's chart. "I've had two heart attacks on the floor in one night. The medical staff has really been working tonight."

"I can imagine," Eleanor said. "Emergency was bouncing when I came in. How is he now?" she asked, drawing the nurse to one side as Gene sat down in the chair by his son's bed.

"Vitals have picked up already," Vicky replied. "He'll do, but he's a very sick man. His father got him here just in time. He's badly dehydrated.''

Eleanor nodded. "Well, I'd better get down to the office so that Mary can give her report and go home to bed. You, too,'' she said with a smile. She glanced at Keegan, her dark eyes more eloquent than she realized. "I'm glad Dr. Welder sent Keegan to my floor. He's sort of a friend of the family.''

Vicky studied her. "Yes. Well, see you tomorrow.''

"Have a nice day.''

"I hope to sleep right through it, thanks.'' Vicky grinned.

Eleanor went to the bedside and touched Gene's shoulder even as she stared down at Keegan's sleeping face. He was still pale, but his color was a little better now, thank goodness. "I have to go on duty,'' she said. "He'll be all right, you know.''

"Thank God.'' He sighed wearily and shook his head. "There's only been one time in his life that he's been really sick, when he was about ten years old and had a bad fall. Otherwise he's been healthy— so healthy that it made this doubly frightening.''

"He'll sleep for a while now,'' she told him. "But you're welcome to stay. I'll check on you later.''

He nodded. "Oh, here.'' He handed her the car keys.

"Thanks for bringing it,'' she said. "How will you get home?''

He grimaced. "The O'Clancys will be right along, I'm afraid,'' he said with distaste. "My houseguests are becoming fixtures. And the last thing he needs is Maureen cooing over him when he can hardly hold his head up.''

"I'll send Nurse Wren down to run them off ten minutes after they get here,'' she said gleefully.

"Nurse Wren?''

"The name is not indicative of her nature, I'm afraid,'' Eleanor told him, and smiled. "She's fifty, hatchet-nosed, and the hospital is her life and her career.''

"Poor O'Clancys,'' he said, and returned her smile.

She winked, glanced once more at Keegan and left him with his father.

It was late afternoon before Keegan regained consciousness. He looked pale and weak, and he could barely lift his head at all. His father had gone home only minutes before, and the O'Clancys had stayed barely ten minutes before Nurse Wren got hold of them. Eleanor almost felt guilty for sending Wren into the room, but it had bothered her—in unexpected ways—to see that Irish woman bending over Keegan so lovingly and kissing his helpless face. She did feel possessive about Keegan; she couldn't help it. She'd shared something with him that she'd never shared with anyone else, that she never wanted to share with anyone else. She hated the thought of that Maureen person touching him, being with him as she had. It was beyond bearing. Seeing Maureen kissing him triggered a horrible emptiness in her. She'd come face to face with reality, with the fact that she'd never really have Keegan. Not his love, or any kind of future with him. He'd marry someone like Maureen, and she would be alone, as she'd been alone since she'd left Lexington four years ago. Despite his desire for her, Keegan would never be able to give her what she wanted most: his love.

She had to force herself to walk to his bed, to take his temperature and pulse and blood pressure with cool professionalism. Especially with those very blue eyes wide open and watching every move she made.

"Out...of uniform," he said weakly, and tried to smile as she pumped up the cuff she'd fixed around his arm and read his blood pressure.

"What?" she asked.

"Your cap."

She sighed. "I left it at home," she replied. "Your father called as I was making breakfast. I barely took time to dress."

He caught her hand as she removed the instrument, holding her fingers despite her feeble effort to free them.

"Thank you," he said quietly.

"It's my job," she replied, and gently took his fingers from hers and put them back over his chest. "Rest now. You've been dreadfully sick."

"Told you...my own cooking would...kill me someday," he murmured drowsily.

"It very nearly did," she said quietly. She reached down and smoothed back his unruly hair. It was cool and damp under her fingers. "Get some rest now. You've had a rough night."

"My stomach is sore." He grimaced, touching it through the sheet.

"I guess so," she said, "with all those spasms. By tomorrow, you'll be much better."

"Stay with me," he whispered, clutching at her skirt.

That went through her like an arrow, that whispered plea. He was sedated and surely didn't know what he was saying; she realized that. But it was so sweet, thinking that he cared enough to want her with him.

She touched his hand with hers and held it until he fell asleep again. Then she tucked it back under the cover and pulled the sheet over him.

Sleep well, my darling, she thought tenderly. She had to force herself to go out the door and leave him. But he hadn't known what he was saying, of course. It was just the aftereffects of all he'd been through.

Gene was back just before three, as Eleanor was going off duty. She told him how Keegan was and mentioned that he was asleep. He said he'd wait until she gave her report and buy her a cup of coffee. She almost refused, but he looked so alone.

"Okay," she relented. "I'll be back in ten minutes. Meet you in the canteen."

Quickly she gave her report and went off duty. Gene was sitting at a table in the small canteen just beyond the waiting rooms.

"It's been a long day," he said with a smile.

"I can imagine." She stared into her coffee cup. "He's better, but still weak. But tomorrow he'll be screaming to get out of here. You wait and see."

"I'll enjoy hearing him scream, after this," he told her. He leaned back in his chair and studied her drawn face. "Still hurts, does it?" he asked levelly.

She lifted her chin. "I'm over all that," she declared.

"Bull," he replied pleasantly. "Not much, you aren't, judging by the way you came running this morning when I called you. You were as horrified as I was, professional training and all."

She smiled miserably. "I guess I was," she admitted. "He's a very special man."

"I think so. He's been spoiled rotten, of course," he told her with a rakish grin. "I'm not sorry, either. I came up rough. I never had anything. So I made up for it with him. If his mother hadn't died giving birth to him, all that might have been different. But after I lost her, he became my whole world. I'd have done anything for him." He sipped coffee. "Women have done their share of spoiling, too, though."

"Yes." She sighed.

He studied her lowered face. "He used to talk about you all the time, after you left Lexington," he commented.

Her face lifted involuntarily, her dark eyes quiet and curious. "Did he?"

"I thought it odd at the time," he confessed, "especially in view of the fact that he'd only taken you out that one time. He was engaged to Lorraine, too. Yet you were the one he talked about."

She sighed. "I found out why he took me out. It was to bring Lorraine up to par, to make her accept his proposal. He manipulated both of us, and it worked."

"Did it? Oh, he got Lorraine all right. But once he had her, he couldn't get rid of her fast enough. He drove her away, Eleanor. He neglected her, ignored her, deliberately baited her until she broke off the engagement."

Her heart began to race. "I hurt his conscience," she said tightly. "He said so."

"He manipulated you both, but it backfired," he said. His blue eyes searched her face. "He cared about you. He really cared. It was a shame you left town when you did."

He couldn't know how that hurt. But she smiled in spite of the pain. "Think so?" she asked, toying with her coffee cup. "Perhaps it was just an attack of guilt."

"Who knows?" he said, watching her. "Don't let that Irish filly drag him off to the altar, Eleanor. She wants him, and he may decide he's got nothing else to hold him here."

"It would be a good match, though, don't you think?" she commented, even though it was killing her to admit it. "She's wealthy and well-bred, and she'd fit into his world very well."

"And you don't think you would?" he shot at her, blue eyes flashing. "Balderdash! I didn't raise my boy to be a snob, Eleanor, and neither am I. You're more than welcome in my home any time, in any way. And don't start throwing that line at me about just being the carpenter's daughter. It won't wash with me!"

"Ferocious old thing, aren't you?" She laughed.

"You bet, when it comes to social warfare." He finished his coffee. "I like you, girl. You've got style and a temper to match my son's."

"I like you, too," she replied. "I have to get home and feed Dad. You'll, uh, let me know if there's any change?" she added hesitantly.

He searched her concerned eyes. "Sure. Care to come back and sit with him tonight?"

She wanted to, desperately. But she shook her head. "You'll do him more good than I will," she said softly. "I'll see you in the morning. Take care. Of both of you."

He nodded. "Thanks again for all you've done."

"I've only done my job," she demurred. Smiling at him, she put the empty cup in the trash can and left.

It was a long night. She paced and paced, until her father mentioned that she might have a game of chess with him. That made it worse, reminded her of Keegan and happier times.

"Go see him, for God's sake, if you're that worried," Barnett suggested.

"I'm not worried!" she snapped.

He shook his head, grinning. "He's tough. He'll be all right. Gene said so. He came by earlier to tell me how Keegan was getting on. Said he didn't know which of the three of you looked worse when the ambulance got there. He was afraid you were going to flake out, too, when you saw Keegan."

"He looked pretty bad," she mumbled evasively.

"I imagine so. He'll probably never eat his own cooking again," he added dryly. "I'm glad the boy's all right. I'm rather fond of him."

So was Eleanor. All too fond. But she said nothing.

Keegan was sitting up in bed when she went on duty the next morning, still pale but bristling with impatience to get on his feet again.

"It's about time you showed up," he grumbled as she walked into the room. His blue eyes glared up at her. "I've been awakened from a sound sleep and forcibly bathed by some horrible old woman with cold hands, I've been poked and prodded by a doctor, someone came and took half my blood with a horrible long needle.... Where were you?''

She had to fight down laughter. "I've been at home sleeping, of course," she replied, going to the bed. "You look much better today. How do you feel?"

"Empty," he said shortly. "How about a steak? On second thought, how about a whole steer?"

She checked his chart and smiled. "Nope. Liquids and semisolids today. If that stays down all right, then we'll see about something more substantial."

"Conspiracy," he accused. "You and that doctor are in league together."

"Of course." She curtsied. "We're your professional health-care team. We have to take good care of you."

"You're starving me to death, that's what you're doing."

"Eating is what got you here in the first place," she reminded him. "Here." She stuck the thermometer in his mouth while she took his pulse. He looked up at her, at the neat fit of her white uniform. His piercing eyes paused on her breasts, and she felt his pulse jump as she took it.

By the time she got to his blood pressure, his watchful gaze was frankly disturbing. She was glad no one was taking her pulse!

She finished reading vitals and jotted them down on his chart.

"When do I get out of here?" he demanded.

"Not today," she said cheerfully. "How about something to read?"

He sighed in frustration. "Dad will bring the *Wall Street Journal* in when he comes."

She lifted an eyebrow. "Well, we do have a local daily paper in Lexington, you know."

"I know who did what," he told her. "The only reason people read the paper is to find out who got caught at it."

"Cynic," she accused.

"I've got more reason to be cynical than most," he responded. "God, you look sweet in that uniform," he added softly.

She avoided looking directly at him. "Would you like something to drink?" she asked.

"The ministering angel of mercy," he said with a smile. "Yes, it suits you. You always did care about people, even when you were a kid. You were forever patching up one of your playmates."

"How do you know that?"

"Your father. We talk about you a lot," he replied, folding his arms over his bare chest. The sheet had slid down around his lean waist, and she was almost sure he didn't have pajamas on under it.

"You're supposed to be wearing a hospital gown," she told him.

"What for?" he asked lazily. "I sleep raw at home, and this is a private room."

"We have candy stripers here," she said. "Young girls who don't exactly need the kind of education they'd get if they came in when you were on your way to the bathroom."

He raised an eyebrow, noticing the way she averted her eyes from his hair-covered chest and muscular stomach. "Do I bother you this way?"

"I went through four years of nurse's training." She looked directly at him. "And I have seen you without your clothes once, if you remember."

"Bravo, honey," he murmured gently. "Do you realize that's the first time you've ever brought the subject up by yourself?"

"As you said once, it was a long time ago," she replied.

"Not so long that I can forget it," he said quietly. He searched her dark eyes. "You haunt me."

"Hire an exorcist," she suggested, then checked her watch. "I have to run. We're overloaded with patients today. Mostly women." She grinned at him. "I imagine they've all come up with various illnesses just because they heard you were a patient."

He smiled, and it warmed her like sunshine. "Think so?" he asked.

"Oh, definitely."

"Do you have to go?" he asked as she paused at the door.

"Afraid so. I'm the assistant floor nurse these days. That means if the supervisor is missing, my head rolls in her place." She grinned.

He tilted his head. "Such a pretty head to meet such a horrible fate," he remarked. "Wouldn't you rather sit and hold my hand instead?"

"Miss O'Clancy will do that for you, I'm sure," she said with admirable indifference. "If you need anything, ring the buzzer."

"I need you," he said softly. "Will you come if I call?"

"Only in case of emergency." She laughed. "See you later."

It was an oddly satisfying day. She popped in and out of Keegan's room as time permitted, and he flirted outrageously with her. She ignored his provocative remarks, though, and was completely professional in her behavior. He seemed puzzled as he watched her go about her duties, competent and secure in a position of responsibility. For once he was on the receiving end of the orders, and she saw him smile at the irony of their reversed positions.

"You're different here," he remarked just after his dinner had been served and Eleanor cleared the dishes away to take his vital signs again. "Very much the career girl. Do you enjoy it?"

"The responsibility gets heavy from time to time," she confessed. "But yes, I do enjoy it."

"You run all the time," he grumbled as she finished with him and tucked her pen back into her pocket.

"I have to," she said, smiling at him. "I have a lot of patients on this floor sicker than you are. There's a heart attack in 4B, and a bleeding ulcer in 4F, and I've got an appendectomy next door, pneumonia down the hall...."

"I get the general idea," he said dryly. "Come here."

Her heart leaped, but she managed a smile. "Why?"

"Because I asked you to," he replied.

"Sorry. We're not allowed to fraternize with the patients," she told him.

"I don't want to fraternize," he replied, and grinned wickedly. "I just want to drag you down here and let you take my pulse again."

The image made her smile. "Lecher," she scolded, shaking her head. "Behave yourself, or I'll send Nurse Wren after you."

He shuddered. "God forbid!"

"Then mind your manners," she ordered, backing toward the door, "or I'll...Oops!"

"Oh, excuse me," Maureen O'Clancy said sweetly as she opened the door right into Eleanor. "I'm sorry, nurse, I didn't see you!"

Nine

Forcing a smile to her lips was the hardest thing Eleanor had ever done. But she managed it.

"No harm done," she said sweetly. "If you'll excuse me, I'll get back to my paperwork."

"Amazing, that you can find time to visit the patients," Maureen said as sweetly, her blue eyes flashing.

"Visiting them is my job," Eleanor reminded her. "And despite the posted visiting hours, we don't like our patients to get too tired," she added in her best floor nurse's tone. "Good day."

"Well!..." Maureen said haughtily as the door closed.

Eleanor couldn't help smiling as she strode down the hall. There was something about that Irish girl....

"Phone call, love!" Darcy called to her from the desk. "It's your Mr. Granger, I think."

"Finally, a bright spot in my day," Eleanor laughed as she took the receiver from her friend's outstretched hand.

"I heard that," Wade drawled in her ear. "Have you missed me? I just heard about Keegan. How is he?"

"Reviving nicely, and at the moment being cuddled and cooed over by his Irish girlfriend," she replied carelessly.

"If I were in his place, I'd settle for you, pretty girl," he laughed. "How about dinner tonight? I'll take you out for spaghetti."

"I'd love it!" she said enthusiastically. "What time?"

"Pick you up at six."

"I'll look forward to it. Bye."

She hung up and hummed a tune as she dealt with supply sheets. Minutes later, Maureen O'Clancy marched past the desk with her nose looking definitely out of joint. She didn't even spare Eleanor a glance as she left the hospital.

"Well," Darcy huffed, "what was that all about?"

"I don't know. Uh-oh, looks like she upset our patient," Eleanor added, glancing at the board: Keegan's light was on. "I'd better go and see about him."

She found him lying back on his pillows looking grim, his arms folded defensively over his chest. He glanced up as she entered the room.

"What kept you?" he snapped at her. "I want my clothes. Now!"

"What brought this on?" she asked.

He sat up straighter. "That Irish bounder O'Clancy is about to talk my father out of Straightaway. For God's sake, he won the Preakness last year, I don't want him sold! And Dad's a sucker for a sob story. O'Clancy will have him charmed if I don't get home!"

"Why not phone your father and talk to him?" she suggested.

"That won't help," he said curtly. "Just get my clothes."

Eleanor leaned back against the door with a sigh. "Do be reasonable. You're just barely off the IV. You're too weak to be running around yet. Besides, are you sure it's the truth, about Maureen's father, I mean? Perhaps Maureen just wants you home again."

Saying that was a mistake. "Do you think so, honey?" he asked softly, his eyes cold and angry. "Maybe it'll be refreshing to have a woman want me for a change."

"Then by all means, we'll send you home as soon as Dr. Welder says we can release you," she replied acidly. "But for now... What are you doing?"

He was climbing out of bed, that's what he was doing, and without a stitch of clothing on his body. He faltered a little, then he straightened and went directly toward Eleanor.

She tried not to look. Arrow-straight body, hair-roughened chest and stomach and thighs, powerful long legs, powerful shoulders without the camouflage of clothing. He was beautiful.

He stopped just in front of her, breathing a little heavily from the exertion. "My clothes," he said quietly. "Or I'll walk out just the way I am."

Eleanor swallowed. "I don't have the authority to release you," she said.

He put his hands against the door on either side of her head and searched her soft dark eyes with his. "Every time I do this, you fight. Or you run. You won't even give me a chance, will you?"

"As you just observed, it might be refreshing to have a woman want you for a change," she said softly. "You might as well give Maureen a whirl, Keegan. She'd fit very well into your life."

Gently he fingered a strand of her honey-brown hair, testing its silkiness. "Snob," he murmured.

"I'm realistic," she corrected.

"Is that what you call it?" He hesitated, searching her eyes for a response. "Ellie, could we kiss each other just once without any coercion at all, do you think? Just for old times' sake?"

"I'm on duty," she protested weakly.

"You don't have anything to be afraid of," he said softly. "Not anything at all. Just close your eyes, little one, and let me do it all this time."

There were a thousand reasons why she shouldn't have listened, but she couldn't think of a single one. Instead she reached her arms up and slid them around his neck, seeing the shock in his blue eyes before they closed and his mouth settled softly on her lips.

"Yes," he whispered hungrily. His arms slid past her waist, bringing her against the length of his bare, warm body. "Yes, that's it, open your mouth...."

She did, letting his tongue probe inside and tangle with her own, feeling the hardness of his body, the sudden heat of him as he pinned her against the door.

"Eleanor," he breathed. His hips moved against her in undeniable need and urgency, and the kiss grew even more passionate—open mouths mingling fiercely together, voices breathing harshly, soft moans.

Eleanor whimpered as the old magic worked on her, as she felt her breasts crushing against his chest, her body aching to join with his. Her hands moved, searching out hard muscle and smooth flesh, working their way down his body, learning it with fingers that trembled softly.

"Yes," he groaned, drawing back, inviting her caresses. "Yes, touch me," he whispered shakily, opening his eyes to search hers. "Touch all of me, baby."

Insanity, she thought, but her hands were insistent, eager. She looked at him, watched the muscles ripple as her hands drew over them warmly, tenderly. He could have died—this might have been impossible. She thought that, and couldn't resist this once to know him, to possess him.

When her hands found and caressed his muscular stomach, he groaned and shuddered. She looked up at his hard, drawn face and exulted as she felt him tremble. He looked down at her, his eyes blazing with desire.

"I wish we were anywhere...except here," he said, his voice low and rough. "I want to do this to you. Touch you, with my eyes and my hands, in broad daylight. I want to be part of you."

"I'm afraid of you," Eleanor admitted at last, her eyes wide and vulnerable in her pale face.

"I'm sorry for that," he replied. "For so many things. I'd take back the past four years if I could. I'd start over with you."

"Once broken, a mirror is never the same."

"I could prove you wrong, if you'd let me," he said softly. "If you'd give me half a chance."

Eleanor closed her eyes in anguish. She wanted that, with him: wanted a new beginning. But there had been so much wounding, so much hurt.

"Come up to the house next Saturday and have lunch with us," he coaxed. "Mary June will be better by then; she'll do something pretty."

"Your houseguests will still be there," she reminded him.

"No, they damned well won't," he said shortly. "Not if I have to drive them to the airport. I've had pretty Maureen up to my neck! I'm sick of being chased. I like to do the chasing myself.''

He always had. Now he was in pursuit of her, and once he caught her it would be just as it was before. Only this time she wouldn't recover.

He held her hands in his, searching her frightened, anxious eyes. ''Trust me, just once. Just this once, Eleanor.''

He sounded sincere. She knew she shouldn't believe him, but the sound of his voice was weakening her, as was this unnerving proximity to his unclothed body. He was so much a part of her already that nothing he did was unpleasant to her.

''All...right,'' she agreed reluctantly.

He smiled. ''All right.'' His blue eyes twinkled. ''Now kiss me and I'll get back in bed.''

''Promise?'' she asked breathlessly.

''Scout's honor.'' He tilted Eleanor's face up to his and brought his mouth down, then kissed her as she'd never been kissed before. It made her go hot all over with mingled, confusing emotions.

''Here,'' he whispered unsteadily. His hands caught hers, moving them to the back of his powerful thighs. ''Now come close,'' he murmured against her mouth. ''Come very, very close and let me feel you....''

His legs actually trembled when she obeyed him. Delicious, exquisite tingles of pleasure throbbed along her nerves as she felt his powerful body surge against her. She jerked a little and he smiled against her warm mouth.

''See how helpless I am with you?'' he whispered. ''Just like a boy, all hot and bothered and out of control. And I think it would embarrass me like hell with any other woman.''

That was flattering. She sighed, then returned his kiss hungrily until he shuddered and gently eased her away.

He drew in a steadying breath, holding her by the waist as he searched her flushed face. Then he smiled slowly, wickedly. ''Knocked the breath right out of you, didn't it? Same here.''

''I...have to go,'' she faltered.

''You'd better fix your face first,'' he said, touching it with gentle fingers. ''You look loved, little Ellie.''

So did he. His red hair was disheveled, his mouth a little swollen, like her own. She felt the smile in her eyes, her lips, as she reached up and traced his eyebrows, his straight nose, his firm chin.

He brought her palms to his lips and kissed them. "That was the best medicine I've had since I was admitted," he whispered.

"And highly unethical it was, too," she teased. She moved discreetly away, her eyes fascinated by the beauty and symmetry of his body.

"It shouldn't embarrass you," he said quietly. "I don't feel like this with most women. I'm not ashamed of the way you affect me."

"No. I'm not, either," she said, surprising herself. She even managed to smile at him as he climbed back under the sheet and drew it up to his waist. "You're beautiful," she blurted out.

His warm eyes swept over her body. "So are you." Suddenly his face hardened. "Make love with me, Eleanor. Let me make the memories sweet. Let me show you how sweet it can be with a man who isn't a selfish brute."

"You weren't all that selfish," she murmured, embarrassed. "I was just inexperienced. I pushed you over the edge too soon."

"Another first," he replied. "Because you were the only woman I ever lost control with. Is that a shock, baby? It's the truth."

It was a shock. So was what she'd just let happen. She turned and went into his bathroom, smoothing her hair and wincing at the sight of her big dark eyes and swollen mouth. Well, she'd have to make a mad grab for her purse. Maybe Darcy wouldn't notice.

"You look fine," he said when she came out again. He held out his hand, and she went to him without a word, letting him press it to his mouth. "Come back and stay with me when you get off duty."

She started to agree, then remembered Wade. "I can't," she moaned. "Wade's taking me out to dinner."

His expression was indescribable. He hesitated a moment, then released her hand and leaned back against the pillows. "Granger again. Well, you can just break the date. I don't want you seeing him anymore."

"Oh, here we go again, slinging orders around like hash in a greasy spoon." She glared at him, stepping back. "Well, Mr. Taber, honey, you just lie here and give all the orders you like, but don't expect me to come to heel. I'm not your personal slave, despite your undeniable expertise at lovemaking. You won't seduce me a second time!''

''Won't I?'' he challenged, bright-eyed. ''Wait and see.''

''You wait. I have work to do.''

She whirled and stomped out the door, hating herself all over again for having trusted him in a moment of weakness.

Darcy pretended not to see the results of Keegan's mouth and hands, but she spent the rest of the day grinning.

''He wants to see you,'' she told Eleanor just before quitting time as she returned from answering Keegan's light.

''I'll have a photograph made, he can look at that. Look at the time!'' Eleanor clucked. ''I have to run. I'll give my report and see you tomorrow, darling. Have a nice evening.''

''Eleanor, you can't strand me with him,'' Darcy wailed. ''He doesn't like me!''

''That's all right. He doesn't like anybody,'' Eleanor assured her with a smile. ''Just don't make any sudden moves, and you'll be fine. See you!''

Wade picked her up at six, and they went to a nice little Italian restaurant, but Eleanor's heart wasn't in it. She picked at her food and made halfhearted responses to Wade's teasing, and was thoroughly miserable.

''Is he getting to you, honey?'' Wade asked sympathetically.

''He's just horrible,'' she muttered, ''and I don't know why I can't manage to put him out of my mind and my life. I feel like such a wimp.''

''It's called love,'' he told her. ''A malady to which we are all vulnerable at one time or another. Chin up, girl, don't surrender now. We're just on the verge of victory!''

''Think so?'' She sighed.

He grinned. ''Well, I hear through the grapevine that the O'Clancys are on their way back to Ireland this very minute.''

''Then as soon as Keegan is on his feet, he'll probably be right behind them,'' she replied.

''Care to bet? Unless I miss my guess, young lady, you're the target, not Maureen.''

''Then he'd better be prepared for a long siege,'' she retorted.

"You said he invited you to lunch Saturday. Go. And while you're there, lay it on thick about how close you and I are getting," he added. "Then stand back and watch the fireworks."

The word "fireworks" brought back vivid memories of that afternoon—of practically swooning in Keegan's arms while he all but ravished her with his mouth. She felt like someone in the grip of a savage fever, burning up with unsatisfied longings, perishing for lack of love. She had no strength at all anymore; Keegan, on the other hand, was very strong—and single-minded.

"Save me from him," she pleaded.

"You don't need saving, beautiful girl," Wade chuckled as he finished his coffee. "He does. You wait. We've got him in a corner now."

"I wouldn't bet on that," she said. "He's slippery. He doesn't really want to settle down."

"I think you're wrong. I think he wants that very much. Why don't you listen to him for a change, Eleanor," he added quietly. "Ask some questions. Be receptive. You might be astonished at the results you get."

She shrugged, and the smile that touched her full mouth was wistful. "All he'd want is an affair. I don't need that."

"You need him," he told her. "How are you going to survive without him? Honey, sometimes it takes a compromise to satisfy both parties. You might think about that."

"I don't mind compromise. But I'm not going the whole way alone," she replied.

He lifted his coffee cup. "I don't think you'll have to. I think very soon I may have to start looking around for a new companion." He sighed. "And I'll never find a girl like you again. I'd have Keegan pushed out of an airplane if I thought it would get me you. But I would like to see you happy. And I don't think you'll ever find what you want with anyone except Keegan."

She was beginning to think that herself. It was kind of depressing, though. She watched Wade drive away an hour later, feeling as if her last friend had deserted her. He hadn't even fixed another date. He seemed to expect that she and Keegan would work it out, but she had reservations. Maureen might be out of the picture—but only temporarily, only until Keegan had satisfied his lust for Eleanor. There were too many differences socially and economically between the Tabers and the Whitmans for anything more permanent. And Eleanor didn't want a backstairs affair. Problem was, she admitted ruefully, she didn't know what to do anymore.

When she went on duty the next day, it was to find that Keegan had checked himself out the night before and gone home. It was a disappointment and a relief.

She worked her shift, dodged Darcy's questions and was emotionally exhausted by the time she went home. Her father was busy in his woodworking shop and didn't question her when she announced that she was going to take a nap before she cooked supper.

She was dreaming. She was being held and touched and loved, and she smiled as Keegan's face came into focus above hers. Then she realized with a start that it wasn't a dream. He was real.

"Don't panic," Keegan said with a soft, deep laugh as he lifted her from the bed in his arms. "I'm just going to take you up to the house to see my new colt."

"But...but I'm asleep," she protested drowsily, wiping her eyes with her hands.

"No, you aren't, pretty thing." His eyes wandered over her. She'd changed into white shorts and a pink button-up sleeveless blouse, and he loved the softness of her tanned body, the sweet weight in his arms. "God, you're pretty."

He bent and kissed her sleepy lips gently. "Wake up, beauty."

She linked her arms around his neck with a stifled yawn and buried her face in his throat. He smelled of Oriental cologne and soap, and she nuzzled closer.

"Don't do that," he said uneasily, "unless you want me to find a satisfying use for your bed."

Her breath caught. She was half-asleep and all too vulnerable, and suddenly the atmosphere in the room was hot and tense and full of promise.

"Your father went up to the house with my dad to see the colt," Keegan said, his voice deep and husky. "I told him I'd bring you along.'' He drew her closer. ''It will take them half an hour to miss us.... Eleanor?''

She drew her head back to his shoulder and looked up at him, and she didn't have time to hide the hunger.

His eyes darkened, shifted to her breasts. She hadn't put on a bra, and he could see the dark, taut outline of her nipples. This wasn't how he'd planned it, but his body was in torment. He wanted her unbearably. And she wanted him.

''We could love each other on that bed,'' he whispered shakily, moving back toward it. ''Cool sheets, hot bodies twisting together like twining vines. I can give you pleasure and watch you give yourself to me, Ellie. I can let you watch me go crazy when the time comes. Let me.''

Keegan set her down on the sheet, holding her as he stripped away the coverlet, his eyes never leaving hers. Then he eased her back down, tossing the pillow to one side. His eyes burned with intent as his fingers slowly did away with buttons and pushed the blouse gently aside to bare her breasts.

He looked down and caught his breath at the mauve-and-pink perfection revealed there. She was fuller than she had been at eighteen, a vision. He reached down and touched the hard tips, rubbing them so that she trembled and bit her lip.

''Cry out, if you feel like it,'' he said huskily. ''You can make all the noise you want to with me. No one will hear us.''

Eleanor arched helplessly. He'd come along at the worst possible time, caught her at her most vulnerable. Years of repressed longing were freed at last, and the ensuing explosion of passion left her powerless to resist.

''Lift up,'' he said gently. ''Let me undress you.''

She let him do it; wide-eyed, she watched him, felt his warm, callused hands easily disposing of her shorts, her lacy briefs, until she lay revealed and yielding on the cool sheets.

Keegan brought her hands to his body, pressing them against him, holding her eyes with his. ''Take my clothes off, Eleanor.''

She didn't know where she found the courage. She'd never in her life undressed a man for this reason, not even Keegan. Most of all she remembered the pain, and her hands hesitated after she removed his shirt and let it drop to the floor.

He tilted her chin up until their eyes met. "It won't hurt this time," he promised. "This time is going to be everything your first time should have been."

She found the buckle of his belt, and even then she hesitated. He laughed softly at her fumbles and got to his feet.

"I'll do it this time," he murmured.

Keegan removed the rest of his clothing, while she watched him, fascinated. Then he turned and stretched out lazily beside her.

"And they say dreams don't come true," he whispered as his hands traveled sensuously up her rib cage to cup her breasts. "They do. Oh, yes, they do.... Turn over and lie against me, little one. I want to feel every inch of you touching my body."

He helped her, bending to kiss her open mouth as his hands moved up and down and around her soft, yielding body.

Eleanor lay still at first, accepting his caresses. But as Keegan found more intimate ways of touching her, she began to writhe. By the time his mouth had worked its way over her breasts and down her hips and thighs, she was crying.

Keegan had never aroused a woman to that state before. Most of them had been experienced, of course, and not as innocently accepting and eager as Eleanor. It excited him unbearably that she was so hungry for him. She must love him, he told himself. She wouldn't be so openly receptive to his loving if she didn't. The thought made him wild. He groaned against her stomach, and his fingers bit hard at her hips, lifting her.

"Want you," she whispered brokenly. Her eyes were closed, her head thrown back, her hands trembling on his hips. "I want you, want you!"

His mouth slid all the way up her body as he settled his weight along her legs and hips and breasts, feeling her soft body press deeply into the mattress. Eleanor trembled a little as he moved his body over hers, and he lifted his head to watch her, to make sure that he didn't hurt her.

"Shhh," he whispered reassuringly, brushing back her disheveled honey-brown hair. Her eyes were huge, frightened. "Relax for me,

Ellie. Yes, like that, just relax and let me do the rest. Yes." He smiled softly, feeling the yielding, the warm softness enfolding him with delicious ease. He shifted closer, feeling her nails bite into his hips as she surged up against him with a gasp.

"Oh, God, this is going to be heaven," he whispered gruffly. "Don't be afraid, but it's going to get a little...rough...now, baby!" He groaned and shuddered as the fever began to burn in him. He clenched his hands under her hips, lifting her. "Baby, baby!"

Eleanor felt the rough movement of his body with a sense of awe, because it wasn't pain she was feeling. It was something unbearably sweet. Her eyes closed in an exquisite shudder as he touched her in a way that made her body ripple with pleasure.

"Yes...do that," she pleaded against his suddenly devouring mouth. "Yes, like that, like that! Keegan!"

She was crying now, whimpering, her soft hands clutching at his hips, his thighs, working magic on the long, damp sleekness of his back as his body rose and fell with hers in the sunlit silence of the bedroom.

Keegan never remembered what happened next. Eleanor was crying and he was on a roller coaster that he couldn't stop. He cried out above her, his voice like that of someone in torment. His body arched like a bow, and his face contorted in exquisite agony as he cried her name.

She reached up, drawing him down against her, comforting him, because she was blazing with tenderness and fulfilled desire, her face wet with tears.

"Keegan," she whispered in wonder. Her lips touched his face, his eyes, his cheeks, his trembling mouth. She smiled. "Keegan."

"Thank you," he whispered shakily. "Thank you for trusting me, for giving yourself so sweetly. I never knew peace, until now. I had to show you, teach you, that it can be magic. A man and a woman can touch the sky."

"Lovemaking," she whispered. Her eyes closed. "You're my lover."

"I've always been your lover," he murmured. "Only me. You've never known anyone else like this, have you?"

"No." She stretched and sighed as he rolled away and leaned over her, smiling.

"Now let's go see my colt," he murmured. "And I'll feed you supper."

She'd wanted something more loverlike than that, and she had to force herself not to ask for it. Could he have loved her that way without feeling something for her? She didn't think so.

"All right," she said. "I'll get dressed."

"What a crime, to cover a body like that," he murmured, watching her put her clothes back on. "My God, just touching you drove me crazy."

"You look pretty good yourself," she said demurely.

Keegan got up with a sigh and put his own clothing back on. When he finished, he pulled Eleanor close and held her against him for a long moment.

"I didn't think," he said quietly. "You aren't on the pill, I gather?"

She swallowed. "No."

He lifted his head, searching her eyes. "If we made a baby, I'll take care of you," he said, his voice deep and quiet.

Eleanor actually blushed. She pushed away from him because it sounded as if he had something other than marriage in mind. "We'd better get up to the farm," she said evasively.

He studied her straight back, frowning.

"I didn't get pregnant before," she pointed out without looking at him. "There's probably nothing to worry about."

"There could be, if it happens again."

"It won't," she said firmly, and walked into the hall. "One lapse doesn't make an affair, Keegan."

"I don't want an affair," he growled.

"Yes, I know." She went out the front door, Keegan at her heels.

"Wait a minute," he said shortly. "Let's get this ironed out right now, Eleanor. You've got it all wrong!"

"No, I haven't!" she returned fiercely. "You have. I'm a grown woman now, not a child. You won't own me by seducing me!"

He seemed at a loss for words. He started to speak, stopped, tried again. "I didn't plan what happened," he said softly. "I didn't mean it to happen...."

"You never do." She laughed coldly. "I'm just handy. Handy, and stupid!"

He grimaced. She didn't understand! She thought he was using her. "For God's sake, it's not like that!" he burst out. "Please, baby, listen to me!"

"Look, there's Dad," she said, watching Gene Taber drive toward the house with her father in the car. She flushed, thinking what they'd have interrupted minutes before. Now, however, she was grateful for the interruption. She couldn't even look at Keegan. How would she ever be able to sleep in that bedroom again?

Ten

"**I** forgot my pipe." Barnett Whitman grinned. "Can't get my ideas together without it, not if I'm going to build a halfway decent barn. Pretty colt, Eleanor, you ought to go up and see it."

"That's where we're headed," said Keegan. He caught Eleanor's unresponsive hand in his.

"Wait, I have to change," she protested.

"I have seen a woman's legs before," Gene Taber teased.

"But it's so informal," she persisted.

"Don't you have a wraparound skirt?" Keegan asked.

Now how had he known that? She nodded and rushed off to drag it out of her closet. She wouldn't let herself think. She didn't dare. There would be time enough for regrets later.

She drew on her white wraparound skirt and tied it, filing out the door just behind her father. Keegan came up to her as she stopped on the porch, and he held out his hand, watching, waiting. With a faint sigh, she put her own into it and felt his fingers contract, warm and possessive.

He smiled.

"Come on," he said, leading her to the car. "We'll drive up behind them."

"You look better," she murmured.

"Since I left the hospital, I expect you mean?" he asked dryly, smiling as she blushed. "Yes, I feel better, too. I never did thank you, did I, for telling Dad what to do."

"He was upset," she said.

He helped her into the passenger seat of the red Porsche. "So were you, I hear," he said, noting her downcast expression as he closed the door.

Eleanor leaned back as she fastened her seatbelt and waited for him to get in and start the engine. Gene Taber had already driven off in his green Buick with Barnett beside him. It seemed the day for a family get-together, but all she wanted to do was…was stay with Keegan and never leave him, she admitted miserably. She couldn't bear the thought of being alone again, of being without him for the rest of her life. Especially now. And what if she did get pregnant?

Involuntarily, her fingers went to her waist, pressing there in wonder as they drove up toward Flintlock. A baby would be nice. Someone to love and care for, someone to look after and fuss over. She smiled.

The man beside her saw that smile and where her fingers were resting, and he smiled, too. He began to whistle softly, glancing sideways at her and smiling.

She glanced at him and looked away again. Smug, wasn't he? she thought bitterly. He'd had his way, and now he was satisfied. He'd be off in search of a new conquest.

"The colt is out of Main Chance, by Straightaway," he told her. "A Triple Crown winner if I've ever seen one. Beautiful conformation."

"Wasn't Straightaway the reason you escaped from the hospital?" she asked slyly.

"I had to. O'Clancy damned near took him home." Keegan pulled into his driveway and followed his father's car back to the garage, pulling in beside the Buick. "Feeling all right?" he asked unexpectedly, his blue eyes concerned as they searched her face.

"Of…of course," she faltered.

"I didn't hurt you, did I?" he asked, his voice softer than satin.

She shook her head, and he nodded, apparently satisfied. He got out and helped her out.

"We're going to look over the layout for the barn," Gene told them.

"Barnett swears he's up to it. Then we'll meet you in the house for supper. Mary June's fixing ham, by the way. She swore up and down that we'd never see another piece of chicken as long as we live after your near miss, son."

Keegan chuckled as he locked Eleanor's fingers in his. "Suits me. I think I'll sell my stock in that chicken packing plant we own shares of, too."

"I don't blame you, boy." Barnett grinned.

The older men wandered off across the yard, and Keegan drew Eleanor along with him into the spacious stable with its wide, wood-chip-covered aisle. He stopped at a middle stall and pushed Eleanor in front of him so that she could look over the gate. There, in the stall, was a sleek, beautiful brown mare with a small, spindly-legged colt.

"Isn't he a beauty?" he asked proudly. He put his hands on her shoulders, idly stroking them. "A fine young devil, all nerves right now. He'll be a sight to behold in a few months."

"He's a champion all right." She sighed. "I've always loved horses, even if I don't know one bloodline from another."

"I could teach you that," he said, his breath fanning her hair. "I could teach you anything you wanted to know. And before you fly at me," he added when she turned, glaring, "I don't mean sex."

That stopped her. She stared up at him breathlessly, her whole body reacting in sensuous pleasure to the intensity of his gaze.

"For God's sake, don't look at me like that," he said harshly. "Don't you realize even now the way you affect me?"

She didn't, but when he drew her against his long, lean body, she got the message.

"Don't pull away," he said quietly. "You belong to me now. You know everything there is to know about my body and how it responds." He smiled at her warmly. "Besides, you're a nurse."

"That doesn't make me any more confident, actually," she confessed. Her hands touched his chest through the shirt and she felt him shudder as his heartbeat increased. She pressed her fingers against him, feeling the soft, bristly pressure of chest hair through the material, feeling him stiffen. She looked up, fascinated by the newness of the relationship they were sharing, by what had happened.

"How do things stand between you and Granger?" he asked.

She shifted restlessly. "I don't have to tell you that."

He tipped her chin up and searched her eyes. "After this afternoon, I have the right to know," he replied. "You gave me something Granger's never had from you."

Something he would never have, but she couldn't tell him that. She bit her lower lip. "I'm very fond of Wade," she said, which was true. She studied his shirt button.

"And how do you feel about me?" he asked.

"I...want you," she confessed, closing her eyes. Well, it was the truth, after all. She did want him. But she wasn't about to tell him the rest of it, that she loved him and she'd never get over him. She'd experienced him totally as a man, and her heart was now his.

His hands smoothed up and down her bare arms, strong, warm, possessive hands. "Only want, Eleanor?" he probed.

She lifted her dark eyes to his. "What are you waiting for, another breathless confession of undying love?" she asked with a harsh laugh. "Wouldn't that be history repeating itself? Isn't physical desire enough for you, Keegan? We're both adults, after all. And I'm sure you're relieved to know that I'm not going to throw my heart at your feet a second time."

He flinched slightly, then lowered his eyes and looked down at her hands, still pressed tautly against his chest.

"Wouldn't you like to try loving me again?" he asked softly. He lifted his eyes back to hers, searching them in silence. "I might be a better proposition this go-around," he remarked at last. "God knows, we're both more mature now."

Eleanor squared her chin and stared at him for a moment. Then, "Desire isn't enough to build a relationship on," she said. "You told me that four years ago, don't you remember?" She laughed bitterly.

His eyes closed. "I remember."

"You did try to be kind, I realize that," she acknowledged. "But you were in love with Lorraine, and you couldn't disguise it. If I'd been a little less infatuated..."

Keegan let her go and turned away to light a cigarette, his back to her. Then he looked up toward the ceiling. "Are you trying to get back at me, Ellie? Is that what this evasion is all about?"

"No, it isn't," she replied. "I'm trying to tell you that what I want now is a stable relationship with a man, some security and a future that doesn't involve stolen moments in the back seat of a car or a deserted house.''

"Oh, God," he cried, bowing his head. "Oh, God, why won't you listen to me?" He turned, his blue eyes dark with pain, and something like defeat. "I'm not offering you some clandestine affair!"

"I don't care," she forced herself to say calmly. "Wade's asked me to marry him." She watched that register, and nodded. "And after today, I'll say yes, Keegan. Because I can't risk letting what happened today repeat itself. I can't seem to say no to you. So I'll settle for a permanent relationship instead."

"You won't be able to give him what you gave me," he said, his voice harsh.

"Of course I won't. But I'll take care of him, and be there when he needs me. I'll have everything I want, and I'll give him children.''

He looked as if she'd cut him with a knife. Abruptly he turned away, his eyes blank and unseeing, his soul in agony. So he'd been wrong. She didn't love him. She only wanted him, after all, and she was so afraid of giving in again that she'd even rush into marriage with a man she didn't love to keep him out of her life. What a horrible, bitter irony: he'd pushed her away when she'd offered him her love, and now that he wanted it, he couldn't get it back. Irony.

"Then I guess that's all there is," he said, his voice dull, lifeless.

"That's all there is," she agreed. She turned away from the stall and walked outside into the sunlight.

Keegan followed her with eyes as cold as death. She was like quick-silver, he thought blankly, impossible to catch and hold. If only he hadn't rushed her, if only he'd held back this afternoon. But he'd wanted her so desperately. He'd thought it would solve everything, show her how he felt about her. All it had done was to push her into a loveless marriage.

"I'd rather not stay for supper," she said when he joined her at the front porch.

"If you leave now, they'll wonder why you left."

She grimaced. "Yes, I suppose so."

He searched her pale face quietly, the smoking cigarette in his hand all but forgotten. "I'm sorry," he said. "Sorry for it all. For the past, for the present. Even for the future. All I seem to do is hurt you, when that's the last thing I've ever wanted to do.''

"You haven't hurt me,'' she said, folding her arms across her breasts. "I was hardly a victim, either time.''

"I seduced you,'' he said, staring down at the cigarette.

"No!'' She touched his arm hesitantly, searching his tormented face. "Oh, no, it wasn't seduction. Not ever. I wanted you.''

"What will we do if you get pregnant?'' he asked softly. "Will you tell Granger the truth?''

"If I get pregnant, I...'' She couldn't go on with the lie. "I don't know what I'll do, except that I'll have it,'' she finished lamely.

He started to touch her face, his fingers slightly unsteady. "I can't lose you twice,'' he whispered.

She frowned. "I don't understand.''

"I...'' he began.

"It's on the table!'' Mary June called out the front door. "Hurry up before I throw it out!''

"Damn,'' Keegan muttered with a sigh. He ground out his cigarette under his heel. "Oh, well, maybe it's for the best,'' he said gruffly. "Come on.'' He guided her up the steps, leaving her to ponder what he'd said.

"Thank God we can sit down to table in peace, with the O'Clancys gone,'' Gene Taber declared jovially as Mary June began serving dinner. "There were nights when I was almost certain that Maureen was going to drag Keegan under the table and rape him between courses.''

Keegan glanced at his father with a faint smile. "I felt that way myself a time or two,'' he murmured. "She was a bit forward for my taste.''

"I had the same fears for Eleanor when Wade came to dinner,'' Barnett Whitman announced, glancing at her with a broad grin. "He was practically drooling the first time.''

Keegan banged his cup on the table, looking grim, as Eleanor flushed and Gene and Barnett exchanged discreet smiles.

"Here it is,'' Mary June interrupted, her black eyes flashing as she put a platter of ham on the table. "No more chicken around this here house,'' she added with a glare at Keegan. "I never seen the like. Folks trying to kill themselves with chicken poison....''

Keegan glared back at her. "I was not trying to commit suicide."

"Any fool who'd put cooked chicken back on the same plate with uncooked chicken pieces deserves just what he gets!" Mary June retorted.

"Miss Perfection," Keegan returned, "haven't you ever made a mistake?"

"Yes, sir," she agreed. "Saying yes when Mr. Gene asked if I wanted to work for him!"

"Stop it, you two," Gene roared, banging the table with his fist. "Can't we have just one peaceful meal in this house without the two of you coming to blows?"

Mary June sniffed. "I don't start it. He does."

"Ha!" Keegan shot back.

"I'll just go and put that chocolate cake I just baked in the trash can," the cook threatened, lips pursed mutinously.

Keegan sighed. He picked his white napkin up out of his lap and waved it back and forth.

Mary June nodded curtly. "Good enough for you," she said. "And see you stay out of my kitchen from now on, if you please. I don't want folks trying to kill themselves in there. Spoils my pantry, it does."

Keegan glared at her retreating back as she hobbled away. "Someday," he threatened. "Someday!"

"Shhhh!" Gene hissed at him. "She'll quit!"

Keegan grinned. "Is there hope?"

"Well, we'd die if we had to depend on your culinary skills, and that's a fact," he told his son.

"Just because I put the damned chicken in the wrong place..." he muttered.

"You should have married Maureen, while you had the chance," Eleanor said with a forced smile. "She'd have baked you cakes."

"She couldn't even buy a decent cake, much less make one from scratch," Keegan said venomously, his eyes narrowed. "And I can pick my own wife, thank you."

Of course he could—some society woman with a family tree as monied as his own. Eleanor smiled faintly at her plate as she tried to eat.

"I wish you'd marry somebody," Gene told his son. "I'm getting old enough to crave grandchildren."

"Adopt," Keegan advised him. He glanced quickly at Eleanor, then looked away again. "I like my freedom."

Eleanor didn't look up, but her heart felt as if it had been cut in two. It was the truth, of course: he didn't want to marry anybody. But why throw it in her face now, of all times, after she'd given in to him?

"He's baiting you, girl," Gene said.

She looked up to find Keegan grinning at her.

"I don't care if he dies an old maid," she said bluntly.

"Heartless woman," Keegan muttered. He finished his meal and sat back in his chair with a long sigh. Why not bring it out into the open? he mused. He could gain an ally or two, and he needed them.

"Why don't you marry me and make an honest man out of me?" he asked her bluntly.

Her fork clattered wildly as it hit the china plate. She retrieved it clumsily, red-faced and breathless as all eyes suddenly focused on her.

"Beast!" she exclaimed.

He pursed his lips and studied her with that possessive smile she hated. "Why not marry me? I'm sexy and filthy rich, I can kiss you stupid without half trying, and you'd get half of the colt to boot."

Gene and Barnett stared at her as she searched for some graceful way out.

"You can't cook," she declared.

"You could teach me," he returned.

"I'm going to marry Wade," she announced defiantly.

"Over my dead body," he replied fiercely. "You're not getting yourself tied to that playboy!"

"Look who's calling Wade a playboy!" she cried. "And you're one to talk about him doing it hanging from tree limbs, when you tried it in a hospital room with nurses coming and going all around us!"

"Eleanor," he chided, nodding toward their fascinated audience, which now included Mary June, "how could you embarrass me like this?"

"I couldn't embarrass you by taking off your clothes in Central Park!"

He smiled slowly. "I'm game if you are. I'll rush right out and buy two plane tickets to New York."

She threw up her hands and got out of the chair. "I give up."

"Marry me, Eleanor, or I'll hound you day and night," he threatened.

She flushed and turned away. "I'm going home."

"I'll drive you."

"No, you won't!" she raged, close to tears. How could he humiliate her like this? She loved him, and he was making some horrible joke out of it.

He saw the tears and wondered if there could be some deep, lingering passion there, if she still cared for him. She was upset, but she wasn't unreceptive. He had her on the run. If he played his hand carefully, he might yet wrench her out of Wade's arms and get her to a minister.

"If you're determined, we'll all go," Gene said, grinning. "Come on, Barnett."

"I won't ride with him," Eleanor said, pointing at Keegan.

Keegan sighed theatrically. "Shoved aside by the woman of my dreams. I'll perish to death for love of you, Eleanor."

"The only thing you'll perish of is your own cooking," she said curtly. "I'm going home. Good night."

She didn't say another word to him. She crawled into the back of Gene's car, and the two older men talked farm business all the way back.

Once home, Eleanor went straight to bed. And that was the worst thing she could have done. The bed still smelled of Keegan, and it always would. She'd been able to strip off and change the bed linen, but she'd never be able to erase the memories…and they haunted her dreams.

Eleven

If Eleanor thought she'd seen the last of Keegan for a while, she was in for a surprise. When she went down to fix breakfast the next morning, he was sitting in the living room with her father, as relaxed as if he belonged there.

He looked up as she entered the room and grinned at her. "Good morning, glory," he teased. "You look pretty in that."

"That" referred to her faded blue jeans and a green pullover knit shirt. Eleanor was off duty today and hadn't expected to find Keegan piled up in the living room like a redheaded snake, just waiting for her.

Now she felt her face going red as she looked at him, remembering yesterday and how easily she'd succumbed. Keegan saw her flush and smiled even wider.

"I wasn't expecting you," she said helplessly.

"I figured that," he replied. "What are we having for breakfast?"

"Did Mary June's ankle get worse?" she asked sarcastically.

"Nope. I just like your biscuits," he chuckled. "And your sweet company, pretty girl."

"She is pretty," Barnett agreed solemnly. "I never could understand why she stayed single so long."

"She was waiting for me, of course," Keegan declared, leaning back in his chair like a conquering general. "Weren't you, Ellie?"

"Don't call me Ellie," she grumbled.

"Okay, honey."

She started to protest, then threw up her hands and went to make breakfast.

Keegan watched her through bacon and eggs and buttered biscuits and homemade apple butter, and she fidgeted helplessly in her chair. After all that had happened between them, she couldn't be casual about their relationship. She just didn't understand what he wanted of her.

"Want to go watch a harness race with me?" he asked Eleanor as she sipped coffee. "Or we could go to the yearling sale at Gainesmore Farm; I saw an Arabian over there that I'd like to bid on."

She cocked her head, puzzled. "You know I'm not that smart about horses, although I'm sure you think that's unspeakable for someone born in Lexington."

"Okay," he relented, "how about a walk in the woods? Or you could get your father's fishing pole and we'll go drown some worms."

"I…I have to work in the garden today," she faltered. "The weeds are killing my tomatoes."

He pursed his lips and shrugged. "So we'll hoe out the tomatoes," he said quietly. "I'm not all that particular about what we do, as long as we do it together."

Barnett Whitman was grinning from ear to ear. He finished his coffee and got up. "I have to go over some blueprints with Gene," he said, beaming at them. "I'm back on the job as of today. My doctor said it was all right, before you start screaming, Eleanor," he added.

She lifted an eyebrow. "Did I say anything?"

"No, and see that you don't," he chuckled. "See you later, kids."

"I'll bet it's been years since anyone called you a kid," Eleanor said after her father had driven away.

"Years since I've felt like one, surely," he agreed. He folded his forearms on the table and searched her face. "Do you really want to spend the day hoeing weeds?"

She glared at him. "No, I won't go to bed with you, if that was the next and very obvious question."

"It wasn't, actually, although I'd rather sleep with you than eat," he said softly, his blue eyes smiling into hers. "You and I do something incredible together when we make love."

Eleanor stared at the coffee cup she was holding. Her heart was going wild, all because he was using that slow, sexy tone she remembered so well.

"I keep wondering what would have happened if I hadn't given in to temptation that night four years ago," he said absently.

"You'd probably have married Lorraine and lived happily ever after," she said dully.

"Do you think so? I don't." He got up, dragged a cigarette from the pocket of his blue-plaid shirt and lit it. "The only thing Lorraine and I had in common was that we both thought she was a knockout."

"All the same, she fit into your life-style very well."

He turned, leaning back against the sink. "So do you," he said quietly.

She laughed. "Not me," she returned, toying with the cup. "I don't know about horses, and I'm certainly not debutante material."

"You're real, though," he said, forcing her to meet his gaze. "That's right. You're honest and stubborn, and you don't back away from things. You have qualities I admire, Ellie. The economics don't matter a damn. They never have."

"They matter to me," she replied shortly. "Look around you, Keegan. This is a nice house, thanks to you and your father, but it's not a patch on Flintlock. I've never worn fancy clothes until recently, and I didn't even know that a champagne buffet meant hors d'oeuvres and drinks. When I first walked onto Wade's property, his mother and sister came at me like spears...."

"Just as I thought," he said darkly. "I've known them for years."

"I gave as good as I got, thank you," she told him, "but the fact is, I don't fit in that kind of society. You were right in the first place when you were warning me off Wade. I'm just a country girl who might someday make a small mark in the nursing profession. But as a—" she searched for a discreet term "—companion for a rich man, I'd be a dead loss."

"I'm not in the market for a mistress," he said, his voice like velvet.

Her eyebrows arched. "Excuse me, but isn't that the position you're offering me? Or do you make a habit of seducing anyone who happens to be handy?"

He sighed wearily as he lifted the cigarette to his mouth. "Eleanor," he said, "what am I going to do about you?"

"You might just leave me alone," she replied, although the thought hurt dreadfully. Still, it was the most sensible course.

"I can't." He held out his hand. "Come walking, Ellie. I want to talk."

She hesitated, but he nodded curtly and she yielded. This would be the last time she obeyed, she promised herself. The very last time.

She took his outstretched hand and followed him out into the sunshine. He locked her fingers with his and went off down a path beside the fence that led to the stream cutting through his property.

"Four years ago," he said without looking at her, "I came by your house on your birthday and asked you out. That night, when I picked you up, you were wearing a blue print dress with puffy sleeves and a low neckline. Your hair was down around your shoulders and smelled of gardenias. I gave you supper at an exclusive restaurant and then I drove you out to the river and parked on a deserted stretch of dirt road."

"Keegan..."

"Shhh," he said gently. He turned her as they reached the shade of a towering oak tree and held her by the arms, studying her face. "And then I started kissing you. And you kissed me back. I put my hand under your bodice and you held it there. We started kissing feverishly then, and somehow I got you into the back seat of that big Lincoln and eased you down, and you let me take your clothes off. It was a warm, clear night, and we made love to the sound of crickets and rushing water, and afterward you told me that you loved me."

She lowered her eyes to his chest. "It isn't kind, reminding me," she whispered miserably.

"I'm not doing it to torment you, Eleanor," he said. "I want to make you understand how I felt. You were barely eighteen, not even a full-grown woman, and a virgin to boot. I was considerably older, practically engaged to Lorraine, and I was torn apart with conflicting emotions. I never meant it to happen at all, but once you let me touch you, I couldn't stop."

"I realize I was as much to blame as you were, Keegan," she replied. "I was crazy about you. I thought, since you were asking me out, that you'd stopped caring about Lorraine and I had a chance with you." She laughed hollowly. "I should have realized that a man like you wouldn't want a shy little country mouse when he could have a fairy princess like Lorraine, but then, I wasn't thinking."

He ground his cigarette out under his heel and took her face in his lean, warm hands. "I never slept with Lorraine," he said, his voice deep and soft. "Part of what I felt for her was sexual. Probably most of it was. Once I had you, though, I wasn't able to want her. That was why I drove her away. I had nothing left to give."

She looked deeply into his blue eyes and was shaken by what she saw. "When you told me why you'd asked me out, I wanted to die," she confessed finally. "I'd practically thrown myself at you.... It was humiliating."

"Not to me," he murmured. "All my life, women had chased me because I was rich. You were the first, and the last, to want me just for myself."

She smiled softly. "You were very special."

"So were you." He bent and kissed her, tenderly, warmly. His mouth opened and poised there; she could taste the smoke on his breath. "Your body haunted me after you left Lexington. Your face. Your voice. I couldn't sleep for feeling your body under mine, those sweet little cries that pulsed out of you. Do you know even now how it excites me to hear you moan when I make love to you?"

"You make it so...so wild," she faltered.

"So do you, honey," he replied curtly. His hands tangled in her thick, soft hair, and he tugged at it. "You make it so much more than a merging of bodies. I think about babies when I take you, Eleanor, did you know?" he whispered, and his mouth found hers even as the words registered in her whirling mind.

She gripped his forearms, trembling as he deepened the kiss; then his eyes opened and stared straight into hers.

"Come close," he said against her mouth.

"I'll hurt you," she whispered hesitantly.

"Yes." He reached down and moved her legs until they touched his, then his eyes closed and his mouth crushed hers in a silence blazing with promise.

He bent, holding the kiss, and lifted her into his arms. "Just once more," he whispered, his voice deep and husky as he carried her into the shade of the tree and placed her gently on the ground. "Just one more time, Eleanor...."

He stretched out against her, and the kiss grew urgent, passionate. His hands caressed her pliant body, molding her breasts, her rib cage, her waist and stomach, her long legs.

"No," she moaned. Her hands pushed halfheartedly at his chest, until they found an opening and pressed into warm, hard muscle and thick hair. His tongue searched inside her mouth, and she felt his heart shaking her with its feverish beat, felt the crush of his body over hers, twisting her against the hard ground as he gave up his control to the passion driving him.

"You want me," he whispered huskily. "I want you. What else matters?"

"I won't...be used," she whimpered. "I won't!"

"Here," he said under his breath, moving her hand against his chest. "Touch me like this."

"Oh, Keegan, this won't...solve anything." She panted, twisting her face away from his.

"Yes, it will," he said. He slid down against her, feverishly pushing up the hem of her shirt, revealing her bare, taut breasts. "God, Ellie, you've got the prettiest breasts," he whispered huskily, then bent his head.

She was lost from the first touch of his open mouth, taking her inside that warm, moist darkness, letting her feel the roughness of his tongue, the soft nip of his teeth. He whispered something she didn't hear, and his lean hands smoothed warmly up and down her rib cage while his mouth made her tremble.

He worked his way down to the fastening of her jeans, pressing his face into her warm flesh, making her burn and ache. His fingers dug into her hips, lifting her rhythmically to the probing of his tongue, the nip of his teeth.

"Please," she whispered helplessly. Her eyes closed and she shuddered. Her hands held his hair, trapping his mouth against her warm belly. "Please, make me stop aching."

"There's only one way to do that," he whispered. He slid up her body, his mouth poised over hers as his hands found and cupped her breasts. He searched her eyes in a lingering scrutiny. "Tell me you love me, Eleanor, and I'll love you in ways you'll never forget as long as you live. I'll make you cry."

"Please." She was beyond arguing. Her body throbbed, burned. She arched helplessly, her legs moving in a wild rhythm on the ground. "Keegan..."

"Say the words, baby," he breathed, toying with the zipper of her jeans. "Come on. Tell me, Ellie."

Her eyes closed. Why not? He owned her, after all. He owned her. "I love you," she whispered achingly, her eyes opening, large and dark and full of pain. "I always have. I always will."

He hesitated, his lips parting, his body shuddering as he looked down at her.

"Isn't that the price?" she whispered brokenly. She lifted her body, sliding her arms under his to press her breasts hungrily against his chest. "Oh, Lord, how sweet it feels to do that," she moaned softly. She rubbed her torso against his and felt him tremble at the silken brush of her skin. "I want you. I want all of you, right here, under the sun, I want to look up and watch you having me...."

His mind exploded. He stripped her with hands that trembled, then shrugged off his own clothing and overwhelmed her with feverish abandon.

She laughed. Laughed, as he held her down and forced his body on hers, and she matched that wild passion, every step of the way. Her eyes open, huge, blazing with the same hunger he was feeling, watched him, gloried in what he did to her with his hands, his mouth, his powerful body.

"I love you," she cried in a voice she barely recognized. Then, as the tension accelerated into something like flying, she felt her body tensing until it threatened to shatter. Her fingers dug into his back while he arched over her and ground her into the dead leaves and grass with the feverish crush of his muscular body.

"Yes, watch me," she said shakily. "Watch me!"

The leaves above them blurred and burst into color. She felt her mouth open, her body turn to liquid and burn with lightning flashes as she throbbed and throbbed and throbbed. She could hardly see his face above her.

"Eleanor," he moaned.

Her fingers trembled as they found his and locked with them. "You belong to me," she whispered.

"Oh, God, yes." His eyes closed and his head fell beside her ear, tortured breaths pulsating out of him with strangled groans as his body tensed and convulsed. "I…love…you!"

It was the passion talking, of course; she knew that, but it was so sweet to hold him, to soothe him, and know that what she'd given him he could find with no one else. For this tiny stretch of time, he was completely, wholly hers.

He trembled in her arms for a long time. And this time, there was no lazy awakening, no moving quickly away. He collapsed against her and lay breathing raggedly until she could feel his skin sticking to hers.

"Yes, hold me, Eleanor," he whispered. One lean hand came up to trace her ear, her cheek, to smooth her damp hair. Somewhere in the tree above them, birds sang sweetly. "Hold me, now."

"Are you all right?" she asked softly.

"Yes. Are you?"

She smiled against his tanned cheek. "I don't know."

He managed to raise himself enough to search her eyes. His were very blue, sated, full of secrets and adoration. Genuine adoration.

"I never stopped loving you," he whispered, kissing her shocked eyes closed. "I didn't realize that I did until it was too late, until I'd driven you away with my own confused indifference. And then I couldn't get you back. I couldn't get to you."

"You love me?" she asked uncertainly.

He lifted his head and touched her mouth softly with his. "You can ask that, after the way I just made love to you?" he whispered.

"Desire…" She faltered.

"Physical love," he corrected quietly. "Because that's what it is, between you and me. It always was, even the first time. I'll never get enough of you."

"But you let me go," she said uncertainly.

He kissed her forehead with lips that were breathlessly tender. "I had to," he said simply. "I'd managed to foul up my whole life by getting myself engaged to Lorraine. I had to force her to break the engagement, and by then you were settled in Louisville. I did write to you, but you wouldn't answer me. I couldn't blame you for that, after the way I'd treated you. But it was a damned long four years, Eleanor."

"You never were trying to make a convenience of me, were you?" she asked wonderingly. "It was this, from the beginning, from the day I came home again."

He nodded, his eyes quiet and sad. "I loved you so much, little one. And every attempt I made to come close just pushed you farther away."

"I didn't know," she said.

"Yes, I realized that. And then Wade Granger started coming around," he said curtly. "And I wanted to kill him."

"He saw through me very quickly," she confessed. "He was my best friend. He knew how I felt about you. He took me out to try and make you jealous."

"He succeeded," he said, his voice quiet. "I was terrified of losing you to him. Especially after yesterday. I lost my head once I got you in my arms in that bedroom. I couldn't have stopped to save my life. And then you said you were going to marry him...."

"He'd have been shocked," she said with a slow smile. "I'd already refused him. It was all a last-ditch attempt to save myself from you."

"And look where it got you," he mused, lifting his head to look down at their locked bodies.

She flushed. "Keegan!"

"You're not embarrassed?" he teased. "Not after the way you were with me this time?"

She swallowed. "Actually, yes, I am. And for heaven's sake, what if someone should come along?"

He sighed ruefully. "We could go inside, and do this in a bed," he said. "Or," he added with a wicked grin as he lifted himself away from her, "we could drive into town and get a marriage license."

Eleanor sat up, gaping at him as he dragged on his jeans and tossed hers over to her.

"Don't look so shocked," he murmured. "Don't you want to marry me? You'd get to sleep in my arms every night. You could even have a son or two with me, if you liked."

She was still gaping. With a resigned sigh, he stuffed her deftly back into her clothing and laughed at her shocked expression.

"A fine lot of help you are," he muttered as he pulled the knit shirt back over her taut breasts. "Shameless woman."

"I'm...speechless," she faltered. "You really want to marry me?"

"Didn't you hear what I told you while we were making love?" he asked. "I love you. What I have in mind is a lifelong affair, not a hurried roll in the hay. I want children with you, you little idiot!"

"Oh."

"Legitimate children," he emphasized. "And don't think I didn't see the way you touched your waist and grinned yesterday. You could already be pregnant. I have a feeling I'm not sterile."

She glanced at him shyly. "I may not fit into your world."

"I'll make a new one, just for us," he replied. He lifted her to her feet and framed her face with his hands. "I love you," he said fervently. "Deathlessly, with all my heart. I want to live with you until I die, and I hope we have sixty years and that when the time comes, we go down into the dark locked in each other's arms. Because I'm afraid of nothing in this world except trying to live in it without you."

Tears stung her eyes as he bent and drew her lips warmly under his. "I feel the same way," she whispered shakily. "I never stopped loving you. There could never have been anyone else. I gave you my heart, and I couldn't get it back."

"Then let's get married," he said.

She smiled. "If you're sure."

"Of course I'm sure," he murmured, smiling. "I'm getting tired of finding excuses to come down here every day. Marry me and we can stay at Flintlock and Mary June will get your breakfast."

"Who'll get Dad's?" she asked suddenly.

"We'll get him a maid of his very own," he chuckled. "Someone who'll make a good nanny as well, when we come visiting."

"Oh, darling," she whispered, lifting her arms around his neck.

"Oh, yes," he murmured, and his strong hands tugged her up against his body in a fierce embrace. "Kiss me once more, and we'll go up to the house and break the news to all concerned. I'll even call your friend Wade and tell him."

"How generous of you," she teased.

"I can afford to be generous now." He kissed her softly. "I've got the whole world in my arms."

She sighed. "I've just thought of something," she said, hesitating.

"What?"

"Darling, all our children will have freckles," she murmured.

He laughed. "Shut up and kiss me."

She was still smiling when he parted her lips with his. As she returned the kiss, Eleanor reflected that she didn't really mind the prospect of freckled children with red hair. They'd stand out in a crowd, just like their handsome redheaded father.

She remembered reading somewhere that revenge was like the eye of a tiger, seeing with narrow vision. She'd seen Keegan that way, hating him for what he'd done to her. But now it all seemed worthwhile. Her tiger had blue eyes, and although she'd never get him into a cage, she was perfectly content to run free with him. She closed her eyes, sighing softly as she touched his cheek with her left hand. In her mind, she could already see the thin gold band he would slide on her third finger, a circle of love without end.

*   *   *   *   *

APACHE DREAM BRIDE
by Joan Elliott Pickart

For Herm Harrison
Professional Football Player!
Superstar!
Hero!
But most of all...my friend.

One

The June day was so perfect, Kathy Maxwell decided, it was as though Mother Nature had reached an agreement with the Prescott Chamber of Commerce to present the small northern Arizona town at its very best.

Kathy took a deep breath of the clean, cool air, and marveled yet again at how clear the bright blue sky was at an altitude of five thousand feet. The lack of smog and exhaust fumes was just one of a multitude of reasons that made her extremely glad she'd moved to Prescott from Chicago a year ago.

"Hi, Kathy," a woman called from across the street. "Are you playing hooky this afternoon?"

Kathy laughed. "You caught me, Beth. Sally is covering the store. I'm going to the craft show on the plaza with Lily."

"Enjoy yourselves," Beth said, waving as she went into a shop.

The people here were always so friendly and warm, Kathy thought as she smiled.

She had spent several summers in Prescott with her cousin, Lily, and had loved every minute of the visits. During her last trip west, she'd found herself consumed with an ever-growing sense of dread when envisioning a return to her life in Chicago.

The violence at the inner-city school where she taught increased each year, making it necessary to spend more time attempting to maintain order in the classroom than teaching the belligerent students.

During the previous school year, she'd lost weight, developed what were diagnosed as stress headaches and had difficulty sleeping. Admitting that she was burned-out had been difficult and had given her a feeling of failure. So, she'd hightailed it to Prescott, certain that a relaxing summer with Lily in the peaceful little town would render her as good as new. But by the end of August she realized it was not to be.

Not a risk-taker, and preferring order in her life, it had taken every ounce of courage Kathy possessed to quit her teaching job just weeks before the fall term began. Gathering that courage, as well as her savings, she had made a permanent move to Prescott and opened her store, The Herb Hogan. Her longtime hobby of growing herbs and studying their various uses had provided her the means to start her own business, which was thriving.

"Kathy, I'm coming, I'm coming," a voice said, bringing Kathy from her thoughts.

She turned to see Lily waddling toward her, moving as fast as anyone who was eight months pregnant could. Her cousin was short, and very round at the moment. She had carrot red hair and a generous supply of freckles.

"Whew," Lily said, stopping next to Kathy. "I'll be so glad when this baby isn't getting free rides anymore. I swear he weighs more than the other three did, despite what the doctor says."

"You didn't have to rush. We have all afternoon to ourselves."

"What a heavenly thought," Lily said as they started down the sidewalk. "Brad was making lunch for the girls when I left the house. Oh, mercy, I don't even want to think about what my kitchen will look like when I get home. Brad is wonderful with the kids, but he's a disaster on cleanup detail." She paused. "So, tell all. How did your date with Roy go?"

Kathy wrinkled her nose. "Ask me anything you ever wanted to know about rodeos. I had a four-hour dissertation on the subject."

"Oh, dear, another dud. That's not good, not good at all."

"Lily, I'm going to say this…again. I've lost count of how many times we've discussed the subject. Are you listening?"

"No."

"Yes, you are. I'm happy in Prescott, very contented. Granted, there are adjustments to make when moving here from a large city like Chicago, but I've settled in quite nicely over the past year. This town is as close to perfection as a place can be.

"However, because it's so small, there isn't an abundance of eligible men. I've accepted that fact, and I'm aware that there's a very good chance that I'll never marry and have children. I'll spoil your kids rotten and be their eccentric spinster aunt. I'd rather live here alone than in Chicago where there were *beaucoup* men. And that, Lily Benson, is that."

"It certainly is not," Lily said with an indignant sniff. "There's a man for you in this town…somewhere. It's simply a matter of staying alert. Prescott is growing, you know. There are people moving here all the time.

"I made Brad promise to tell me if any bachelors retain him as their attorney. You've got to work on your attitude, Kathy, or you're liable to miss seeing a real hunk of stuff when he's right in front of your nose."

"Lily…"

"And," she went on, "let us not forget your many attributes, my dear. You're tall, disgustingly slender, have naturally curly blond hair, gorgeous blue eyes, and not one freckle, because I have your share. You're twenty-seven, intelligent, have your own business, adore children…. The list goes on and on. You're a super catch, Kathy Maxwell, and a fantastic man is going to come out of the ether and realize that."

Kathy rolled her eyes heavenward but kept silent, knowing it was useless to argue the subject further with her lovable and stubborn cousin.

The plaza, also called the square, was located on the main street and was a block long on each of its four sides. A majestic courthouse sat in the center, surrounded by trees and lush green grass. A charming gazebo had been built on one section of the lawn. Ongoing activities took place on the plaza, Kathy's favorites being the craft shows.

Handmade items were on display in the seemingly endless number of booths edging the grass of the square. Some of the people manning the booths were local citizens, others had come from across the country.

Kathy was slowly collecting items with Southwestern, as well as native American, themes to decorate her tiny cottage, which she adored. The one-bedroom house had a white picket fence, a tall juniper tree on one side, and a large backyard, where she grew herbs. Her home was "cozy and cute," she often told Lily, and it suited her needs perfectly.

"My stars," Lily said, "would you look at all the people on the square? What a crowd. See? I told you that Prescott is growing, and there's the evidence of it. Well, let's plough in and ogle the goodies."

"Did it ever occur to you that a majority of those folks are tourists?"

"Hush. Don't be negative. Mark my words, they live here."

"Yes, ma'am," Kathy said, laughing. "Anything you say, ma'am."

Late that night Kathy stood next to her double bed, a hammer in one hand. She cocked her head to one side, then the other, finally nodding in approval. She was delighted with the purchase she'd made at the craft show, and now it was properly placed on the wall just above her pillow.

"A Dream Catcher," she said, smiling. "I love it."

The native American creation was comprised of a three-inch circle covered in soft pink felt. Minute, taut webbing crisscrossed the interior of the circle, leaving a small hole in the center. Several felt streamers, six and eight inches long and decorated with beads and feathers, hung from the circle.

The legend of the Dream Catcher was enchanting, Kathy mused. Hung above where a person slept, the ornament would catch dreams that floated through the night air. Only good dreams would be allowed to pass through the hole in the center, while bad dreams were snared in the webbing and would perish at dawn's light.

"Pleasant dreams guaranteed," she said with a decisive nod.

She put the hammer away, locked the doors, then went to bed. She looked at the Dream Catcher once more before turning off the small lamp on the nightstand. With a sigh of contentment, she snuggled into a comfortable position.

What a lovely day it had been, she thought. As more and more time passed, she was emotionally reassured that she'd made the right decision when moving to Prescott. Her life was once again in order and her health restored. Everything was fine.

Except…

Kathy sighed. If she was totally honest with herself, she'd have to admit that she often yearned to have a special man to share with, to laugh and talk with; someone she loved and who loved her in return.

She wished to marry, have children, and still continue to nurture her growing business. She wanted it all, fairy-tale perfect, greedy person that she was. But the man, his love and the subsequent babies were missing.

She was learning to accept that fact. She refused to allow that empty place in her life to diminish her happiness and the sense of *rightness* about the choice she'd made to leave Chicago.

Who knows, she thought sleepily, maybe her Prince Charming *was* out there somewhere. He'd suddenly appear in her life and fall madly in love with her as he captured her heart.

Maybe…maybe…

Kathy drifted off to sleep.

She was standing in a field of glorious wildflowers, the vibrantly colored, fragrant blossoms dancing in the breeze as far as the eye could see. Her simple dress of pale yellow cotton fell to the tops of her bare feet. A sunbonnet covered her hair, tied loosely beneath her chin.

She was comfortable in the clothes, knew they were hers and were the proper attire for the West in 1877.

Raising one hand to shield her eyes against the brilliant sun, she stared into the distance with a sense of wondrous anticipation and excitement.

He was coming. Yes, she could see him now, racing toward her on his gleaming horse. Closer and closer he came, becoming clearer with every rapid beat of her heart.

Bronzed and beautiful, he rode bareback, clad only in buckskin pants and moccasins. His broad, tawny, muscled chest was glistening, his shoulder-length hair shining like ebony. His eyes were as dark as a raven's wing, and his features were bold, rough-hewn, with high cheekbones that were further evidence of his Indian heritage.

This was her love, her magnificent brave; proud, strong, riding like the wind, and coming to her, only her. He pulled the horse to a stop and dropped to the ground, striding toward her with sensual grace.

She opened her arms to receive him into her embrace.

"Hurry," she whispered. "Oh, please hurry, my love."

He was one step away, reaching for her, desire radiating from the depths of his obsidian eyes.

Then...

Kathy jolted upward in bed, her heart pounding. She heard the insistent shrill of the alarm clock and smacked it off.

"Blast," she said aloud. "I missed the best part of my wonderful dream."

She looked over her shoulder, intent on glaring at the Dream Catcher for not poking the dream through the hole earlier so it wouldn't have been cut short by the rude ringing of the alarm.

But the Dream Catcher wasn't there.

"Darn it," Kathy said, tossing back the blankets and leaving the bed.

She was certain she'd secured it firmly with a nail tucked through the loop at the top. Apparently, though, both nail and Dream Catcher had fallen to the floor during the night.

"That's strange," she said, seeing the nail still in the wall.

Kathy dropped to her knees and peered under the bed, discovering only a few dust bunnies. Rising, she slid her hand between the mattress and the wall. Nothing.

Where on earth had the Dream Catcher disappeared to?

"Coffee," she mumbled, starting toward the door. "Coffee, then a more thorough search."

She yawned just as she reached the foot of the bed, then stopped, statue-still. Her mouth remained opened from the now-forgotten yawn and her eyes widened. A strange squeak escaped from her throat, and she snapped her mouth closed. The sound of her frantically beating heart echoed in her ears.

The missing Dream Catcher was on the floor between the bed and the wall.

But it was no longer three inches around. It was six feet across!

And there, caught half in and half out of the center hole, lying on the carpet with his eyes closed, was the Indian brave from her dream!

Her trembling legs refused to hold her for another instant, and Kathy sank onto the edge of the bed, her horrified gaze riveted on the enormous Dream Catcher and the man caught in the webbing. He hadn't moved. The steady rise and fall of his chest were the only indication that he was even alive.

No, Kathy thought frantically, he *wasn't* alive. Well, he wasn't dead, either. But he was most definitely not alive in the sense that he was actually there in her bedroom. That was ridiculous. Impossible. Absurd.

Kathy jumped to her feet, stomped back to the head of the bed, then yanked her Mickey Mouse T-shirt straight over her bikini panties. After getting into bed, she pulled the blankets up to her chin and squeezed her eyes tightly closed.

That Indian, she told herself, that absolutely gorgeous-beyond-belief man, was *not* in her bedroom because she was still asleep and dreaming. It was one of the most wide-awake-seeming dreams she'd ever had, but it was a dream, nonetheless. The alarm would go off at any moment now and she'd begin her daily routine on a perfectly normal Monday morning. Fine.

Several minutes passed as Kathy stayed ramrod stiff under the covers. Then she very tentatively opened one eye to sneak a peek at the clock.

"Oh, dear heaven," she said, with a near-sob.

It was long past time for the alarm to ring *because it had already rung!*

She was awake. *She was honest-to-goodness awake.* The empty nail on the wall above her head seemed to scream at her that the pretty little three-inch Dream Catcher was no longer *there,* because it was now six feet around and holding fast to the most magnificent man she had ever seen.

Kathy Maxwell, she admonished herself, stop it. Just cut it out. This was *not* really happening, because things like this *didn't* really happen. There was a perfectly reasonable explanation for this nonsense, but, oh, mercy, she wished she knew what it was.

She eased herself slowly upward, hardly breathing, then crawled on her hands and knees toward the end of the bed.

There was, Kathy told herself, nothing on that floor but a section of brown carpet that needed vacuuming.

As she came to the foot of the bed, she closed her eyes, causing her to nearly fall off the end.

Slowly, very slowly, she opened her eyes. At that exact same moment, the Indian opened *his* eyes and looked directly at her.

"Aaak!" Kathy screamed.

She scrambled off the side of the bed and came to a stop at the man's feet. He turned his head to stare at her, a frown knitting his dark brows.

"Oh. No. Oh, dear," Kathy said in a voice that was more of a whimper. She hopped from one foot to the other, wringing her hands. "No, no, no."

"A death dance?" the Indian said. "I'm dead. So be it."

Kathy stopped in mid-hop, and leaned slightly forward. "My goodness, you have a marvelous voice. It's so deep and rich. Well, that figures. You're a big man and your voice is exactly right for your size. I suppose your tan is natural, what with your being a native American and... No! I'm not talking to you. I refuse to say another word, because you're not really here. Are you getting this, mister?"

"I'm dead," he said, then sighed. "I thought I had lived my life with honor befitting a Chiricahua Apache, but apparently I have angered the gods. I have been sentenced to spend my eternal beyond with a shrieking witch-woman."

Kathy planted her hands on her hips and narrowed her eyes. "That was very rude. I am *not* a shrieking witch-woman, for Pete's sake.

How would you feel if your Dream Catcher grew from three inches to six feet and plopped a guy from *your* dream on the floor in your bedroom? Huh? Answer that one. You'd be shook up, too.''

"Dream Catcher?" he repeated, glancing at the apparatus surrounding him. "Yes, this is a Dream Catcher, but I have never seen one this large. Why am I being held captive in this enormous Dream Catcher?"

"Beats me," Kathy said, shrugging. She giggled, realizing at once that there was a hysterical edge to the sound. She pressed one hand to her forehead. "No fever. Drat. But, darn it, this is *not* happening. It just can't be.''

The Indian began to shift, struggling to escape from the tight webbing surrounding the center circle where he was held fast.

"Don't you move," Kathy said. "I'm warning you, I'll call the police, and the sheriff, and the fire department, and...and... I mean it, you stay right there.''

The Indian glowered at her and continued to wrestle with the Dream Catcher. Kathy inched backward until she thudded against the wall, then wrapped her hands around her elbows in a protective gesture.

She watched with wide eyes as the man worked his way free.

One part of her exhausted brain was terrified at the thought of what he might do to her.

Another section of her frazzled mind was mesmerized by the intriguingly sensuous and blatantly masculine play of the bunching muscles beneath his taut, tawny skin.

Yet another piece of her mind continued to deny that this bizarre scenario was taking place.

"Mmm," the Indian said as he accomplished his goal. He rolled to his feet in a smooth, graceful motion, standing close to six feet tall.

"Don't kill me," Kathy said, her voice trembling. "Don't scalp me. Don't do anything, except go away." She flapped her hands at him. "Shoo. Be gone. Disappear. Right now.''

"Woman," he said gruffly, crossing his arms over his broad chest, "you talk too much. I must be dead. There's no other explanation for this. Unless..." He narrowed his eyes. "It is possible, although I seriously doubt it, that you possess magical powers that you combined with those of the Dream Catcher. Indian legends and folklore should not be tampered with. Not ever.''

Kathy shook her head. "I don't have any magical abilities. And I certainly didn't tamper with the powers of the Dream Catcher." She paused. "I hung the Dream Catcher above my bed, deciding its legend was enchanting. Then just before I fell asleep I was thinking about how wonderful it would be if a special man... I had a dream about... Oh, dear heaven. No, forget it. This whole thing is impossible.''

"I agree. Therefore, I am definitely dead.''

"No," she said, sighing, "you're not dead. I can't explain this. I don't really believe it, but...I wish you'd crawl back into that Dream Catcher and transport yourself to 1877 where you belong.''

"If I am not dead, if I am actually here, I would prefer not to be. But I do not possess the power to command a Dream Catcher." He shook his head. "No, I refuse to believe this is happening.''

Kathy inched her way carefully around him to sink onto the edge of the bed.

"Look," she said, "we agree that this really isn't taking place, but repeating over and over that it can't be true isn't getting us anywhere. Let's just stop for a minute and take the approach that it *did* happen. That's probably very foolish, but I'm getting a tad desperate here.''

The Indian shrugged. "It *is* foolish, but I do not have a better idea right now.''

"Fine. We'll just calm down and discuss this like mature adults. I suppose I should introduce myself. I'm Kathy Maxwell. Do you have a name?''

"Dakota.''

"Dakota what?''

"Dakota what?" he repeated, obviously confused.

"Don't you have a last name? Two names?''

"One man. One name.''

"Oh, well, that's reasonable, I guess, considering the fact that no one in your tribe would be putting together a telephone book.''

"Pardon me?''

"Never mind. Dakota, this is not 1877. It's 125 years later than that, give or take a handful.''

"That is ridiculous."

"I know, but for now we're pretending that it isn't ridiculous. Okay? Do you remember what you were doing before you woke up here?"

He nodded. "I was riding my horse on open land. There were wild-flowers in all directions. My thoughts were—" He stopped speaking and frowned. "An Indian brave deals with his own problems, solves them privately."

"Dakota, please," Kathy said gently, "I understand and respect that, I truly do, because I often keep troubling things within myself, too. But this is so important. Share with me, tell me what you were thinking as you rode through the wildflowers. Your inner feelings are safe with me, Dakota."

He stared at her for a long moment, and she met his gaze directly, aware that he was weighing and measuring, deciding if he would do as she'd asked.

"Yes, all right," he said with a weary-sounding sigh. "I was dwelling on the condition of my life, the emptiness of it, the loneliness. My people have all gone to the reservation, but I chose not to go, not to be penned up like an animal. I could not survive like that, and I knew I had to stay behind. Yet at that moment, I was wishing I had a place to belong, somewhere I could call home."

"Oh, Dakota," Kathy said, hearing the pain in his voice, "I'm so sorry."

He cleared his throat. "My thoughts were interrupted as I saw a woman standing in the distance. A white woman. I did not know her, but then...I *did* know her. I was going to her, she was waiting for me. This does not make sense, because I would never approach a white woman."

Kathy got to her feet. "Yes, it *does* make sense, because that was my dream. Oh, my gosh, Dakota, don't you see what this means? I somehow connected to your airwaves, or brain waves, or something. That was *me* standing there in that yellow dress. Do you understand?"

"Then you *did* tamper with the powers of the Dream Catcher."

"Not intentionally. I bought it at a craft show because I thought it was pretty and I liked the legend it represented. Dakota, I hate to say this, but I think we'd better start accepting the fact that you really were transported through time in the Dream Catcher.''

"I do not know, I just do not know. How is it that you speak Apache?''

"I don't. I'm speaking English and so are you.''

"No. I know only my native tongue.''

Kathy threw up her hands. "This is more evidence that this whole thing is true. We're both talking in our own language, but we can understand each other. That must be part of the Dream Catcher's power.''

"I will have to think about this,'' Dakota said, shaking his head. "I speak so you can understand me in this era, yet I wear my own clothing.'' His gaze slid over the soft T-shirt Kathy wore. It clearly outlined the swell of her breasts. "Is that your usual attire? Is that an image of the god you worship?''

For the first time since the bizarre beginning of the morning, Kathy became acutely aware of her scanty attire. The Indian's dark eyes seemed to be peering through her shirt, scrutinizing her bare breasts beneath.

She could feel the heat from his penetrating gaze. It touched a place deep and low within her, churning, swirling, causing a flush to stain her cheeks. She was pinned in place, unable to move, having to remind herself to breathe.

This man, she thought hazily, was real. He was there. Denying his existence was foolhardy. There was no lingering doubt in her mind that he had been flung through time and space to arrive in the present from the past.

She had somehow managed to dream about a living, human being, rather than a creation of her imagination. The potent powers of the Dream Catcher had then captured him and brought him to her.

But why?

The magnitude of what had taken place was too enormous, too overwhelming, to be chalked up to some weird cosmic glitch.

Why had this happened to her and Dakota?

"Kathy?''

"What? Oh, my clothes. I don't go outside like this. I wear this to sleep in, that's all."

"And that image? Is that who you worship?"

"Heavens no," she said. "That's Mickey. He's not a god, he's a mouse." She paused. "Dakota, the only way that I can deal with all of this is to accept the facts as they stand and give it all a semblance of reality, even if it's not reasonable reality. Oh, dear, I'm not making sense. What I'm saying is, until I have just cause to change my mind, I'm going to believe you were transported from 1877 to now through the Dream Catcher."

"You have the right to do what you wish."

"And you? What do *you* believe is happening here?"

Dakota sighed. "I do not want to believe it. There's no purpose to my being here. Yes, I was feeling lonely, alone, but there's no life for me here in the future, in the white man's world. I do not belong here, Kathy."

"We don't know that, Dakota. If we accept this scenario as being the truth, as being what actually happened, then we have to move on to the question of *why* it occurred."

"The why is because you tampered with the powers of the Dream Catcher. The question is not why, it is how. How do we send me back to my own time? I don't want to be here, Kathy, and I have no intention of staying."

"Dakota," she said quietly, "maybe there is something important that you're supposed to do here. Yes, all right, to be fair to you we should be trying to figure out how to send you back. But I truly believe we should also be considering the question of why you are here, what it all means."

"Mmm," he said, frowning.

"Will you think about both issues? Please, Dakota?"

He stared at her for a long moment before answering.

"Yes," he said finally, "I will think about both. That will enable me to postpone, at least for a while, the bleak thought that we may never know the answer to either of those questions. We may *never* know."

Two

Why?

The question beat against Kathy in time with the water from the shower.

Perhaps she was placing too much emphasis on that question, adding to the situation further complexity that didn't need to be there.

It could very well be that it was all a fluke, an unexplainable event that had been created by the powers of the Dream Catcher. There was no mysterious, hidden meaning and purpose to discover. It had simply happened.

The magic of the Dream Catcher had interwoven with the thoughts she'd had just before falling asleep of wishing for a special man in her life. She'd dwelled on what was missing from her life, rather than counting the blessings that she had. Her musings had created the dream of seeing Dakota in the field of wildflowers.

Back in time Dakota had been thinking similar thoughts, acknowledging his loneliness, yearning for a place to belong, a home that was once again his.

Like a silken thread from a tapestry, the Dream Catcher had woven through her dream and onto Dakota's thoughts, pulling them together, uniting them.

But why?

Oh, darn it, Kathy thought as she dried herself with a fluffy towel. She couldn't seem to move past believing that there was an important and definite reason for what had happened.

She stopped for a moment and stared at the bathroom door.

What if she'd imagined the whole thing? She'd return to her bedroom, the pretty little Dream Catcher would be hanging on the wall and there would be no Dakota, because he didn't exist.

What was more terrifying? That Dakota was really there, or that he wasn't, meaning she was slowly but surely losing her mind?

"Fine, Kathy," she muttered, "ask yourself some more questions to boggle your brain."

Dakota. If he was real, truly there, she was going to have to be very, very careful. For that one brief moment he'd had an unsettling effect on her. Man to woman. Like nothing she'd ever experienced before.

That was not going to happen again.

Dakota stood in Kathy's bedroom, his eyes darting around. He felt claustrophobic in the small space and had to draw on inner strengths to keep from finding the way to the outdoors as quickly as possible. Even the windows were covered in some sort of hard, clear substance that he could see through, but which sealed the room further.

He moved to the end of the bed to stare at the giant Dream Catcher where it lay on the floor, a frown on his face.

The powers of a Dream Catcher were well known and respected by his people. He had, indeed, been carried far into the future to a place like none he'd seen before and was held captive there.

He dragged both hands down his face, then shook his head.

No, he didn't want to believe that, because he did *not* want to be here. This was the white man's world that offered him nothing but danger and a lack of acceptance. He would be feared and, therefore, hated.

Dakota laughed, the sound harsh and short, having a bitter ring to it.

It was no different for him in his own time. He faced danger at every turn from the soldiers who sought him. Indians of all tribes were feared and, thus, hated for the color of their skin and the way they chose to live their lives.

He had told Kathy Maxwell that he wanted to go back to where he belonged. Belonged? He belonged nowhere, as everything he had possessed had been taken away and was no longer his to have.

The white people were greedy and cruel. They'd claimed the Apache land for their own, sending the Indians to reservations like penned animals.

But he hadn't gone. Not Dakota. For many, many moons now, he'd been alone, roaming the land, hiding whenever he saw soldiers riding near. He'd not spoken to another living being in a very long time.

Until Kathy.

She was the first white woman he'd seen up close, and he'd been startled by the blue of her eyes. It was as though the gods had given her pieces of sky to see with. Pretty eyes. Eyes like the sky, hair like the sun. *Very* pretty. She would give a man fine sons.

Kathy.

Her name was moving easier through his mind now; and did not seem quite so strange. When he first beheld her, looked at all of who she was, which was the custom of his people, he had felt the shaft of heat streak within his body to coil low and tight. He'd wanted to join with her, man and woman.

That thought *must* be ignored. The matter of importance was to find a way to have the Dream Catcher send him back to where he'd come from. It was lonely and empty there, but at least he knew it for what it was.

Dakota narrowed his eyes as he stared at the Dream Catcher, willing it to speak to his mind, give him the answers he needed.

But the Dream Catcher was silent.

His attention was drawn to the carpet, and he hunkered down, running one hand over it.

How did Kathy grow soft, brown grass in her house? What manner of soil had she packed hard for her floor to have produced this crop of vegetation?

He placed his hands on his thighs and pushed himself upward to stand staring at the Dream Catcher again.

"Dakota?"

He spun around at the sound of his name being spoken in a quiet voice.

He saw Kathy in the doorway, wearing a red shirt of some sort, and man-pants of dark blue. She'd painted her mouth with light red, and her short, sun-colored hair was damp, curling over her head and brushing her pale cheeks.

The heat of desire rocketed through him again. Was she casting a spell over him, causing him to lose control of his basic needs, the command of himself, that he took great pride in?

"Are you all right?" Kathy asked.

"Yes, I'm all right."

"While I was dressing I thought perhaps I'd imagined—" she swept one arm through the air "—all of this, you, the huge Dream Catcher. But what has happened to us is true. You *are* here, Dakota, and we have no choice but to deal with that fact."

"Mmm."

Kathy sighed. "I'm exhausted. The day has hardly begun and I'm so tired. This has been a very draining experience. I... Oh, my gosh, I have to get to work. I'm going to be late opening the store."

She started from the bedroom, then halted her step, turning to face him again.

"I can't leave you alone all day," she said. "There are too many things here that would be new to you and you might hurt yourself. Besides, we need to concentrate on finding a solution to this...this mess. I'll call Sally and ask her to cover the store."

She hurried into the living room and telephoned Sally, who cheerfully agreed to run The Herb Hogan.

"I'll be fine tomorrow," Kathy said. "I don't feel well because...because my allergies are bothering me."

"I didn't know you had allergy problems," Sally said.

"I didn't, either. Life is full of little surprises," Kathy said. And six-feet-tall surprises, too.

"We have herbs for helping allergies, Kathy."

"Oh, yes, of course. Silly me. I forgot. I'll probably come into the store later and fix myself up as good as new. Thanks for covering on short notice. Bye.''

As Kathy replaced the receiver she turned to see Dakota standing in the doorway.

"Where is your man?" he said.

Kathy blinked. "My man? I don't have one."

"He died?"

"No, I've never been married. In this time era, women often live alone."

"Then who protects you? Feeds you? Makes a home for you?"

"*I* do," she said, splaying one hand on her chest. "I take care of myself."

"That's not the natural order of men and women. Women do not have the skills or strength to do men's work. Wearing man-pants won't help you achieve what you are not capable of doing."

"Man-pants? Oh, you mean my jeans. It's appropriate for women to wear...well, man-pants. These," she went on, lifting one foot, "are tennis shoes. They come in all colors. I have on white ones, but I own a blue pair, a red pair, a... Never mind. I have a feeling you don't give a hoot about tennis shoes."

Dakota shrugged.

"You're positive you feel all right?" Kathy said. "It occurs to me that it might be very hard on a person to be hurled through time."

"I'm fine, except for being hungry."

"You need some food? Well, all right. Maybe if we do something ordinary like having breakfast we'll be able to approach this whole thing more calmly. Yes, that's a good idea. When in doubt...eat."

In the kitchen, Kathy immediately decided that if she attempted to explain to Dakota what a stove, refrigerator and microwave were, they'd never get around to eating. For now, she'd just let him be totally confused about all the paraphernalia.

She opened the refrigerator and removed bacon, a carton of eggs and a quart of milk. A few minutes later, the bacon was sizzling in a frying pan as she wire-whipped eggs and milk in a bowl.

Out of the corner of her eye, she saw Dakota tentatively touching things, sometimes leaning forward for a closer look, before moving on to the next item that beckoned.

This kitchen, Kathy thought, was too small. Well, that wasn't exactly true. It wasn't big enough when she was sharing it with Dakota. There was more than just his size causing her to feel suddenly crowded and unsettled, it was also the aura of masculinity emanating from him. His raw, earthy, male essence was sensuously overwhelming.

She was acutely aware of her own femininity to the point that her skin tingled. Dakota was man. She was woman. Those facts should be nothing more than simple data. But it *wasn't* simple for some mysterious reason.

No, she'd covered that topic while she was getting dressed. She was not going to fall prey to Dakota's male magnetism. He wasn't a man, he was a problem to be solved.

With a sigh, Kathy forked the bacon onto a pad of paper towels, drained the majority of the grease into a coffee can at the back of the stove, then poured the frothy egg mixture into the pan. Staring off into space she stirred the eggs in a steady rhythm with a slotted spoon.

A problem? Oh, dear, that was putting it mildly. She wished she could decide that this whole scenario couldn't possibly have taken place and, therefore, it hadn't. But she'd run out of ways to attempt to convince herself that it wasn't true. Dakota was most definitely there.

"Smoke," Dakota said, from where he stood behind her.

"What?" Kathy said. "Oh, my gosh, I've burned the eggs."

She quickly lifted the frying pan to another burner on the stove, muttering under her breath as she vigorously stirred the eggs.

"Woman," Dakota said, "you don't cook well. I think perhaps you've spent too much time trying to do men's work and have neglected learning how to properly perform your duties."

"That's great, just dandy," she said, glaring at him. "I have a 1877 chauvinist on my hands. So, okay, this meal is a disaster, but I'm not my usual organized self this morning. This *is not* the way I ordinarily start my day. Got that? And don't call me 'woman'."

"You *are* a woman."

"I realize that, but the way you say it is demeaning. My name is

Kathy.'' She paused. ''Oh, Dakota, I'm sorry. I didn't mean to be so cross with you. I'm upset by all that's happened. Let's take a deep breath and eat breakfast, such as it is.''

She carried the meal to the table. Dakota followed her and stared at a chair. He watched Kathy settle onto one, then splayed a hand on the seat, pressing down on the smooth wood to determine its strength.

''It will hold your weight,'' Kathy said. ''Trust me.''

Dakota eased himself onto the chair, his muscles tensed should he find it necessary to move away quickly. A few minutes later he relaxed and scrutinized the offering on his plate.

The bacon was crisp, but the eggs were burned in spots and runny in others. He looked at Kathy, and watched in fascination as she shoveled eggs onto a fork.

''What is that tool?'' he said.

''This? It's a fork.'' She poked it into her mouth, pulled it back out empty of eggs, then chewed and swallowed. ''See? It's a way of getting the food where it needs to go. Try it.''

He wrapped one large hand around the fork handle, jammed the prongs into the eggs, then jerked his hand upward, spilling the contents.

''Slowly, Dakota, gently. Try it again.''

''Mmm,'' he said, glaring at her.

Kathy smiled as she watched him attempt to master the strange tool called a fork. He moved cautiously this time, and she could see him assessing the challenge with intelligence and determination. Yet, there was also an endearing, little-boy quality to the scene that caused a warm, fuzzy feeling to tiptoe around her heart.

''You did it,'' she said, clapping her hands as Dakota chewed a delivered forkful of eggs.

He swallowed, then frowned. ''This tastes terrible.''

Kathy shrugged. ''If you don't like it, don't eat it. It's up to you.''

''I need the nourishment. Bad cooking is better than nothing, I suppose.''

''Don't push me, Dakota.''

''Push you?'' he said, looking directly into her eyes. ''I would never harm you, Kathy. I am an Apache. I respect women, I respect you. I wouldn't push you, beat you or strike out at you.''

"Oh, I didn't mean…''

"If you have your nose split someday, it would be by your choice.''

"Pardon me?''

"An Apache woman who commits adultery has her nose split so everyone will know what she has done, that she was not true to her man.''

"That's gross. Just eat the awful eggs.''

They finished the meal in silence, each lost in their own thoughts.

"Dakota,'' Kathy finally said, "do you have any knowledge, understanding at all, of how to get the Dream Catcher to reverse what it did?''

"No.''

"Great,'' she said with a sigh. "What if I have to actually dream about sending you back to where you belong? That would be impossible. A person can't dictate to their subconscious like that.'' She paused. "What if we both sat on the floor by the Dream Catcher and concentrated on the same message? You know, kept mentally repeating 'Send Dakota back to 1877.'''

Dakota shrugged.

"Do you want to try it?''

"The idea has merit,'' he said, nodding. "I must heed nature's call first.'' He got to his feet.

"Wait,'' she said, jumping up. "I have to explain about bathrooms and… This is so bizarre. Oh, well, come on. I've got a nifty little room to show you.''

Two hours later, Kathy flopped back onto the living room carpet and closed her eyes.

"I'm exhausted,'' she said. "Brain dead. I can't concentrate anymore. We've been sitting on the floor forever next to this giant menace, and it's not working.''

"No, it's not,'' Dakota said. "This plan is not the answer.''

Kathy got to her feet, then slouched onto the sofa. "Now what?''

"I don't know.''

"Dakota, are there people worried about your disappearance. I mean, do you have a family? A...a wife? You said that you were riding alone through the wildflowers but..."

"I don't have a wife. I have no one now," he said quietly. "My people have gone to the white man's reservation. I refused to go. I have been alone for many moons."

Kathy straightened to look directly at him. "I'm sorry. You're from 1877. Yes, I'm remembering my history. The Indians in this area were moved to reservations around 1875. Someone who wouldn't go was called a Bronco Apache, meaning one who is alone, no longer a part of a tribe." She paused. "I can only imagine what it has been like for you, Dakota. The image in my mind is so stark and empty. An existence of such chilling loneliness."

Dakota stared at the Dream Catcher, but didn't reply.

"Maybe I'm wrong," she said. "I'm viewing it from how I'd feel. You were having thoughts about loneliness, but on the whole you may have been perfectly happy living like that. You might not need other people."

"My body can survive if I am alone, but my spirit suffers. A man who is truly a man is complete enough within himself to have room for others. There's an emptiness in solitude that goes on for too long. I have needs, Kathy. I have needs."

He turned his head slowly to meet her gaze.

I have needs, Kathy.

His words echoed in her ears and a reply was whispered again and again from her heart. *I have needs, too, Dakota.*

Dakota nodded slowly, and Kathy registered a flash of panic, suddenly wondering if he could read her mind. If not, then what blatant message of desire was radiating from her eyes and visible on her face?

She felt stripped bare, vulnerable, with no defenses against the potent masculinity of this man.

I have needs, Kathy.

And wants? she thought. Was he as aware of her as a woman as she was of him as a man? Or did he see her as nothing more than an annoying product of the powers of the Dream Catcher?

Oh, Kathy, stop it, she admonished herself. What Dakota did, or did not, think of her was not important. Her reactions to him as a man meant nothing, would not be allowed to mean anything. No.

She had concentrated as hard as she could as they'd sat by the Dream Catcher, sending their mutual message that Dakota be transported back to 1877. She'd tried her best.

Or had she? she now wondered.

Had she held something back from the focus of her thoughts? Had the tiny portion of her heart that didn't want him to leave...not yet, please, not yet...been more powerful than the truth of what must be done?

Oh, she didn't know. She was confused, tired, excited, frightened, all in one jumbled maze.

She had *so many* questions with no answers.

Three

———

Dakota suddenly rolled to his feet, startling Kathy back to attention.

"The Dream Catcher," he said, "must be kept in a safe place. I don't want to stay here, in this world, and if anything happens to the Dream Catcher, I'll have no hope of returning to my own time."

"We can slide it under my bed," Kathy said, pushing herself off the sofa.

"Fine."

Kathy stopped and looked directly at him. "I realize that this whole scenario is overwhelming. Your traveling through time, and encountering all the new and strange things that you've never seen before, must be very unsettling. Even so, I can't help but wonder if you've considered staying here."

"No."

"Dakota, what would you be going back to, other than loneliness and danger? Do you really want to spend the rest of your life on the run, hiding from the soldiers, never able to settle in one place?"

He splayed one hand on his chest. "*I* didn't choose the way of my existence, it was the white man's doing. The choice I *did* make was not to go to the reservation with my people. I'm prepared to live with the consequences of that decision."

"But you don't have to, don't you see? You'd be accepted here, judged only by who you are as a man, not by your heritage. Oh, Dakota, you've said yourself that the Dream Catcher has great powers. Couldn't it be possible that you were *meant* to be here for some reason?"

"Such as? Do your people need to be taught how to live off the land, fish and hunt for their food, build shelters to live in?"

"Well, no, but..."

Dakota shook his head. "Then the Dream Catcher has no purpose for my being here."

"You don't know that to be true."

"Kathy, there's no point in discussing this any further. I intend to do everything possible to enable me to go back to 1877."

"But..."

"That is enough! Let's put the Dream Catcher under the bed."

Kathy sighed, then they carried the Dream Catcher into the bedroom and carefully maneuvered it beneath the bed.

Back in the living room, Dakota folded his arms across his chest and frowned as he looked at Kathy.

"There's something disturbing me that I cannot put to rest," he said. "Why are you alone? Is there something about you that doesn't please the men of this time? I beheld you, which is Apache custom. I have seen you on the outer side and sensed who you are within. You please *me,* Kathy Maxwell. I would give serious thought to making you my woman."

"I..." Kathy started to reply, then snapped her mouth closed as she realized she had no idea what to say.

A strange warmth swept through her as Dakota's words echoed in her mind. What he had said was one of the most exciting, yet frightening, things she had ever heard. *Dakota's woman.*

Oh, stop. She wasn't going to dwell on it a second longer. Dakota was simply curious about the customs and social structure of this era.

You please me, Kathy Maxwell.

Kathy, she scolded herself, just cut it out right this second.

"Well, you see, Dakota," she said, wishing her voice was steadier, "choosing a life's partner is much more complicated now. It's done more slowly, carefully. I have to be as pleased, as you put it, with the man as he is with me. Just looking at someone, beholding them, isn't enough.''

''Why not?''

''Because there are discoveries to be made first.''

''Such as?''

''Well, values. You know, your stand on truth, trust, fidelity. Then there's stuff like what do we have in common? How do you spend your leisure time? How do you feel about security, a home, children, a woman who has her own business and wouldn't give it up for the world? Then there's... Oh, good night, you aren't really interested in all of this, are you?''

He nodded. ''It fascinates me. You've listed what people in this time must discover about each other, and most of it is reasonable.'' He paused. ''No man has pleased you as you made these discoveries?''

Kathy shrugged. ''No. Emotions come into play here, too, you know. There has to be love that is real and rich and deep. But, no, I haven't found the man I want to spend my life with.''

''*I* please you.''

Kathy blinked. ''I beg your pardon?''

''You beheld me. I can tell from what I've seen in your eyes that you desire me. You have had thoughts of joining with me, man to woman.''

A flush of embarrassment heated Kathy's cheeks. ''Well... um...you're a very handsome, well-built man, Dakota. I'm a healthy, normal woman who... Oh, for Pete's sake, this is ridiculous.''

''No, it isn't,'' he said, shaking his head. ''I did not ask to come here and I do not intend to remain. However, while I'm here I wish to understand this world. To learn and enrich my mind. A man who isn't constantly attempting to add to his knowledge is lazy, worthless. You have customs that are new to me, things you can teach me during my stay.''

''But what if when you go back you don't even remember having been here?''

''So be it. It's important that I live for the moment I am in. That's the Apache way. Each beat of our heart is to be cherished.

"Apaches also pride ourselves on our patience. If we encounter an enemy who outnumbers us and it would mean certain death to engage them in battle, we withdraw to fight another day when we will be assured of a victory. That isn't cowardly, it is wise. We place high value on life, living. We don't treat lightly the gift of the body we were given to walk the earth in."

"That's a lovely philosophy," she said quietly. "People in this time era could use some of that kind of common sense."

"I haven't betrayed the Apache way," Dakota went on, "but I've had to struggle to maintain my patience. My people were robbed of their land, their way of life. They were herded like animals to the reservation, never again to be free. Patience will change nothing."

"I'm so sorry about what was done to the Indians back then. I've only read about it, but I realize you're suffering the pain of it right now."

"I've been alone these many moons," he said, his voice gritty, "and questions with no answers have plagued me. Now I've been brought here where I don't wish to be, but at least I can ask questions and have them answered. I can learn.

"I am a man, Kathy, a proud Apache brave. All I wanted was a place, a home, a sense of self and worth. I wanted a woman of my heart and sons of my seed. The white man hasn't killed my body. *I won't let them crush my spirit.*"

Tears filled Kathy's eyes as she heard the raw emotion in Dakota's voice, saw it on his face and in the depth of his expressive dark eyes. Before she'd realized she had moved, she had wrapped her arms tightly around his waist and rested her head on his chest.

"No one is going to crush your spirit," she said, tears echoing in her voice. "We won't let them, Dakota. *We won't.* I'll teach you whatever you want to know about this era, if that's what you want, if that will make you feel better about being here."

Dakota encircled Kathy with his arms, then buried his face in the soft tumble of her curls, savoring the fragrance of flowers.

"We haven't solved the mystery of the Dream Catcher's powers," he said. "We don't yet understand the Dream Catcher's spirit call to enable us to send me back. So while I'm here we will live for the moment we hold in our hands.''

Dakota's words echoed in Kathy's mind as she stayed nestled against his warm, massive body. He felt wonderful, smelled wonderful. Being held in his strong arms was wonderful. Desire was beginning to churn hot and low within her.

But there was more than basic physical yearnings involved. Dakota was touching an emotional place deep within her that she hadn't even known existed. She was beginning to feel connected, bonded to him. She had *felt* his pain as he'd spoken of what had been done to his people. The chill of his loneliness as he'd roamed the land alone was an icy fist within *her*.

While I am here, we will live for the moment we hold in our hands.

Did she have the courage to actually do that? Could she live for the moment, treasure what they might share, then be prepared to let him go? How long would she ache for him when he was gone? How long would she cry?

Oh, she couldn't think straight. Too much was happening so quickly that she was off kilter and terribly confused. She was going to put her emotional turmoil on hold, she had to.

Dakota inhaled Kathy's feminine aroma once more, then moved her gently away from him.

''What discovery do you want to make first?'' he said.

Kathy laughed in spite of herself. ''You make this sound like research for a term paper.''

''A what?''

''Never mind. I'm such a wreck that a dose of practical thinking is called for. Therefore, we'll shift our focus. You need some clothes.''

''I have clothes.''

''Yes, but you don't have a shirt. Men in this era are free to go without a shirt, but not all of the time. You need a shirt.''

He shrugged.

''So, I'm going shopping and buy you a shirt. I'll get you some jeans, too. Man-pants. Do you shave?''

''What?''

''Do you grow hair on your face that you cut off each day?''

"No," he said slowly. "Kathy, are you talking nonsense?"

"No. White men grow hair on their faces. I've read that most Indians don't, and I guess it's true. Okay. Cancel the shaving cream and razor. Do you—" she paused, feeling the now-familiar warm flush creep onto her cheeks "—use underwear?"

"I don't know the meaning of that word."

Dandy. Go for it, Kathy. "Do you have anything on beneath your pants?"

Dakota frowned. "For what purpose? Do white men wear pants under their pants?"

"Well, yes."

"Strange. No, I don't have this underwear you speak of."

"Good. I've never bought Jockey shorts in my life. Dakota, listen to me. You must promise that you'll stay inside the house while I'm gone. You can't go wandering around until I think of a way to explain who you are and why you're here."

"I need to breathe fresh air. The walls are closing in on me."

"Oh, dear. Well, all right. Let's go into the backyard and have a stroll. I'll show you my herb garden. Then will you be able to stay inside while I go shopping?"

"Shopping is what you do to get me a shirt?"

"Bingo. I mean, yes, that's correct."

He nodded. "I'll agree to your plan. We'll see your herb garden now."

They left the living room, went through the kitchen, then Kathy stopped on the enclosed sun porch beyond.

"This is where I dry my herbs," she said, sweeping one arm in the air.

Dakota looked at the multitude of plants covering the walls of the sun porch. Kathy had designed, then hired a handyman to build, the drying walls with pegs where she hung the herbs, utilizing every spare inch of space.

"I can't grow everything I need for the store," she said, "but I'm pleased with what I'm able to add to the inventory myself. I get most of my teas from a woman in Sedona, and the oils and lotions from Flagstaff. I also sell commercial vitamins.

"I dry the herbs here, then put them in brown paper bags because they must be kept in a dark, dry place. I take the bags to The Herb Hogan. That's the name of my store."

"It's good," Dakota said, nodding. "You've tended to your herbs as it should be done. No Apache woman could do better."

"Oh, well," she said, smiling, "thank you. That was a very nice compliment."

She was pleased to the point of ridiculous by what Dakota had said. It shouldn't matter what he thought of her talents, but the warm, fuzzy feeling she was registering was evidence that it did. She was as adept as an Apache woman would be at growing and caring for herbs? Goodness, wasn't that something?

Dakota continued to scrutinize the herbs, then finally nodded again.

"Are you ready to go outside?" Kathy said.

Dakota started toward the door, then stopped, looking through the window.

"No. It's too open, with nowhere to conceal myself if the soldiers come."

"Dakota, there aren't any soldiers trying to find you to take you to the reservation. Your people are free now. Free. They can go anywhere they want to. They live, work, play, right beside white men if they choose. Some are still on Indian land, on reservations, but it's because they want to be, not because they're forced to stay there. You have nothing to fear by leaving the shelter and safety of this house."

He looked at her for a long moment. "I'll trust what you say, Kathy. These are peaceful times?"

"Not everywhere, I'm afraid, but here in Prescott it's peaceful."

"Mmm," he said, then followed her out the back door.

It was another picture-perfect day. The air was clean, the sky a brilliant blue with a sprinkling of fluffy white clouds.

Dakota spread his arms wide, closing his eyes as he inhaled deeply, then slowly exhaled. Opening his eyes again, he swept his gaze over the multitude of neat rows of Kathy's herb garden.

"This is good," he said, nodding. "The soil is rich here?"

"Yes, it's excellent. I have it tested to be certain it's in proper balance. This year I added some iron."

"Mmm," he said, walking forward.

Kathy watched as Dakota started along the first row of the garden. He stopped often, hunkering down to gently grasp a leaf between his thumb and forefinger, then rose again and went on.

He moved with such a smooth flow of motion, she mused, like a graceful animal in the wilds. He was comfortable in his own body, his command and control over it a given.

Kathy had dated several men in Chicago who worked out regularly at health clubs. But now, looking back, she realized they wore their bodies like merit badges to be recognized and fawned over.

But there was more than just the "realness" of Dakota's physique that was giving her food for thought. His openness and honesty when he talked to her was also far different from what she'd known.

Dakota spoke from his heart, holding nothing back. He'd shared his pain and loneliness with no concern for an image of machismo. He wasn't caught up in modern-day posturing, the real-men-don't-eat-quiche syndrome.

He was so real, so rare, so special.

Dakota, Dakota, she thought. *What are you doing to me?* No, she wouldn't dwell on Dakota, the man himself. She mustn't allow herself to do that because it was dangerous and foolish. He didn't even want to be here. He was sort of "on loan" from the past until they could master the mysteries of the Dream Catcher.

Great, she thought dryly, now she was making him sound like a library book she needed to return. But in a way, that was true. He had to go back to 1877, where he belonged.

"Feverfew," Dakota said, bringing Kathy from her tangled thoughts. "It has a bitter taste, but eases head pain."

"Yes, it works wonders for headaches and migraines. A few drops of peppermint in the drink helps the flavor. Of course, peppermint is worthwhile on its own. It aids digestion, reduces nausea and vomiting, and is often soothing to peptic ulcers." She laughed. "I sound like a commercial on television."

Dakota frowned.

"Oh, my, you don't know about television. I don't watch it much, because I'd rather read a good book. I enjoy football games during the season, but... I'm confusing you terribly, Dakota. I'm sorry.''

"There's a great deal to learn about this time you live in.''

"That's true,'' she said quietly, "but I'm beginning to think you have things to teach me, too. People now seem so caught up in their possessions and appearances. What they have is often more important to them than who they are. *Really* are.''

Their eyes met as he walked slowly toward her, finally stopping directly in front of her.

"Are we making discoveries?'' he said.

"Yes, Dakota,'' she said, smiling, "we're making discoveries.''

"Good. Well, I've breathed the fresh air and escaped from the walls that were closing in on me. I'm renewed. I'll stay inside while you go shopping for the shirt you say I must have.''

"I'll go right now,'' Kathy said, "and get back here as quickly as I can.''

After Kathy left the house, Dakota sat on the floor in front of the box she had described as being a television. He glanced at the picture that showed people moving and talking, but didn't really see it, his thoughts turned inward.

A part of him, he knew, was angry that he had been transported from his world to this one. Wasn't it enough that the white man had been controlling his existence, without the powers of the Dream Catcher taking hold of his destiny, as well?

What purpose could possibly be served by his being here in this time? None. Yes, he could learn, enrich his mind with knowledge he hadn't had before, but as far as he could tell it wouldn't be useful information once he returned to 1877.

Kathy was convinced there was a definite reason for what had taken place, a meaning, a message, that they didn't yet understand. Was she right? He didn't think so.

Kathy. Kathy Maxwell.

The concept she'd outlined of a man and woman making discoveries about each other was interesting. He fully intended to explore that theory further, to discover more about Kathy.

She pleased him. She made his blood run hot, his manhood ache to join with her womanly body. He liked the color of her eyes and hair, her aroma, the way she fit so perfectly against him when he'd held her in his arms.

A sudden chill swept through Dakota, pulling him from his thoughts, and causing him to stiffen as a wave of dizziness followed the cold. He drew a rough breath, then shook his head to clear away the dark mist that had begun to dim his senses.

What was wrong with him? He'd never felt such a strange sensation. Was he ill? He was a strong, healthy brave who was rarely sick. Whatever it had been that had assaulted him was gone, leaving no reason to dwell further on it.

Dakota shifted his attention to the television and concentrated on what there was to see in the box.

Less than an hour later, Kathy drove toward Lily's house with the fervent wish that her cousin would be at home.

Kathy had bought Dakota two western shirts with pearl snaps. One was royal blue, which she thought would look wonderful with his bronzed skin. The other was black and gray in a typical western-shirt pattern of stripes and plaid. She'd also purchased two pairs of jeans, which she hoped would fit him. She had not, thank goodness, had to buy him any underwear.

As she approached Lily's house, she rehearsed an explanation as to who Dakota was and how he'd come to be in her home.

After three attempts, she mentally threw up her hands in defeat. No matter what she said, she was going to sound like a loony tune. What if Lily refused to believe her, decided Kathy had slipped over the edge and hauled her off for professional help?

So, don't tell her, Kathy argued in her mind. No, that was dumb. She and Lily saw each other often, were in and out of each other's homes. Lily would *definitely* notice that a tall, dark and handsome Apache had taken up residence in Kathy's cottage.

Besides, she needed Lily and Brad's input and suggestions as to how it might be possible to send Dakota back to his own time.

Don't start, Kathy Maxwell, she told herself. She had to ignore how thoroughly depressing the thought of Dakota's leaving was becoming. The fact remained that he had to go, because he didn't belong here. Even more, he didn't *want* to be here.

But…

"Kathy, shut up," she said aloud as she pulled into Lily's driveway.

Her cousin had the inner door opened and the screen locked. Kathy rang the bell, and two little girls instantly made a beeline to answer the summons.

"Hi, Aunt Kathy," one of them said.

"Hi, sweetheart. Can you unlock the door?"

"No, Mommy says I have to get her if someone comes. Bye." She turned and ran across the room.

"But it's me, your Aunt Kathy," she called after her. "Oh, well. How are you, Holly?" she said to the other child.

"Two," the toddler said, holding up that many fingers.

"No, not how *old* are you, just how are you? Never mind, Holly. You're two, and that's great. I wish I was two, and didn't have any problems except refusing to be potty trained."

"Two. Two. Two," Holly said.

"Kathy," Lily said, lumbering toward the door. "What's wrong? Why aren't you at The Herb Hogan?" She unlocked the screen door and pushed it open. "Come in, come in. What's going on?"

Kathy entered the large living room decorated in attractive but very sturdy furniture meant to withstand the wear and tear of an active family. A generous supply of toys cluttered the carpeted floor.

"I took the day off because—" Kathy paused "—because I took the day off. Oh, dear."

"Sit," Lily said, pointing to the sofa. Kathy slouched onto it. "Girls, play with your toys so I can talk to Aunt Kathy."

"Cindy is in school," the older girl said, "'cause she's six. When I'm five, I can go to school, but I'm four. I want to be five, Aunt Kathy."

Kathy smiled. "You'll be five next year, Mary Kathy. The time will pass very fast, you'll see."

"Mary Kathy," Lily said, "take Holly into the family room, please. You're building a castle out of blocks, remember?"

"And I'm the princess of the castle, Holly," Mary Kathy said, taking her sister by the hand. "You can't be the princess 'cause I am."

"Two. Two. Two," Holly said merrily, allowing Mary Kathy to lead her from the room.

"Now, then," Lily said, sitting down in a chair and automatically resting her hands on her protruding stomach. "Speak."

"Yes, well, I... Well, um... Lily, I... Oh, dear heaven."

"Good grief, Kathy, what is your problem?" Lily said, frowning. "I've never seen you so befuddled. What on earth is the matter?"

Kathy sat up straighter on the sofa, cleared her throat and lifted her chin.

"Okay, here goes," she said. "When we were at the craft show yesterday I bought that pretty little Dream Catcher, as I'm sure you recall. I was intrigued by it, and not only was it lovely, but the legend was so enchanting. So! I hung the Dream Catcher above my bed to do its thing. You know, only let nice dreams through the hole in the center, and snag the nasty dreams in the webbing. That's how it works, you see. Well, I went to sleep..."

"Kathy," Lily yelled, "take a breath."

Kathy jumped at Lily's sudden outburst.

"My stars," Lily said, "you're talking a hundred miles an hour. You have to be about drained of oxygen. You'll scare the bejeebers out of the girls if you pass out on the floor."

"Oh. Sorry. I'm a tad shook up." Kathy took a deep breath and let it out slowly. "There. I'm fine." She pressed one hand on her forehead. "No, I'm not. I'm a wreck, a total wreck."

Lily leaned as far forward as her stomach would allow. "Why? What wrecked you?"

"Dakota."

"Who?"

"Oh, Lily, you've got to believe me. I had a dream about a gorgeous...I'm talking magnificent here...Indian brave, who was riding across acres of beautiful wildflowers to come to me. Me! Goodness, I wonder if Dakota is worried about his horse. The poor animal must be terribly confused. One minute Dakota was there, then...poof...he was gone. Would a horse notice something like that?"

"Kathy!"

"Oh. Yes, well, there I was, dreaming my nifty dream. The Indian was walking toward me, ready to take me into his arms…and the alarm clock went off."

"Damn."

"That's what I said. At first. But then. Oh, dear heaven, Lily. Dakota…that's the Indian's name…was on my bedroom floor! The Dream Catcher had grown to about six feet across, and he was caught in the hole in the center. It's true, I swear it. He's at my house right now. I explained what a television was, told him the people weren't really in that little box. I *think* he understood.

"Anyway, I left him watching TV so I could go shopping for him, buy shirts and jeans. He doesn't use underwear. I cooked him breakfast, which was a culinary disaster, but he said I grow herbs as well as an Apache woman, which pleased me to no end. We tried to send him back through the Dream Catcher, but it didn't work. I need your help, and Brad's, too. Okay?"

Lily sank back in her chair and stared at Kathy with wide eyes. She opened her mouth to speak, shook her head and closed her mouth again.

"You don't believe me," Kathy said, her shoulders slumping. "I can tell by the look on your face."

"I'm mulling this over," Lily said.

"Mull faster."

"Kathy, a couple of years ago my friend, Elsie, was very unhappy. She'd just gone through a messy divorce, she had no idea what to do with her life, she felt useless, with her self-esteem at rock bottom."

"And?" Kathy prompted.

"I convinced her to go to a craft show on the square with me to get her mind off her problems for a bit. There was a native American selling strings of Spirit Bells in one of the booths. They're colored beads and bells attached to cords. Each color of bead is supposed to bring you different rewards when you hang the Spirit Bells in your house. Red is for love, yellow is prosperity, green is for plentiful crops, and on the list goes.

"Well, Elsie was really taken with the whole idea. Blue is for peace and tranquillity. That's what she yearned for, inner peace, instead of the emotional turmoil she was in. So, she asked the Indian if he would make her a small string with bells and only blue beads. We strolled by the rest of the booths, then went back to get Elsie's custom-made Spirit Bells.''

''What happened?'' Kathy said, now sitting on the edge of the sofa cushion.

''From the moment that Elsie hung the Spirit Bells in her house, things began to change. Out of nowhere it seemed, she began to come up with solid plans for her future. She enrolled at Yavapai College, saying she had a long-buried dream to become a teacher.

''She polished her typing skills so she could work as a secretary while going to school. She sold her house and moved into a cute condo that wouldn't overwhelm her with upkeep. She found her inner peace. To this day, she believes it's because of those blue beads. And I believe it, too.''

''Oh, my,'' Kathy whispered.

''Kathy Maxwell,'' Lily said firmly, ''I do hereby declare there is a gorgeous Indian in your house who was transported from the past through your Dream Catcher. His name is Dakota, and he doesn't use underwear.''

''Oh, thank you, Lily, thank you.''

''What on earth are you going to do with him?''

While he's here, Kathy thought, we'll live for the moment we hold in our hands.

''Kathy?''

''Who? Oh. What am I going to do with him? During the time he's here he wants to learn about this era, and he's teaching me about his people, his beliefs. We're...we're sharing, discovering.

''He doesn't want to stay here, Lily. He sees no purpose for his being here, yet I find myself more and more convinced that there's a definite reason this happened.

''Oh, I don't know. It's all so confusing, so hard to comprehend. At first I refused to believe he was real and had actually traveled through time. But it's true. He's really here.''

''Amazing,'' Lily said. ''But I believe it, too. Indian powers are very strong, Kathy. You must have some kind of power yourself to have been able to connect with Dakota through the Dream Catcher. Goodness, this is really something.''

"I know," Kathy said, getting to her feet. "I've got to get home because I don't want to leave Dakota alone too long. There are so many things for him to explore that he's never seen before. I'm afraid he might injure himself."

"Good thought." Lily pushed herself to her feet with less-than-graceful form.

"Lily," Kathy said, "could you get a sitter on such short notice so you and Brad could come to my house tonight? Four minds working on a dilemma are better than two."

"Brad is in Phoenix for a dinner meeting. We could come tomorrow night, though."

"All right. Thank you." Kathy frowned. "Attorneys are very logical people. Is Brad going to believe this story?"

Lily laughed. "No problem. He handled Elsie's divorce and knew what condition she was in mentally and emotionally. My husband, the logical attorney, now has Spirit Bells hanging in his office, with every colored bead that has a purpose. He said he was going for the whole nine yards. After this baby is born, I intend to inform him he's to remove the purple beads from those cords.''

"What is purple for?"

"Passion."

Kathy laughed. "Oh."

"I don't want Brad to turn into an ice cube, you understand, but four kids is enough." She lowered her voice to a whisper. "This one," she went on, patting her stomach, "was conceived in Brad's office. I walked in and... Well, the purple beads go, or I'm never visiting him at his office again. We'll be over tomorrow night, Kathy. Brad will definitely want to meet Dakota. So will I, for that matter. Gorgeous?"

"Incredible."

"Very interesting."

"Thank you so much, Lily," Kathy said, giving her as much of a hug as was possible. "I'll see you tomorrow night."

"Two. Two. Two," Holly shouted, toddling into the room.

* * *

As Kathy drove away from Lily's, a sense of anticipation began to blossom within her.

She was going home.

She was going home to Dakota.

Four

Kathy entered the house through the front door and dropped her packages and purse on the nearest chair. Dakota was sitting cross-legged on the floor in front of the television and did not acknowledge her arrival.

That was an appropriate position for an Indian, Kathy thought, smiling. Oh, goodness, she was glad to see him. She'd never "come home" to anyone before, and it felt so right. No, it was more complex than that. It felt right because it was Dakota.

"I'm back," she said cheerfully. "Did you enjoy yourself while I was gone?"

"Mmm," Dakota said, still staring at the television screen.

Kathy crossed the room to stand behind him, curious as to what program he was watching that held his undivided attention.

"A soap opera?" she said. "Oh, heavens, Dakota, people don't really have that many crises in their lives. Well, maybe some do, I suppose, but not the average person. On the soaps, everyone is shown to extreme. You know, the nice people are very, very nice, and the crumb-bums are very, very crummy. I'm not sure that soaps are the appropriate thing for you to watch because you'll get a distorted impression of..."

Kathy stopped speaking and blinked in surprise as Dakota suddenly rolled to his feet and turned to face her. He gripped her upper arms, pulled her close and covered her mouth with his.

Kathy's eyes flew open in shock, but in the next instant her lashes drifted down and her arms encircled Dakota's waist. She slipped her tongue between his slightly parted lips to seek and find his tongue, feeling him tense for a moment at her bold intrusion.

The kiss deepened and heat thrummed within Kathy, deep and low. Hot. So very hot. It began to pulse in a maddening, tantalizing tempo that matched the beat of her racing heart.

She slid her hands upward, splaying them on his bare back, savoring the warmth of his skin and the feel of the taut muscles beneath her palms.

Dakota dropped his hands and wrapped his arms around her, nestling her to his body. Her breasts were crushed against the solid wall of his chest, creating exquisite images in Kathy's mind of Dakota soothing the sweet pain with his hands and mouth.

She could feel his arousal pressing against her, hard and heavy, and her passion soared even more. A hum of pure womanly pleasure whispered from her throat.

She was on fire, Kathy mused hazily. Going up in flames.

This kiss, this incredible kiss, was like nothing she'd experienced before. Her senses were heightened. The feel, the taste, the aroma, of Dakota were magnified. She was acutely aware of every inch of her own body, as well, rejoicing in her femininity.

Dakota, her heart and mind sang.

He broke the kiss and released her so abruptly that she staggered for a moment. They each drew a ragged breath, then their gazes met, desire radiating in eyes of sky blue and eyes of ebony.

"That," Dakota said, his voice raspy, "was definitely a discovery."

"It certainly was," she said, a rather wistful tone to her voice.

"What is this called, this joining of mouths we just shared?"

The last of the sensual mist encasing Kathy dissipated. "A kiss. We were kissing. What do the Apaches call it?"

"We don't...kiss."

Kathy's eyes widened. "You've never kissed anyone before?"

"No. I saw it done by the people in the box, the television. It seemed to give them pleasure. One man spoke of wanting his woman after they'd kissed and she agreed, said she wanted him, too. I assumed this was part of the ritual that takes place before men and women join their bodies. I wanted to discover what it felt like to share it with you. This kissing is, indeed, pleasurable.'' He nodded. ''Yes, I like it.''

Kathy moved around him and turned off the television. ''I think you've seen enough for one day. I must say, Dakota, that for someone who has never kissed anyone before, you did a sensational job of it.''

''It pleased you?''

''Oh, my, yes.''

''Good. Then I'll kiss you again,'' he said, reaching for her.

''No,'' she said, taking a step backward. She thudded against the television. ''I don't think that would be a terrific idea.''

''Why not? You said it pleased you.''

''It did, but it made me feel... That is, I wanted to... Well...'' Her voice trailed off, and a warm flush stained her cheeks.

''Mmm,'' he said, appearing extremely proud of himself. ''You wanted to join with me. That's good, very good. Kissing was an excellent discovery. We're moving closer to the time of joining.''

''No, we're not,'' she said, her voice rising. ''Yes, okay, I want you, I want to join with you. It's called making love, if the proper emotions are involved. But it isn't going to happen between us, Dakota.''

''Why not?''

She folded her arms over her breasts. ''Listen to me carefully. I do *not* take the act of joining, making love, lightly.''

''Nor do I.''

''Fine. Then you should be able to understand that it's too risky. What if I... Darn it, what if I fall in love with you and then you zoom back to 1877? What then, Dakota? I would miss you. I would cry. I have to protect myself from that kind of heartbreak.''

''I would miss you, too, Kathy,'' he said quietly. ''My heart would be heavy, sad.''

Kathy nodded. ''Then you understand why we mustn't kiss anymore, and why we're not going to make love, join. This discussion is over.''

''For now.''

Kathy sighed, shook her head, then hurried to the chair where she'd placed the packages.

"Try on your new clothes," she said. "That's safe enough."

She turned to see Dakota inching down his buckskin pants.

"Wait a minute," she said. "Stop that."

"How can I try on new clothes if I don't remove my old clothes?" he said.

"You can't take off your clothes in the middle of the living room, for Pete's sake. You do it in private, alone, behind a closed door."

Dakota frowned, digesting what she'd said, then shook his head.

"No, that's wrong," he said, his voice low. "We're supposed to be on a journey of discovery. We've discovered a great deal already, Kathy. One of those things is that kiss. Another is that we want to join, make love, but you have fears to put to rest first."

"Dakota…"

"Hear me," he said, raising one hand. "I agree with the reasons for this journey of discovery, and I feel there's no shame in your viewing my body naked, in its natural state. Don't you see, understand the importance of the discoveries we would make if you stood naked before me, and I before you? It's the way it should be."

She was dying, Kathy thought frantically. She was dissolving. Her bones were melting. Dakota's voice seemed to be caressing her like rich velvet, the sensual words fanning the embers of desire within her into leaping flames once more.

But there was even more involved than just the sexual aspect of what he was saying. There was also the simplistic honesty that was so real and pure that he was introducing to her world from another era.

When, how, in the decades since Dakota's time, had everything changed, become so complex? The honesty was now buried beneath games played between men and women, beneath the struggle for equality, then on to the battle for power and control.

Dear heaven, she thought, what a precious gift Dakota was giving her by just being himself. It was as though he was sweeping away the cobwebs so she could see, *really* see, the truths of her world.

What she had always accepted, she now questioned. The way it was, was not necessarily as it should be.

She needed to take an inventory of herself, discover not only things about Dakota, but rediscover herself, as well.

She'd been awakened from complacency.

She would never be the same again.

She would never want to be.

Because of Dakota.

"Kathy?" he said, bringing her from her reverie.

"Dakota, I heard what you said, I listened. I need to think it all through, because what's very simple to you is terribly complex for me.

"Please be patient with me while I'm attempting to unravel the maze in my mind. Would you please go into the other room to remove your clothes?"

Dakota looked directly into her eyes, then nodded slowly. He gathered the packages and left the room.

"Oh-h-h, my," Kathy said, sinking onto the chair. "Who are you, Kathy Maxwell? What do you want?"

She sighed, leaned back in the chair, forced herself to blank her mind and waited for Dakota.

When he reentered the living room, Kathy's breath caught as she stared at him. She got slowly to her feet, her gaze sweeping over him.

"You look..." she started, then swallowed. "Wonderful."

The jeans appeared as though they'd been custom-tailored just for him. They hugged his narrow hips and muscled thighs with delicious perfection.

He'd chosen to wear the royal blue shirt, which did, indeed, do fantastic things for his bronzed skin and marvelous physique. His shoulder-length black hair shone like polished ebony as the sunlight pouring through the window cascaded over him.

"Do you like those clothes?" she said.

"Mmm. The pants are stiff, not soft like my own, but they're acceptable."

"New jeans are always stiff. Why don't you go put your own pants back on, and I'll wash the jeans. That will soften them a bit."

"Do you still want me to be naked where you can't see me, or was once enough?"

"Go," she said, laughing, flapping her hands at him. "No, wait," she added, in the next instant. "You should see how great you look. I have a full-length mirror hanging behind my bedroom door."

"To see how I look as a man of *this* time?"

"Well, yes, you *look* like you belong here. You could walk around downtown with me and no one would be the wiser. But, oh, Dakota, you aren't like us, the people of this era. You're special and rare, like a treasure that should be cherished. You're what man once was, but has forgotten how to be. Don't change. Oh, God, Dakota, don't change.''

''What are you talking about?'' he said, frowning.

''Never mind,'' she said, waving one hand in the air. ''I know I'm not making sense but... Come on, let's go into the bedroom.''

In the bedroom, Kathy closed the door to reveal the mirror.

''Okay, step over here by me,'' she said.

Dakota moved to stand beside her, and they both looked at the mirror.

''Oh, merciful saints,'' Kathy whispered.

She grasped Dakota's arm, her eyes widening in horror as she continued to stare at the mirror.

Dakota wasn't there.

The mirror reflected only her, her hand in the air, holding nothing.

''Dakota?'' she said, a ring of panic in her voice. ''What does this mean? What's happening? Why can't we see you in the mirror?''

''Now I understand why I felt so strange before. I thought for a moment that I was ill,'' he said, a muscle jumping along his tightened jaw. ''I was transported to your time through the Dream Catcher. My body is here. But, Kathy, my spirit stayed in the place...in the place where I belong...and must return to.''

Kathy's heart raced as she looked into the mirror again, then back at Dakota.

''Your spirit, your soul,'' she said, her voice trembling, ''was separated from you? It remained in 1877? Why?''

Dakota took a step backward. ''I don't know, Kathy. My head pains me and I need some solitude, some peace. The walls are closing in on me again. I'm going outside to the garden.''

Kathy watched him as he strode from the room, then she stared at the mirror, wrapping her hands around her elbows as a chill swept through her.

How terrifying it had been to see only her own reflection when she *knew* Dakota was standing beside her. She felt as though a part of *her,* as well, had been torn from her, ripped away.

Why had this happened to Dakota?

Was it due to the magical powers of the Dream Catcher being tampered with, instead of respectfully left alone?

Or had Dakota, himself, been subconsciously struggling against the forces hurling him forward in time?

What had he meant when he said he'd felt strange, thought he was ill?

More questions. More questions without answers.

Kathy massaged her temples with her fingertips.

Now *she* was getting a headache. She and Dakota needed a break from all of this. As soon as he returned from the herb garden, she'd suggest they go for a relaxing drive, beyond the city where Dakota wouldn't have to see anyone.

Yes, that was a good idea. They'd seek solace in the peacefulness of nature, pretend they were the only two people in the entire world.

Five

Deciding that she and Dakota would have a picnic supper, Kathy retrieved a white wicker hamper from the front closet shelf and set it on the kitchen counter.

As she prepared sandwiches, she moved often to where she could see through the sun porch window to the yard beyond. Dakota had settled onto a small patch of grass, sitting Indian-style and staring into space. His back was ramrod straight, and his hands were fanned on his knees.

He'd withdrawn and was turned inward after the startling episode with the mirror, Kathy mused. And so had she. They were each lost in their own thoughts.

As Kathy sliced pickles, she sighed. Then she sighed again, becoming aware of how often she was producing the sad sound.

Darn it, she scolded herself, *cut it out.* She *knew* Dakota had to return to his own time in history. That fact had been a given from the very beginning of this bizarre experience.

But the incident with the mirror had spelled things out in painful reality, leaving nowhere to hide from the stark truth.

Dakota could *not* stay here.

With her.

"Oh, damn," she said, then sniffled.

She was acting so ridiculous, it was disgusting. She'd only known Dakota for a handful of hours. He'd arrived unexpectedly, he'd leave as soon as the mystery of the Dream Catcher was solved, and that would be that.

"Fine," she said, then reached for a bag of potato chips. "No, it is *not* fine."

As she continued to pack the hamper, she gave herself a stern lecture on not behaving like an adolescent. She told herself to accept things as they were, to get her act together instantly.

"Forget it," she mumbled. "I'm not listening to one word I'm saying."

She was Kathy Maxwell, but she was not remotely close to being the same Kathy Maxwell who had hung the pretty little Dream Catcher above her bed and gone blissfully to sleep. She was changed.

It was difficult to explain even to herself, but, somehow, in the few short hours they'd been together, Dakota had become an important, intricate part of her life.

He had looked at her and really *seen* her. He had beheld her and knew who she truly was. For him, all she had to do was *be,* and it was glorious.

Oh, Lord, she was miserable, she thought, filling a thermos with lemonade. The image in her mind of Dakota disappearing back through the hole in the center of the giant Dream Catcher was devastating. She would miss him so much, so very much.

Kathy closed the lid on the hamper just as Dakota entered the kitchen. She took a steadying breath and turned to look at him, forcing a lightness to her voice when she spoke.

"I thought it would be nice to get out of the house for a while," she said. "We can drive beyond the city to a quiet place and have a picnic."

"Picnic?"

She patted the hamper. "Supper."

Dakota nodded.

A short time later the hamper and a blanket were on the back seat of Kathy's blue compact car. Dakota stood next to the passenger door, his arms folded tightly over his chest, a deep frown on his face.

"Dakota," Kathy said, "*please* get in the car."

"No."

"It's perfectly safe," she said, flinging out her arms. "I drove it when I went shopping for your clothes, and I came back all in one piece. Remember? This automobile is an example of the type of transportation we use now. It's a modern-day horse." She paused. "Or whatever."

"Mmm."

He glared at her, then walked slowly around the car, peering at the tires, looking in the windows, rapping his knuckles on the hood.

"I don't like it," he said, shaking his head. "Why would anyone go willingly into a metal, egg-shaped box to be held captive while it moves on the road with other metal eggs? There's no sense in this, Kathy."

"You've got a point there," she said thoughtfully, then blinked. "No, you don't. Please, Dakota, trust me." She opened the passenger door. "Get in. Okay? It's comfortable, just like a chair."

After giving her one more dark glower, he moved tentatively onto the seat.

"You're a tad scrunched," she said, "because you have such long legs." She reached across him and clicked the seat belt into place. "There. Snug as a bug."

She closed the door, then ran around to the driver's side. After getting in and fastening her seat belt, she turned the key in the ignition. Dakota tensed even more as the engine roared.

"Stay calm," she said, shifting into reverse. "Here we go, nice and easy."

As she backed out of the driveway, then drove slowly, very slowly, away from the house, Dakota began to relax.

He did *not* like this metal egg, he reaffirmed in his mind, but there seemed to be no alternative but to sit there, tied in place like a captured coyote.

His instincts told him that Kathy should not be in this thing, either. She had no man to take care of her, keep her from harm. While he was there, *he* would protect her. *He* would be her man.

He was her man, his mind echoed. She was his woman. There was a bond between them, something special, like nothing he'd experienced before. He wanted to join with her to make love, yet it was more than that. He cared about Kathy. He wished to see only happiness in her eyes of sky blue and on her lovely face. Kathy Maxwell had become very, *very* important to him.

A chill swept through Dakota as he glanced at Kathy.

He now knew that he had no spirit, no center. It had not come with him when he'd been transported through the Dream Catcher. And it wasn't there to provide him with the ongoing flow of the essence of who he was.

He had to go back to his own time.

He had to leave Kathy.

And he knew, just somehow knew, that she would cry when he left her.

He turned his head to stare out the side window in a futile attempt to catalogue all the new and strange sights he was seeing.

Nothing really registered, as his mental vision was filled with images of his life in 1877. He saw himself alone, roaming the land, hiding from the soldiers. With the pictures, came the ache of loneliness.

He closed his eyes to draw courage and strength from deep within himself, to accept his fate with the quiet dignity befitting an Apache brave.

But thoughts tumbled through his mind in a confusing maze of contradictions. He didn't want to stay in this era, in the white man's world that was so difficult to understand. His own time was simple; man united with nature and lived in harmony with the land. Yet the thought of going back to the existence he'd had was bleak, dark and very empty.

Why? Why had all of this happened to him? Why had the Dream Catcher snared him and brought him here? Why had he been connected with Kathy by the magical powers? He didn't know the answers to any of his questions. He just didn't know.

Dakota blanked his mind by force of will, and directed his attention to the scenery beyond the window of the car.

For the picnic, Kathy selected a secluded area tucked beneath towering trees. It was high above the city, providing a breathtaking view for miles.

The only sounds were chattering squirrels, chirping birds and the rustle of leaves on the trees as an occasional breeze whispered through on its way to somewhere else.

Seated on the blanket, Kathy and Dakota consumed every bit of the delicious meal. They hardly spoke, each intent on relaxing, allowing the tension and stress within them to ebb.

When their appetites were satisfied and the debris placed in the hamper and set off to one side, they both took deep breaths and released the air at the same time, causing them to laugh in unison. The joyous sound seemed to echo through the crystal-clear air, cascading back over them tenfold.

"This was a good plan," Dakota said, smiling. "Thank you."

"You're welcome." Kathy paused. "You have a marvelous smile, Dakota. You should use it more often. Native Americans... Indians...are often thought of as being stoic, not revealing their emotions, but feel free to smile whenever the mood strikes."

He chuckled. "I'll remember that." He laid back on the blanket, lacing his hands beneath his head.

Kathy sat cross-legged next to him, sweeping her gaze over the glorious view.

"Strange," Dakota said.

"What is?" she said, turning her head to look down at him.

He freed one hand from under his head and extended it toward her.

"Come down here by me," he said. "I want to show you something."

Kathy hesitated for a moment, then did as he asked, stretching out next to him. There was just enough room between them for their entwined hands.

Was this a smart idea? Kathy asked herself. The heat emanating from Dakota's massive body seemed to weave over and through her, swirling and thrumming low within her. He was just so male, and just so there, and she was just so aware of every rugged inch of him.

"The sky," Dakota said quietly.

"Who? Oh. Yes, it's very blue, isn't it?"

What a brilliant thing to say, she thought, mentally rolling her eyes. She was going to shut up before she said something else as equally dumb.

"Yes," Dakota said, chuckling, "it's very blue."

Oh, good night, Kathy thought. That sexy sound of his was sinful. The heat within her was now pulsing, tightening in a spiraling coil.

Dakota's smiled faded. "Ever since I was a boy I'd steal moments like this to lie in a bed of grass and stare at the sky. It gave me a sense of peace. It always had a calming effect on me.

"No matter what was happening in my life, the sky was consistently there. It was something I could count on to steady me, like a rock. Does that make sense?"

"Yes," Kathy said softly. "Yes, it does."

"Your eyes remind me of the sky, Kathy. I've never seen eyes as beautiful as yours. Blue, so blue. Sometimes I gain an inner peace by looking into your eyes. Other times they cause me to burn with the want of you."

"Well, I…" Kathy started to say, then stopped speaking as she realized there wasn't a rational thought within her reach.

"Looking at the sky now," Dakota went on, "it struck me that it's the same as it is in my own time. That's what I meant when I said it was strange. I expected it to be different somehow, but it's not. It makes me feel…connected. Yes, that's the word. Connected."

"To 1877? To where you…belong?"

He released her hand and rolled up on his side, bracing himself on one forearm and looking directly into her eyes.

"No. It makes me feel connected to *your* time in history. To where I am now. Connected to you."

"Oh," she whispered, unable to tear her gaze from his mesmerizing dark eyes.

Dakota raised his hand and began to trace her features with the tip of his index finger. Kathy shivered from the tantalizing foray. Dakota's fingertip was callused, but his touch was so gentle. Her heartbeat quickened.

"I have never," he said, his voice raspy, "felt such soft skin as yours. Apache women spend hours each day in the sun, and their skin becomes dark and leathery at an early age. Your face is as pale as a new moon, and feels like the pussy willows that grow by a stream. Soft, so soft."

Then he slowly, so slowly, lowered his head to claim her mouth with his. His tongue slipped between her slightly parted lips to seek and find her tongue, stroking it sensuously with his own.

Kathy's arms floated upward to encircle his neck, her fingers weaving through the thick, silky depths of his hair. She urged his mouth harder onto hers.

She didn't think. Couldn't think. Didn't wish to think. She wanted only to feel, to give full rein to the passion and emotions flowing through her.

Dakota shifted on top of her without breaking the kiss, catching his weight on his forearms. Kathy could feel his arousal heavy against her, a promise of what he would bring to her as a man.

She savored the taste of his mouth, his aroma of fresh air, soap, and the musky scent of building desire. She heard the rumble of want escape from low in his chest, and rejoiced in the knowledge that he wanted her as she did him.

Her breasts ached to be caressed by his strong but gentle hands. Her femininity pulsed with heat, the flames licking through her. A whimper of need fluttered in her throat.

Dakota tore his mouth from hers to draw a rough breath.

"I want to join with you. To make love," he said, "here, beneath the blue sky, in nature's bed."

"You once said," Kathy said, hearing the thread of breathlessness in her voice, "that while you are here, we'll live for the moment we hold in our hands."

"Yes."

"I wondered if I could do that, if I had the courage, because I'm not a risk-taker. I will choose the safe road whenever I can. But, oh, Dakota, I do want you so much. I've changed since you came into my life. I *do* have the courage to live for the moment, *our* moment."

Dakota looked at her, simply looked at her. The intensity of his desire was there for her to see and believe in. Kathy trembled.

He shifted off of her, and with hands not quite steady, they removed their clothes.

Don't you see the importance of the discoveries we would make if you stood naked before me, and I before you? It's the way it should be.

And it was.

They discovered. They rejoiced in the beauty of each other, the perfection, the wondrous differences that made Kathy, woman, and Dakota, man. They burned with the want and need to mesh their bodies into one entity.

Dakota stretched out again next to Kathy, then kissed her deeply once more.

Discovery.

With hands and lips they journeyed, explored the mysteries the other's body revealed, then cherished each other as precious treasures. Tastes, textures, aromas, all mingled together. Desire built to a fever pitch.

"Dakota," Kathy whispered. "Please."

"It is time," he said quietly. "*Our* time. This is the joining of our marriage bed. From this moment, for the moment we hold in our hands, we are one."

He moved over her then, catching his weight again on his forearms. "Kathy."

"I'm yours, Dakota."

He entered her body, the moist heat receiving him, welcoming him, all of him. For a long moment he was still, as they savored.

Then slowly at first the tempo began, the dance, the ritual as old as mankind, yet new and theirs alone.

Kathy matched Dakota's rhythm in exact synchronization, lifting her hips to meet him, clinging to the taut muscles of his arms.

Harder. Faster. Pounding in a cadence that stole their breath and caused their hearts to race.

It was ecstasy.

It was beyond description in its splendor, a union like nothing either had ever known. They no longer knew where their own body stopped and the other's began. They were truly one, joined.

The tension grew in tightening coils deep within them, swirling, churning. Creating a near-pain so exquisite it brought the name of the other to their lips in awe and wonder.

On and on. Discovering, discovering. Higher. Hotter.

Then...

"Oh, Dakota!"

Kathy was flung into glorious oblivion. Shattered into a million pieces, each as vibrantly colored as the wildflowers had been when she'd first seen Dakota. She called his name over and over, clinging to him with a grip far greater than her normal strength.

Seconds later he joined her there, as his life's force spilled from him into her, granting his release from passion's hold. He threw his head back with a roar of masculine pleasure. He, too, saw the multitude of colors, knew they were the wildflowers where Kathy had beckoned to him, and exalted in the knowledge.

They hovered there as the last rippling spasms swept through their bodies. Then they began to drift slowly down, into the welcoming sea of the fragrant, bright flowers, then further yet to come to a reality still encased in a hazy, sensual mist.

His strength spent, Dakota collapsed against Kathy, then instantly rolled onto his back, taking her with him. She stretched out on top of his glistening body, nestling her head in the crook of his neck.

Neither spoke.

Thoughts that might have become words floated lazily into their minds, then were dismissed, none adequate to describe what they had just shared.

So no words were spoken.

But they knew.

Then bodies cooled and heartbeats quieted. Kathy shifted reluctantly off of Dakota but stayed close to his side. He encircled her with one arm, wanting her there.

"Oh, Dakota," she finally whispered.

He kissed her on the forehead. "Yes, I know."

Minutes ticked by, and the sweet bliss of peaceful slumber began to drift over them.

"Dakota?" Kathy said, a sleepy quality to her voice.

"Mmm."

"How could we have shared what we did, something so beautiful, so rare and rich, so honest and real, if your spirit wasn't here with you? Maybe we misinterpreted what we saw in the mirror. You *are* here, Dakota. I would know, now, if you weren't, if a portion of you had been missing."

"The spirit flows through the entire man, Kathy. It's part of him, his heart, his mind, all that he is. But the actual spirit, the essence of who he is, is at his center, the place of his self, his being. Who he is.''

"If it flows all through you, then can't you stay here in this time? You *do* have your spirit.''

"No, you don't understand. It's like a lake of pure, crystal-clear water that flows out into many streams, nurturing as it goes. But if the center, the lake, disappears and I'm empty, then soon there will be no streams. Now do you see?''

"Yes, I guess I do.'' She paused. "Dakota, what will happen if you don't go back to where your center spirit is? What will become of you?''

Several minutes passed, but he didn't answer.

Kathy raised her head to look at him. "Dakota? What will happen to you?''

He drew one thumb gently over her lips, then across the soft skin of her cheek, before meeting her troubled gaze.

"Kathy,'' he said quietly, "I will die.''

Six

Kathy stirred, opened her eyes, then frowned as she realized she had no idea where she was.

"Oh," she said in the next instant.

Darkness had fallen, and the sky was a spectacle of beauty with millions of stars glittering like diamonds on black velvet. The luminescence from the heavens made it possible for her to see Dakota, who was sleeping peacefully next to her.

A soft smile touched her lips as she gazed at him, marveling at the power of his magnificent body evident even in slumber.

She shifted slightly and was immediately aware of a foreign yet exquisite soreness in her body that was the result of the lovemaking shared with Dakota.

As vivid, sensual pictures of their joining began to form in her mind's eye, heat began to pulse deep within her. She wanted him again, still, forever.

Forever, her mind echoed, and she frowned. There would be no forever with Dakota.

I will die.

Dear heaven, they had to solve the mystery of the Dream Catcher before it was too late. They had to find a way to send Dakota back to his own time to be united with his spirit.

When he had told her what would happen to him if he remained separated from the center of his spirit, Kathy couldn't speak as unshed tears filled her eyes.

She'd clung to him, holding fast, with the wild, irrational thought that she could keep him with her, safe, if she didn't let go. She'd kissed him, covering his mouth with hers before he could say any more that she couldn't bear to hear.

They were consumed instantly with passion, and all thoughts mercifully fled. Their lovemaking had been urgent, frenzied, with a near-desperate need to become one entity that could not be torn apart by outside forces.

How strange, Kathy mused, still staring at Dakota as he slept, that she could be feeling such joy and such sorrow at the same moment.

She sighed in contentment, allowing the warmth of her happiness to flow through her like a gentle brook.

But then the chill of sadness came, clutching her heart with an icy fist.

I will die.

She hadn't asked Dakota how long they had to discover the hidden magic of the Dream Catcher, because she hadn't been prepared to hear the answer. When he awoke she'd gather her courage and ask the dreaded question.

Dear God, she thought, tears misting her eyes, she didn't want Dakota to leave her. She cared deeply for him, and she wanted to continue on the journey of discovery of what they might ultimately have together.

But he had to go so that he could live. His life was more important than her aching heart, and she would muster all her strength to enable her to bid him farewell with dignity. Somehow.

"Dakota," she said, jiggling his arm, "wake up."

He responded instantly, sitting bolt upward, which caused Kathy to fall back onto the blanket.

"Goodness," she said, "when you wake up, you really do a job of it."

"Mmm."

"We have to leave here." She glanced at her watch. "It's nearly nine o'clock. Clothes. Where are my clothes?'' She sat up and began to scoop the garments together.

"I'd like to spend the remainder of the night under the stars,'' Dakota said, looking heavenward.

"I don't know if this is an official campsite, or what the rules are about that. Besides, it's getting chilly. We'd better go back to the house.''

"Kathy, wait.''

"Yes?''

"You *do* know that you're my woman, my wife, now, don't you?'' She placed one hand on his forearm.

"No, Dakota,'' she said gently, "I'm not your wife. We made love. We're lovers. But we're not married. We're not husband and wife.''

"Yes, we are. This was our marriage bed and our joining made us one. You're my woman. I'm your man. We're married. That's the way of the Apaches.''

Kathy sighed. "But it's not *my* way. To be married, people sign official documents, speak vows before someone authorized to perform the marriage ceremony. Not only that, Dakota, but I would never marry unless I was in love. Unless I was prepared to make a commitment to forever, to spending the rest of my life with my husband.''

"You don't care for me?''

"I care for you very, very much. You've become so important to me so quickly, but I need more time to discover all there is to know about you, to nurture those feelings and see if they grow into love. I can't believe that you love me, either.''

"Caring is enough for marriage,'' he said, his voice rising. "The love comes as days and nights pass. You need time to discover more about me, to nurture the feelings you now have? We don't have a lot of time.''

Kathy got to her feet and began to dress.

"I realize that,'' she said. "I drew on my courage and made the choice to live for the moment we hold in our hands. I have no regrets about what we shared here, none at all. But I'm not your wife, Dakota. We're not married, because I'm not in love with you. Plus, we have no future together, no forever.''

Dakota rolled to his feet and gripped her shoulders.

"You won't honor me as a man by being my wife while I'm here?"

"It has nothing to do with honoring you. I can't, I won't, allow myself to think beyond the moment. You've got to go back to your own time, Dakota.

"Oh, don't you see? It's going to be difficult enough for me when you leave. Somehow, *somehow,* I'm going to make certain I don't fall in love with you. I hope, pray, a person can control their own emotions in the arena of love. Dakota, I am *not* your wife."

He narrowed his eyes. "You are refusing to acknowledge that we are married? You're dismissing what took place in our marriage bed?"

Kathy stepped backward, forcing him to drop his hands from her shoulders. She continued to dress.

"Please don't do this," she said. "You're spoiling everything by asking more of me than I can give you."

"You gave *yourself* to me." Dakota began to pull on his clothes with rough, angry motions. "Doesn't that mean something to you?"

"Of course it does. I don't take lovemaking lightly. I don't engage in casual sex. Darn it, you were the one who said we should live for the moment, and now you want a lifelong commitment from me. This doesn't make sense, because you know as well as I do that you can't stay here."

"So you'd have me return to my time dishonored, an Apache brave who shared his marriage bed with his woman, only to be told you refuse to be my wife? You would do that to me?"

"Dakota, look, we're arguing about customs and rituals that are different because we come from different worlds, different cultures."

He stopped dressing and looked at her for a long moment.

"Too different," he finally said quietly.

"No, I don't believe that. If you were staying here and if we fell in love, we'd find a way to mesh our worlds. But there's no point in discussing it because you've got to leave. I don't want to spend what time we have left arguing. Please, Dakota? Can't we put this issue of marriage aside, not address it?"

"You don't understand the importance of it. You don't understand *me*."

"And you're not understanding *me*. We haven't had time to make all the discoveries we need to."

"That may be true, *but you are my wife*."

"All right! You follow your customs and consider me your wife. I'll follow mine and know I'm *not* your wife. How's that? Will that do?"

"No!"

Kathy sighed. "We're just going in circles here. If you won't put the issue aside for good, let's at least agree to talk about it later when our tempers are under control. There's something of a far greater magnitude that we should be concentrating on."

"Which is?" he said, still frowning.

Well, Kathy thought miserably, there was no excuse for postponing this any longer.

"Dakota, how long… What I mean is, how much time… That is… Do you know how long we have to figure out how to send you back through the Dream Catcher before you…before you…die?"

He sighed and closed the distance between them, framing her face in his hands.

"No," he said, "I don't know. Once, many years ago, a brave in my tribe lost his wife and two sons to a fever. He grieved deeply. Within days he began to lose the strength in his body, became weak, unable to eat, could hardly walk. The shaman spoke over him to rid him of the sickness holding him."

"What happened?"

"The shaman finally said that the center of the brave's spirit had perished with his wife and sons, and there was no way to stop the remainder of his spirit from flowing out of him. He died, went to his eternal beyond, two weeks after he'd buried his family."

"Oh, God," she whispered.

"That's the only time I witnessed such a happening. I can't say exactly how long I have, because the powers of the Dream Catcher are intertwined. But after what I witnessed those years ago, Kathy, I don't think I have much time. I believe that there are not many days left for us to be together."

"I see," she said, trying desperately to blink away sudden tears. "Well, we certainly don't want to spend those hours arguing, do we? No, of course we don't." She paused. "Come on, Dakota, let's go home."

* * *

Home. Let's go home.

The words echoed in Kathy's head as she drove toward the city, envisioning her little cottage in her mind. She'd found such inner peace and contentment in that house during the last year. It was her safe haven, a place that emphasized the rightness of her decision to move from Chicago to Prescott.

But now the mental image of the house after Dakota was gone was a picture of empty rooms and lonely hours.

Let's go home.

Would it still seem like a *home* when Dakota was no longer there? Or would it be just a structure where she slept, ate, spent her leisure time? Would she continue to be capable of accepting as fact what was missing from her life: a husband, children, a *home?*

A flash of anger sliced through her, and her hold on the steering wheel tightened.

Darn it...no, *damn it*...she wished none of this had happened. She wished Dakota hadn't been transported from the past to the present by the Dream Catcher.

Why her? Many people had purchased Dream Catchers at the craft show, then proceeded blissfully on their way.

But Kathy Maxwell? *Her* Dream Catcher had gone nuts, and because it had she was in the midst of a confusing, unsettling, bizarre mess. If she could turn back the clock, she'd march past the booth of Dream Catchers without a sideward glance.

She sighed.

That wasn't true and she knew it. What had happened with the Dream Catcher was a blessing, not a curse. She would cherish every memory, every precious moment, spent with Dakota.

She knew he had to return to 1877. If he didn't he would die. *Dear heaven, he would die.* He couldn't stay here. Even more, he didn't want to. He viewed their worlds and beliefs as being too different, too far apart. He'd rather exist alone and lonely in his own era.

She'd hurt him by refusing to acknowledge that she was his wife, and his pain had shown itself in the form of anger. They'd each stood their ground, stubbornly declaring that their stand on the subject was the way it should be.

Had she been wrong? Knowing they had to find a way to send

Dakota back, should she have graciously accepted the title of his wife for the duration of his stay? No, she couldn't do that, she just couldn't.

Why not? Kathy asked herself. Oh, enough was enough. She was mentally exhausted and just couldn't think anymore tonight. She'd address the issue again later. Fine.

At the house Kathy emptied the hamper, put it away, then sat down on the sofa. Dakota had settled cross-legged on the floor.

"Dakota," she said, "my cousin, Lily, and her husband, Brad, are coming over tomorrow evening to meet you, and to help us try to solve the mystery of how to transport you back to your own time through the Dream Catcher."

"Mmm," he said, nodding.

"Would you like to go to The Herb Hogan with me tomorrow, instead of staying here alone all day?"

He nodded again.

"Oh, Dakota, I'm sorry I hurt you, I truly am. I just can't agree to saying that I'm your wife. Please don't let this issue ruin what time we have left together."

"I'm trying not to, Kathy."

"Thank you." She paused. "It's not all that late, but I think I'll go to bed. Where...where do you want to sleep tonight?"

"With you. I wish to sleep with you in our marriage bed."

"Dakota..."

He raised one hand to silence her. "I can't view it any other way. I'm not referring to the titles of husband and wife. I am talking only about the bed."

"Which is intertwined with the titles we're not discussing, but so be it." Kathy got up from the sofa. "If you can separate things, then so can I. I don't want anything to tarnish what time we have left."

Dakota rolled to his feet, drew Kathy against him and captured her lips with his. The searing kiss was urgent and rough, his tongue plummeting into her mouth to meet her tongue.

Kathy answered the demands of Dakota's mouth in kind. The hunger, the need, to blot out all that threatened them consumed her with an overwhelming intensity.

She wanted to fly to the place of ecstasy where only she and Dakota could go…together. Nothing, nor no one, could intrude upon the private world they created when they were one entity, their bodies meshed.

Dakota broke the kiss and lifted her into his arms, carrying her into the bedroom. He set her on her feet and they quickly shed their clothes, hands immediately reaching for the other once again.

Kathy moved into his embrace, pressing tightly against him as he kissed her. She clung to him, feeling his arousal, meeting his tongue and stroking it, crushing her breasts to the hard wall of his chest.

They tumbled onto the bed, and in one powerful thrust, Dakota entered her. Filling her, he instantly began a pounding rhythm that she met beat for beat. It was wild, like a storm gathering force. It swept them up and away from the threatening truths of reality.

They reached the summit a breath apart, calling to each other, glorying in the splendor of the brightly colored place they'd been flung to. The wildflowers, *their* wildflowers, welcomed them once again.

They lingered there, not wishing to return. Minutes passed as they savored what they'd shared, held fast to what was now another cherished memory.

"Did I hurt you, Kathy?" Dakota said finally. "I was rough when I should have been gentle."

"Oh, no," she said, splaying one hand on his chest, "you didn't hurt me. It was wonderful. When we make love, Dakota, only the two of us exist in the entire universe. We go to *our* place, where no one can find us. I wish there was really somewhere we could hide."

"There isn't."

"I know," she said with a sigh.

"Are you sorry you bought the Dream Catcher that day? Sorry you hung it above your bed? Do you wish I had never come into your life?"

"No, I'm not sorry." She laughed softly. "I tried to be. I attempted to get rip-roaring mad about it, but that lasted about three seconds. If I could turn back the clock to the moment I stood in front of that booth on the square and saw the Dream Catchers, I'd pick the pretty little pink one and hang it carefully above my pillow. Do *you* wish I'd walked on past that booth?"

Dakota shifted so he could look directly into her eyes.

"No."

"That's all you have to say on the subject?"

"That's enough."

"Yes," she said, sleepily, "it is."

Holding fast to each other, they slept.

The Herb Hogan was part of the downtown area of Prescott. The row of buildings in the block dated back to the turn of the century with weathered charm.

Inside the store Kathy turned on the lights, flipped the sign on the door to Open, then went behind the counter, placing her purse in a drawer. Dakota stood just inside the door.

Kathy watched him as he swept his gaze slowly over the expanse.

This shop was her pride and joy, she mused, the fulfillment of a dream she'd nurtured until it had become a reality. She was so proud of The Herb Hogan, had made it the focus of her existence, her purpose.

She had dealt with the realization that the trade-off for choosing to live in this delightful little town would very likely be that she would never marry and have children. She refused to settle for any man, just to have a man, and the selection in Prescott was extremely limited. Her maternal instincts would be satisfied by lavishing affection on Lily and Brad's daughters.

She'd not been lonely in her aloneness, and she was prepared to live out her life as it was.

But then…Dakota.

Now she knew the meaning of caring deeply for someone, of wanting to discover all and everything about one special man, of sharing and being connected, while still maintaining a sense of self.

Yet as quickly as these wondrous things had come into her life, they were going to be snatched from her grasp when Dakota left her. Oh, dear heaven, the image in her mind's eye of her existence without him was cold, so horribly cold and empty.

Enough, Kathy, she scolded herself. She'd end up thoroughly depressed if she dwelled on the fact that Dakota must return to his own era in history. She'd be so busy feeling sorry for herself that there wouldn't be room in her emotional treasure chest to place each precious memory of the time spent with this man.

She forced her gloomy thoughts into a dusty corner of her mind and watched as Dakota scrutinized The Herb Hogan. She attempted to see it fresh as he was.

The store was bright and cheerful, the gleaming front windows allowing sunlight to pour in. The shelves were dust-free and neat with various bottles, jars, pouches and packets lined up in precise order. Every inch of space had been utilized, but she had been careful not to present an image of overwhelming clutter. There were shelves behind the counter, as well, and a back room beyond a closed door.

Dakota nodded. "This is excellent. I don't know what a lot of these things are, but I recognize others. This is a fine store, Kathy."

Kathy felt a rush of warmth suffuse her from Dakota's praise, and she smiled.

"Thank you," she said. "I'm very proud of The Herb Hogan, and it means a great deal to me that you approve of what I've done."

She paused and frowned. "No, that didn't sound quite right. I'm proud for myself, within myself, for what I've accomplished. I don't need anyone's approval, per se, to affirm what I've done. But your praise is lovely, like a warm, fuzzy blanket. An extra bonus. Do you understand what I'm trying to say?"

Dakota walked slowly across the room and behind the counter, a thoughtful expression on his face.

"What you said is far different than the customs of my people. Women are held in high regard, respected, but the work they do, the tasks they perform, are done for the approval of their fathers, then later their husbands. They're given their worth by those they've hoped to please."

"Mmm," Kathy said, frowning.

"I never questioned it, because it was how it had always been. Yet, now that I think about it, isn't it better that a woman be complete within herself, her spirit whole, as she comes to her man?" He nodded. "Yes, I believe it is."

Kathy slipped her arms around his waist. "Oh, Dakota, do you realize what you just did? You opened your mind to new ideas, a new way of viewing things. It's the way things are here, in this time. That's wonderful.''

He encircled her with his arms and pulled her closer to his body.

"It's not really important, Kathy. I can't stay here.''

She sighed. ''I know. Come into the back area and I'll show you my workroom. You can fill jars, packets and pouches with dried herbs if you want to.''

"In a minute,'' he said, then lowered his head and claimed her mouth.

The smoldering embers of desire within Kathy burst instantly into licking flames as she returned the kiss in total abandon.

The sound of a tinkling bell as the front door was opened caused her to jerk in surprise. She attempted to step free of Dakota's embrace, but he released her slowly, causing a blush of embarrassment to stain her cheeks.

She turned to greet a woman in her mid-thirties, who had entered the store and was staring at Kathy and Dakota with wide eyes.

"Well, my goodness,'' the woman said, coming to the front of the counter. She smiled at Kathy. ''Having a nice day? I'm sorry I interrupted. You'd probably like to strangle me.''

"Hi, Sharon,'' Kathy said, then cleared her throat. ''I'd like you to meet Dakota. He's an old…friend.''

"I'm pleased to meet you, Dakota,'' Sharon said, beaming at him. ''How long do you plan to be in Prescott?''

"I'm not certain,'' he said.

"Well, maybe you should consider staying here,'' Sharon went on. ''You and Kathy are obviously very glad to see each other.'' She raised her eyebrows. ''Old *friend?* I'm thinking perhaps Kathy is more than just your friend.''

"Kathy is my wife,'' Dakota said.

"Oh, good Lord,'' Kathy said.

"Wife?'' Sharon repeated. Her eyes darted back and forth between Kathy and Dakota.

"Yes,'' he said, nodding, ''but she's reluctant to accept the title, so we're not discussing it to avoid an argument.''

"Did that make sense?'' Sharon said. ''Kathy Maxwell, did you get married and not tell me? Why won't you acknowledge that you're

Dakota's wife? Are you on some liberated woman kick or something? Married. I'm so thrilled for you.''

"Sharon, wait, halt,'' Kathy said, raising both hands. "Things aren't exactly as you think they are. What I mean is... Well, Dakota and I... But I really can't explain because... Oh, for crying out loud.'' She rolled her eyes heavenward.

"Dakota,'' Sharon said, "is this cute person your wife—'' she pointed at Kathy "—or isn't she?''

"She is,'' he said, folding his arms over his chest.

Kathy closed her eyes and shook her head.

"I love it, I love it.'' Sharon glanced at her watch. "Darn it, I've got to dash. This weekend is Territorial Days, you know, and I'm on the committee. The town will be packed with tourists, per usual. I've got so many last-minute details to tend to.

"I came to get my usual stash of vitamins, because I'm going to need every ounce of energy I have to get through this event. But that's okay, because I love Territorial Days.''

In a flurry of activity, Sharon collected what she wanted from the shelves, dumped them onto the counter, then after paying for the purchases, scooped up the bag Kathy had put them in.

"I'm off,'' Sharon said. "Listen, as soon as Territorial Days are over, we'll talk about a wedding party for you and Dakota. Fantastic.'' She looked at Dakota. "You were pulling my leg about not knowing how long you're staying in Prescott, you bum. Of course you're here for good. You're Kathy's husband.''

Dakota frowned. "I didn't touch your leg.''

"What?'' she said, obviously confused.

"Don't worry about it, Sharon,'' Kathy said wearily. "Have a nice day.''

"You, too. I'm off. Are you two coming to Territorial Days? Of course you are. Everybody does. Bye, guys, and best wishes. Married. I love it.'' She hurried out the door.

As the sound of the tinkling bell above the door faded, an oppressive silence settled over The Herb Hogan. Kathy took a deep breath, let it out slowly, then turned to face Dakota. He still had his arms crossed on his chest, and Kathy lifted her chin to a determined tilt.

Do not yell, she told herself. She would slowly and patiently explain to Dakota what was on her mind, what she needed to say. Fine.

"Dakota," she said, attempting to produce a smile that didn't materialize, "you really shouldn't have told Sharon that I'm your wife."

He frowned as he looked at her. "Why not? You *are* my wife. Why would I deny the truth? You may feel differently about it, but I spoke what is true to me. Honesty is very important to me, Kathy."

"Of course it is, and it's important to me, too. It's a major part of my value system. I'm not suggesting that you lie, but sometimes the truth is better left unsaid. You and I don't agree on the subject of my being, or not being, your wife. Therefore, you should have kept silent. Understand?"

"No."

"Dakota," she said with a sigh, "the news flash that you and I are married will spread through Prescott like a prairie fire. People are going to come streaming in here with a zillion questions. How long have we known each other? Where did we meet? When were we married? Where do we plan to live? Are you going to be running The Herb Hogan with me? And on and on."

Dakota shrugged. "We'll answer only the questions we wish to. We'll say we shared our marriage bed, joined, made love. I see you as my wife, but you don't view me as your husband. That's clear enough."

"Oh, good grief. Dakota, listen to me. Even if I *did* consider myself your wife, it would be foolish to tell people that we're married, because you can't stay here. After you're gone..." Oh, what a chilling word...*gone*. "Everyone will be wanting to know where you went, why you didn't stay with me. They'll look at me and wonder what's so wrong with me that caused my new husband to disappear. Do you see what I mean?"

"Are you saying," he said, his voice ominously low, "that what other people think is of more value to you than honesty, truth?"

Kathy opened her mouth to retort, then snapped it closed again.

Mercy, she thought, Dakota's interpretation of what she had said was *not* flattering. It made her sound cold and superficial, placing her public image higher on her list of importance than honesty.

That wasn't true.

Was it?

No, no, no, it wasn't. Dakota just didn't understand how it was in this era. Things weren't so complex in his time, his place in history. These days a person had to...

"Oh, dear," she said, massaging her now-throbbing temples.

She was becoming all muddled up again. So confused. In this era...what? she asked herself. Honesty only came first if it was convenient, if it wouldn't rock the boat? At the first sign of trouble, were truth and honesty quickly shoved aside by outright lies, or lies of omission? Was that what she was attempting to get across to Dakota, and urging him to agree to?

Yes.

"Dakota," she said quietly, "I'm sorry. I humbly apologize for asking you to do something that's so very wrong, asking you to deny what to you is the truth. I'll deal with the ramifications of what you told Sharon as they come. I won't attempt to change you. You've taught me a great deal by just being you. I thank you for that, and I *am* truly sorry."

Before Dakota could reply, the door opened and two women in their sixties entered The Herb Hogan.

"Hello, Olive, Alida," Kathy said, smiling. "You must be running low on your teas and lotions."

"We are, indeed," Olive said, "but we would have stopped in, anyway. We just bumped into Sharon and she said..."

"Yes," Kathy interrupted, "I'm sure she did. Ladies, I'd like you to meet Dakota. In his world, his culture, we're married. In mine, we're not."

"Pardon me?" Olive said.

"That is all we have to say on the subject," Dakota said, looking directly into Kathy's blue eyes. "Is this compromise?"

"Yes," she said, smiling at him warmly. "This is compromise."

Seven

Business was steady through the day at The Herb Hogan. As the hours passed, more people heard about Dakota's sudden presence in Kathy's life and the rather confusing explanation being given as to the status of their relationship. Most left the store with purchases and bemused expressions.

In the late afternoon, Dakota sat at the table in the back room, filling pouches with various dried herbs.

He was amazingly relaxed, he realized, and had been during the entire day.

Once he'd stopped tensing each time the door opened and someone entered the store, he'd begun to look forward to observing each new person. The diversity in their clothing, coloring, even the way they spoke, was intriguing.

And all of them had smiled and greeted him with sincere warmth.

It was as Kathy had told him; he was safe here, no one was searching for him to kill or capture him. He was being accepted simply as a man. Kathy's man.

Was that why he had been transported here by the Dream Catcher? Had the gods decreed that he wasn't to spend his remaining days like a hunted animal and hurled him forward in time to a place where he was accepted?

If that was true, why had Kathy been intertwined in the process of giving him a new life? And if it was true, why had his center spirit not come with him? Why was he being forced to find a way back to his era?

"Mmm," he said, frowning.

A new life. A *temporary* new life. If he stayed here, he would die. So what had been the purpose for all of this? It made no sense, none at all.

Except....

Kathy.

He liked her smile, the sky blue of her eyes, the sunshine color of her hair. He valued her honesty and sincerity, respected her ability to work in harmony with nature when growing the herbs in the garden. She was a fine woman among women.

He did, indeed, consider her his wife. Their joining was satisfying beyond measure. When they were one entity, it was exquisite. She gave of herself willingly, totally, each time they came together.

He rejoiced in seeing her naked before him, and touching, tasting, every inch of her soft skin. Her breasts were lush, and one day his son would suckle there, receiving the nourishment of mother's milk. He would...

His son?

Dakota snorted in self-disgust. Such foolishness to be envisioning Kathy bearing his son. His stay in this world was going to be brief, not long enough to witness his seed growing bigger within Kathy, producing a fine, healthy boy.

He had to leave here.

He would never see Kathy again.

That thought caused a knot to tighten in his gut, and Dakota shifted on the chair. The hot coil that had swept through him as he dwelled on the lovemaking he shared with Kathy was now a cold current consuming him, clutching his heart in an icy fist.

Oh, why, why had he been brought here to this haven of peace, found the woman he now considered his wife, and yearned to have her grow big with his child, only to be forced to return to a hostile, lonely existence in order to live? Why were the gods tormenting him like this, teasing him so cruelly?

Was this the way it was meant to be? Was he being given a reprieve, a rest, from his world to restore his strength? Were the differences between his beliefs and Kathy's too great for him to remain here forever?

So many questions, he thought, shaking his head. So many answers that remained beyond his reach.

Dakota sighed and reached for another pouch.

Kathy finished recording the totals from the cash register in a ledger, put it away, then crossed the room to lock the door. She flipped the sign to Closed, then wrapped her hands around her elbows. Taking a deep breath, she allowed the silence to cascade over her like a comforting blanket.

As the hours of the day had passed, she mused, she'd become more and more gloomy, finally ending up thoroughly depressed. Her initial joy when she and Dakota had compromised on the issue of her being, or not being, his wife had slowly dissipated until it was completely gone.

They were so very different in their beliefs. Their worlds and cultures were miles apart. How many compromises could two people put into operation and expect them to work? How many were *too* many, creating far too much tension and stress? It was a disturbing, unsettling question.

But her depression, Kathy knew, had hit her full force when she realized the elusive answer didn't matter, because Dakota couldn't remain there. He had to go back to his own time. *He had to.*

Oh, dear heaven, she wanted him to stay.

She *needed* him to stay.

Stop it, Kathy, she ordered herself. She would *not* let her mind travel down the road it was approaching. She would *not* dwell on what she and Dakota might have if he didn't leave. She would *not* entertain the idea that she might eventually fall deeply and forever in love with him.

No!

She shook her head sharply in an attempt to clear her mind of her jumbled thoughts, then headed for the back room to tell Dakota it was time to go home.

Home, her mind echoed. Forget it. She wasn't going to start thinking about home versus house again. She was depressed enough, thank you very much.

After a dinner of hamburgers and French fries, which Dakota declared to have merit, Kathy shooed him into the living room so she could make a dessert to serve to Lily and Brad.

At seven o'clock the doorbell rang and Kathy hurried to answer the summons, greeting Lily and Brad as she opened the door.

As the pair came into the house, Kathy gave them a quick hug. Brad Benson was about five-foot-ten, trim, wore glasses, and was slowly losing his hair, a fact he didn't care one whit about. He was rather nondescript until he smiled. Then his entire face lit up and his eyes twinkled. Kathy adored him.

"Lily and Brad," Kathy said, "I'd like you to meet Dakota."

They all turned toward Dakota, who was standing across the room.

"Oh, my stars," Lily said, awe evident in her voice. "You didn't do him justice. He's... Gracious me. This is, indeed, a pleasure, Dakota."

"Pleased to meet you," Brad said, smiling. "You had quite a journey to arrive here, Dakota. Welcome to our world. It must seem very strange to you."

"I'm being rude," Lily said. "I'd like to welcome you, too, Dakota. All of this—" she swept one arm in the air "—must be rather overwhelming."

Dakota walked slowly forward to stand directly in front of Lily.

"Ever since I was a small boy," he said, "I have known if a woman carried a girl child or a boy. The shaman in my tribe told me it was a gift, but I found it a nuisance when I was young because the women would pester me to tell them what the babe within them would be."

"Really?" Lily said, smiling. She patted her stomach. "Well, this is a boy. Guaranteed."

"What would you do to determine the sex of the child?" Brad asked.

"Place my hand gently on the woman's stomach," Dakota said.

"Lily?" Brad said. "How about it? Would you like Dakota to check out your boy theory?"

"Go right ahead, Dakota," Lily said. "This will prove that women know what's going on. This baby is a boy."

Dakota lifted one hand and splayed it on Lily's large stomach. A moment later he nodded.

"You will have," he said, dropping his hand to his side, "a fine, healthy daughter very soon."

"Daughter?" Lily said. "It's a boy, I'm sure of it. Did you ever make a mistake, Dakota?"

He shook his head.

Brad hooted with laughter. "Lily, if I was a betting man I'd put my money on what Dakota said. It's another cute-as-a-button baby girl."

"But I want a boy!"

"Perhaps your next child will be a son," Dakota said.

"Oh, no, you don't," Lily said. "There aren't going to be any more babies after this one."

Dakota frowned. "You're going to refuse to join with your husband? He'll have no choice but to take a second wife."

"Dakota," Kathy said, "that's not how it works now. Lily didn't mean she was planning to refuse to... Oh, good grief, let's all sit down, shall we?"

Lily sat in a straight-backed chair that Brad brought to her from the kitchen table. He settled in a rocking chair, and Kathy and Dakota took places on the sofa.

"Kathy," Lily said, "Sharon called me just before we left the house and said..."

"Yes, yes, I know what she said," Kathy interrupted. "Dakota and I have been dealing all day with the issue of whether or not I'm his wife."

"Well?" Lily said. "Are you his wife?"

"Yes," Dakota said.

"No," Kathy said. "Let's not get into that right now, okay? That's not the issue at hand. We know why we're here. We have to find a way to send Dakota back through the Dream Catcher to his own time."

"Why?" Lily said. "Why can't he stay? You like it here, don't you, Dakota?"

He nodded. "Mmm."

"So," Lily said, throwing up her hands, "stay."

Yes, yes, yes, Kathy's heart sang.

"No," she said, "he can't."

"Why not?" Brad said seriously.

"Because of the mirror," Kathy said.

She quickly related what had happened when she and Dakota had stood in front of the mirror, and Dakota's explanation of what it meant.

"I see," Brad said. "I'm sorry to hear that."

"This is terrible," Lily said.

A heavy silence fell over the room as gazes shifted from one person to the next, each seeking but not finding, a solution to the dilemma. Brad finally spoke.

"Dakota," he said, "if it got right down to it and the choice was yours, would you choose to go back to 1877, or stay here?"

Kathy was hardly breathing as she looked at Dakota, waiting to hear his answer. Seconds ticked by that seemed like hours.

"Apaches face the truth as it is," Dakota said. "Do I wish to go? Stay? It does not matter. I *must* return to my own time to be united with my spirit."

"You'd make a good attorney," Brad said, smiling. "You don't allow your facts to be swayed by emotions, your personal feelings."

"Just for the record, though," Lily said, "would you prefer to stay or go?"

Dakota turned his head to look directly at Kathy. Her heart skipped a beat as she saw the warmth and tenderness in the ebony depths of his eyes.

"I would choose to stay," he said quietly.

Oh, dear heaven, Kathy thought. Oh, Dakota.

"Then we have to find a way to make that possible," Lily said. "We have to. Brad, think of something."

"I need some time to analyze this," Brad said, "to give it more thought. Well, let's take a look at this Dream Catcher of yours."

The group got to their feet and started toward the bedroom.

Dakota wanted to stay, Kathy's mind echoed. He wanted to stay with *her*. Was that wonderful? Or was it terrifying? What exactly were his feelings toward her? He considered her his wife, said caring was enough to get married, and that love would grow as days and nights passed. But was he considering the conflicts between them, the obstacles they faced?

Oh, what difference did it really make? Dakota could *not* stay with her. He was going to leave. She'd be alone. And she would cry.

In the bedroom, Kathy and Dakota slowly and carefully slid the Dream Catcher from beneath the bed.

"My stars," Lily said, "that's unbelievable. I saw you buy it when it was so small, Kathy, and look at it now. Incredible."

"I know," she said.

"Amazing," Brad said.

They pushed the Dream Catcher gently back into its safe place.

"Well, there's obviously no instant solution here," Kathy said, "but at least we'll know you two are thinking about it. Four minds are better than two. Let's go have some dessert."

They were soon sitting around the kitchen table enjoying cherry cobbler topped with dollops of whipped cream. Kathy registered a tremendous sense of pride at how well Dakota managed his spoon.

It was as though he'd used utensils for years, she thought. And it was as though he'd been a part of her life forever.

"Delicious, Kathy," Brad said, leaning back in his chair. "Thank you." He paused. "Well, we need a plan of action. I have a fairly light day scheduled tomorrow. I'll go to the library and see what I can find out about Dream Catchers. I doubt seriously that there's any documentation on an episode like what happened to Dakota actually taking place. But there might be something on the beliefs surrounding the thing."

"If this had happened before," Lily said, "and was made public knowledge, it would have been in every newspaper in the country."

"I shudder to think what it would have been like for the poor person who had been transported here. He wouldn't have a moment's peace or privacy. The press would hound him unmercifully, as well as scientists, historians, even government agents, for all we know. We *must* protect Dakota from that sort of thing."

"Good point," Brad said. "Secrecy is extremely important."

"Sharon asked me what Dakota's last name was," Lily said. "I told her it slipped my mind. She thinks I'm a dunce."

"Native Americans of Dakota's era didn't have last names," Brad said, "but we'd best give you one, Dakota. We want you to appear as though you're a regular citizen. Smith. Dakota Smith. How's that?"

"Two names for one man," he said, smiling. "I'm adopting many of the white man's ways."

Oh, that sinful smile, Kathy thought. He didn't use it often, but when he did, it curled her toes.

"Dakota Smith?" Lily said. "Really, Brad, don't you have more imagination than that? Smith is so boring, ordinary. Dakota is *not* ordinary."

No joke, Kathy thought dryly.

"Smith will do fine, Lily," Brad said. "If you want to spend time dwelling on names, you'd do well to decide on one for our soon-to-be-here daughter. Calling her Michael Bradley Benson isn't going to cut it."

"*She* was supposed to be a *he*," Lily said.

"No," Dakota said. "You don't carry a son. Not this time."

"Don't start *that* again, Dakota Smith," Lily said. "This is the *last* time."

"Mmm," he said. "Perhaps."

Lily glared at him, Brad chuckled, and Kathy fought against threatening tears.

Oh, look at this, she thought, swallowing past the lump in her throat. There they sat, all of them, sharing dessert around the kitchen table. They were comfortable together, a family, two couples: Lily and Brad, Kathy and Dakota. Anyone peering in the window would see a lovely scene.

How empty that chair where Dakota sat would seem when he was gone. How empty her life would be. *Oh, Kathy, please, just stop it.*

"Well, we'd better go," Brad said. "I'll let you know what I find out in the library. Lily, are you ready to take that baby girl home and set the sitter free from the clutches of our other daughters?"

Lily patted her stomach. "So much for Michael Bradley. Oh, well, sugar-and-spice little girls are certainly wonderful. Do you like the name Julie? Susan? Tracey? How about..."

"It's home and bed for you, madam," Brad said, getting to his feet.

Goodbyes were said at the door, then Kathy turned to look at Dakota.

"Well," she said, smiling, "I hope you liked Lily and Brad."

Dakota nodded. "Yes. They're real, honest, with no false fronts."

"Yes, they are." She cocked her head slightly to one side, a thoughtful expression on her face. "You can tell if someone is being open and honest with you, can't you?"

He nodded again. "In my time, having that ability can mean the difference between life or death. It can mean trading and bartering to provide for my people, or being fooled and giving what I have, with not enough gained in return.

"I refused to go to the reservation because I didn't believe the false promises of a prosperous and comfortable life in another place. The soldiers weren't speaking the truth and I knew it. The Apaches are a proud and brave people, but at that moment they were exhausted and frightened. They couldn't hear me when I spoke. And so, they went."

"I'm so sorry, Dakota."

"I stood hidden in the trees and watched them go, my heart heavy, my spirit filled with sorrow. As they disappeared, leaving only the stirred dust in the air, I heard the call of an owl. That sound, that bad omen, was the final proof that my people would never again be free."

Kathy closed the distance between them and placed one hand on his arm.

"They're free now, Dakota," she said softly, "just as I told you. Does that ease your pain, even a little?"

He covered her hand with his. "Yes, it does, and I thank you. You give me many gifts, Kathy."

The gentleness in their eyes as they continued to look at each other began to shift and change. The embers of desire within them glowed brighter, then burst into flames of heated passion.

Invisible threads of sensuality wove around them, encasing them in a cocoon where only they could be. It was their safe haven, where no one could intrude, where the reality of what they faced could not touch them.

"You would really stay here if you could?" Kathy whispered.

"I would stay." He drew his thumb over her lips. "I would stay here with you, my wife."

Kathy knew in the far recesses of her mind that she should voice objection once again to the title of wife that Dakota insisted on giving her. But that knowledge was clouded by the sensual mist consuming her ability to reason.

No, she couldn't think. Not now. It had been a long and exhausting day, and she just couldn't think anymore. She could only feel. She was awash with desire, the heat of it burning low within her, pulsing with a tempo as wild as the beating of her heart.

She felt cherished, respected, appreciated for doing nothing more than being. There was no question as to the honesty of what he was saying, for he knew no other way to speak. He was honoring her with the title of being his wife, and that was a precious gift she would treasure always.

Reality seemed to suddenly tap her on the shoulder, bringing her from her sensuous haze.

"Dakota," she said, "why would you wish to stay here with me as your wife? You were the one who said our worlds were too different, that they couldn't be meshed."

"I spoke those words in anger. I've since seen the merit of compromise. I believe you care deeply enough for me to be my wife. I'm content with that. You need more before accepting the title of wife. You have to be in love with me. That's your right and I respect it." He nodded. "Compromise."

"I see," she said thoughtfully.

"There's nothing left for me in my time, Kathy. Everything I had, who I was, has been stripped away. It no longer exists. Here? I have you, people who accept me, and I don't have to fear for my life."

"But what about all the other differences between us, our cultures, our worlds? I know I said that compromising could solve all of our problems, but now I wonder if that's really true. How many compromises can a relationship withstand?"

"What are *all these differences* that you refer to?"

"Oh, well, you know, like..." Kathy stopped speaking and frowned. "There's a whole list of them, but I'm too tired to click them off right now."

"A list."

"Yes."

"Is there? Are you positive of that?" Dakota sighed. "This conversation is useless. I have to go back, and we both know that. I wish

I knew why I was transported here by the Dream Catcher. To come, then be forced to leave, makes no sense to me. I don't regret it, but I don't understand it.''

"There's a great many things I don't understand,'' Kathy said wearily. "I'm so exhausted.''

"Then let's go to bed and get the rest we need. I don't have the energy I'm accustomed to. It's flowing out of me and there's no center spirit to replenish it.''

"Oh, Dakota, I...''

"Hush. No more talking tonight. It's been a long, tiring day.''

Several hours later, Kathy lay wide wake next to a sleeping Dakota. Despite her fatigue, she was unable to sleep, to shut off the cacophony of jumbled thoughts that chased each other in an endless, tangled circle in her mind.

Why *had* the Dream Catcher brought Dakota here and left his spirit behind? What had been the true purpose of all of this?

She shifted into a more comfortable position, willing herself to allow sleep to claim her.

When Dakota had asked her what obstacles stood in the way of their being together, her mind had been a complete blank. There *was* a list of differences between them, potential sources of problems.

Kathy yawned.

So, okay, she hadn't been able to say what they were when Dakota had pressed for an answer. That made sense because she was so tired. She'd remember them in the morning.

Wouldn't she?

Eight

In the light of the new day, Kathy decided that dwelling on the list of reasons why she and Dakota could not have a future together was a waste of valuable mental energy.

The issue that had to be focused on was how to transport Dakota back to 1877. He was already experiencing the physical effects of his spirit flowing from his body.

They were rapidly running out of time.

In the late morning, Lily came into The Herb Hogan for a quick hello, saying she wouldn't stay long as she had the two youngest girls with her. They possessed, she declared, the busiest fingers in the West and were hazardous to the health of Kathy's store.

Lily had received several more telephone calls from people inquiring if it was true that Kathy was married, and asking Lily for the juicy details.

"I winged it," she said merrily, after Kathy had exclaimed over how far the story had spread. "Due to the fact *I* was confused, I've probably thoroughly confused everyone else. Knowing me, I didn't say the same thing twice. Oh, well."

"There will be a new piece of gossip by tomorrow," Kathy said. "Dakota and I will be old news."

"However," Lily said, pointing one finger in the air, "do remember that our mothers are planning to fly in from Florida when this baby is born. They're not going to be put off as easily as folks here. They'll be into when, where and how in a big way, and most definitely will demand a straight answer regarding your marital status."

"Oh, good grief," Kathy said, rolling her eyes heavenward. "Don't have the baby too soon, Lily. I have to think about what I'm going to tell them."

"Oh, okay," Lily said, laughing and patting her stomach. "The message has been sent to this human cargo. *She* has been told. Dakota, are you absolutely positive that I'm carrying a girl?"

"Mmm," he said, nodding.

"Since you wanted to name a boy Michael," Kathy said, "why don't you call the new baby Michelle?"

"That's a thought," Lily said. "Holly, no, no, sweetheart, don't touch Aunt Kathy's pretty bottles. Come on, girls, we've got to go."

"Lily, wait," Kathy said. "Have you talked to Brad? He was planning to go the library to investigate Dream Catchers."

"No, I haven't talked to him since this morning but I'm sure he'll be in touch with you later. Bye for now."

Just minutes before closing time, Brad entered the store.

"Hi, Brad," Kathy said. "Would you lock the door and flip the sign to Closed, please?"

Brad did as instructed, then came to the counter.

"I waited until now to come by so we wouldn't be interrupted," he said.

"Good idea. Let's go into the back room and sit down," Kathy said.

Settled on chairs at the table in the rear area, Kathy and Dakota looked at Brad questioningly.

"Well, I have good news and bad news," Brad said. "The bad is that the reference material at the library was about what I expected. The history and legend of the Dream Catcher is fully documented. I even found instructions for how to make them. There was nothing to help us with your situation, though, Dakota."

"And the good news?" Kathy said, leaning slightly toward Brad.

"I found an article about Dream Catchers written by a Dr. John Tucker. He's a professor, retired from Northern Arizona University, and he still lives in Flagstaff. He taught courses for many years on native American history, culture, folklore, customs, the whole enchilada."

"The what?" Dakota said.

"Oh, sorry, Dakota," Brad said. "The man knows a great deal about Indians. The thing is, there was a subtle message in the article that Indian folklore should not be taken lightly, that it was not given the proper respect. I got the distinct feeling that this Dr. Tucker truly believes in many of the legends."

"And?" Kathy said.

"I took a chance and called him. Oh, yes, indeed, the good professor believes in Indian legends. I crossed my fingers, hoped I wasn't making a mistake, and told him how Dakota had gotten here."

"Oh, dear," Kathy said, reaching over to grasp Dakota's hand.

"Dr. Tucker didn't flicker. He was excited about what I was saying, was totally accepting, and said it was bound to have happened eventually since the surge of popularity of people owning Dream Catchers. He was surprised it hadn't occurred before now."

"I'll be darned," Kathy said.

"Can he be trusted?" Dakota said.

"Yes," Brad said. "He understands the importance of secrecy, said he cringed at the thought of what would happen to Dakota if this became known publicly."

"Brad, did you explain to him about Dakota's center spirit not traveling through the Dream Catcher with him?" Kathy said.

Brad nodded, then sighed. "Dr. Tucker said that you can't survive here, Dakota, without the center of your spirit."

"I know," Dakota said.

Kathy tightened her hold on his hand.

"Did Dr. Tucker say what we should do to return Dakota to his own time?" Kathy said. Oh, no, please, no. She didn't want him to leave her.

"He's going to do some research on it," Brad said. "He knows a great many native Americans and can ask questions about the Dream

Catcher, without them wondering why he's interested, because he's gathered data from them for many years.''

"When will you be speaking with him again?" Kathy asked.

"He and his wife are coming over on Saturday for Territorial Days. Dr. Tucker is very eager to meet Dakota, and we're to connect with them at Sharlot Hall at two in the afternoon. I'll recognize him because his picture was printed with the article."

"This is only Wednesday, Brad," Kathy said. "There are precious days being wasted until Saturday."

"Dr. Tucker will call if he discovers something before Saturday. He realizes that time is of the essence, but he feels he's in for a real challenge as far as finding out what we have to know. He needs the days until Saturday, if not longer."

"We don't know how much longer Dakota has," Kathy said, her voice trembling.

"Calm down, Kathy," Dakota said. "Brad has done all he can, and I'm grateful for that. We will have to be patient until we can meet with Dr. Tucker."

"I didn't come equipped with Apache patience," she said, sighing. "Thank you so much for everything you did today, Brad."

Brad got to his feet. "Well, we'll see what happens on Saturday. I'd better get home to my harem."

Kathy and Dakota stood and the two men shook hands. Brad left the store, and a few minutes later Kathy and Dakota were driving toward her house. Neither spoke, each digesting all that Brad had said.

Inside the house, Kathy started toward the bedroom.

"I'm going to change into jeans," she said, "then I'll fix dinner."

She stopped suddenly, turned, and hurried back to where Dakota was still standing in the middle of the living room. She wrapped her arms tightly around his waist, looking up at him.

"I want to hold fast to you," she said, unable to keep tears from filling her eyes, "to somehow keep you safe. I'm so worried that we won't find the answers we need in time."

Dakota encircled her slender body with his arms.

"We have to hope that Dr. Tucker will discover the mysteries of the Dream Catcher, and send me back so I can be united with my center spirit."

"Dakota, what if…what if we asked Dr. Tucker if there is a way to transport your spirit from there to here? If he discovers how to send you back to your spirit, doesn't it make sense that he could do it in reverse?" She rested her head on his chest.

"Yes," he said, "I suppose. There's no harm in asking him."

But a frown knitted his brows, and an expression of deep sadness settled over his features. He buried his face in Kathy's silky curls and tightened his hold on her, not wanting to let her go. Wishing to stay with her in her world. Forever.

Hours later, just before Kathy drifted off to sleep, she nestled closer to Dakota, placing one hand on his chest to feel the beat of his heart beneath her palm. He was asleep, the steady rise and fall of his chest giving her a sense of well-being.

They had both executed maximum effort to push aside the cloud of gloom and fear hovering over them so they could enjoy the evening together.

Kathy had laughed in delight at Dakota's shock as he tasted ice cream for the first time. After his second bowl, he declared the dessert to have great merit.

They'd weeded and watered the herb garden, removed some of the dried herbs that were ready to go to The Herb Hogan from the drying wall, then watched a movie on television.

And then they'd made love, Kathy remembered dreamily. It had been exquisite, so beautiful. Nothing was allowed to intrude into their private world of ecstasy, of sharing, of being one glorious entity.

Kathy closed her eyes and slept.

Early the next afternoon, a man entered The Herb Hogan with several small rugs draped over one arm. Kathy greeted him pleasantly.

"The name is Sam Spander," the man said. "I'm down from Nevada to have a booth on the square for Territorial Days. I came in early to make the rounds of the merchants, give you a chance to sell authentic Navajo rugs out of your own stores. I have enough other inventory to allow you to deal in the rugs."

"They're lovely," Kathy said.

Sam spread the rugs out on the counter.

"I can let you have them at a good price. I have some Navajos who weave these exclusively for me. Authentic Navajo rugs are hard to come by, but I have a steady supply. Are you interested?"

"Well..." Kathy said, staring at the pretty rugs.

"No," Dakota said, then folded his arms tightly over his chest.

"Dakota?" Kathy said, looking at him in surprise. "Mr. Spander, this is Dakota Smith."

"I'm Apache," Dakota said.

"Nice to meet you," Sam said, eyeing him warily.

"Kathy doesn't want your rugs," Dakota said.

"I don't?" she said. "Why don't I?"

"Because those were not made by Navajos," Dakota said, a steely edge to his voice.

"Now, wait just a damn minute," Sam said.

"Dakota," Kathy said, "how do you know these aren't authentic Navajo rugs?"

Dakota pointed to the end of one of the rugs.

"They have fringe. Navajos weave with one continuous strand on a loom. Their rugs are smooth on all sides, and never have fringe. The Navajo's prayer is 'to walk in beauty,' and they make rugs with no frills, no fringe. They are an expression of simplistic beauty. No, these are not Navajo rugs."

"Well, well, Sam," Kathy said, "now what do you have to say?"

Dakota narrowed his eyes as he looked at Sam. "You've tried to cheat my woman, my wife. An Apache brave doesn't stand silently by and allow such a thing to happen."

Sam's eyes widened in fright. "Now, don't get excited, Dakota...Mr. Smith." He snatched up the rugs and began to back toward the door. "This is just a little misunderstanding, that's all. I'll get out of your way. No problem."

"Leave Prescott before the sun sets," Dakota said.

Sam stopped in his tracks. "I've paid for a booth on the square for the weekend."

"No," Dakota said. "You'll be gone. You won't cheat people in this town, or diminish the honor of the Navajo by presenting inferior rugs as being made by them. Do you understand me?"

"You bet. I'm gone. Out of town," Sam said, turning toward the door. "You never saw me." He hurried out of the store.

Kathy burst into laughter. "Oh, Dakota, you were wonderful. Did you see his face? I think he had images of your scalping him, or some grim thing."

"Mmm," Dakota said, still frowning. "No one will treat my wife poorly. If they do, they answer to me."

"My hero," Kathy said, smiling at him warmly.

"Your husband," Dakota said with a decisive nod.

An hour later, Kathy received a telephone call from one of her homebound customers, requesting a new supply of the herbs she used for brewing tea, as well as her favorite lotion. Kathy promised to deliver the products after regular working hours.

She went into the back room where Dakota was filling pouches with herbs, and explained that they'd drive to the woman's house before going home for dinner.

"Oh, you're filling pouches with cinnamon tea," she said. "I recommend it for morning sickness, among other things."

Dakota looked up at her. "Tea brewed from the root of the ginger plant is best for the sickness at dawn that comes with carrying a child."

"Gingerroot?" Kathy said, frowning. "That's for ailments resulting from circulation problems."

Dakota shrugged. "It's used by my people for the dawn sickness."

"Let me look it up in my reference book."

"Kathy," Dakota said, his voice very low, "*I* have said that gingerroot is what is best for dawn sickness."

"And *I*," Kathy said, her blue eyes flashing with anger, "have never heard of it being used for that."

She went to the front, then returned with a large book that she thunked onto the table. After shooting Dakota a stormy glare, she began to flip quickly through the pages until coming to the *G* section.

"Ginger," she muttered, drawing one fingertip down the column of small print. "Ginger, ginger. Ah, here we go. Gingerroot." She quickly read the information, her eyes widening. "Oh."

"Oh?" Dakota said.

A flush of embarrassment stained Kathy's cheeks.

"Gingerroot tea *is* used to relieve morning sickness," she said. "Well, Dakota, I'm sorry. You were right and I apologize."

Dakota got to his feet and crossed his arms over his chest, frowning deeply. "An Apache wife would never question the words of her husband. It doesn't demonstrate the proper respect due a man. You shouldn't have doubted what I said to you."

Anger erupted in Kathy like a volcano. She opened her mouth, realized she was so furious she was unable to string two words together, and looked like a puffing goldfish. She snapped her mouth closed, then turned to the table and began to drum her fingertips on the surface in an erratic rhythm.

"Did you understand me, Kathy?" Dakota said, a cold edge to his voice.

That did it.

She spun around, her blue eyes flashing like laser beams.

"Don't you dare speak to me in that tone of voice, Dakota Smith. You're talking to me the same way you did to that sleazeball with the phony rugs. Don't even think about doing a 'me Tarzan, you Jane' routine on me."

"Who?"

"Forget that part," she said, flipping one hand in the air. "Dakota, women in this era have a voice."

Dakota stared at her for a moment, then laughed. "A *loud* voice. All right, Kathy, you've definitely made your point."

"I did?" She blinked. "Well, fancy that." She matched his smile. "This is a perfect situation for some culture training. You see, Dakota, when two people have an argument, they holler a tad, end the nonsense, then make up."

"Oh?"

"Yes, indeed. This is very important."

"What's this making-up process?"

"Well," she said, "I'll demonstrate it for you, sort of like show-and-tell."

She wrapped her arms around his neck, molded herself to his rugged body, and covered his mouth with hers in a searing kiss. Dakota encircled her with his arms and returned the kiss in total abandon, meeting her questing tongue eagerly with his own.

Kathy sank her hands into his thick, silky hair, urging his mouth harder onto hers, savoring his taste, the feel of his aroused body pressed against her, inhaling his special aroma.

When she finally ended the kiss, they stayed locked in each other's embrace. Desire radiated from Dakota's obsidian eyes, matching the ardor shining in Kathy's blue eyes.

"This making-up has merit," Dakota said, his voice raspy.

"Great, huh?" Kathy laughed. "Make love, not war." She nestled her head on his chest and sighed in contentment.

They stood silently for a long moment, savoring.

"Kathy?" Dakota finally said.

"Yes?"

"Who is Tarzan?"

"This will be fun, Dakota," Kathy said as they drove away from The Herb Hogan. "The delivery I'm making is on a side of town you haven't seen yet. So, sir, I'll be your tour guide."

Dakota chuckled.

"Oh, do you understand about traffic lights?" Kathy said, pressing on the brake.

"You've stopped because the red light came on. When the green one glows, you'll start off again. The yellow in the middle means you press your foot harder on the pedal and race forward before it changes to red."

"Oh, dear, shame on me. Some people stop the instant they see the yellow light, but I... Never mind, that's boring. Now, then, on your left is the old armory, which is ancient and constructed of stone. Isn't it marvelous? It's used for all kinds of activities. It has a gymnasium where people play basketball and stuff, take classes in dancing, aerobics, martial arts and..."

Kathy chattered on, directing Dakota's attention to the left, right, then back to the left. He couldn't understand all the words she was using, but didn't interrupt for definitions. Kathy looked so happy, her blue eyes sparkling, and he enjoyed looking at her far more than the landmarks.

After the delivery to the homebound customer had been made, Kathy drove away from the woman's house. A beautiful sunset was just beginning to streak across the sky in vibrant colors, acting as a backdrop to the mountains in the distance. The air was clear and clean, and a cool breeze carried an aroma of flowers and freshly cut grass.

Kathy glanced over at Dakota, smiling at the mere sight of him, then paid attention to the traffic again.

"Have you had enough commentary for now?" she said. "Oh, one last thing. On the right up ahead is the Veterans Hospital. It's built on the site of where Fort Whipple once stood.

"See the wooden wall with the stone pillars topped by old-fashioned lamps? Those huge, metal gates between the pillars were found in the weeds, and a group of people took on the project of restoring and reattaching them to the pillars. There was a special ceremony held to rededicate the gates and mark the 130th anniversary of the fort."

"Fort Whipple," Dakota said, his voice harsh. "Stop the car, Kathy."

Kathy snapped her head around to look at him, and her breath caught as she saw the tight set to his jaw, the pulse beating in his temple, the fury radiating from his narrowed eyes.

"Dakota, what..."

"Stop the car!"

She glanced quickly in the rearview mirror, then eased off the road, driving down a narrow road to park at the gates. She turned off the ignition, then had to hurry to unfasten her seat belt, as Dakota was already out of the car. She caught up with him at the gates, seeing the ramrod stiffness of his body.

"Dakota," she said, "what's wrong? Why are you so upset?"

"I've never seen this fort, but I've known of it for many years," he said, a rough edge to his voice. "Word reached my people where we lived in the Chiricahua Mountains that General Carlton of the Santa Fe soldiers had issued General Order Number 27, which stated that Fort Whipple should be built.

"Through these gates, soldiers rode out time and again to massacre the Apache and Yavapai Indians. These are gates of death, Kathy. *Gates of death.*

"The Apaches who lived up here were not of my tribe, not Chiricahua. They killed many white men who came here after gold was discovered in the Bradshaw Mountains. The Yavapai suffered the consequences of the Apache's actions, and were sent to the San Carlos reservation a few years ago.''

He shook his head as though to clear it.

"No, not a few years go. I'm not in my own time." He paused. "Fort Whipple. I hate the very sight of those gates."

"Oh, Dakota, I'm so sorry," Kathy said, her voice trembling with unshed tears. "I never would have mentioned it if I... It's history to me, something that happened so long ago. I didn't mean to cause you this pain, I swear I didn't. I'm so, so sorry." The tears spilled onto her cheeks.

"It's strange to stand here," Dakota said, glancing around, "and realize the soldiers won't appear, prepared to kill me because I'm not of their blood.

"My people wished only to live as we always had, Kathy. The white men came to *our* land, took *our* game to feed themselves, leaving us hungry. They pushed us away like worthless insects who annoyed them. All that was ours, they claimed as their own. What choice did we have but to push back, fight to protect the only way of life we had ever known?''

"Please, Dakota, let's leave here. I apologize for... Oh, God, how could I have been so insensitive, so thoughtless? What is history to me, is your reality. You trusted me and what did I do? I can see the pain in your eyes, on your face."

She dashed tears from her cheeks and struggled to stop crying.

"Different cultures, different worlds," she said, a sob catching in her throat. "This is a perfect example of that. You consider me your wife? Someone who has hurt you like this, just blissfully announced that nifty Fort Whipple was right up ahead? I won't ask you to forgive me, Dakota, because how could you?"

"It's all right," he said, then sighed wearily.

"No, it's not. I feel as though I betrayed your trust in me. The thing is, I'm liable to do it again and again because I forget you're not of this time. You've adapted to this era so wonderfully. You're open and receptive to all the new things you've had to deal with. So what do I do?" She shook her head. "I make certain you don't miss seeing good old Fort Whipple."

"I know you didn't purposely cause me this inner pain, Kathy."

"There's no excuse for what I did. I've started taking your existence here for granted, the way you've adjusted as a given. I've got to remember how different we are, how far apart our worlds are. *I can't forget that.*

"You wanted to hear the list of differences between us?"

She swept one arm through the air. "There's one of the things, Dakota. Those gates, and my lack of sensitivity to who you are, really are. Your wife is supposed to be your best friend. Well, friends don't cause each other pain. They don't."

She moved around him and ran toward the car.

Dakota stood statue-still, staring at the gates, then drew a deep, steadying breath.

There were no soldiers beyond those gates, he told himself. They were not suddenly going to appear and attempt to kill him. He was safe here in Kathy's world.

He turned and started slowly toward the car.

Kathy was being very hard on herself for having mentioned the existence of Fort Whipple, he mused. He could forgive her easily, because he knew in his heart she hadn't intentionally caused him pain. But she knew that, too. She knew it had been an innocent mistake, a momentary lack of judgment on her part.

But...

It was as though she was gathering the incident around her, using it as a shield between them. She was now insisting that it was a perfect example of how different their worlds were, a concrete reason why they couldn't have a future together if they found a way for his spirit to be brought forward in time.

Why was she doing that?

What was she afraid of?

Nine

During the next day and on into Saturday, tension began to build in Kathy and Dakota as the meeting with Dr. Tucker drew near.

Dakota turned his emotions inward and spent more time than usual in the herb garden. He sat cross-legged on the ground, his hands draped loosely over his knees. His back was ramrod-stiff and he appeared to be hardly breathing.

Kathy handled her increasingly frazzled nerves in an opposite manner. She slammed cupboard doors, polished the furniture with a vengeance and muttered a great deal.

After lunch on Saturday, she indulged in a leisurely bubble bath with the hope that the lazy soak in the fragrant, warm water would be soothing. It wasn't. With a cluck of disgust she got out of the tub and began to dry herself with a fluffy towel.

Good grief, she was a wreck. What a helpless, frustrating, vulnerable feeling it was to acknowledge that her entire future rested in the hands of a stranger, a faceless man known to her only as Dr. Tucker.

Kathy hung up the towel, then stilled, staring into space.

This was how Dakota and his people must have felt when the settlers, then later the soldiers, invaded their land. The Indians were at the mercy of others. They no longer had a voice in how and where they would live, or what the future held.

Kathy began to dress slowly, her mind focused on the past, on what she had read in history books.

How incredibly sad it all was, she mused. The white settlers had gathered their courage and come to a harsh new land, searching for better lives and the fulfillment of their dreams for a prosperous future. They had come with hope in their hearts, not hate.

But mistakes born of ignorance had been made. They had moved onto land already claimed by native Americans long before. Fear, then anger, resulted in atrocities being committed by both groups of people. Lives had been lost and dreams destroyed.

Dakota had suffered such tremendous losses, she thought as she left the bathroom. Yet he hadn't hardened his heart to the point of being unable to care deeply for her. He didn't blame her for what had happened, despite her being a descendent of the people who had driven him from his land.

Kathy's mind began to drift toward the memories of the incident with Dakota at the gates of Fort Whipple.

No, she told herself, she wouldn't relive it, not again. It was haunting her. It had become a nightmare that plagued her during the day, as well as in her dreams at night.

After she and Dakota had gotten home that night they had not discussed what had happened at the historic gates. But she couldn't forget it, nor forgive herself for what she'd done.

There was nowhere to escape from the fact that it had been a glaring, painful example of the differences in her and Dakota's worlds.

In the bedroom, Kathy found one tennis shoe, but the other eluded her. She dropped to her knees and peered under the bed.

"Dear heaven," she whispered, then scrambled to her feet. "Dakota!" she yelled.

He appeared a moment later, wearing the blue western shirt, jeans, and a frown.

"Why are you shrieking?" he said.

"The Dream Catcher," she said, her voice trembling.

"What about it?"

"Oh, Dakota, it's not as big as it was." She dropped to her knees again and slid the Dream Catcher carefully from beneath the bed. "See?"

Dakota hunkered down, balancing on the balls of his feet. His frown deepened.

"It was easily six feet across the morning you came here," Kathy said, "but now it's... I don't know for sure, but it appears to be less than five feet in width."

Dakota nodded slowly.

Kathy clutched one of his arms with both hands.

"What does this mean?" she said, a frantic edge to her voice.

"I'm not certain, and I can only guess. I think the powers of the Dream Catcher that were in full force when I was transported here are now diminishing. Why? I don't know."

He looked at Kathy.

"We're fighting the enemy of time twofold now, Kathy. I must be united with my center spirit before it's too late and I die. And, the mystery of the Dream Catcher must be solved before its remaining powers are gone. I don't hold much hope in my heart for a victory."

"Yes, you do," she said, tightening her grip on his arm. "You *won't* give up, Dakota. Do you hear me? We don't know what Dr. Tucker is going to tell us, but I sense that we'll need to be strong, to believe in what he says, to enable us to do our part."

"And if he has no answers?"

"He will, Dakota. *He will.* Come on, let's go. We have to meet Lily and Brad. Oh, blast, where's my stupid shoe?"

As they drove to Lily and Brad's, Kathy chattered on about Territorial Days, unable to bear the tension-laden silence in the car.

Held every year, she related, Territorial Days were very popular with Prescott residents, as well as the multitude of tourists who drove up the mountain to attend.

The main event was held a block from the town square on the grounds of the Sharlot Hall Museum complex.

One of the buildings besides the intriguing museum was the original residence, built back in 1864, of the Territorial Governor, John Goodwin, and the Secretary of the Territory, Richard McCormick.

Another structure built in 1864 had been a general store that later belonged to Judge John Howard, who sentenced frontier criminals for their offenses. Since the judge dispensed "misery" to the miscreants, the little house was called Fort Misery.

Kathy rambled on about the other buildings, some of which had been carefully moved onto the site to preserve them for future generations.

"You'll see people in costumes depicting the times when the buildings were actually in use," she said. "Women will be dipping candles, operating spinning wheels, cowboys will make biscuits over a campfire, all kinds of things. It's fun."

"Mmm" was all Dakota had to say about Kathy's dissertation.

At Lily and Brad's, Lily said she didn't have the energy to go with them.

"It's so crowded,and I'm having an 'I'm totally exhausted so don't mess with me' day. I'll stay home with the girls. You find Dr. Tucker and his wife and bring them here for lemonade and cookies. You can't have a serious discussion in the mob down there."

"I could wait here with you, Lily," Kathy said.

"No, no, you'll be a nervous wreck and you'll drive me nuts. You go on with Brad and Dakota. Shoo. You don't want to be late meeting Dr. Tucker, and finding a place to park will be a good trick." She flapped her hands at them. "Goodbye, goodbye."

As the trio trudged the last block to the Sharlot Hall complex, Brad chuckled.

"We should have walked from the house," he said, "considering how far away we had to park. We're meeting Dr. Tucker and his wife at the front entrance of the museum. They were planning on coming over early to have time to enjoy all the Territorial Days doings, so they'll be ready to leave with us."

Kathy slipped her hand into Dakota's and held fast.

"Let's cut across here," Brad said. "We'll be in the middle of the crowd, but Dakota will be able to see some of what's going on. It's very unique, very clever and authentic. These folks really give it their all. You'll feel as though you've already been transported back in time, Dakota."

"Mmm," he said.

As they stepped off the sidewalk onto the lawn, they were immediately caught up in the crunch of people. Dakota's fingers tightened around Kathy's.

There were too many people, his mind hammered. They were surrounding him, pressing in from every direction. He'd never been in a place where so many were gathered. It was too loud, too confining.

"Dakota?" Kathy said as they maneuvered their way slowly forward. "Are you all right?"

"I can't breathe here, Kathy," he said, beads of sweat dotting his brow.

"Ah, damn," Brad said, "where was my mind? I'm sorry, Dakota, I just didn't think. I don't imagine you've ever been in a crowd like this one."

"No."

"I'm to blame," Kathy said miserably. "I can't believe I did this to you again, Dakota. Bringing you here was as thoughtless and insensitive as my showing you the gates of Fort Whipple." She shook her head in self-disgust. "I'm hopeless. I can't seem to handle the differences between our worlds at all. I continually cause you pain and…"

"Kathy," Brad interrupted, "I don't know what happened at Fort Whipple, but let's not stand around discussing it. We have to get Dakota out of this crowd."

"Yes, of course," she said. "I'm sorry. Oh, dear, I continually do things that I have to apologize for. I *am* sorry, Dakota."

"Come on," Brad said. "Keep moving as quickly as possible. If we can get through this section, we'll be at the sidewalk leading to the museum."

Dakota nodded, but his eyes continued to dart back and forth. The wild tempo of his heart echoed in his ears.

His urge to run, to flee to safety, was nearly overwhelming, requiring every ounce of willpower he possessed to continue to place one foot in front of the other.

Remain calm, he ordered himself. He must stay calm, reach deep within himself for courage. He was in no danger there. There were too many people, *too many*, but they were friendly. They were not his enemies. They weren't hunting for him, they weren't even paying any attention to him. He could see the walkway up ahead. Calm. *Remain calm.*

Suddenly Dakota halted dead in his tracks, every muscle in his body tensing. Kathy turned her head to see what Dakota was staring at beyond her.

"Oh, dear heaven," she whispered.

Ambling toward them were two men dressed in the blue uniforms of frontier cavalry soldiers and carrying old-fashioned rifles.

"Run, Kathy," Dakota said, his voice rough. "Go. Your safety comes first. I'll delay the soldiers while you find a place to hide. Go. Now."

She moved quickly in front of him and gripped his arms.

"Dakota, listen to me," she said, a frantic edge to her voice. "Those men are not really soldiers. They dressed in those uniforms to be part of Territorial Days. It's all pretend, Dakota. It's not real."

"Run!" he yelled.

Several people turned to look at him curiously.

"Dakota..." Brad said.

"Please, listen to me, Dakota," Kathy said. *"Look at me."*

He slowly shifted his gaze from the still-advancing soldiers to look directly into her eyes.

"You consider me your woman," she said softly, "your wife. I know I've made terrible mistakes, caused you much upset, but I'm asking you to trust me one more time, believe in me. No one is going to hurt you. Those soldiers aren't real. They're no threat to you. *Hear me.*"

Dakota stared at her for another long moment, then drew a shuddering breath that rippled through his body. His shoulders slumped as the tension ebbed from his muscles, then he squared his shoulders again.

"I hear you, Kathy," he said, a gritty quality to his voice.

The soldiers strolled past them.

"Howdy, folks," one of them said. "Enjoying yourselves?"

Brad let out a pent-up breath. "Oh, yes," he said dryly, "we're having a terrific time."

"Way to go," the soldier said.

"I'm such a lamebrain," Brad muttered.

"Are you all right now, Dakota?" Kathy said.

"Mmm," he said, nodding.

"You put my safety first," she said, a ring of awe in her voice. "You told me to run and hide while you fought off the soldiers."

"I'm an Apache brave of honor. I protect my woman from harm at any cost. That's how it's meant to be."

"Fancy that," she said, managing to produce a small smile. "If I were you, I wouldn't even speak to me, let alone protect me."

"Let's hurry up," Brad said.

They left the lawn and started along the sidewalk toward the museum.

Dr. and Mrs. Tucker, Kathy decided, looked exactly as a retired professor and his wife should.

John Tucker was short and round with thick gray hair and wire-rimmed glasses. He had a smile that caused crinkling lines to form by his eyes, and there was a warm and friendly aura emanating from him. He introduced his wife, Evelyn, who was a carbon copy of him in female form.

"You have no idea how much of a pleasure this is, Dakota," Dr. Tucker said, shaking Dakota's hand. "I've been counting the hours until I could meet you." He released Dakota's hand and glanced around. "I wouldn't have thought you'd be comfortable in this atmosphere."

"There are wise men," Brad said, "and there are dumb men. Color me dumb."

"Well, let's leave, shall we?" Evelyn said. "I'm sure Dakota has had quite enough of Territorial Days."

Brad gave Dr. Tucker directions to the house, saying they would rendezvous there.

Twenty minutes later, they were all settled in Lily and Brad's living room, sipping lemonade.

"Dr. Tucker," Kathy said, "before you tell us if you've discovered anything that will help us, I want to say that it's our fervent hope that Dakota's center spirit can be transported here, rather than sending him back to 1877. There's nothing left for him in his own time. It's gone, everything he had, the existence he knew. He wants to stay *here*."

Dr. Tucker looked at Kathy, then at Dakota, back at Kathy, and nodded.

"Am I assuming too much," he said, "to believe you are now married by Apache custom?"

"Kathy is my wife," Dakota said.

"Oh, well, I..." Kathy said, feeling the heat of embarrassment on her cheeks. She threw up her hands in defeat.

"Oh, bless your hearts," Evelyn Tucker said.

Brad leaned forward in his chair, rested his elbows on his knees, and made a steeple of his fingers.

"What have you discovered since we talked on the phone, Dr. Tucker?" he said. "Have you solved the mystery of the Dream Catcher?"

Please, Kathy begged silently. *Say yes. Dr. Tucker, please, say yes.*

"No," the professor said, frowning.

"Oh, God," Kathy whispered, then pressed trembling fingertips to her lips.

"Now wait," Dr. Tucker said, raising both hands. "*I* don't have the answer, but after talking to a multitude of native Americans I know in Flagstaff, I've gathered information that *might* be the solution. There's no guarantee about this. I want you to fully realize that."

"We'll try anything," Kathy said. "Dakota will die if he isn't united with the center of his spirit."

"Yes, my dear," John Tucker said, "he will. I was told that more than once during my interviews. Time is of the utmost importance."

"There's something you don't know," Kathy said. "We haven't even told Lily and Brad yet because we found out just as we were leaving the house."

"What?" Lily said. "What is it?"

"The Dream Catcher," Dakota said quietly, "is becoming smaller. It's less than five feet across now."

"Why?" Lily said, her voice rising. "What does that mean?"

"Let me tell you what I've managed to find out," Dr. Tucker said. "First of all, it might surprise you to learn that none of the native Americans I spoke with had any doubt that someone could be transported through time with a Dream Catcher."

"John presented it hypothetically, of course," Evelyn said. "No one he interviewed even suspected that he was dealing with an actual situation.''

"Correct," John said. "An old gentleman told me that it's very common for two people who are meant to be together, soul mates, if you will, to be kept apart by time, by where they exist in history, due to a subtle shift in the moon when they were born.

"That, the old gentleman said, is why there is so much unhappiness in the world, such discord in marriages. The person they were meant to be with is in another era, never to be known to them.''

Kathy blinked. "What? Are you saying..." Her voice trailed off as she stared at Dr. Tucker.

"Yes, dear," Evelyn said, smiling, "you and Dakota are soul mates, you belong together.''

"It's very complex," John said. "Three things have to be in perfect synchronization. The people must be thinking at exactly the same moment about what is missing from their lives. They must be wishing to feel complete. Obviously you two were doing that.

"The third ingredient is to have the means to unite those people.'' He lifted both hands palms up. "The Dream Catcher.''

"My stars," Lily said, "isn't that something? Kathy and Dakota are soul mates, are each other's...destiny. Yes, that's an excellent word.''

Dakota crossed his arms over his chest and nodded. "So be it.''

"Now, wait a minute," Kathy said. "Just hold it here.''

"Yes, dear?" Evelyn said. "What do you wish to say, Kathy?''

"Well..." Kathy shook her head. "I have no idea. It's too much to comprehend, to believe.''

"*I* believe it," Dakota said.

"Dr. Tucker," Brad said, "if all this is true, then why didn't Dakota's spirit travel with him through time?''

"Because a part of him was still holding on to life as he'd known it before he was longing for what was now missing. He was emotionally struggling against the reality of his present existence.''

"Oh, darn," Lily said, "that makes sense, it really does.''

"Why is the Dream Catcher shrinking?" Kathy said, a rather frantic edge to her voice.

Dr. Tucker sighed. "I was told about such a thing happening, but didn't know it applied here until now. The diminishing in size of the Dream Catcher means that one of the pair is fighting against what has taken place, what has happened. For reasons known only to them, they aren't accepting the other person's role in their life. That is draining the Dream Catcher of its power.''

''All right, you guys,'' Lily said, glaring at Kathy and Dakota, ''which one of you is gumming up the works?''

''My darling wife,'' Brad said, chuckling, ''that is none of your business.''

''Oh,'' Lily said. ''Well, what if said unknown person gets their act together...quickly. Will the Dream Catcher stop shrinking?''

''I really don't know,'' Dr. Tucker said. ''No one I spoke with knew how to stop the shrinking, only what was causing it. To be safe, we'll have to proceed assuming the Dream Catcher will continue to decrease in size.''

''Mmm,'' Dakota said, frowning.

''We're now facing two races against time,'' Dr. Tucker continued. ''We must accomplish our goals before the remaining spirit within Dakota is depleted, and before the Dream Catcher becomes nothing more than the small ornament it was when Kathy originally bought it.''

''What are we to do?'' Kathy said, clutching her hands tightly in her lap. ''Dr. Tucker?''

''There is, supposedly,'' he said, ''an old shaman living down in the Chiricahua Mountains. I say 'supposedly' because no one I spoke to has actually seen him, nor knows anyone who has. The majority had heard of him, though. He's believed to be very powerful, a true shaman. The consensus was that if anyone could control the Dream Catcher's magic, it would be that shaman.''

Dakota nodded.

''You must take the Dream Catcher,'' Dr. Tucker said, ''go down to the southern part of the state to the Chiricahua Mountains, and find that shaman.''

''As quickly as possible,'' Evelyn interjected.

''Indeed,'' John said, patting her knee. ''I'll draw you a map of the general area in the Chiricahua Mountains where the shaman has been rumored to have been seen.''

"I know the Chiricahuas," Dakota said. "I'm a Chiricahua Apache. Those mountains are...were...my home."

"Dr. Tucker," Lily said, her voice unsteady, "we don't want to lose Dakota, none of us do. This baby—" she rested her hands on her stomach "—is to be named Michelle Dakota Benson."

"I'm honored to have your child hold my name," Dakota said.

Kathy pressed her fingertips to her aching temples. "I feel so overwhelmed. It's too much to take in. I need time to sort through all of this."

"If there's one thing we're short of, it's time," Brad said. "Dr. Tucker, in your honest opinion, sir, what do you think the chances are of Dakota surviving this?"

"I don't know, son," he said quietly. "I just don't know."

Ten

To Kathy's relief, the remainder of the afternoon and on into the evening was filled with activities that would make it possible for her to leave town for an undetermined length of time.

When she telephoned Sally to inquire if she would be available to run The Herb Hogan, her assistant immediately assumed that Kathy and Dakota were finally going on their honeymoon.

"Yes," Kathy said quickly, pointing one finger in the air. "That's it, that's exactly what we're doing. A honeymoon trip. Good idea. What I mean is, aren't you the clever one to have figured that out? There's no keeping a secret from you, Sally."

"Ha! You've tried to keep the secret of your marriage to Dakota from everyone, you sneaky person, with you saying you weren't his wife and him declaring you were. You're so silly sometimes, Kathy. Anyway, I hope you have a fabulous honeymoon. Stay away as long as you like and don't worry about the store."

"Well, Dakota and I will take more herbs to the store later today. There are shipments due in from Flagstaff and Sedona, so you'll be all set. I have a neighbor boy coming to water my garden. I just don't know for certain when we'll be back."

Nor did she know if she'd be returning to Prescott alone, she thought dismally. No, no, she wouldn't dwell on that now.

"Oh-h-h, this is so romantic," Sally said. "I don't suppose you're telling anyone where you're going."

"No."

"I don't blame you. You and Dakota want to be alone, just the two of you."

And an old shaman, Kathy mused, who held the key, the only hope, for saving Dakota's life.

"Yes, just the two of us," Kathy said quietly. "Thanks a million, Sally. It's wonderful to be able to go away and know the store is receiving your tender loving care. You're a wonderful friend."

"It's my pleasure. Enjoy your trip. Bye for now, Kathy."

Kathy and Dakota stocked The Herb Hogan to overflowing, then stopped to purchase two more shirts for Dakota, plus travel-size personal items. Back at the house they ate dinner, managing to keep the conversation light, then Kathy packed a small suitcase, leaving out last-minute things they'd use in the morning.

As darkness fell, Kathy spread out a map of Arizona on the kitchen table.

"Okay, let's see," she said. "We're here. It's about a two-hour drive to Phoenix, another two to Tucson, and two more to Douglas, down on the Mexican border. If we stay overnight in Douglas, we can start out fresh for the Chiricahua Mountains on Monday morning. Does that sound all right to you, Dakota?"

She turned to look at him where he stood next to her by the table.

"Yes," he said, nodding. "Your plan is…" Suddenly he grabbed the back of a chair as he pressed his other hand to his forehead. "I… The room moves… I…"

"Dakota?" Kathy said, flinging her arms around his chest. "Are you in pain? Are you dizzy? What is it? Talk to me."

"I have to sit down," he said, sinking slowly to the floor.

Kathy moved with him, anxiously watching his face. He closed his eyes, shook his head slightly, and drew a deep breath. He opened his eyes again tentatively.

"The room has stopped spinning," he said. "I feel stronger now. For a moment I was very weak. I didn't have the strength to stand. This was much worse than the other time I felt strange."

"Dear heaven," Kathy said, her eyes widened in horror, "then it's happening faster, isn't it. Your spirit is flowing out of your body and can't be replaced because the center isn't there."

"Yes." He stroked her cheek gently with his thumb. "I'm sorry."

She encircled his neck with her arms and nestled her head on his chest.

"*You're* sorry?" she said, her eyes filling with tears. "I've spent the day doing everything but facing the truth of what Dr. Tucker said."

"My center spirit didn't travel with me through the Dream Catcher because I was still clinging to my existence in the past."

"That's true, but you know that is not what I'm talking about. The Dream Catcher is shrinking because one of us hasn't acknowledged the other's role in their life. That's me, Dakota, and we're both aware of that fact. You consider me your wife, but I won't accept the title because..."

"You don't love me," he interrupted quietly. "That's not your fault. You can't force emotions upon yourself, they have to just come. Just be there."

A sob caught in Kathy's throat. "But I care so deeply for you. I want you to stay here with me more than I can even begin to tell you. There's so much for me to deal with, Dakota, and it's all confusing and frightening. What if I really do love you, but I'm such a muddled mess I don't realize I do? Oh-h-h, I can't stand this."

"Don't cry," he said, stroking her back in a soothing motion. "I have sensed your fear of loving me, Kathy. What are you afraid of?"

"We haven't had enough time together to make discoveries. We're from different worlds, different cultures. Twice now I've caused you pain by being thoughtless and insensitive because I forgot you were from another time. *Forgot*."

"Did it ever occur to you that you've accepted me so completely into your life that it's a natural and wonderful thing that you forget that I arrived here from another era? Ah, Kathy, are we really all that different? We're man and woman, united, one. With the concept of compromise you've taught me, I truly believe we can mesh our worlds *if* we want to badly enough."

Kathy shifted slightly so she could look directly at him.

"Well," she said, tears echoing in her voice, "I *did* think about the fact that you could be my partner at The Herb Hogan if you wanted to. You know all about herbs, their uses, how to grow and dry them. We might even be able to open a second store in Prescott Valley or Chino Valley, the next towns over.''

Dakota nodded. ''That plan has great value.''

''But... Oh, Dakota, to marry? To make a commitment to forever? It's so risky, so dangerous, because we've had so little time together. I...'' She shook her head as a sob caught in her throat.

''I understand. I can't fight your demons of fear for you, Kathy. They are yours, within you, and there's nothing I can do, despite my skills as an Apache brave. That battle is yours...alone.''

''I'm so sorry, Dakota,'' she said, crying openly. ''*I'm* causing the Dream Catcher to shrink. It's *my* fault. You must be so hurt because of that, so angry at me. You must be close to hating me.''

''No, Kathy,'' he said, ''I'm not close to hating you at all. I love you, Kathy Maxwell. My caring for you enough to name you my wife has grown. I love you.''

Kathy dashed the tears from her cheeks, then took a trembling breath.

''You...you love me?'' she said. ''You're *in* love with me?''

Dakota nodded.

''Oh, dear, I don't know if that's wonderful, or terrible. I'm so confused, so...''

''Hush,'' he said, then brushed his lips over hers. ''There's no purpose to be served by discussing this further now. We've both been open and honest with each other about our feelings.''

''And they don't match, don't mesh.''

''So be it.''

''Oh, Dakota, I'm sorry, so sorry.''

''Let's get off the floor. Do you know that when I first came here I thought you'd grown this carpet in here? I've learned a great deal. Perhaps you should give thought to what *you've* learned.'' He released her and rolled to his feet.

Kathy scrambled up next to him. ''Do you feel strong enough to stand?''

''I'm fine now. I don't know how this will progress, Kathy. I've only seen it happen once before many years ago, and it may differ from person to person. What *is* clear, is that we're running out of time very quickly.''

"Yes," she said softly, "I know. Well, we'll go to bed now, get a solid night's sleep, then start out fresh at dawn tomorrow. Dakota, we have to believe that we'll find the shaman in time and he'll have the answer we need. *We have to believe that.*''

Dakota nodded, then encircled her with his arms and captured her mouth in a searing kiss. They went to bed and made slow, sweet love, going together to the place that held the beautiful wildflowers.

Just before Kathy fell into a restless sleep, Dakota's words echoed in her mind.

Perhaps you should give thought to what you've learned.

They awoke at dawn to the sound of a soft, steady rain. While Kathy usually enjoyed a rainy day as much as one brilliant with sunlight, the weather seemed a dark omen that heightened her fears.

They spoke little as they ate breakfast, cleaned the kitchen, then loaded the car.

"Well, it's time to collect the Dream Catcher," Kathy said finally, failing to produce a lightness to her voice that she'd been striving for.

"I'll get it," Dakota said.

As he walked away, Kathy closed her eyes and took a steadying breath.

She had to gain control, she told herself. She felt as though she was falling apart by inches. Her world, the very essence of who she was, was chipping away, piece by piece. There were hours of driving to be done, then a trek into the Chiricahua Mountains. She had to be strong, not only in body, but in mind, as well.

What she would *not* dwell on was that Dakota loved her. *Loved her.* That fact, combined with her muddled emotions, was too much to deal with now, just too much.

"Kathy," Dakota said, bringing her from her tormented thoughts.

She looked up and a gasp escaped from her lips.

Dakota was holding the Dream Catcher.

And it was no more than three feet wide.

"Oh, dear heaven, Dakota," she said, her voice trembling.

"Well, it will fit easily in the back seat of your metal egg known as the car," he said.

"Oh, Dakota," she said, managing a small smile, "you'd find the bright side of the bleakest day." The Dream Catcher was getting smaller and smaller, and it was her fault! "Are you ready to go?"

He came to the middle of the living room and glanced around, his gaze touching each piece of furniture in turn.

"This is my home now," he said quietly. "I want to return here, to live out my days and nights with you." He looked at Kathy. "Let's get started on our journey. We have a long way to go."

"And a shaman to find."

"Mmm," he said, nodding.

The rain continued to fall as they drove down the mountain toward the valley below that held the huge city of Phoenix. As Kathy came to each section of the road that was comprised of twisting, turning curves, she directed her full attention to driving.

Approaching Phoenix, the rain lessened, then stopped. The number of cars on the road increased, and they were soon caught up in bumper-to-bumper traffic. She glanced quickly at Dakota and saw the deep frown on his face.

"I know it's crowded," she said, "but we're going around the edge of the city on this highway. We'll be back in open country soon, and you'll be able to see all the way to the horizon during the drive to Tucson. We'll stop at a rest station on the far side of Phoenix and stretch our legs. Would you like to listen to some music?"

"Mmm," Dakota said.

Kathy tuned the radio to a country western station and began to hum along with a familiar song. A few minutes later she realized Dakota was scowling at the radio.

"What's a 'thang'?" he said.

"A who?" Kathy said. "Oh, he's saying 'thing.' The words of the song are 'love is a wonderful thing.'"

"No, he said, 'Love is a wonderful thang.'"

"Yes, I know, but…" She pressed a button on the panel. "Let's go for easy-listening music. Explaining country western to you would exhaust me. If they played 'Achy Breaky Heart,' you'd be totally confused."

After they left the rest station, Dakota sighed and leaned his head back on the top of the seat.

"Dakota?" Kathy said. "Is something wrong?"

"I need to rest."

"Are you having another attack of weakness?"

"Mmm. I'll sleep now, Kathy."

"Yes," she said, her hands tightening on the steering wheel. "Yes, good, that's good. Rest, sleep, so you can regain your strength."

She pressed harder on the gas pedal.

Hurry, her mind screamed. They were going too slow, using up too much precious time getting to the Chiricahua Mountains. Dakota's spirit was flowing from his body, the Dream Catcher was shrinking in size and... *Hurry.*

She shook her head in self-disgust and eased up on the pedal.

Getting a speeding ticket wasn't the solution, she admonished herself. They were doing the best they could, covering the maddening distance one mile at a time. But would their best be enough to save Dakota's life?

It had to be. It just had to be. Please!

By the time they reached the border town of Douglas, darkness had fallen and Kathy was thoroughly fatigued from the long drive.

Dakota had awakened from an hour's nap to assure her that he was once again feeling fine. They'd chatted on and off about rather mundane topics, but always there was the ever-building tension born of the knowledge of why they were making the trip.

They ate dinner at a small café, then checked into a motel, placing the Dream Catcher carefully on top of a table that sat in the corner of the room. Kathy was asleep within moments of her head touching the pillow.

Dakota stared up at a ceiling he couldn't see in the darkness, the fingers of one hand entwined with Kathy's. He sighed, feeling as though he was being crushed by the weight of his despair.

Kathy, his mind whispered. His woman. His wife. He loved her, honored and respected her, wished for her to bear his son, the many children, of his seed.

But he was dying.

He'd been overcome with the weakness again while Kathy had been in the shower. He'd managed to remove his clothes and get into bed before she came out of the bathroom. His spirit was leaving his body more quickly now, and there was nothing he could do to stop it.

Nothing.

As an Apache brave he wasn't afraid of death, of going to his eternal beyond. No, it wasn't fear that consumed him, it was sorrow. He didn't want to leave Kathy. He wanted to stay with her for all time.

He had only himself to blame for the fact that his spirit was flowing from him. At the moment Kathy's yearnings for a soul mate had intertwined with his through the Dream Catcher, he'd been clinging to the past, to what he'd once been, the way of life that had brought him happiness, fulfillment and inner peace.

Like a child holding stubbornly to a toy that wasn't his, a small portion of his mind had been refusing to let go of all he had ever known.

Because of his foolishness, his spirit had been left behind when the Dream Catcher flung him forward in time to be united with Kathy.

But the shrinking of the Dream Catcher?

It was diminishing in size because Kathy Maxwell had declared that she didn't love him as he loved her. And that hurt. It caused an ache in his heart beyond measure.

They needed more time to make discoveries, she'd said. To determine if the differences in their worlds could be overcome by compromise. She cared deeply for him, but she wasn't in love with him.

She was telling the truth as she knew it. She would never lie to him, but he was certain she wasn't being honest with herself. Her true feelings for him were buried beneath the fear of loving, of making a commitment to forever.

And there wasn't anything he could do about it.

Dakota's free hand curled into a tight fist of anger and frustration. He felt like a helpless infant, unable to gain control over his own destiny.

In his era, he'd been dictated to by the soldiers who hunted him with the intention of killing him.

Now?

He was held in the web of the mysteries of the Dream Catcher, and had been rendered completely vulnerable.

The Dream Catcher had worked its magic and brought Kathy and him together in the place where they both belonged. But their human frailties were destroying the gifts of the Dream Catcher, which were offered to very few.

Their only hope was the shaman. A true shaman was filled with wisdom beyond common man. Perhaps *his* powers would be stronger than the weaknesses of Kathy Maxwell and Dakota Smith.

They had to find that shaman!

Dakota finally slept, but he was restless, tossing and turning through the long, dark hours of the night.

When Kathy and Dakota awoke the next morning, the Dream Catcher was only two feet wide.

Eleven

It had rained during the night, and the day was hot and humid. Kathy reaffirmed in her mind that she definitely preferred living in mile-high Prescott, with its clear, cool air.

For breakfast they went to the same café where they'd eaten dinner the night before. While they ate, Kathy studied the map that Dr. Tucker had drawn for them. When the friendly waitress returned to the table to refill their coffee cups, Kathy smiled at her.

"Excuse me," Kathy said, "but I was wondering if you've ever heard of anyone seeing the old shaman who reportedly lives in the Chiricahua Mountains?"

The waitress stilled the coffeepot in midair and planted her other hand on an ample hip.

"Well, I've sure heard tell of him," she said. "There's been rumors of that old guy for years. Folks have come down here for the sole purpose of finding him, but no one ever has, as far as I know. I think it's just a wives' tale that there's an Indian medicine man in those mountains. Nope, I don't believe he exists, I truly don't."

She looked at Dakota.

"Is he supposed to be a relative of yours or something, sugar?"

Dakota shook his head.

"We need to find him," Kathy said. Her eyes widened as she realized the waitress had actually batted her eyelashes at Dakota. "It's very important."

"Well, good luck to you," the waitress said. She slid a glance at Dakota. "Is there anything else you want? For breakfast?"

"No," Kathy said, unable to stifle a burst of laughter. "Thank you."

"You bet," the woman said, then sashayed away.

"You have just been flirted with, Mr. Smith," Kathy said, smiling.

Dakota frowned. "If she doesn't change her ways, she'll end up with her nose split."

"Oh, good heavens, don't get started on that gruesome stuff." She paused, all traces of her smile gone. "Are you feeling all right this morning?"

"I'm fine."

"That's good. Well, according to this map, it will take more than an hour to drive to the mountains and as far in as we can go by car. We'll have to walk the rest of the way to where Dr. Tucker's friends said the shaman lives."

"Mmm," Dakota said, nodding.

Kathy leaned forward and covered one of his hands with hers on the top of the table.

"Dakota, you must promise me you'll stop and rest whenever you need to. It's hot and humid, and Dr. Tucker said the Chiricahuas are rough-going in places. Don't be all macho and tough. Tell me when you need a break. Okay?"

"It's not difficult to move through the Chiricahuas. I've done it my entire life."

"Oh, that's right. You live...lived...there. Well, I'd still appreciate it if you'd promise me you won't push yourself. Please?"

"I hear you, Kathy. Let's go. We're wasting time." He paused. "I love you, Kathy. We will find the shaman, and he'll know the answer to the mystery of the Dream Catcher. Everything is going to be fine."

They looked at each other for a long moment, each desperately wanting to believe what he had said, each knowing it might not be true.

"Come," he said finally, getting to his feet.

Kathy tried to enjoy the beauty of the area through which they drove, but with every passing mile she grew more tense, her breakfast sitting like a heavy stone in the pit of her stomach.

The going was slow for the last several miles as she inched the car over a dirt road that was an obstacle course of deep ruts. The road ended in a grove of tall trees and enormous rocks.

"Well, this is the end of the trail," she said, turning off the ignition.

"The Chiricahuas," Dakota said, his gaze sweeping over the area. "I know this land."

After locking the car, Kathy slipped the keys into the pocket of her jeans. They clipped the water-filled sports bottles to their belt loops, then Dakota tucked the Dream Catcher under one arm. Kathy studied the map, looked around, then scrutinized the paper again.

"That way," she said, pointing to the left. "I think."

Dakota stood behind her and looked over her shoulder at the map.

"You have it upside down, Kathy," he said. "If we go to the left, we'll eventually end up back at the paved road we were on."

"Oh," she said, flipping the paper around. "Well, I never claimed to be Daniel Boone."

"Who?"

"Never mind. Let's see here. Okay, we go to the right." She looked in that direction. "How can we do that? There are huge boulders in the way."

"We climb over them."

"You can't be serious. When Dr. Tucker said it was rough-going in places, I didn't realize he meant we were in for actual mountain climbing."

"The rocks aren't going to move out of the path just because you don't want to climb them, Kathy. We'll come to much steeper terrain before we reach the area Dr. Tucker marked on that map."

"Oh, good grief," she said, rolling her eyes heavenward. "This is going to be hard work. I'm not into exercise, Dakota. My idea of a walk is going to my mailbox, or strolling around the town square in Prescott." She sighed. "Well, let's get started. You'd better lead the way. I have a feeling I'd have us thoroughly lost in ten minutes or less."

"Definitely less," he said, starting forward.

"Thanks a lot," she muttered.

"You are welcome."

A little over an hour later, Kathy moaned.

"Dakota," she said, "slow down. No, even better...stop. I've got to rest."

He halted and turned to look at her.

"Again?" he said, raising his eyebrows. "This is the third time since we started."

She sank onto the ground beneath a tall tree. "Who's counting? Oh-h-h, my legs, my feet, my entire body, are screaming for mercy."

Dakota chuckled and sat beside her.

"You're not even out of breath," she said, glaring at him. "You move up and over those boulders as though they weren't even there. Worse yet, you only have one free hand because you're carrying the Dream Catcher. That's borderline rude, Mr. Smith." She leaned her head against the trunk of the tree and closed her eyes. "Oh-h-h."

"I'm very accustomed to this country, Kathy."

"I'm ethnically disadvantaged," she said, not opening her eyes. "Translated that means I'm a wreck because I'm not an Indian."

"Mmm," Dakota said, nodding. "That conclusion has merit."

Kathy opened her eyes and looked at him.

"Have you had any waves of weakness or dizziness?" she asked.

"No, nothing. In fact, I feel very strong. I wonder..." His gaze swept over the area. "Perhaps I've stopped the flowing out of my spirit for a while by coming to the place of my birth, the place where I was raised and lived. I don't know, but it's possible, I suppose."

Kathy lifted her head from the tree. "That would be wonderful, Dakota. It would mean we have more time to find the shaman." She looked at the Dream Catcher where it lay on Dakota's thighs. "The Dream Catcher isn't any smaller than it was when we left Douglas."

"No."

"We probably should have wrapped it in something. It could snag on a bush or tree and be damaged. I should have thought of that and protected it."

"No, I don't think so," he said slowly. "I believe, although I'm not certain as to why, that it shouldn't be covered. It has great powers, and a true shaman has great powers."

"You mean the shaman might sense that the Dream Catcher is near him? He might pick up some kind of vibes from it, or whatever?"

"Maybe." He looked up at the trees surrounding them. "The trees are much taller now than when I lived here. It's strange to see this."

"Yes, I imagine it is," she said quietly, then paused. "How much farther do we have to go before we reach the area where the shaman is supposed to be? *And* how large of an area do we have to search through?"

"At the speed you travel, it will be a while yet before we're in the section where the shaman is believed to be. That area, though, isn't large because it's surrounded by steep rocks forming a small canyon. He'll either be there, or he won't."

"He'll be there," Kathy said decisively.

"The woman in the café said many others have sought him, Kathy, but no one has found him. They no doubt had the same knowledge we have."

"I don't care. *We* will find him." She got to her feet. "Come on."

They trekked for another hour, Kathy only allowing herself two stops to rest. The terrain was becoming rockier, and Dakota had to reach down and extend his free hand to her time and again to pull her up and over a huge boulder. The trees were thicker, closer together, and the going was frustratingly slow.

As they emerged from an extremely dense group of trees, Dakota suddenly stopped dead in his tracks, causing Kathy to bump into him from behind. She moved to his side to see what had caused his abrupt halt.

She saw a clearing the size of a football field, where no trees grew. There were bushes spotting the area, some wildflowers and clumps of weeds.

"Dakota?" she said, looking up at him questioningly.

"This…" he started, then shook his head. He cleared his throat, took a deep breath, then let it out slowly. "This was where I lived, where my people had their camp. I was born here, grew up here. It was from this place that my people were driven away. They had to leave here when they went to the reservation."

"Oh, Dakota," she whispered, seeing the pain in his eyes, hearing it in his voice.

"I can envision it all," he went on. "Our homes, the children playing, the women working, the fires burning to cook our food. I lived there." He pointed to the right. "Our horses were kept in that area." He swept his hand in another direction. "Meat was smoked over a fire at that far end."

"Dakota…"

"I can hear them. The voices of my people are reaching me, Kathy. The echo of their sorrow is carried on the wind. There is no laughter, only the sound of crying, of deep sadness."

"Oh, Dakota, don't do this to yourself. Let's move on. This is so painful for you."

"I stood in those trees on the other side," he said as though she hadn't spoken, "and watched them leave with the soldiers. My people walked tall, straight. Proud Chiricahua Apaches even in their hour of defeat.

"In a single line they went, not speaking. Even the children were silent. Even the babies made no sound. And as they left, not one of them turned to look back upon what had been theirs, what they would never see again."

A sob caught in Kathy's throat, and she covered her mouth with one hand.

Dakota stood ramrod stiff, staring at the clearing, reliving it all, the memories beating unmercifully against his mind. A shudder ripped through him with such painful intensity it caused him to take a sharp breath.

Thunder rumbled in the distance, snapping him back to the present, causing the past to release him from its cold, tormenting fist.

"It's threatening to rain," he said, his voice still husky with emotion, "and it comes quickly in these mountains. We'll have to take shelter, Kathy, because the lightning that accompanies summer storms is very dangerous among these trees."

"But we'll lose time, Dakota."

"It can't be helped. See how the sky darkens? We only have a few minutes."

"Where will we go?"

"I know a place where the rocks form a type of cave. We'll be safe there." He looked at the sky again, then reached for her hand. "We'll have to run. We'll cross… we'll cross the clearing that was my home, move through those trees beyond, then we'll be a short distance from the cave. Come on, Kathy. Hurry.''

They ran.

Dakota had to shorten his stride so Kathy could keep up. The dark clouds rolled across the sky like a wild current in a raging river, roaring with thunder as they came. Lightning streaked through the heavens in jagged, bright slashes, then large drops of rain began to fall.

They ran across the field of memories into the woods beyond, then emerged on the other side to find huge boulders in their path. Dakota veered to the right, then upward over the rocks, still holding tightly to Kathy's hand. The rain increased, soaking them to the skin and drenching the Dream Catcher.

It was becoming darker, like dusk inching toward night, and the noise was deafening. The thunder rumbled, the lightning crackled, wind whipped the trees into a frenzy and seemed to moan like the voices of a multitude of ghosts as it tunneled through the crevices between the rocks.

Kathy's heart pounded, not only from physical exertion but from fear, as well. The storm had materialized so quickly with a ferociousness that was frightening. It was like a wild beast intent on attacking, swooping down and devouring them.

''There it is,'' Dakota shouted above the cacophony.

The rock shelter built by nature's hand was about five feet across and high, and six feet deep. They bent over and hurried under the protection, moving as far back as possible before turning and sinking to the dry ground.

Kathy gasped for breath, waiting for the burning in her lungs to dissipate. Dakota propped the Dream Catcher carefully against the side wall.

''The Dream Catcher is wet,'' he said, ''but none of the webbing is damaged. If the wind shifts, we'll be pelted with rain, but at least we're in no danger from the lightning.''

Kathy nodded, then pulled up her knees and wrapped her arms around them. A shiver coursed through her.

Dakota put one arm around her shoulders. ''Are you cold, Kathy? The temperature has dropped more than twenty degrees, I imagine.''

"Yes, it's chilly," she said, "but I'm scared, too. It was so peaceful, Dakota, with birds singing, squirrels chattering to one another, the leaves of the trees rustling gently when a breeze feathered them. Then… I don't know. The storm is ominous, a bleak, dark message of some kind."

"No," he said, then kissed her on the temple. "There's nothing to be frightened of. This is a typical storm in the Chiricahua Mountains. I've sought shelter right here in this cave countless times and waited for the weather to clear. I won't let anything happen to you, Kathy."

She turned to meet his gaze, then snuggled closer to him, resting her head on his shoulder. They watched the storm rage beyond the opening of the little cave.

Her fear, Kathy realized, was gone. She was with Dakota, and they were in a dry cocoon where no harm could touch them.

The storm had appeared out of nowhere, it seemed. It had just suddenly been there, not to be ignored. It wasn't ominous, it was symbolic. Dakota, too, had entered her existence with a dramatic and unexpected arrival. And Dakota most definitely could not be ignored.

The rain that now fell, she mused, would nurture the trees, grass, flowers and animals. It would provide what they needed in order to flourish as they were meant to. Dakota's emergence into her life had nurtured *her,* as well, made it possible for her to grow, achieve the maximum potential of her femininity, be all that she was capable of being as a woman.

She shifted her gaze to the Dream Catcher, seeing that it was slowly drying and returning to its soft-pink color. It was still two feet wide, as it had been when they left Douglas that morning.

It was so delicate, she thought, such a beautiful handmade creation. Yet the powers it possessed were almost beyond the scope of her imagination. It was shrouded in mystery and held the keys to the doors of life or death for Dakota.

And it was *her* fault that it was shrinking.

Kathy sighed, a sad-sounding sigh, then looked again at the pouring rain coming down in near-solid sheets.

Somewhere out there was the shaman, the only one who could turn the key to the proper door and make it possible for Dakota to stay in this time.

They would find the shaman.
Wouldn't they?

Twelve

During the next hour the rain began to slacken, finally diminishing to a fine mist. It was not as dark, nor as cold, and thunder no longer rolled across the heavens.

"We'd better leave," Dakota said. "We're still going to get wet, but that can't be avoided. The danger from the lightning is over, though. We'll have to move slower because everything will be slippery."

"What if we can't find the shaman before nightfall?" Kathy said, a slightly frantic edge to her voice. "What will we do then?"

"Don't worry about what hasn't yet happened, Kathy."

"Mmm," she said, glaring at him.

They left the cave, and Dakota filled his lungs with the fresh scent of rain, savoring it. While he indulged in nature's wonders, Kathy wistfully envisioned a warm bubble bath followed by deliciously dry, soft clothes.

With the Dream Catcher tucked securely beneath Dakota's arm, they started off.

Three hours went by without Kathy having to ask to rest, clearly indicating to her how slowly they were moving. The rain had stopped, their clothes had dried stiff as boards, but the temperature remained mercifully cool.

In the late afternoon they ate the energy protein bars they'd tucked into their pockets, washing them down with the tepid water in the sports bottles.

They continued on, and Dakota reached down yet again to extend his hand to Kathy to assist her to the top of the rock where he stood. When she was next to him, he swept one arm in the air.

"Down there," he said, "is the canyon we've been looking for."

"It is? All I can see are tops of trees and a whole bunch of very big boulders."

"If the shaman exists, as some people believe, he'll be in that canyon."

"*Some* people believe?" Kathy said. "*We* believe he's there."

Dakota stared at the area below.

"Dakota? You *do* believe that, don't you?"

Without speaking, he turned and walked away. Kathy sighed and trudged after him, deciding she just didn't have the energy to argue the point. She was thoroughly exhausted and had to concentrate on putting one foot in front of the other.

It took nearly an hour to weave their way down the rocky slope to the floor of the canyon. Kathy was nearly numb with fatigue, but was aware of the icy fingers of fear that were inching around her heart and mind.

This was it, she thought, staring at the mass of trees before her. The shaman was in there. Somewhere. He was. He had to be.

Dakota went forward and Kathy followed him, frowning at his broad back as he made a narrow path through the thick foliage.

Something was wrong, she thought. Dakota hadn't spoken to her since they'd seen the canyon from the top of the ridge. It was as though he'd withdrawn and erected an invisible barrier between them. She felt alone and lonely, and very, very frightened.

It was hot in the midst of the dense trees and extremely humid. A branch tangled in Kathy's curls, and she yanked it free, pulling painfully on her hair. Tears filled her eyes, and she had to struggle not to wail at full volume.

She was hot and tired. Her clothes were scratchy against her skin. She was scared, lonely, and Dakota was being as comforting as one of the unyielding rocks they'd been battling all day.

She wanted to go home, have a bubble bath, a good long cry, and be finished with this awful nightmare. She'd drag Dakota out of there by the back of the shirt and tell him in no uncertain terms that enough was enough. She'd fall madly in love with him and they'd live happily ever after. The end.

A wobbly little sob escaped from her throat.

That was what she wanted, but it wasn't remotely close to reality. If they didn't find the shaman, Dakota was going to die. It was too much to handle, all of it.

Two tears slid down her cheeks, followed by two more, and she sniffled. A few feet ahead of her, Dakota stopped, and she dashed the tears from her cheeks.

"What..." she started to say.

"Shh," he said, raising one hand but not turning to look at her.

She glowered at him, which didn't make her feel one bit better.

"The shaman," Dakota said, his voice low. "The shaman is here."

Kathy's eyes widened, and she hurried to stand next to Dakota, looking up at him eagerly.

"He is?" She glanced around. "Where? I don't see anything, anyone. How do you know he's here?"

"Shh."

"Darn it, Dakota, don't you dare tell me to be quiet," she said, none too quietly. "I've been in this frightening mess with you every inch of the way, and you're suddenly treating me as though I'm as unimportant as one of those crummy trees. Talk...to...me."

He looked down at her and narrowed his eyes. "Shh."

That did it.

Kathy burst into tears.

Dakota blinked, opened his mouth, shut it again, then frowned. Kathy covered her face with her hands and wept. He set the Dream Catcher against the trunk of a tree, then wrapped his arms around Kathy, holding her tightly to him.

"I'm sorry," he said gently. "I turned inward, attempting to control my fear and the pain I feel when I realize I might have to leave you, that I might die, and you'll be alone, crying. I centered on myself and I'm sorry."

Kathy tilted her head back to look at him. He raised one hand to wipe the tears from her face.

"It just all caught up with me," she said, her voice trembling. "I'm so tired, and so scared and... Oh, dear God, Dakota, I don't want to lose you. Is the shaman really here? How do you know?"

"I sense his presence. I feel his power. He's very near."

She stepped back out of his embrace. "Then let's find him, let's hurry. Get the Dream Catcher and..." She looked at the base of the tree. "No! Oh, no. Dakota, the Dream Catcher...the Dream Catcher... No!"

He spun around and snatched it up.

It was only one foot wide.

Dakota grabbed Kathy's hand and began to move through the trees again, Kathy having to scramble to keep up with him. Ten minutes later with no warning, they suddenly emerged from the thick growth into a small clearing about the size of Kathy's living room. They stopped dead in their tracks.

The shaman.

He was sitting cross-legged on the ground behind a low-burning campfire. Clad in buckskin pants and shirt, he wore his gray hair in two heavy braids that hung to the middle of his chest. His face was a deep bronze, partly from heritage, but also from years spent in the sun. His skin was a mass of wrinkles, his age undeterminable, but he was obviously very old. His dark eyes met Dakota's.

"You have come, Dakota," the shaman said.

"I have come, mighty shaman," Dakota said.

"Dear heaven," Kathy whispered, tightening her hold on Dakota's hand.

"Sit," the shaman said. "Your woman may share my fire, as well."

They moved forward, and Kathy sank gratefully to the ground, her legs refusing to hold her for another moment. Her heart was racing as she stared at the shaman.

"I have waited for you, Dakota," the shaman said. "You have been honored, chosen, by the mystical powers of the Dream Catcher. It holds the ability to send you to your eternal beyond. Are you prepared to die, Dakota?"

"Yes."

"No," Kathy said. "Please. No. Can't you help us? Don't you know the answer to the mystery of the Dream Catcher? Can't you bring Dakota's center spirit here to him, so he can stay with me?"

"Tell your woman," the shaman said, still looking at Dakota, "that she may share my fire but she is not to speak."

Dakota squeezed Kathy's hand. "I have told her."

Kathy sighed.

The shaman frowned. "She should not have spoken, but I heard her words. Do you wish to stay in this era, Dakota? It is not yours. You don't belong here."

"It *is* mine now, the place where I belong," he said. "There is nothing left for me in my own time. My people have gone to the reservation, but I refused to go."

"Bronco Apache," the shaman said.

"Yes. This woman is my wife. I wish to remain with her. My spirit flows from my body. My center spirit did not travel with me through the Dream Catcher. I must be united with the center of my spirit, or I will die. Time is very short. I feel the weakness. The Dream Catcher is growing smaller."

"I know most of what you're telling me," the shaman said. "I saw the visions in the smoke of my fire. What I did *not* learn from the smoke pictures was that you wished to stay in this time."

"That is my wish."

"Mmm," the shaman said, shifting his gaze to stare at the fire.

Please, Kathy silently begged. *Oh, please.*

Several long minutes passed, then the shaman looked at Dakota again.

"All is not as it should be," the old man said. "The Dream Catcher diminishes in size because your woman is troubled. She is afraid and does not listen to the voices of her heart." He shifted his gaze to look directly into Kathy's eyes. "Perhaps you should give thought to what you've learned, as Dakota told you. I heard the echo of his words. They are wise. Turn inward, Dakota's woman, seek the truth. Then you may speak."

Kathy's heart raced, and another chill of fear swept throughout her. She wanted to run as fast and as far as she could, but she was held immobile by the mesmerizing dark eyes of the shaman.

Then slowly, slowly, a calmness settled over her, a sense of peace like nothing she'd experienced before. The chill was replaced by a warmth that suffused her, moving through her like a gentle whisper caressing her heart, mind, her very soul.

The voices in her mind that had plagued her with confusion, doubt and fear, quieted, then were still. She heard only one message that was clear, and rich and real.

She was in love with Dakota.

And Kathy Maxwell was filled with the greatest joy she had ever known.

"I was afraid," she said softly. "My fear of the risks of loving spoke in a voice louder than that of my heart. I used the differences in my world and Dakota's as a shield to protect myself. But now I know, believe, that we can overcome any obstacles in our path as long as we stand together, united. One."

She turned to meet Dakota's gaze.

"I love you, Dakota," she whispered. "I love you so very much, with all that I am as your wife."

"And I love you, Kathy, with all that I am as your husband."

She smiled at him warmly, gently, with love shining in the sky-blue depths of her eyes. It was a purely feminine smile of a woman grown. Understanding, glorying in the knowledge and rejoicing in its gifts.

"It is good," the shaman said, nodding. "You are now one, as it should be."

"I wish to stay in this time with my wife," Dakota said, looking at the shaman again.

"My father was a shaman," the old man said, staring into the fire, "as was his father, and the fathers for countless generations that came before. The teachings were passed from father to son, as is our Apache custom. The Dream Catcher has always been held in high esteem, for its powers are great." He paused. "I have never performed the ceremony of the Dream Catcher."

Kathy stiffened in fear, but Dakota slid her a quick glance, cautioning her with his eyes to keep silent.

No, no, no, her mind screamed. She loved Dakota. She was deeply in love with him, she knew that now. They couldn't have come all this way, actually found the shaman when no one else had been able to, only to discover that he didn't have the answer. That he didn't know the mystery of the Dream Catcher. *No! Dakota was not going to die.*

"You haven't performed the ceremony of the Dream Catcher," Dakota said, "but was it taught to you by your father?"

The shaman nodded.

Hope surged within Kathy.

The shaman met Dakota's gaze again. "It was taught to me, but…" He shook his head. "It was believed that if someone was touched by the Dream Catcher's powers and was hurled through time into the future, they would wish to return to where they belonged. The ceremony is for that purpose."

"You are very wise, mighty shaman," Dakota said. "Don't you possess the knowledge to reverse the ceremony? To bring my center spirit to me here?"

"I don't know. The risks are many. The ceremony is ancient, sacred. To tamper with what has always been might result in your death. I can be certain of nothing."

"I hear your words," Dakota said. "I would speak with my wife."

The shaman nodded and raised one hand in dismissal.

Dakota got to his feet, pulled Kathy to hers, and they moved to the edge of the clearing. He placed his hands on her shoulders and looked directly into her blue eyes, seeing the tears shimmering there.

"You've heard the shaman's words, Kathy," he said quietly.

"Yes," she said, tears echoing in her voice. "It's perfectly clear, Dakota. You must go back to your own time. It's too dangerous to attempt to reverse the ceremony. I love you too much to have you run that risk." Her breath caught on a sob. "You have to go back."

"No."

"But…"

"Listen to me," he said, tightening his hold on her shoulders. "*You* are here. *You* are my life. If I go back, Kathy, I would have nothing. Oh, yes, I'd be alive, but would I? Really? It would be a living death. Empty. Lonely. Cold. I'm going to ask the shaman to attempt to reverse the ceremony of the Dream Catcher."

Kathy grabbed the front of his shirt. "You might die. He said that.

You might die, Dakota.'' Tears streamed down her face. "I don't want...don't want...you...to die.''

He pulled her close, resting one cheek on the top of her head.

"Would you wish me to go back to a world so empty, Kathy, that I can feel the pain of it by merely envisioning it in my mind?''

"No, but...''

"Kathy, I must do everything possible to stay here with you. I must. Now, hear me as I tell you what *you* must do. If...if I die, you will cry tears of healing to soothe the sadness of your spirit. Then you'll stand tall, proud, befitting the widow of an Apache brave who has gone to his eternal beyond.

"And, Kathy? Just as when my people did not look back upon what had been when they left the reservation, you will look only to the future. If I die, you will live on with dignity. You'll open your heart, your center spirit, to love, to laughter, to life. Do you understand?''

"Dakota, please, I can't...''

"Do you hear my words, Kathy?''

She nodded, feeling as though her heart was shattering into a million pieces.

"Come. We mustn't show a lack of respect by keeping the shaman waiting. I love you, Kathy Maxwell.''

"I love you,'' she whispered. *Forever. Only you. For all time.* "I love you, Dakota Smith.''

They returned to sit in their places opposite the shaman. The old man looked at Dakota.

"It is my humble wish,'' Dakota said, "that you perform the ceremony of the Dream Catcher in reverse, mighty shaman. I honor and respect my wife. I love her and she loves me. We are one, united, until death and the eternal beyond separates us. I would stay in this world with her. I understand and accept the risks involved in what I am asking of you.''

The shaman nodded. "So be it. You have decided on the proper course, Dakota, the one befitting a true Apache. To desert your wife because it would be of lesser risk to you has no honor. If you die because of your choice of action, your memory can be held in high esteem by your widow who shall weep.''

"Mmm,'' Dakota said.

No! Kathy thought. Dakota was *not* going to die. She felt so help-less, so useless. There was nothing she could do but sit silently by and watch the events unfold. *Oh, Dakota.*

"We must go to the stream that runs past this enclosure," the sha-man said. "There we will be in harmony with earth, air and water." He got to his feet. "Bring the Dream Catcher."

The shaman walked slowly but steadily, his firm step one of a much younger man.

They went around the end of the boulders edging the small canyon, then moved again through tall trees. A few minutes later they emerged to find a stream of crystal-clear water that flowed lazily over a bed of rocks. Lush grass grew on both sides of the stream.

"Wild raspberries," Dakota said, pointing across the brook. "They grew here when I was a boy and still flourish. I would come here, eat my fill of berries, drink the cool water, then lie in the grass and watch the clouds make pictures in the sky. I was at peace here."

"It's beautiful," Kathy said softly. "I can see you in my mind's eye coming here as you must have been as a boy. It *is* very peaceful."

The shaman went to a spot beyond the grassy section and made a small circle of rocks. Within minutes, a fire glowed in the center.

Dusk was beginning to fall, and a sunset was streaking across the sky in vibrant colors, casting a golden hue over the area. The shaman motioned for Dakota and Kathy to sit across from him, the circle of rocks separating them.

"Give me the Dream Catcher," the shaman said. "Do not touch your woman, nor is she to touch you. Turn into yourself, Dakota. Focus on the place within you that is empty, where the center of your spirit must come. See it. Feel it. Will it to return to you. I go now to my altered state. What happens beyond this moment is not under my con-trol."

Dakota draped his hands on his knees as Kathy had seen him do many times in her backyard. He closed his eyes.

Wait! she thought frantically. *Please! Wait!* She wanted to hold him one more time. Kiss him one more time. Declare her love one more time.

But it was too late.

The shaman sat as Dakota did, the Dream Catcher on the ground in front of him. His eyes were closed as he took three deep breaths, releasing each through an open mouth.

Kathy jerked in surprise as the shaman began to chant in low, rumbling tones, the sounds having no discernible meaning to her.

Then slowly, slowly, a funnel of smoke began to swirl from the small fire, growing bigger and denser with every beat of Kathy's racing heart.

A gasp escaped from her lips as she stared at the spiraling smoke with wide eyes.

Forms were taking shape within the funnel. She could see them! She saw Dakota's face, and hers, then the image of the Dream Catcher became clear. The funnel moved, thicker, darker. The images vanished as the funnel encased Dakota in its depths until she could no longer see him. The shaman chanted on, louder now, the cadence faster.

Kathy was frozen in fear, unable to move, hardly able to breathe.

Dakota! her mind screamed. *Dakota! I love you. Stay with me. Bring your center spirit to you here. Here, Dakota. Don't leave. Don't go back in time. Stay. Stay, my love. Dakota…Dakota…Dakota…*

The smoke continued to whip around Dakota, then the top of the funnel grew and flung itself over the shaman, the Dream Catcher and the circle of rocks. It was only inches from Kathy, but didn't touch her.

She was alone and terrified outside the thick, spiraling wall of darkening smoke. She could no longer hear the shaman's chant, the only sound a humming noise created by the smoke funnel.

Time lost meaning.

Tears streamed unnoticed down Kathy's face. Her mind echoed Dakota's name over and over.

Dakota…Dakota…Dakota…

The smoke became dark as night. Churning. Swirling. Humming.

Dakota…Dakota…Dakota…

Suddenly Kathy felt as though she'd been struck by a powerful force that knocked her over, flat on her back on the ground. She struggled for air as black dots danced before her eyes. A wave of dizziness washed over her, and she closed her eyes, still gasping, trying to breathe.

She slipped away…into oblivion.

* * *

Kathy stirred and opened her eyes, blinking in confusion as she stared up at a night sky that twinkled with the diamondlike lights of a million stars. The brilliance of the heavens cast a silvery luminescence that was nearly as bright as day.

Where was she? What...

Dakota!

She scrambled to her knees, her heart beating so wildly it was actually painful.

Dakota was on the ground near her, his eyes closed. The shaman, the Dream Catcher and the circle of rocks were gone. There was no visible evidence that a fire had ever burned there.

"Dakota," she whispered.

She moved quickly to kneel beside him, placing her hands on his rugged cheeks, willing him to open his eyes. She moved one hand to his chest, rejoicing in the feel of his steady heartbeat beneath her palm.

"Dakota," she said, then increased the volume of her voice. "Dakota, it's Kathy. Wake up, my love. I'm here, waiting for you. Please, Dakota, please come to me. Dakota?"

He slowly opened his eyes, then drew a deep breath that shuddered through his body.

"Kathy?"

"Yes," she said, smiling even as tears filled her eyes. "Yes."

He struggled to sit up, took another deep breath, then shook his head slightly to clear it. He glanced around.

"The shaman?" he said.

"He's gone. The Dream Catcher is gone, too, and the rocks by the fire. Oh, Dakota, what happened? I was so frightened. There was a funnel of smoke that covered you, and I couldn't see you, or the shaman. I think I fainted, but I'm not sure. Do you remember anything?"

"I was...I was above the earth, being pulled in two directions at once. There was pain, intense pain, as though I was being torn apart. Images were everywhere. I saw my people, the soldiers, then you, your house, then back again to my people.

"But then... Yes, I heard your voice calling to me. Over and over you said my name, begging me to stay, to bring my center spirit here, to this time and place. I clung to your words like they were tangible objects. I held fast, endured the pain and refused to release my hold. Because of you and your love for me, Kathy, I'm here.''

"Oh, Dakota," she said, dashing the tears from her cheeks. She paused and her eyes widened. "Your center spirit. Is it with you? How will we know if the ceremony really worked?"

Dakota frowned, then looked at the stream. "The truth can be learned if I look in the water."

"Your reflection," she whispered. "We couldn't see you in the mirror in my bedroom because you didn't have the center of your spirit."

"Yes. Go stand by the stream, Kathy, and look at your reflection. The stars will make it bright enough for you to see yourself. I'll join you in a moment, and we'll learn the truth of what has taken place."

"What are you going to do here while I go to the stream?"

"I must give humble thanks and say farewell to the shaman."

"Where did he go?"

"I don't know. His powers are far greater than anything I can understand. I now believe that no one else ever saw him because he wasn't here until we came, until we needed him. He won't return to this place. Ever."

"He took the Dream Catcher."

"Mmm," he said, nodding. "If my center spirit isn't within me, there's no more to be done. The Dream Catcher has no further purpose now. Go to the stream, Kathy." He brushed his lips over hers. "Go."

On trembling legs, Kathy did as Dakota had instructed her. At the edge of the stream, she stared at her reflection, which was clearly visible in the sparkling, silver-toned water. She wrapped shaking hands around her elbows.

And waited.

Her heart pounded and her throat ached.

She waited.

Within minutes she would learn what the future held.

She waited...for what seemed like an eternity.

Then...

Dakota!

His reflection was there in the water as he came to stand behind her. He lifted his hands to place them on her shoulders, and she felt his warm, gentle touch at the same glorious moment it was mirrored in the stream.

She spun to face him and flung her arms around his neck, crying openly with joy. He held her tightly to him, tears streaming down his cheeks, as well. They rocked back and forth, saying each other's names, happiness dispelling the lingering shadows of fear within them.

Then Dakota sought and found her mouth, kissing her deeply, urgently. Desire rocketed through them, their passion as hot as the flames of the fire the shaman had built in the circle of rocks.

"Kathy," Dakota said, close to her lips. "I want to make love with you here, by this stream that has told us we're to spend the remainder of our lives together."

"Yes. Oh, yes, my love."

They shed their clothes quickly, each appearing to the other like an exquisite statue crafted from fine silver. And there on the plush grass they joined, meshed their bodies, were one.

It was ecstasy.

It was the beginning of their forever.

Afterward they lay close, entwined, listening to the lilting song sung by the gentle ripple of the brook.

Dakota splayed one hand on Kathy's stomach, then shifted up to rest on one forearm so he could look directly into her eyes.

"Kathy, my wife, you have conceived my son on this night. He rests here, within you, beneath my palm."

"I... Your son? Are you sure?"

Dakota nodded. "You carry my son. Are you upset, unhappy, that this has happened?"

"Oh, no, Dakota, no. It's wonderful. I'll be very proud to bear your child, Dakota. It's perfect, so special, that he was conceived here in this place. Thank you, Dakota. Oh, how I love you."

"And I love you."

He kissed her, then they settled again in the soft grass, both realizing how exhausted they were from the incredible events that had transpired.

"We'll spend the night here in nature's bed," Dakota said. "In the morning we'll feast on wild raspberries and drink the clear water of the stream.

"Then, Kathy, we'll leave the Chiricahua Mountains for the last time. I'll never return. My life as I knew it here is over. The now and the future are of importance, not the past. Our son may wish to see this place some day, but that will be his choice to make."

"Yes, my love," Kathy said. She snuggled closer to him and placed one hand on her stomach with a sense of wonder and infinite joy. "In the morning we'll go home, together." She smiled. "The three of us."

Epilogue

Kathy stood in front of the full-length mirror in Lily and Brad's bedroom and stared at her own reflection.

She was wearing a white gauze dress with a scooped neckline that came to just above her breasts and stopped at the edges of her shoulders. Bright wildflowers had been embroidered across the bodice and on the wide border of the street-length hem. It was nipped in at the waist with a gauze belt.

It was a lovely dress, beautiful in its simplicity.

It was her wedding dress.

Kathy smiled, a soft, gentle smile, as she splayed both hands on her flat stomach. Love for the baby being nurtured there, the child created by the meshing of Kathy's body with Dakota's, suffused her.

"Your father and I became husband and wife according to the customs of his people," she whispered to the baby. "Now we'll be married by the rituals set forth by mine. Both of those worlds will be yours to discover and rejoice in, little one. Oh, you are loved beyond measure already. You're a miracle and we'll cherish you."

"Kathy?"

She turned to see Lily in the doorway.

"Are you ready?" Lily said. "You look wonderful." She crossed the room to hug Kathy. "I'm so happy for you and Dakota."

"Thank you, Lily." Kathy smiled. "I'm happy for us, too."

"Here's your bouquet. Wildflowers, just like you wanted. The gazebo is threaded with wildflowers, too. Your parents and mine are beaming, as though they're taking credit for you and Dakota being together. They adore your man, you realize."

"Well, they might be a tad nervous if we'd told them the truth about how he came into my life," Kathy said, laughing. "Parents don't have to know everything."

"Amen to that," Lily said. "Well, here we go, Mrs. Smith. You're about to become Mrs. Smith...again. This family-only ceremony is the final, perfect touch in blending your world with Dakota's. Oh-h-h, I'm going to weep through the whole thing, I just know I will." She threw up her hands and marched from the room.

Kathy followed more slowly, allowing a sense of peace and contentment to caress her mind and soul, while the love for Dakota nestled warmly around her heart.

When she stepped into the backyard, she didn't see the pretty gazebo with the minister standing inside, nor her parents and Lily's. She wasn't aware that Brad was holding a sleeping Michelle Dakota, or that the other three little girls were wiggling like excited puppies. Lily's sniffling into a lace-edged hankie didn't register.

She saw only Dakota.

He was dressed in a butter-soft, white doeskin shirt, pants and moccasins. Wildflowers were embroidered on the cuffs of the shirt. His shoulder-length hair gleamed like polished ebony in the sunlight.

She moved toward him, her gaze locked with his. She walked alone, not on the arm of her father as was more traditional. She'd gently explained to her dad that he really couldn't 'give her away,' because she belonged only to herself, was an entity unto herself.

"When did you become so wise?" he'd said, smiling at her.

"When I fell in love with Dakota."

Kathy came to the gazebo and smiled up at Dakota. He matched her smile, then they turned, went up the three steps, and crossed to stand in front of the minister.

"Friends," the clergyman said, "we have gathered here today as witnesses for Kathy and Dakota as they repeat the vows that will unite them as husband and wife."

The words flowed around Kathy as she looked directly into Dakota's eyes, seeing there all she needed to know, seeing there all she needed.

Time lost meaning, then suddenly Dakota was kissing her, they wore simple gold wedding bands, and everyone was hugging, or kissing, or shaking hands, with everyone else.

"I love you," Dakota said, close to her ear.

"I love you, too, but I sort of floated away during the ceremony. I missed the whole thing."

"Does it matter?"

"No. I'm your wife. I will love and cherish you until the day I die. We have a whole lifetime together to explore, Dakota."

"Discoveries," he said, nodding. "That has merit."

"Oh, I must show you something before we have cake and punch," Kathy's mother announced to the group. "I bought it yesterday at the craft show on the plaza, but we were so busy getting ready for the wedding that I forgot about it. It's fascinating and really very pretty."

She opened an enormous purse and withdrew a small tissue-wrapped package. Brushing back the paper, she held up her newly acquired, bright blue, three-inch-wide treasure.

"Isn't it lovely?" she said. "It's called a Dream Catcher. I'm going to hang it on the wall above my pillow when we return home to Florida. Don't you think that's a marvelous idea?"

"No!" Kathy, Dakota, Lily and Brad said in unison.

"Well, why on earth not?" she said, obviously confused.

Lily launched into a speech listing every reason imaginable why her aunt should hang the Dream Catcher in the kitchen, because one generally didn't sleep, thus dream, in the said room.

"Dream Catchers *do* have merit," Kathy said to Dakota.

"Mmm," he said.

And then they smiled, love shining in their eyes.

*   *   *   *   *

#1 *New York Times* bestselling author

NORA ROBERTS

brings you more of the loyal and loving, tempestuous and tantalizing Stanislaski family.

The Stanislaski Sisters
Natasha and Rachel

Coming in February 2001

Though raised in the Old World traditions of their family, fiery Natasha Stanislaski and cool, classy Rachel Stanislaski are ready for a *new* world of love....

And also available in February 2001 from Silhouette Special Edition, the newest book in the heartwarming Stanislaski saga

CONSIDERING KATE

Natasha and Spencer Kimball's daughter Kate turns her back on old dreams and returns to her hometown, where she finds the *man* of her dreams.

Available at your favorite retail outlet.

Where love comes alive™

Tyler Brides

It happened one weekend...

Quinn and Molly Spencer are delighted to accept three bookings for their newly opened B&B, Breakfast Inn Bed, located in America's favorite hometown, Tyler, Wisconsin.

But Gina Santori is anything but thrilled to discover her best friend has tricked her into sharing a room with the man who broke her heart eight years ago....

And Delia Mayhew can hardly believe that she's gotten herself locked in the Breakfast Inn Bed basement with the sexiest man in America.

Then there's Rebecca Salter. She's turned up at the Inn in her wedding gown. Minus her groom.

Come home to Tyler for three delightful novellas
by three of your favorite authors: Kristine Rolofson,
Heather MacAllister and Jacqueline Diamond.

HARLEQUIN®
Makes any time special ™

LINDSAY McKENNA

continues her most popular series with a
brand-new, longer-length book.

And it's the story you've been waiting for....

Morgan's Mercenaries:
Heart of Stone

They had met before. Battled before. And
Captain Maya Stevenson had never again
wanted to lay eyes on Major Dane York—
the man who once tried to destroy
her military career! But on their latest
mission together, Maya discovered that beneath
the fury in Dane's eyes lay a raging passion. Now she
struggled against dangerous desire, as Dane's command
over her seemed greater still. For this time, he laid claim
to her heart....

Only from Lindsay McKenna and Silhouette Books!

"When it comes to action and romance,
nobody does it better than Ms. McKenna."
—*Romantic Times Magazine*

Available in March at your favorite retail outlet.

Silhouette®
™ *Where love comes alive*™

From bestselling
Harlequin American Romance author

CATHY GILLEN THACKER

comes

TEXAS VOWS

A McCABE FAMILY SAGA

Sam McCabe had vowed to always
do right by his five boys—but after
the loss of his wife, he needed the small-town security
of his hometown, Laramie, Texas, to live up to that
commitment. Except, coming home would bring him
back to a woman he'd sworn to stay away from.
It will be one vow that Sam can't keep....

On sale March 2001

Available at your favorite retail outlet.

HARLEQUIN®

Makes any time special ™